JUMPER
CABLE

TOR BOOKS by PIERS ANTHONY

PIERS ANTHONY

JUMPER CABLE

A TOM DOHERTY ASSOCIATES BOOK

NEW YORK

JUMPER CABLE

Copyright © 2009 by Piers Anthony Jacob

All rights reserved.

Map by Jael

A Tor Book
Published by Tom Doherty Associates, LLC
175 Fifth Avenue
New York, NY 10010

www.tor-forge.com

Tor® is a registered trademark of Tom Doherty Associates, LLC.

Library of Congress Cataloging-in-Publication Data

Anthony, Piers.
   Jumper cable / Piers Anthony—1st ed.
       p. cm.
   "A Tom Doherty Associates book."
   ISBN 978-0-7653-2351-4
  1. Xanth (Imaginary place)—Fiction.   I. Title.

   PS3551.N73J77 2009
   813'.54—dc22

                                        2009016765

First Edition: October 2009

Printed in the United States of America

0 9 8 7 6 5 4 3 2 1

Contents

JUMPER
CABLE

1
PROPHECY

Jumper was going about his business as usual, hunting succulent bugs to eat. He had happened upon a puddle of ointment, and knew there would be flies in it. He was just about to nab a fat fly, taking care not to get stuck in the slimy stuff himself—whereupon a hook swung down from the sky and caught him by the scruff of his chitin. It hauled him up, up, and away, dizzyingly.

Then it dropped him into another scene. This was strange beyond his experience. The ointment was gone, and with it the delectable fly. The plants were thick-stemmed and woody, reaching into the sky, sheathed in clusters of green leaves. Some were small green blades hugging the ground. There was a bird, but no threat to him because it was so small as to be no bigger than a mite. Weird!

Jumper suffered a tweak of memory. His great-to-the-nth grandfather, the original Jumper, had had experience with such a realm. Where was it?

There was a scream. Jumper reacted before he thought, getting there in a single bound. Jumping was of course his nature; he could cover many times his body length per jump, and make a perfect landing. He was, after all, a free-ranging spider.

It was—his distant tenth-hand memory tweaked—a man, grabbing a girl. Girls needed protecting. So he extended a foreleg, caught the man by the scruff, heaved him up, and threw him away. The man landed in a prickle bush, yelped, looked at Jumper, yelped again, and fled.

"Xx, xxxxx xxx!" the girl cried, getting to her two thick feet.

Jumper clicked his mandibles in confusion. He did not speak girl talk. He was trying to figure out what a girl was doing in this scene. Girls were properly of the giant realm.

She gazed at him, then went to the side and fetched something squirmy. She brought it to him. She held it up with one of her forelegs.

Jumper reached out a foreleg and took it. It seemed to be a writhing nest of greenish leaves. What was he supposed to do with it?

The girl made a gesture as of putting something in her mouth part. Oh—this was edible? He lifted it to his own mouth, to taste it. But the thing immediately squirmed into his mouth and filled it with twisting strands.

"Oh, thank yew!" the girl exclaimed, exactly as before.

"You're welcome," Jumper said.

Then he paused, astonished. Not only had he understood her, he had replied in her own language. How could that be?

"It's the tongues," the girl said. "I gave yew the gift of tongues. So we could talk."

"Tongues?" he asked, perplexed. There was something funny about the way she talked, without any clicking of mandibles; could this explain it?

"It's a kind of plant," she clarified. "It enables a person to relate to any language. Yew saved me from getting abused by that village lout, and I wanted to thank yew. So I had to enable yew to talk. Yew can spit out the tongues now, if yew want."

He considered that. "First, can you tell me where this is? I am not familiar with this scene."

"Well, yew woodn't be. Yew're a spider, aren't yew? A big one. Yew must bee from far away. This is Xanth proper."

"Xanth proper! That's where my ancestor was."

"I dew knot know about him, but yew came in on a narrative hook. I saw it drop yew here. I was so surprised that I was knot careful, and that lout caught me. Then yew rescued me. I really dew appreciate that. Most creatures woodn't have bothered."

"A narrative hook?"

"It's a device to catch someone up in a story right away. Once it hooks yew, yew can't leave the scene."

Jumper wasn't satisfied with that, so he changed the subject. "Why wouldn't someone else have bothered to help you? You seem like a nice girl, for your species."

"My species. There's the rub. Yew see, I'm knot really a girl."

"You're not? You look like one."

"From the front."

"You seem to have a nice front." She was bare, and shapely. He was remembering the descriptions handed down to the descendants by the original Jumper. Girls were supposed to have thin forelegs, thick hind legs, and fleshy cones on their torsos. She did.

"But I'm really a woodwife."

"Wood? Trees are wood. They have wives?"

"No, silly! I am made of hollow wood. See." She turned around.

Jumper stared. From the back he saw that she was indeed hollow. Her round limbs and cones were empty, as was her head. Her shaped front outside was all there was of her.

She completed her turn and faced him again. "So you see, I am something else. I wish I could bee a real girl, so I could make some real man happy, and not bee stalked by village louts who dew knot care what's inside as long as they can poke it from outside. But that simply is knot my nature."

"I . . . see," he said, orienting about three of his eight eyes on her. It didn't help; she remained the shell of a woman.

"And that is knot the worst of it. Com Pewter wants to make me into a Mother Board to fix his obsolescence. Because my animation is all in my wood shell. I could knot stand being shut up like that, so I'm fleeing civilization. Knot that I was ever part of it; I am an innocent woodland creature."

"I understand. I wouldn't like it either."

"But that's no concern of yewrs. Yew saved me this time, and I'll bee more careful next time. I'm really grateful. Is there any favor I can dew yew in return?"

"Can you tell me how to return to my own realm?"

She shook her head. "Yew can knot return, once yew've been hooked. Yew have to finish the narrative."

"But I was about to catch a succulent fly!"

"I'm sorry about that—what's your name?"

"Jumper."

"I'm sorry, Jumper. I'm Wenda. Wenda Woodwife, a fantasy female. I dew knot know why the narrative hook caught yew and put yew here; maybe it was just an accident. But yew're stuck in my world for the duration."

"But I'm not comfortable here!" That was an understatement, but he wasn't sure how to fill it out to full strength.

"I understand, I think. I'm knot comfortable being a fake girl; yew're knot comfortable being in an alien environment. Too bad we can knot solve each other's problems." Then she paused, looking at him. "What is that?"

"My carapace?" he asked. "I wear my skeleton on the outside. Not that I have much of one. I am mostly soft body and hard legs."

"No, that thing stuck to yewr back." She stepped forward and reached for it. It turned out to be a square paper with markings on it.

"I didn't know about that," he said, surprised.

"It's like a label, identifying yew."

"I know who I am. A lost spider."

She studied it. "I think yew had better read it, Jumper. It seems to relate to yew." She handed it back to him.

Jumper took it with one foreleg and oriented an eye on it. To his surprise he found he could read. The tongues really were versatile.

PROPHECY
A Hero unfurls the Bra & Girlls
The Good Magician will set the mission
Like the Ogre beware rogue her

Win Heart and Mind but be not blind
The Unicorn betrays the scorn
And Button Ghost unmasks the Host.

Jumper looked up. "This makes little if any sense to me. What hero? What girls? What Ogre? What Unicorn? What Ghost?"

"I dew knot know. It may bee part of your problem I can knot solve." She smiled. "Maybee it is part of the tangled web yew weave to confuse people."

Jumper folded the mystical note and tucked it under a fold of his carapace. "I think I could solve your problem, at least. All you need is girl clothing and someone to watch your back to make sure no one else sees it."

"Clothing! Woodwives dew knot wear clothing."

"So it would make you seem more like a real girl."

Her little mouth dropped open. "It wood, woodn't it? I never thought of that."

"Well, you're a forest creature. It shows in your speech."

She considered. "Clothing makes me think of the anti-streaking agent."

"The what?"

"It is something to put in wash water. It messes up the fauns and nymphs something awful, because then they can knot streak."

"I don't understand."

She paused, assessing his incomprehension. "It is complicated. But I might bee able to solve yewr problem, or tell yew how to. I thought it was just chance that brought me here right when yew arrived, but maybee that hook had a reason to drop yew near me. Because maybee we can help each other. What yew need to dew is go ask the Good Magician, as yewr Prophecy suggests."

"I don't believe I know him, or even where he is. Would he know the answer?"

"He knows the answer to everything. All yew have to dew is ask. Only then he makes yew pay for it with a year's service, or equivalent. So maybe that's knot for yew."

Now Jumper considered. "If the alternative is to stay here in this foreign habitat, I might be better off with that year." Then he reconsidered. "Except for one thing."

"One thing?"

"Spiders of my type live only about six months."

"But yew're much bigger now. Shouldn't yew live longer? At least in this realm? Maybee six months in yewr realm is sixty years in this one."

He wasn't sure. "Maybe so. If I knew where to find him."

"I am beginning to think that maybee we can after all help each other, as I said. I wood like to ask the Good Magician how to become a full girl instead of a half girl, and how to escape Com Pewter, who can change reality in his vicinity. But it's a dangerous trip, and there are many louts along the way. I wood never make it on my own with my innocence intact. But if I traveled with yew, no lout would bother me."

"You know the way there?"

"Yes. An enchanted path leads to it. I wood be happy to show yew."

"Then let's do it."

"Let's dew it," she agreed.

He thought of something else. "The lout was afraid of me. Why weren't you?"

"Because spiders suck the juices out of succulent bugs. I'm knot succulent. I'm made of wood. I merely look succulent from the front. The front of a girl is all a lout cares about."

That explained it, to an extent. "But if you aren't soft and juicy, how can the louts hurt you?"

"They dew knot suck. They inject. I am soft enough from the front."

Jumper still did not quite understand, but decided to let it be. "Then let's get you dressed. Do you have any clothing?"

"I know where all the clothing plants are. There's a shoe tree nearby, and a pantree, and a hat rack, and all."

Jumper followed as she busily harvested assorted clothing. Then he helped her put it on. It fit well in front, but hung loose behind. They had to put a leafy branch behind her, which he fastened in place with sticky web. That supported her panties and bra, which he also taped in place.

Then she donned a shirt and skirt, similarly tacked down. Finally she put on lady slippers from another obliging plant, and a dainty feminine hat that helped anchor her hair to conceal the hollow back of her head.

They went to a calm pool of water and looked down. "Oh!" Wenda exclaimed, delighted. "I look ravishing!"

"Good enough to eat," Jumper agreed. Then he reconsidered. "Not that I would."

"Knot that yew wood," she agreed, laughing. "I'm inedible."

They set out for the Good Magician's castle. "This magician—I know nothing of him. My ancestors did not mention him. Is he a formidable character?"

"I understand he's a grumpy old man who does knot give clear answers. But somehow they always work out."

"I hope so. I am not comfortable in this odd realm."

"We will locate an enchanted path that will not only lead us there, it will guarantee that there are no bad dangers. That's the point of the enchantment: to protect innocent travelers. So yew won't have to worry about danger."

"But then why did you say the trek is dangerous?"

"Dangerous for me, because of the louts. They think that all girls want to be hugged and kissed indiscriminately. That's only the beginning. The enchantment does knot consider the loss of innocence a threat."

"Spiders aren't much for hugging and kissing," he agreed. "But I thought human girls liked it."

"Only with the right man. A lout is knot right. A lout would just yews me, knot make me a woman."

"Couldn't you just tell him not to?"

"Louts dew knot listen well. That's why they're louts."

This was evidently more complicated than he understood. "I can keep the louts from you."

"Thank yew."

An innocuous creature approached them, clearly no threat to anyone. But Wenda was alarmed. "Dew knot let it close!"

"But it is harmless," he protested as she guided him to a place behind a big tree.

"No. I know the forest predators. That's a No gard."

"I don't understand."

"Backwards for Drag on. He's pretending to bee harmless, putting yew off yewr guard until he can get close enough to chomp yew."

Sure enough, as the creature passed by the tree and they saw the other side of it, it was a horrendous toothy smoky reptilian creature. Quite big enough to chomp Jumper. A dragon.

"You saved me," Jumper said.

"Well, yew saved me first."

He experienced a largely unfathomable emotion. "I . . . feel good about you. I don't know why."

"Yew like me," she said. "And I like yew. We are becoming friends."

"Spiders don't have friends."

"Maybee they dew when they are in our realm."

That was evidently the case. "What do friends do with each other?"

"They help each other, and enjoy each other's company, and are sad when they part."

"Friends," he agreed, satisfied.

They came to a clearing in the forest. Suddenly a wind stirred up. It caught one of Jumper's legs. "Ouch!" he said, expressing discomfort in the human tongue.

"Oh, it's a biting wind," Wenda said. "We'll have to go around this region."

Jumper would have preferred to bite the wind back, but there was nothing to chomp on. So they circled the clearing, going behind trees, where the wind could not get at them well enough to bite.

As they completed their circuit, one of Jumper's eight sharp eyes spotted something to the side. It looked like a bare human leg. But it was gone before he could get a second eye on it.

"Something may be stalking us," he said.

"The woods are full of stalkers," Wenda said. "How big is it?"

"All I saw was a leg, perhaps the size of yours."

"That could bee anything from a goblin to a troll. Dew knot let it come close; they're even worse than louts."

"I will remain alert. If I catch it, is it all right to eat it?"

"Well, I guess so. But I understand goblins taste awful. At least the ugly male ones dew."

"They probably don't much resemble fat bugs," Jumper said with regret.

"The enchanted path is knot far from here. Then we'll bee safe from such threats."

They came across a human man sitting under a tree. He looked up and saw Wenda. "Well, now," he said. Then he saw Jumper. "Stay away!" he cried. "My name is Oxalate. I can change the amount of oxygen in the air. If you come close I'll smother you."

"What are yew talking about?" Wenda demanded.

"If I increase the oxygen enough, the air may burst into flame. If I decrease it, no one can breathe, and it can stifle a fire. So don't let that monster come close."

"This is Jumper," Wenda said. "He is knot going to eat yew."

"Well, I don't want to risk it."

"Then we will leave yew alone," Wenda said, and walked on. Jumper followed her.

"Why did you do that?" he asked when they were alone again.

"Yew are my friend, are yew knot? He was knot being nice to yew."

Jumper thought about that, and concluded that he liked this wood-wife even better than before.

In due course they intercepted the enchanted path. Once they stepped on it, other threats faded, knowing they couldn't do anything. That was a relief.

"Now all we have to dew is follow this until we reach the Good Magician's Castle," Wenda said confidently.

Jumper wondered whether it could be that simple. He really didn't quite trust this odd realm. He wished there were a magic path leading back to his own realm.

Sure enough, they had hardly started walking along the enchanted path when a large bird coasted in for a landing before them. "What is that?" Jumper asked as the thing braked to a sliding stop on the path, blocking their way.

"Oh my hollow head!" Wenda exclaimed. "It's a stork!"

"There is something wrong with a stork?"

"Knot exactly. They deliver babies."

"Small humans? Why would they do that?"

"It's complicated to explain. Just be satisfied that the stork has no business with us."

"It looks as if it has business," Jumper said. For the bird was walking toward them.

"I'd better talk to it," Wenda said. "There's been some mistake."

The stork hailed them. "Greetings, fair nymph, monster spider."

"We dew knot want any," Wenda said. "I never even let a lout touch me."

"I am not looking for you, nymph. I am looking for Maeve Maenad. There's a special delivery for her."

"A maenad?" Wenda asked, astonished. "They dew knot signal storks! They're wild bloodthirsty bare women who would as soon bite a man to death as kiss him."

"That may be the case," the stork agreed, "but we received a definite signal from one of them, and the delivery must be made. I am the supervisor, here to resolve an awkward situation. It is very unusual to lose a potential mother. Have you seen her?"

"We have knot," Wenda said. "And we hope knot to. Maenads are dangerous."

"Thank you. But keep an eye out for her." The stork reoriented, ran down the path, spread his wings, and finally managed to take off. In two and a half moments he disappeared into the sky.

"Keep an eye out?" Jumper asked.

"The bird wants us to keep on eye on the maenad, in case she shows up."

"I have eight eyes, but I need them all. I don't want to put one on anyone."

She smiled. "That is knot literal. Knot in this case. It just means to watch for her."

"Oh." Jumper was relieved. "So we have to look for her?"

"Knot really. We dew knot want to find her. But maybee she will bee like an inanimate object."

"How is that?"

"They always hide in the last place yew look for them."

Jumper was confused again. This was one really strange realm! "So let's not look."

"Of course," she agreed.

Jumper was glad that was settled, and that he didn't have to risk any of his eyes looking for something they did not want to find.

They resumed walking. "That's weird," Wenda said. "A stork looking for a maenad. There must be a glitch in their paperwork."

So it seemed it wasn't quite done with. "I am not clear what this is about."

"Oh. That's right. I guess yew wood knot know. Yew see, sometimes two humans—a boy and a girl, usually—get together and signal the stork, in that way telling it they want a baby. The signal goes out in the form of an ellipsis. That's three dots loaded with significance. The stork bureaucracy is very inefficient, and it takes them anywhere up to nine months to deliver the baby. They follow the path of the dots back, locate the mother, and give it to her."

"You're right. That does seem complicated."

"But maenads dew knot signal the stork. They use their sex appeal to lure men close so they can pounce on them and bite them to death. Even most village louts know better than to get close to one of those bloodthirsty creatures. So it's ridiculous for a stork to try to deliver to a maenad. It has to bee a mistake."

"It must be," Jumper agreed. This realm was proving to be every bit as weird as it first seemed.

"Oh, there's a campsite," Wenda exclaimed. "Let's stop there."

"There is something there we want?"

"Food. Rest."

Jumper realized that he was getting tired, and certainly he was hungry. He hoped there would be fat bugs there.

They entered the camp. It was very nice, with all manner of pie plants, and a pleasant shelter.

And there was a beefsteak tomato plant. Jumper picked a beefsteak and brought it to his mandibles. It was delicious. One of the pie plants had a shoe-fly pie; he threw away the shoe and ate the fly. This camp was all right.

Meanwhile Wenda found a small acorn tree and chewed on several acorns. Jumper remembered that she was made of wood, so must need wood food to sustain her substance. He wasn't sure how she assimilated it, because her mouth opened on emptiness inside, but concluded that was her business.

They entered the shelter. There was a bloodcurdling scream. Jumper fell back, as curdled blood didn't work well for his system.

"Someone's in there," Wenda said. "A girl. She must have thought yew were going to eat her."

"Actually I prefer fat bugs."

"I will talk to her." Wenda went on in.

Jumper inspected the adjacent pond. Something leaped out of it and sailed through the air. Jumper snagged it with a loop of web and reeled it in: a flying fish. So he stripped away the ing fish and ate the fly. Yes, this would do.

Wenda emerged. "This is complicated," she said. "Yew had better come in and listen. I have told her yew are knot for eating."

She seemed to have it garbled, but he let it be. "Told who?"

"It's Maeve Maenad," she whispered. "Hiding from the stork."

He was astonished. "The one we didn't see! We should inform that stork."

"No. That wood be telling."

"I don't understand."

"Yew woodn't. Take my word: storkly secrets are knot bruited about. We must help her."

"But you said maenads are dangerous."

"They are, normally. But Maeve has become a maiden in distress. That's different. I am similar, in my fashion. I must help her if I can."

Jumper clicked his mandibles in perplexity. It remained a very strange realm. "So we help her."

"Yes. We'll take her to the Good Magician, since we're going that way anyway, so she can ask him how to escape the stork. Meanwhile we'll have to hide her from the stork. That's why we need to hear her story. So we know exactly how to help her."

What could he do? "We listen," he agreed.

They entered the shelter. This time there was no scream. There was a succulent morsel of a bare girl, with wild hair and a feral smile.

"Jumper, this is Maeve Maenad," Wenda said. "Maeve, this is Jumper Spider. We are meeting in peace."

"Peaches and cream!" Maeve swore. "He's mouthwateringly fat."

"And she's saliva-dribbling fleshy," Jumper replied. He realized that Wenda had not misspoken when she said he was not for eating: the wild woman really would have attacked him. Of course then he would have bitten her head off and sucked out its juice. It was a nice head, surely very tasty.

"Yew both wood like to eat the other," Wenda said. "Yew must knot. We need to get along together."

"Why?" Maeve asked. Jumper couldn't have put it better himself.

"Because yew both need to see the Good Magician, and yew can get there better together."

Maeve sighed, making her body jiggle in a truly appetizing way. Her flesh, unlike Wenda's, was edible. "If we must, we must."

"Now tell us yewr story," Wenda said. "So we can figure out how to help yew."

Maeve grimaced, then launched into it, while they listened.

She was dropped into the central pool of bloodred wine with a resounding splash, with her name tag tied to her wild hair: Maeve, she who intoxicates. She immediately gulped some of the wine and got drunk and vicious: a true maenad. Gorged on wine, she soon grew into the flower of her wildness, racing with the other maenads to capture, tear apart, and consume any creature that strayed near Mount Parnassus. Especially anything male.

But as she grew older, reaching her teens, she discovered a new aspect of her situation. Her body changed, becoming thicker through the hips, thinner through the waist, and developing mounds on her chest. At first she was disgusted, because it made her slower when running; her proportions had become ungainly, and the flesh on her chest flopped at high speeds. Then she happened to see a picture of a woman left by a man who had been routinely consumed, and it was just like that. It seemed that men really liked to see that awkward flesh on women. A bulb flashed over her head as she understood.

Maenads weren't just wild women, they were sexy wild women. That was why human males came to their region. She wasn't sure what a man actually wanted to do with a maenad if he caught her, because they always chased down and tore apart any men they spied, biting off gobbets of hot flesh and swallowing them in a feeding frenzy. That was, after all, the purpose of a man, wasn't it? To be torn up and eaten. But it annoyed her when an occasional man was wary, and fled before the maenads could run him down. Perfectly good meat going to waste.

So she experimented. Once when she spied a man near the fringe of the mountain, and he spied her, she didn't run after him with spittle flying. She stood and watched him. He came closer, eyeing her warily. He obviously knew her nature.

But he did not come all the way up to her. He got nervous, and was about to turn to go. That was when she might have run him down and bitten his leg to lame him, so that she could then finish him off at leisure. He represented a huge meal she might have all to herself. But instead she lifted her arms, put her hands on her head, and half turned. This had the effect of outlining her chest, a body part he seemed to be looking at.

He did look, and took a step toward her, licking his lips. But then he hesitated again, justifiably nervous about getting too close.

So she inhaled. That made her chest expand, and her mounds stood out. The man's eyes glazed over and he panted. But then he shook himself, tore his eyes away, leaving tatters of eyelids behind, and started to turn away.

So she turned away herself, pretending she wasn't chasing him. With luck he would be deceived, and then she could whirl and pounce. But there was another effect. He stared at her bottom, and this time his eyes completely glazed. He had freaked out.

Good enough. She whirled and pounced, catching him before he could recover his sight and flee. She tore a bite from his neck, then landed on his back as he collapsed on the ground. Soon she was tearing delicious gobbets of flesh out and gulping them down. Before long there was little left of him except bones, and her belly was so full she had to go hide in a tree to digest it all. What a successful hunt!

While she digested, she reviewed the process by which she had caught him. Her chest had almost done it, but in the end her bottom had finished it. Why these things should so fascinate a man she didn't know, but philosophy was not her forte. She just wanted to know what worked. Chests worked, bottoms worked. But could they be improved upon?

When she was lean and mobile again, she went to spy on a human household beyond the maenad demesnes. It wasn't safe to hunt here; the humans were too likely to cut off her retreat and slaughter her. But she might learn something useful just by watching.

She did. She saw a farm girl eyeing a passing village lout. Evidently the girl was interested in the lout. Maybe she was hungry. But the lout was too stupid to pay attention, and was walking on.

"Hey, lout!" the girl called.

"Huh?" he asked, turning to look at her.

She turned away from him, pulled up her skirt, and flashed her panties.

The lout was stunned. He just stood there, eyes glazed, until the girl dropped her skirt and went inside her house. He remained for some time, like a statue, until finally a wood-bee sat on his nose, startling him back into activity. He departed, trailing crumbs of glaze as his eyeballs recovered.

This was a revelation to Maeve. So it was clothing that did it! Panties freaked out men.

She went to a small pantree and harvested a panty. She put it on, then admired herself in the reflection of a pond. It did do something for her bottom. It could be a secret weapon.

She took it off and hid it away, because it wouldn't be secret if the other maenads caught on. Then when she was alone, and spied a man, she used it. He freaked out just like that, and she had no trouble catching and eating him.

Thereafter she became the most successful huntress of her kind, though still a teen. The other maenads were jealous, but couldn't figure out how she did it. She made sure never to use the panty when any other maenad was near.

There was only one mishap. That was when she flashed a man, and he came to her, and she bit at his throat—and bounced off. So she bit at his arm, and missed again. Finally she bit at his leg, but still got nowhere. "Sweet violets!" she swore. "What is wrong?"

The man shook his head sadly. "Nothing with you, maenad. It's me. My magic talent is to have an impenetrable shield that prevents any living creature and most inanimate things from touching me. It is the bane of my existence."

"Then how do you eat and drink?" she demanded, hoping to find an avenue she could exploit to get at his flesh.

"It lets in only food, water, and air—that sort of thing. So I survive. But it won't let me touch a woman, so I can't kiss her or do anything else with her."

"So why did you come to me?"

"I hoped that the savagery of a maenad would be too much for the shield, and we could touch maybe just enough. Alas, it's not so."

"Just enough for *what*?"

"You don't know? Ah, maenad, your prison may be as bad as mine. I suppose I will just have to go to petition the Good Magician for an Answer."

And with that mysterious remark he turned and walked away. She hadn't even learned his name, not that she cared about that.

Fortunately that was the only balk. She was able to satisfy her hunger with other men. But still she wondered: who or what was this Good Magician? Was he edible?

By the time she emerged from her teens, she was not only truly full figured from her excellent diet, she was in contention to become the leader of the maenads, because of her hunting prowess. She was really proud of herself.

Then came disaster. It started simply enough. If only she had known! It was a handsome man who came to drink at the maenads' wine spring. He came when the other maenads were out hunting, and only Maeve remained to guard the spring. This was no coincidence, she learned later—way too late. He had come then because he was interested in her.

She stood before him in all her bare splendor. He gazed at every detail, but his eyes did not glaze. He seemed to be immune. So she donned her panty and turned her back. But while she was doing that, he was donning dark glasses, that fudged the image so it was too vague to freak him out.

She tried moving her body in the ways that normally affected men. He watched, evidently appreciating it, but still not freaking out. This was most frustrating!

Then he spoke. "Hello, lovely nymph! I am Harbinger, a binge-drinking messenger with some harpy ancestry. Who are you?"

She was so surprised that she answered. "I am Maeve Maenad. Why aren't you freaking out?"

"Because I came prepared, knowing that otherwise you would tear out chunks of my living flesh. You are far too lovely to be wasted that way. Know, O delightful damsel, that wine dulls my vision so that I can't freak out."

"Then why do you need those glasses?"

He smiled. "I don't. They are merely a prop." He removed the glasses and gazed at her, unfreaking.

Her amazement continued. "What do you want of me?"

"I want what any man wants of a beautiful woman."

This was stupid, but he was so handsome that she really wanted to know. "What is that?"

"Love."

"I don't know that word."

"Then I will be glad to teach you its meaning. Come with me, Maeve, and we will make beautiful music together."

"I don't know anything about music."

He laughed, as if she had said something fully. "You don't need to. Come." He started walking away from the pool.

And such was her bemusement, she walked with him. After all, she could pounce on him and tear him apart any time, as long as he remained close. After she satisfied her curiosity.

He led her o'er hill and dale to an unfamiliar glade with its own pleasant pool. "Let us swim together," he said, removing his human clothing.

"Swim?" That was his idea of love? Swimming was something a maenad did to catch a person trying to escape across water.

"It is a pleasant diversion. We can get close together in the water."

She stared at his bared body. What a handsome specimen he was, with firm lean meat on his arms and chest! Her mouth was watering already. And of course he would be easier than ever to catch in the water.

She removed her panty, because water wasn't good for it, and waded into the water with him. He reached out and took her hand, and she let him.

And something odd happened. Suddenly she was overflowing with an emotion she had never remotely experienced before. She stepped into Harbinger and kissed him. A real kiss; she didn't even try to bite. That was quite unlike her. Unlike any maenad.

He wrapped his arms around her, and she delighted in that touch. He was right: it was fun being close together in the water. But also very strange. She found herself with urges she had never experienced before.

And he was indulging them. They had a gloriously weird experience together, amazingly pleasant.

Then it was done, whatever it was. He separated from her. "Thanks, Maeve. It's been fun. Now I'll be on my way."

On his way? "But I have just gotten interested in you," she protested.

"Get over it." He dried, donned his clothing, and walked away.

She stood chest deep in the pond, staring after him. What had happened? She hadn't even tried to bite him, let alone tear out any of his flesh. She had just hugged him and done something oddly new, and now he was gone.

Finally she waded out of the pool, picked up her panty, and walked back home to the wine pool.

The other maenads had returned. "Where were you?" one demanded. "The spring was unguarded."

"A—a man took me away," Maeve said haltingly. "To a pool."

"And you didn't tear him apart?"

"No."

"What did you do, then? Club him to death and hide the body so we couldn't share the meat?"

"I—I kissed him. And swam with him. And hugged him. Sort of."

They stared at her in shock. Then an older maenad asked an irrelevant question. "Exactly where was this pool?"

Maeve pointed. "That way."

The maenad nodded. "That's a love spring."

"A what?"

"Water that makes any male and any female fall in love with each other, at least for a while, and signal the stork."

Maeve was appalled. So that was what they had done! "Why, that miserable deceiver! I didn't know."

The older maenad sighed. "It's not the sort of thing our kind normally knows about. He tricked you into it, then had his way with you. You should never have trusted him."

"I didn't trust him! I was going to eat him."

"Well, let's hope the stork didn't get the signal."

They resumed their normal existence. But unfortunately the stork had gotten the message, and just about nine months after the incident came looking for her. Her worst fear had materialized.

Maeve fled. The other maenads, understanding her horror, tried to cover for her, pretending that she was still among them. But the stork wasn't fooled. It knew exactly which maenad it wanted. When it didn't find her by the love spring, it widened its search.

"And now wherever I go, that stork is close behind," Maeve concluded. "I can't let it catch me."

"We'll take yew to the Good Magician," Wenda said. "He'll know what yew can dew about it."

"The Good Magician!" Maeve exclaimed. "I have heard that name. Who is he?"

"He is a gnome who solves people's problems, for a price," Wenda explained. "Yew have a problem. He will know how to make that stork stop pestering yew."

"But I can't go outside by day! The stork is watching."

"We'll hide yew. Make yew look like someone else. Knot a maenad. So the stork will knot recognize yew."

Maeve began to have hope. "Not a maenad," she repeated.

Jumper was impressed. Wenda truly seemed to care about other people, even spiders and bloodthirsty wild women. As a spider he had never really liked or disliked anyone else, but now he was coming to like Wenda more than ever. Friendship. That was an unfamiliar but actually rather pleasant feeling. If she was right, the Good Magician would solve all three of their problems.

They worked on Maeve. Wenda sent Jumper out to harvest assorted clothing, while she worked on Maeve's wild hair. When Jumper returned with a pile of apparel, he almost didn't recognize the maenad. Her hair was now neatly coiffed, in the manner of a human girl, and she looked oddly pretty. He could almost understand why a human man might want to kiss her, if he could safely do so.

When they added her clothing, she looked totally different. Her savage beauty was muted. Except for her teeth, which were sharply pointed, for tearing flesh. There seemed to be no way to hide those, unless she kept her mouth perpetually closed.

Then Jumper found a wax tooth plant, and harvested an upper and a lower set. Maeve put these under her lips, and had a beautiful set of slightly protruding unpointed teeth. She couldn't talk very well with them in, but maybe she wouldn't need to.

"We can tell strangers yew're very shy," Wenda decided. "And with those wax teeth in, yew won't bee able to bite anyone, if yew happen to forget. Yew can knot afford to act like a maenad."

"Mmmph!" Maeve said angrily.

"She's right," Jumper said. "You need to be nothing like a maenad. You must be a nice, sweet, innocent human girl."

Maeve spat out her teeth. "And suppose a lout makes a move on me?" she demanded. "Wanting to get another stork chasing me?"

Wenda exchanged a glance with one of Jumper's eyes. "Then Jumper may have to throw him away," Wenda said. "But meanwhile yew must bee a helpless maiden without a bloodthirsty thought in yewr dainty little head."

"Growr!" Maeve growled, jamming the teeth back in. At least she understood the necessity.

They settled down for the night, the two maidens sleeping on either side of Jumper, trusting him to protect them. He felt oddly flattered.

2
Bra & Girll

I n the morning the girls, getting along tolerably well, did their things and made ready to travel. So did Jumper.

The trek along the enchanted path was routine. On occasion they passed people going the other way. Jumper garnered some wary looks, but his presence on the path indicated that he was probably not as dangerous as he looked.

Near noon they paused by a flute tree that serenaded them with lovely music. Beyond it was a set of pear trees; they always came in twos. Maeve went to pick two pears.

"And who might you be, wench?" a voice demanded.

"Who are you calling a wench, stink tail?" Maeve demanded in return.

Jumper and Wenda got over there in a hurry. The other person was a harpy, part bird, part woman, perched on one of the twin branches of the tree.

"We apologize," Wenda said. "We did not realize it was yewr tree. We are merely traveling through."

The harpy was only marginally mollified. "It is not my tree. I merely dislike being disturbed when I'm snoozing."

"We will move on," Jumper said.

"It talks!"

"I was given the gift of tongues," Jumper explained. "Come on Maeve; we don't want to intrude on her nap."

"Oh, I'm awake anyway, now," the harpy said with grudging grace. "Take your two fruits."

"You're a harpy," Wenda said. "Why are yew knot swearing?"

"I am a high brow harpy," she replied, raising her brows. "I don't use fowl language."

"A high brow harpy," Maeve said, shaking her head. "I never heard of that."

"Naturally not."

Maeve bridled. "Is that a cut, birdbrain?"

The harpy eyed her scathingly. "That depends on whether you have the wit to appreciate it, floozy."

Maeve made a growling sound as she ripped out her false teeth to expose the gleaming pointed ones. But both Wenda and Jumper dived in to separate the two. "Let's exchange introductions," Wenda said, desperately changing the subject as she shoved a juicy pear at Maeve. "I am Wenda Woodwife."

"A woodwife! But you look rounded."

"My friend Jumper here helped fill me out with cloth and webbing. I really am hollow. And this is Maeve Maenad."

"A maenad! In clothing?"

"What's it to you, featherface?" Maeve demanded.

The harpy inspected her more closely. "Those teeth. You *are* a maenad. In that case you're no vapid nymph, but a savage creature to be respected. We harpies have long admired the viciousness of the maenads."

"Is that an apology?" Maeve demanded.

"It resembles one. I am Haughty Harpy."

"We are glad to meet yew," Wenda said quickly.

The harpy inspected the three of them. "Pardon my curiosity, but why would a hollow woodwife, a bloodthirsty maenad, and a giant spider be traveling together peacefully? You should be trying to consume or squish each other."

"Oh, we woodn't care to burden yew with our problems," Wenda said.

"Unfortunately for me, I am atypical of my species in that I am a curious bird. Suppose we exchange problems? That is, information on them."

Wenda looked at Jumper. "I suppose a harpy woodn't be eager to bruit secrets about, wood she?"

Jumper didn't know anything about harpies, so he temporized. "Maybe not if she had a secret of her own she didn't want shared."

"Exchange of hostages," Maeve said, replacing her wax teeth now that she had finished demolishing her pear and wasn't about to tear the harpy apart.

"Fair enough," Haughty said. "I will show you mine if you show me yours."

"Agreed," Jumper said, now curious about her secret. The two girls nodded.

"Harpies have half talents," Haughty said. "We can't use them well unless we find and cooperate with folk of other species who have the other halves. Since we hate to cooperate with anyone, even other harpies, this renders us effectively talentless. But sometimes our magic manifests anyway."

She paused, because her paragraph had ended. Then a new paragraph arrived, neatly enclosed in quote marks, and she resumed.

"Mine is, of course, obnoxious. It is that I change at times to my alter ego, Hottie Harpie, who is all the things I'm not, but definitely not my better half. She seeks males of either the avian or mammalian persuasions, and shamelessly seduces them. I hate that, because of course if she catches the stork's attention on her watch, that stork will in due course seek me on mine. I hate babies! They bawl endlessly and are chronic bundles of demand. 'Tis a fate devoutly to be abhorred."

"Yes!" Maeve said in the pause between paragraphs.

Then another paragraph arrived, as neatly packaged as the first two, and Haughty had to continue. "So now I am trying to travel to the Good Magician's Castle, to prevail on the old f**t for an Answer to my

Question, which is how the bl**p do I stop my worser half from being so obnoxious?"

"I didn't catch that word," Wenda said. "An old what?"

"Fart," Maeve said zestfully. "She actually bleeped most of it out. She even bleeped out bleep.

"As I said, I do not employ gutter terminology."

"You are one weird harpy!"

"Thank you. Now I believe it is your turn, maenad. Why did you exclaim between paragraphs?"

"Because I agreed with you, harpy. Babies are abominations. A stork is pursuing me, because of an embarrassing incident in a love spring, and if it catches me I'll be stuck with one of those howling blobs myself. So I'm going to ask the Good Magician to hide me from that nemesis."

Haughty nodded. "You would surely make just as bad a mother as I would."

"If not worse," Maeve agreed. It was evident that the two were starting to get along, having a basis for understanding.

"And yew're going to see the Good Magician too," Wenda said. "But why are yew perching instead of traveling?"

"Because the confounded path enchantment is out just ahead," Haughty said. "I am heavy-bodied for my size, and can't soar at great heights, so must fly from perch to perch near the ground. That's dangerous, so I follow the path for safety—and now can't. I am explendiferously p**ved."

"Peeved," Maeve murmured. She seemed to have a knack for censored vocabulary.

"The path is out?" Jumper asked.

"You're not much for attention, are you, spider?" the harpy remarked sagely. "Yes, it seems that a sphinx lost its balance and fell, rolling across a section of the path and squishing the magic flat. So now nothing remains but a fuzzy indentation and a frenzy of hungry monsters lurking for trusting travelers. Until it is repaired, no one can safely repair across it."

"But we need to cross it," Wenda protested.

"Then you must wait, as I am doing, woodwife." The harpy eyed her. "By the way, I don't recall hearing your story."

"It's a hollow one. I am fleeing civilization so as knot to bee made into a Mother Board, dodging village louts along the way. I want to bee a whole woman, knot half reared."

"So your problem relates to males too."

"Yes. Especially machine and human males. I am hoping the Good Magician will have an Answer for me."

The harpy turned to Jumper. "And you are perhaps the strangest of this motley assemblage. What is your story?"

"I was caught by a narrative hook and dumped into this narrative. I am hoping the Good Magician can return me to my natural realm."

"So we are all going to the same place. Perhaps we could travel together."

"Why should we let yew join us?" Wenda asked cannily.

"I know a detour where the monsters aren't lurking. It's not really safe, but it's feasible."

"That helps," Maeve said.

"Let's take a look at that break," Wenda said. "Maybee we can forge across quickly."

They went on along the path to the break. It was merely a flattened section, looking innocent enough.

"I'll show you," Haughty said. She folded her wings and hopped onto the edge of the flattened area.

A monster zoomed across from a hiding place to the side, jaws snapping hungrily. Haughty leaped straight up, spreading her wings and flying clear. But a winged monster swooped down, jetting fire. Haughty barely made it back to the safe zone.

She had made her point. "We'll take the detour," Wenda agreed.

"That passes the Bra & Girll," Haughty said. "I hate that place, because it's where Hottie goes slumming. But it's well traveled, so the monsters won't notice a few more people. We can loop past it and take the unenchanted path that intersects the enchanted one farther along. It should be routine."

"It can't bee, or yew woodn't bee seeking our protection," Wenda said cannily. "What's the catch?"

"Sometimes there are storms. Then folk have to stay at the Bra. It's really an inn."

"That name," Maeve said. "Shouldn't that be Bar & Grill?"

"It should," Haughty agreed. "But the proprietor has a problem with his Rs. They don't stay in place well. They tend to switch places with adjacent letters."

"Even on the sign?"

"Even there. Now it's established. It does serve good food, though. But I hope we can pass right by it. Because it would be better to be somewhere else when Hottie appears."

They let her lead them on the detour. All went well, at first.

Then there was a rumble in the sky. "Bl**p!" Haughty swore. "Fracto has noticed us."

"Bleep," Maeve translated helpfully.

"Who?" Jumper asked.

"Cumulo Fracto Nimbus, the worst of clouds. He exists to rain on parades, wet on dry laundry, blow important papers away, and make a complete nuisance of himself."

"A simple cloud?" Jumper asked incredulously. "I am not impressed."

"That's his nature." Haughty looked around. "D**n! I don't see anywhere else to take shelter."

"Darn," Maeve said, once again filling in the blanks.

The cloud swelled ominously, evidently having overheard their dialogue. Jags of lightning radiated from it, and more thunder sounded. Gusts of wind rattled the leaves of nearby trees, getting the range. The first fat drops of rain spattered on the nearby leaves.

They clustered under a spreading acorn tree, but the storm intensified. Colored hailstones bounced off the leaves and piled up on the ground.

"I haven't seen those in a long time," Wenda said. "Fracto is really working at it."

"To the Bra," Haughty said regretfully. She led the way, flapping ahead of them, pursued by hailstones. "Maybe Fracto will lose interest before nightfall."

The others held small branches over their heads to shield them against the hailstones and hurried after Haughty. The storm hurried after all of them. A few stones caught them, but Fracto couldn't orient fast enough to catch them with the worst while they were moving.

Maeve turned back for a moment to stick out her tongue at the storm. "Nyaa, fogface!"

"You shouldn't have done that," Haughty said. "Now he'll never let us be."

Indeed, the fury of the storm redoubled. The hailstones welled to the size of pears, bashing trees and ground alike.

However, they soon came to the Bra & Girll, the sign exactly as described. The house seemed nice enough, and inside there was a bar for food and beverages.

"Hello, Haughty," the proprietor called. "Who aer yoru firends?" He was a huge man, shaped somewhat like a spent volcano.

"Hello, Crater. We are going to the Good Magician's Castle," Haughty replied. "These are Wenda, Maeve, and Jumper." She was being careful not to identify their species.

"That would be Carter," Maeve murmured. "It must be only one R per word that strays."

Crater stared at Jumper, whose species could not readily be masked. "You look mighty big fro a spidre. Are you safe to be aorund?"

"Safe enough," Jumper replied. "I eat bugs, not people."

Crater returned his attention to Haughty. "They'er welcome, porvided they can pay."

"Oh, s**t," Haughty said. "I forgot: Crater charges for room & board."

"Spit," Maeve murmured.

"Orom & broad," Crater agreed jovially.

"But we dew knot have anything to trade," Wenda said. "Maybe we can move on."

Maeve looked out the window. "Rain is blasting down outside. We're stuck."

It was true. The window was awash with water, and thunder shook the inn. They would have to stay the night.

"Maybee we can bargain," Wenda said. "Crater, is there anything we can offer yew in exchange for yewr hospitality?"

The innkeeper looked at her, then at Maeve, who bridled. "Besides that!" Maeve snapped.

"Besides what?" Jumper asked, mystified.

"Never mind," Haughty said. "You wouldn't understand."

She had him there. He had no idea what they were talking about. "Maybe if you explained?"

"He was looking at their bras," Haughty explained. That hardly helped. After all, this was the Bra & Girll. Why shouldn't he look at such things?

Meanwhile Crater was considering. "Well, I do have a couple house wrokers who would like to visit the Good Magician, if they could just tarvel three safely."

"Workers travel there," Maeve murmured. She had become a general translator.

"Male or female?" Haughty asked alertly.

"Female. They'er nice girls. They make the beds, clean the oroms, peel potatoes, sevre the food, and so on, eanring theri keep while they wait. I think yoru big spidre might be able to portect them form molestation. Undrestand, they can portect themselves, in theri fashions, but that seems unladylike, so they hesitate."

"Wrod ovelroad," Maeve muttered, frustrated.

Haughty looked at Jumper. "This seems promising. Can we add two more to the party?"

"Let's meet them," Wenda said warily. "Before we decide what wood bee best."

Crater put two fingers to his mouth and made a piercing whistle. In a moment two young women came down the stairs.

"Ladies, we may have a company to take you to the Good Magician's Castle," Crater said. Then, to Jumper: "This is Phanta, who can become a ghost."

"In fact I have no choice," Phanta said. "It happens in darkness."

This was interesting. "Why do you want to see the Good Magician?" Jumper asked.

"To stop Gheorge Ghost from chasing me. He wants to lock me up in darkness to possess me forever."

"The lout!" Wenda exclaimed.

"He should be torn apart and eaten," Maeve agreed.

"I have to keep a candle constantly burning at night, so I won't get caught. Because once I'm a ghost, I can't make a light."

"You poor thing," Wenda said.

It seemed Phanta was satisfactory. "You may come with us," Jumper said.

"And this is Olive Hue," Crater said, introducing a greenish complexioned young woman. "She can make imaginary firends with eral talents."

"Olive Hue—I love you," Maeve murmured. She seemed to have a talent for translation of any type.

"Now that's different," Haughty said. "But why do you need to see the Good Magician?"

"Because my imaginary friends are temporary. They fade out when my attention flags. I want a friend I can keep."

"Can't you imagine the same one again?"

"Yes, but it will fade out again. The Good Magician should know how to make them permanent, if I want them."

That made sense to Jumper. He used several of his eyes to exchange glances with the others, then said, "You may come with us."

"Vrey good," Crater said. "Welcome to my humble establishment fro the night."

Haughty winced.

"What bothers you?" Jumper inquired.

"Night is when Hottie takes over. I can't prevent it."

"Ah, Hottie Haprie," Crater exclaimed. "We love hre hree."

Which was, of course, the problem. Then a bright bulb flashed over Jumper's head. "Maybe Olive can help."

"With what?" Olive asked.

"At night Haughty becomes Hottie, who it seems fascinates men. But if she signals the stork, Haughty may share the mischief. Could any of your imaginary friends help, Olive?"

Olive nodded. "Maybe the Censor, temporarily."

"Temporarily?"

"Someone always finds a way around his spells after a day or so. But one might suffice for one night."

"Please summon him."

"All it takes is imagination." Olive concentrated, and a sour-looking man appeared. "Hello, Censor," Olive said.

"Xxxx xx xxx," he replied gruffly.

"Same to you," Maeve murmured, translating.

"Censor doesn't like anything," Olive explained. "And all his words are automatically censored out. But I can understand him, because he's my friend." Then she addressed the man. "Censor, this harpy has a problem. When night comes she will become most indelicate. Can you keep her decent for the night?"

"Xxxx'x xxxx," he agreed.

"That's easy," Maeve said.

"Thank you. Keep an eye on her, because night is approaching."

"X xxxx."

"I will," Maeve said.

Crater served a fine evening meal complete with rhed whine and candy corn. There was even a fat July bug for Jumper. The man was an excellent host. Phanta donned a small tight uniform and waited on their table while Olive went to the kitchen to wash pots. The two obviously were earning their keep.

Maeve had to remove her wax teeth to eat. She did so, and tore zestfully into her gory undercooked steak.

Several other travelers came from their rooms to join in. One was Gene Blue, a blue man with the talent of making blue jeans. Another was Jamie, a short chubby man whose talent was to make things heavier. Fortunately he didn't have to; he did it only when something needed it, like a table that needed not to be blown away. Jumper noted that the eyes of both men tended to follow the motions of the waitress, especially when her little skirt flounced as she moved. Maybe they were concerned that she not mislay their portions.

"You know, Phanta, you'd look good in jeans," Gene remarked. "I could make you a really tight-fitting pair."

"They'd only make me blue," she replied, flouncing away from him.

Again, Jumper feared he was missing something. These humans had nuances that were beyond the understanding of spiders.

And as they feasted, night fell.

"Well, now."

Haughty Harpy was gone. In her place was Hottie Harpie. She was prettier, with glossy long hair, perky tail feathers, a prominent bare bosom, and a challenging gaze.

"You're looking blue, handsome," Hottie said to Gene Blue as she hopped over to his section of the counter. "I'll bet I can cheer you up." She inhaled, lifting her bosom almost under his nose. Harpies had essentially one anatomical feature of interest to human males, but that was impressive. There was a lot of good meat there. Not that Jumper would ever eat it, however succulent it might be. It wouldn't be polite.

Gene's eyes widened, seeming about to crystallize. Apparently he was noticing her body.

Then something odd happened. Her bosom fogged. It was still there, just concealed in puffs of cloudlike froth. Hardly any meat showed.

Gene lost interest.

"What the bleep is this?" Hottie demanded, her naughty word making the air around it glow despite the way it had been bleeped out.

Jumper caught on. "You have been censored."

"Outrageous! No one can bleeping censor me!"

But the Censor could. He smiled obscurely and faded out. He was imaginary, but his talent was real, and lingered after his departure, and Hottie's hottest anatomy remained fogged out.

Hottie swore up a storm that threatened to rival the one outside, but she had been effectively nullified. Finally she went to perch sullenly in a corner.

"Thank you, Olive," Jumper said.

"Just get me safely to the Good Magician."

"We will certainly try."

Gene's male eye wandered to Maeve. She met his gaze and drew her lip back in a pointed-tooth snarl. His eye hastily retreated.

They concluded the meal. Then Olive imagined some friends with bodies like cans in skirts, but nice arms and legs, and they did a rousing cancan dance that the men watched avidly. It seemed that they admired the dancers' ability to lift their legs really high, showing their cans. Jumper had just about given up trying to comprehend the interests of human folk.

The girls went upstairs to their rooms. Jumper was too big to fit on the stairs, so he settled down at their base and closed five or six of his eyes to snooze. He tried never to close all his eyes at one time; a fat bug might escape his notice.

In the night there came a faint scream. *Jumper! Help!*

All eight eyes snapped awake. It was completely dark, but he could see well in darkness. There, coming down the stairs, was a ghost. It looked like a man, carrying a bundle over his shoulder. It was the bundle that was screaming.

Jumper didn't move, but he inspected the bundle as it passed by one of his eyes. It was Phanta! In her ghost form. She looked the same, just less substantial. That meant the male ghost must be her nemesis, Gheorge, the one who stalked her. Somehow he had caught her in darkness.

Jumper knew he had to stop this abduction. But how? The ghosts lacked substance; he couldn't simply grab them.

He followed them as they passed through the wooden door. He had to open it to get out, because he didn't want to break it down. The storm had cleared and the stars were out. And Phanta was being borne helplessly away.

What could he do? He quickly spun a loop of web, whirled it around, and lassoed them. But the web passed through them without effect.

Then he had an idea. He rewound his lasso and hurled it straight up at the sky, very high. It snagged on a star. He hauled the star down. It was really quite bright as it got near the land.

He whirled it around and flung it at the ghosts. Suddenly they were illuminated.

And Phanta reverted to her solid living state. Gheorge had no further power over her. All he could do was slink away into the darkness as the captive star lay guttering on the ground.

"Oh, thank you, Jumper!" Phanta cried, planting a kiss on his mandibles. "You saved me from a fate worse than death!" Her bosom was heaving with excitement.

"Well, I did what I could. But how did you get caught in darkness? I thought you always kept a candle burning."

"I do. I think he blew it out."

"He can do that?"

"He must have learned how. He caught me off guard. I would have been lost, but for you. He would never have let me see light again. I'm so grateful!" She kissed him again.

"We'll have to find a light that can't be blown out."

"I'm not sure there is any, in Xanth. Unless I can find a fresh plant bulb."

"We'll look for one."

Jumper hauled up the guttering star, that seemed distinctly unhappy on the ground. He dangled it by his web loop. It was trying to burn through the loop and escape, but the web material melted without ever quite letting go.

"The poor thing," Phanta said.

"I will free it once we have other light. I don't want Gheorge Ghost to return for you."

"That makes sense," she agreed, shuddering. "One thing about you, Jumper, I know you don't want to do to me what he wanted to."

Jumper wasn't quite sure what she meant, so he didn't question it. Human beings had their own special ways.

They walked back to the inn, where a light had come on. "What's out three?" Crater bellowed. He was wearing a nightcap and held a club, ready for trouble.

"Me, Phanta, with Jumper," Phanta called back.

"You have a thing for spidres?" Crater demanded, surprised. "Or is he tyring to eat you?"

"Not exactly. Gheorge tried to abduct me. Jumper saved me. He's a great guy."

"Oh. Well. That's all irght, then." He put away the club.

They reached the inn. "Now I will free this star," Jumper said. He whirled it around on the end of his cord, then hurled it back up into the sky. It flared happily as it went, glad to return safely home.

"Bye, star!" Phanta called after it, and it flared again, faintly.

"You did not keep a candle bunring?" Crater asked Phanta.

"I think he blew it out. Candles are no longer safe."

"So you need to get to the Good Magician soon."

"Yes. Thank you so much for arranging this, Crater."

Crater fetched a storm lantern and lit the wick. "Let's see him blow this out," he said grimly. "But I'm sruprised a ghost can blow at all."

"He's really after me," Phanta said. "I don't know why."

"Because you'er a good-looking wench," Crater said gruffly. "Why else do you think I have you sevring food?"

"Because your last waitress married a patron and retired to easy living?"

"That too," he agreed.

"And the one before her quit when someone goosed her?"

"Well, men will be men," he said, seeming embarrassed. "If any tyr that with you, let me know and I'll boot them out."

"No need. They can't goose me."

"They can't?" he asked, surprised.

She smiled. "Try it, Crater."

"Nuh-uh! You've got one cute bottom, but I don't want you to quit too."

"I'm departing tomorrow anyway, remember? So you can risk it."

"Well, if you'er suer." He reached out and took a hold of her bottom as she closed her eyes. And his hand passed right through it. "Hey!"

"I turned ghost for a moment," Phanta explained, opening her eyes. "I can do that by shutting my eyes. I solidify again when I open them."

"So it seems dark to you," Jumper said. "But then how can you sleep without becoming a ghost?"

"I do turn ghost then, but I solidify the moment I wake and open my eyes. So it's safe, as long as there's a light."

"I never knew," Crater said, amazed

"Well, you never tried it." She smiled obscurely. "Of course I might not have ghosted with you."

The man blushed, for some reason. "So tarvelers have been tyring it all along?"

"Yes. But I watch them, and blink when they touch. Of course that's when I'm not holding a dish."

"That's why you sometimes dorp dishes! You can't hang on to them when you'er ghosting."

"Sorry about that," she said apologetically.

"And that mug of gorg that landed in that tarveler's lap—that was why?"

"Yes."

"He never complained."

"Because he knew I would tell why, and you would boot him."

Crater shook his head. "Dran! I wish I could keep you."

"You're sweet."

"But we're wasting the night," Crater said. "Back to bed."

"I think I'll stay down here with Jumper," Phanta said. "Just in case Gheorge does find a way to blow out the lantern."

"As you wish," Crater agreed, and returned to his room.

"There is much I think I don't understand," Jumper said.

"Well, you're a spider. Your male eyes don't glaze at this sight of well-filled panties."

"Should they?"

"Here's the thing, Jumper: when a human man sees a human girl's panties, he freaks out. It's part of the background magic of Xanth. It happens to a lesser extent when he sees things like Hottie's bare bosom or a girl's full bra. But men are so crazy, they actually try to see these things. So we girls show them only as we choose, usually just enough to get their attention without getting them all worked up. When we find a man we want to keep, we show more, reeling him in. It can be a fine line, and sometimes we misjudge."

"That's when they duck you!" he exclaimed.

"Well, close enough," she agreed, smiling. "They aren't supposed to goose, but travelers can be uncouth. Fortunately I can prevent them."

"You said you might not have ghosted with Crater, and he blushed. I don't understand that either."

"I was teasing him. The rule is, a man may look but not touch, unless a girl wants him to. He follows that rule. But when I hinted I might want him to, he couldn't help getting all excited. Men are foolish that way."

"Would you really let him touch?"

"I might. He's a good guy. It depends on my mood at the time."

"Teasing—is this nice?"

She considered. "Sometimes. Sometimes not. Now that I ponder it, I think maybe I shouldn't have teased him. Especially since I'm leaving."

"There's not much to be done about it now."

A dim blue bulb flashed over her head. Jumper recognized it: not an idea bulb, but a decision bulb. "There you're wrong. I'm going to go untease him, just for tonight. A kind of going away present."

"Untease?"

"I'm going to let him touch me. He'll like that."

"I don't see how a duck—I mean, goose—would make much of a difference."

"You wouldn't," she said. "This is more than that. I'll see you in the morning, Jumper. Thanks for everything." She departed, heading for Crater's door.

Jumper settled down again for the night, marveling at the obscure ways of human women. He continued to wonder as he heard muted noises coming from Crater's room. It sounded as though they were wrestling. That made no sense at all.

"And I thought *I* was hot," Hottie Harpie said from the corner. Jumper had forgotten she was there. "That's the one thing I envy full-human girls: their legs."

"You have legs," Jumper reminded her.

"Bird legs don't freak human men."

He realized that must be true. Maybe some day he would figure out why human legs did.

In the morning they gathered: five maidens and Jumper. Crater packed them a knapsack with food for the journey. He looked surprisingly cheerful, as if he had had an excellent night. Jumper glanced at Phanta with a single eye, but she gave no sign.

"I'll miss you grils," Crater said. "I hate having to do all the wrok myself."

"There will surely be other girls," Phanta said.

"Not like you."

"If I didn't know better," Olive murmured privately to Jumper, "I'd suspect he was smitten with her. But of course he likes the way she brings in travelers."

"She does that?" Jumper asked.

"They come from all around to gawk at her skirt."

This did not match what Hottie had said. "Not her legs?"

For some reason she laughed. "Those too."

Maybe he was destined never to understand.

"Who carries the pack?" Haughty asked. "*I* can't."

A glance circled around. "I can try," Wenda said. But when she tried to put it on, it sagged so badly around her hollow back that she couldn't. Phanta tried it, and it fit reasonably well, but when she blinked it dropped to the ground. It seemed that even the briefest closing of her eyes had the ghost effect. Olive tried it, but turned out not to be strong enough to carry it well. Maeve put it on, and she was strong enough.

"But it's pretty heavy," Jumper said. "I might carry it more readily."

They rigged a harness and fastened it to his back, and Jumper had no trouble carrying it.

Maeve made an effort. "I'm trying to be girlish, to mask my nature," she said. "To thank you for taking the pack, I'll try to kiss you without biting." She approached Jumper, put her mouth to his mandible, and jerked her head back just before her teeth snapped together. "Sorry about that. I have not yet conquered my nature."

They marched out into a beautiful morning. There was a path leading to the enchanted path. It wound through field and forest, o'er hill and dale, past rocks and rills, enjoying the sights as it went. "We'll be there in another hour," Haughty said.

Then suddenly there was a blast of thunder. A storm was zooming out from cover behind a large tree.

"F**k!" Haughty swore. "Fracto ambushed us!"

"Flak," Maeve murmured. "Harpies hate antiaircraft fire."

The dark cloud spread out in seconds, and lightning flashed. They were about to get drenched, or worse.

"Maybe I can help," Olive Hue said. "One of my friends has a special talent."

"Make it fast," Phanta said. "Fracto means to wash us out."

A young man appeared. "You look worried, Olive," he remarked.

"We need protection from Fracto," Olive said. "We need to get safely to the enchanted path."

"That's my specialty," he agreed. He concentrated.

"This is my imaginary friend Jestin," Olive said to the others. "He conjures a portable section of an enchanted path."

"Hello, Jestin," Phanta said, switching her little skirt about. His eyes started to glaze. There just seemed to be something about that skirt despite its smallness. As it was, it was barely big enough to cover her panties.

Olive hastily got between them, blocking off Jestin's view. "Wait until he finishes the path," she said urgently.

"Oh." Phanta toned it down.

The path appeared. It looked ordinary, except that it was undisturbed by the rising wind. They crowded onto it just as the storm let loose half a deluge of rain. The water sluiced away, not touching them.

Now Phanta approached Jestin again. "Thank you so much for your help," she said, kissing him. She could do what Maeve could not: kissing without biting.

Then, before she could freak him out, Jestin faded. "We can't have a distraction," Olive snapped. "We have to make our way to the permanent enchanted path before this one breaks down from the strain."

"One might almost suspect that one girl is a tiny bit jealous of her friends," Haughty murmured.

"Almost," Jumper agreed.

They followed the path, but soon it ended. Ahead the storm was intensifying, with lightning striking trees and wind battering them, and of course water beginning to flood.

"We pick up the rear section and carry it forward," Olive said. She put her hands down, and a section of the path came up. She carried it to the front and aligned it with the section they were on. Then they all stepped onto that.

In this manner they advanced slowly toward the regular enchanted path, while Fracto raged all around them. Not one jag of lightning struck them, not one wash of water soaked them, not one fierce gust of wind blew them away. It was a great way to travel through an otherwise treacherous region.

In due course they made it to the regular enchanted path. Fracto, defeated, blew off elsewhere.

"Thank you, Olive," Jumper said. "Your friend Jestin really came through."

"My friends generally do," she agreed, flattered.

They resumed their interrupted trek along the path. At noon they paused to eat from the pack Crater had packed. Jumper reached back a foreleg and swung it down to the ground.

It turned out to be far more bountiful than they had anticipated. It was a veritable feast, with something for each of them, ranging from a really juicy bug for Jumper to a really gory leg of bovine for Maeve. There was also a big jug of rhed whine.

They tried a sip, then a cup, then several cups, and finally finished the jug, though they had not meant to. This led to some things that seemed odd only in retrospect. Jumper and Haughty did an impromptu dance, with him jumping high in the air and her plummeting almost to the ground to zoom under him as they whirled crazily around. Wenda, Maeve, Phanta, and Olive threw off their clothing and danced in a circle around them, jiggling ferociously front and rear. Wenda was of course fine from the front, but from behind her hollowness was completely exposed. The others took turns "trying her on," stepping into her from behind so that it looked as though she were full-fleshed.

Then they were too tipsy to stand, let alone walk, and had to make camp right there on the path, in the middle of the day. They weren't even up to doing that properly. Instead they collapsed into a pile, with Jumper on the bottom and Haughty on the top, the others draped somewhere in between. What a meal!

Late in the afternoon they recovered, one by one. Jumper was the first, he thought maybe because being the largest, he had taken a smaller portion of rhed whine relative to his size than the others had. Even so, he felt as if he had eaten a rotten zombie fly.

Maeve was next. "That whine's not the same as what our home pool has," she said, making a wry face. "More impurities. But the wildness— it was good to experience that again."

"We're just lucky no human males were present," Wenda said, extricating herself from the pile.

The others shared a shudder as they got to their feet, and searched out their scattered clothing from the surrounding bushes and tree limbs. "We'd have been ruined," Phanta agreed.

This perplexed Jumper. "All we did was have some fun dancing. What is wrong with that?"

A female glance circled one and a quarter times. It landed on Olive Hue. "When men see bare girls, especially inebriated ones, they get all excited and grow about four extra hands, and that's not all. It quickly gets complicated, and the girls are lucky if the storks don't take out after them."

"The stork!" Maeve exclaimed, hastily diving into her clothing, doing her hair, and putting in her wax teeth, seemingly all in one motion.

Phanta squeezed her head between her hands as if it hurt. "Let's not have such a party again. The hangover's awful."

"What is hanging over?" Jumper asked, not seeing anything.

"Never mind," Wenda said. "It's knot relevant, and anyway, we finished the jug."

"It means we have headaches, and our mouths taste like dragon p**p," Haughty explained.

"Pulp," Maeve murmured. "Not the best tasting part of a dragon."

Jumper didn't see how that related to hanging over, but let it pass. There were just too many human nuances for him to keep up with.

In due course they resumed walking along the path, and by night-fall they were close to the Good Magician's Castle. But by mutual consent they decided to spend one more night on the road, in part to get the taste of dragon pulp out of their mouths.

They washed in the safe pool, foraged in the enchanted campground, and had a nice meal without whine. "Now all we need is some eye scream for dessert," Haughty said. "But we don't have the eyes."

"Or the scream," Maeve said.

"I have a friend who makes ice," Olive said.

"There are cream puffs growing by the pond," Phanta said. "I'll harvest some." She went off to do that.

Olive's imaginary friend appeared, a somewhat cold-looking woman. In fact, her hair seemed to be formed of icicles. "Hail Mary," Olive called. "We're making eye scream. May we have some of your hail?"

Mary gestured, her hair flared, and a small pile of hailstones dropped among them. "Eat, drink, and be Mary," she said as she faded.

They gathered up the hailstones before they melted and put them in a pot. Phanta returned with the cream puffs, and they carefully opened each and poured its cream into the pot. Then they stirred it up until it screamed. Sure enough, it had formed a single eye. It was ready.

It turned out to be great eye scream, and it didn't make them run around bare or get mouths tasting of dragon pulp.

Then they settled in the shelter for the night. "You know," Maeve said, "I'm not much for civilized socializing. I am doing it only because I have to hide from that bleeping bird. Otherwise I would be running wild on Mount Parnassus and tearing flesh from anyone I caught. But I find I am enjoying the company of you folk. Don't you dare tell the other maenads that."

"I feel much the same," Haughty said. "Normally I peer down my nose at ground-bound j**ks, but you can be good company."

"Jacks," Maeve murmured. "They are used to lift heavy things up."

"You're all okay," Phanta said. "But my favorite is Jumper, because he saved me from Gheorge last night."

"He did?" Wenda asked. "I did knot know about this."

"Yew wood knot," Phanta said with a smile. "Yew were asleep, wood-wife. Gheorge blew out my candle and hauled me away, but Jumper lassoed a star and saved me."

Phanta and the others gazed at Jumper with all ten of their eyes. That made him uncomfortable, as he had only eight eyes. "I was just trying to help."

"We do like each other," Olive said. "It's too bad we'll have to separate and go our own ways tomorrow."

"Maybee we can meet again, some day," Wenda said. "I wood knot want to miss that."

"We are becoming friends. But I am going back to my own realm," Jumper said. "I can't just go back and forth. That's why I need the Good Magician's help."

"Can a ghost reach your realm?" Phanta asked.

"Maybe. Mainly, it's much smaller than this one. In fact, maybe it's the same realm, only on a different scale."

"Maybe we'll find a way," Haughty said.

At that point night fell with an inaudible clank, and there was Hottie Harpie. "And I could give you such a good time, if only you had bird or man parts."

Jumper tried to blush, but didn't succeed, because he was a spider and anyway had no idea what she was talking about. The others laughed; they *did* know, and found it funny. Or something.

3
CHALLENGES

I n the morning they approached the Good Magician's Castle. It was a solid edifice with a broad moat, high walls, and
not much else. A path led down to the drawbridge, which
was invitingly down. A number of exotic plants grew beside the path,
and Wenda identified some as they went.

"Cottonwood," she said, indicating a small tree covered with white
puffs. "One of the most useful trees in the forest. In the spring yew can
harvest cotton balls from it; in the summer, cotton candy. In the fall,
cotton socks. And in winter yew can burn the wood and get cute little
puffs of white smoke."

Beside the tree grew tall reeds. "Fen-fen, from the Ogre-fen-Ogre
fen. The ogres eat it to lose weight, but now they find it is causing heart
attacks. Not even ogres much like getting pelted by flying hearts. Apparently they are guardians of the fen."

Sitting on a branch of the tree was an oddly shaped collection of
fruit. Olive tried to touch it, but it suddenly spread wings and flew
away.

"That's a fruit bat," Wenda explained. "It was afraid yew'd eat it."

"I did have something of the sort in mind," Olive confessed, embarrassed.

"Getting in is supposed to be a challenge?" Maeve asked. "This looks easy. Nothing but harmless plants."

"Don't you believe it, maenad," Olive said. "I have heard about this castle. The Good Magician is a recluse who hates to have his time wasted by folk demanding favors, so he makes it hard for them to get in, and then he demands a year's service or the equivalent in exchange for an Answer few can figure out anyway. So it really isn't worth it, unless you're desperate."

"I *am* desperate," Maeve said. "If that stork catches me, I'll be, as Haughty would put it, sc****d."

"No, that's backwards," Phanta said. "The stork comes after the sc***ing."

"Scraping?" Wenda asked, stifling half a smile.

"Scalping," Haughty said, suppressing a chortle.

"Scheming," Olive said.

They looked at Jumper. "Scalding?" he asked.

They all laughed. "Just keep that bleeping bird away from me," Maeve said. "Anyway, I'm game. I'll go on in, and the rest of you can take your turns after you see how it goes."

Olive shrugged. "Try it your way."

Maeve set forth. The others followed, with Wenda continuing to admire the special plants. She seemed to know them all. Jumper realized that the rest of them weren't actually trying to follow; they were standing in place. But somehow they remained close to the maenad. Indeed, this garden wasn't quite as innocent as it appeared.

"Weird," Haughty said. She spread her wings and tried to fly back, but nothing happened. "What the h**l!"

"Haul, I think," Wenda said. They missed Maeve's translation. "We're being hauled along after her."

"Another detail," Olive said. "Querents can't use their talents. Haughty can't fly, and it seems Maeve can't separate from us. We must be slated to tackle the challenges as a group, though I haven't heard of that before."

"So the first challenge is already upon us," Jumper said. "And we are learning the rules."

"Maybe *you* are," Maeve called back. "I'm not good at rules." She plowed determinedly on, and they paced her, involuntarily.

"There's a soul food plant," Wenda said. "That's a rare one. Normally it grows only near the Black Wave Village, where they guard it carefully."

"That one?" Phanta asked, reaching for a brown horn.

"Dew knot touch that!" Wenda cried, alarmed. "No, the soul food is the other side of the path."

A goblin stepped out onto the path ahead of Maeve. He was big-headed, big-footed, knobby between, and ugly, as all goblin men were. "Well now, sweet maiden," he said. "So nice of you to visit."

"Beware," Olive murmured. "Goblin males are never polite. It has to be sarcasm."

"What the bleep do you want, knobhead?" Maeve demanded politely.

The goblin laughed nastily. "Take off your clothing and I'll show you, cutie."

Maeve considered. "If I do, will you get out of my way?" Obviously she was trying to handle this peacefully, though it plainly went against her nature.

"Har har har!" he laughed. "Maybe after I'm done with you, you luscious little piece."

"Uh-oh," Olive murmured. "She's getting annoyed."

"That is not good enough," Maeve said, small sparks glinting in her eyes. "You have to promise."

"Har har har! Enough flirtation, you hot little package. Get 'em off now or I'll rip 'em off. I'd like that."

"That does it," Maeve snapped. She quickly stepped out of her clothing, unbound her wild hair, threw off her gloves, and spat out her wax teeth. Then she leaped at the goblin, her pointed teeth snapping, her uncovered claws raking.

And suddenly a whole clot of goblins appeared. It was a trap.

Maeve took a bite out of the first goblin, and he screamed in pain. But the others laid hands on her arms, legs, and torso. They jammed a sponge into her mouth so she couldn't bite and held her spread-eagled.

"So we've got us a maenad," their leader said zestfully. "Oh, won't this be fun!"

"They're going to sc**w her!" Haughty exclaimed. "We have to do something."

Jumper realized he might be about to find out what the word really meant, but this wasn't the way he wanted to learn it. He started forward, about to tackle the goblins.

"Wait!" Wenda stooped beside the path and picked something up. It looked like a discarded animal horn. In fact it was the plant she had warned Phanta against touching. She hurled it forward. It arced onto and into the crowded goblins, landed on the ground, and broke open. Brown mist puffed out.

"Hold yewr noses," Wenda said. "Dew knot breathe if yew can help it."

"What are you talking about?" Phanta demanded. Then she caught a whiff. "Oh, no!" She grabbed her nose.

"Gas attack," Olive said, grabbing her own nose.

Then Jumper smelled it: the foulest imaginable stench. It reeked of rotten excrement mixed with spoiled vomit, shaken, not stirred, plus less attractive substances. And he was only at the edge of the expanding cloud.

The goblins were at the center. Already they were turning ghastly green as they tried desperately to scramble out of range, but they had been coated with the vapor. They were doomed.

"Stink horn," Wenda said with satisfaction. "A forest plant. I can knot think why it is knot more popular."

She glanced at the others. "Hold yewr breaths and hurry through before it dissipates and the goblins return."

They needed no second warning, as the gut-wrenching stench was thickening. They gulped foul air and ran forward.

Jumper spied Maeve gasping helplessly on the ground. He picked her upper section up with two legs and ran with the other six, dragging her feet along. When he had her well clear of the stench, he set her down and turned to go back for her clothes. But the vile brown cloud rose up menacingly, oozing feculence, and he reconsidered.

"Don't bother," Maeve gasped. "I wouldn't want those clothes anyway."

Then they saw another figure coming down the path. It was a cloaked person . . . no, a tall bird . . . no, it was the stork! It was coming after Maeve, having spotted her in her natural state. It carried a bundle.

Then it got into the cloud, and abruptly it was coughing and turning green. The bundle did the same. The bird retreated, looking as if it was about to be very sick.

Maeve laughed. "Serves it right!" she gasped. "By the way, Jumper, thanks for rescuing me. What a smell! Rotten carrion is sweet in comparison."

"You are welcome," he said. "But won't the stork catch you, now that it knows where you are?"

"Not if I get to the Good Magician first and get my problem solved."

"So we had better move on before that noxious gas clears."

"We had better," she agreed, struggling to her feet. "But it may be hours before that stork tries again to pass it. I'm just lucky I have a tolerance for decayed flesh." Even so, she looked distinctly sick. Jumper made a mental note to stay away from stink horns.

They rejoined the others, who were waiting a bit farther from the rampaging cloud of stench.

"I think we have navigated the first Challenge," Haughty said. "By invoking Xanth's worst f**t."

"Fret," Maeve said. "Something that truly disturbs people. Like that gas."

Phanta choked back something that might in better times have resembled a laugh. Was that really the word the harpy had used?

They came up to the moat. The moat monster lifted its head from the water and surveyed them hungrily. Snappish little fish crowded close to the bank, hoping for tasty flesh to bite. No crossing there; it was hard enough just to wash the remaining stink off. Fortunately they could use the drawbridge.

But when they approached the drawbridge, they discovered that there was a woody curtain hanging across its near end. A number of lengths of wood were bound together to make a flexible barrier. Jumper was about to draw it aside so they could pass, but Wenda stopped him. "Dew knot touch it! That's bamboo."

"Isn't that a type of wood?" Olive asked. "That should be harmless."

"Knot bamboo," Wenda said. "It is dangerous. I'll show yew." She picked up a small stone and flipped it at the curtain.

The wood struck one piece, and it detonated. BAM! The explosion rocked the whole heavy curtain and blew out a blast of hot air that pushed them back. Wenda was right: they did not want to touch it.

"But we can throw more stones, and make it all explode," Olive said. "Then it won't be in our way."

"Knot bamboo," Wenda repeated. "Watch."

In a moment, maybe even half a moment, BOOM! and the fragmented section of bamboo regenerated and was whole again. They would never be able to detonate all the pieces fast enough to get past them before they were dangerous again.

"Again, your expertise has identified a woodland project we need to know about," Olive said. "We're lucky this environment didn't nullify your knowledge as well as your magic."

"By the way, what is your magic?" Haughty asked.

"Being hollow yet animated," Wenda said. "I could knot function this way if I weren't magic. So yew could call it my talent. I call it my curse."

"So we can't cross the drawbridge," Jumper said. "We need to find some other way across the moat."

"As I understand it," Olive said, "there is normally some way at hand to handle the Challenges. Just as there was a stink horn, waiting for Wenda to recognize it and use it. We just have to find the key to getting across the moat."

"Let's walk around it," Jumper suggested. "And see if we can find that key."

They started walking. There was a parklike strip outside the moat, with a convenient path through it. This must be what they were supposed to do. If they circled all the way around the castle without finding the key, that might signal their failure. Then they wouldn't get to see the Good Magician, and would be stuck with their assorted fates. Not to mention a wasted prophecy. So they needed to be alert.

A woman came running toward them, laughing. They gave her room, and she ran right on by, still laughing. But something odd happened: each person she passed burst into similar laughter. Soon they were all collapsing in spasms of mirth, even Jumper, who didn't know what was so funny.

After a while they gradually subsided. So he inquired: "What was so funny, to make us all laugh like that? I didn't even know spiders could laugh."

"Nothing," Haughty said seriously. "I seldom laugh. Yet I was overcome."

"It's as though it spread from her to us," Phanta said. "That's weird."

"Infectious laughter!" Olive said. "That's her magic!"

Haughty shook her head. "So it must be. But how is that relevant to our need to cross the moat, either as help or hindrance? Because everything is relevant, isn't it?"

"It is supposed to be," Olive agreed. "Maybe if we were smarter, we could figure out how it relates."

They went on, nonplussed if not nonminussed. And soon another person came running, this one a man. He looked as if he were about to be sick. They let him pass—and choked up, feeling ill in the throat, unable to speak.

After a few uncomfortable minutes they recovered. None of them had actually upchucked, but all had been silenced.

"And what was that?" Haughty wheezed.

"A running gag," Olive said. It seemed she was good at puns.

The others groaned, and not because they found it very funny. In fact they were not amused. They got up and resumed their walk around the moat.

They came across a small group of people at the bank of the moat. Two were children, a boy and a girl, plainly unhappy, while the third was a merman trying to console them.

Jumper, leading the way, paused. It bothered him to see anyone unhappy, especially a child. "What is the matter?" he inquired.

If the children were surprised to be addressed by a big talking spider, they didn't show it. "I am Mercury," the merman said. "My talent is to change the temperature of water. I can make it hot, cold or comfortable in my vicinity." He swished his tail in the water. "These children also have talents relating to water, but they aren't happy with them. I am trying to encourage them, but they don't believe me."

"Any talent surely has some use," Olive said to the children. "What are yours?"

"I am Caitlin," the little girl said. "I can turn wine to water. But nobody likes me to do that. They say it would be better if I could turn water to wine, and I can't."

"Have you tried it with reverse wood?" Olive asked.

The girl's mouth fell open. "Do you think that would do it?"

"I think it might," Olive said. "Reverse wood reverses most things. Of course you can never be sure how it reverses them, so you just have to try it and see. But it might work."

"I'll try it," Caitlin said, pleased.

"And what is yours?" Olive asked the boy.

"I am Ian," he said. "My talent is pushing water away from my body. People say that's no use at all."

That obviously set Olive back. Reverse wood might just get him soaked. She looked helplessly at the others. They shrugged, not able to offer anything.

"There must be something," Olive said at last, defeated. "If we think of it, we'll let you know. Meanwhile, would a kiss cheer you somewhat?"

Ian considered. He was a child, but there were some pretty girls here. Maeve, bare, was especially fetching, but Phanta was quite pretty too. "Maybe."

"Choose one of us," Olive said.

"Her," Ian said, pointing at Haughty.

Haughty almost fell over with surprise. "But I'm a harpy! No one wants to be kissed by a harpy."

"I think harpies are great," Ian said. "They have all these bad words."

Oh. Boys did tend to be naughty.

"Well, I'm not saying a bad word to a child," Haughty said.

Ian started to cloud up.

"Oh, h**l," Haughty said, disgusted.

"Heel," Maeve murmured too faintly for the boy to hear. As a result, he imagined a much worse word.

"Great!" Ian exclaimed. "H**l! I love it."

"You're welcome," Haughty said, touched. She flew across and kissed the top of his head as she passed over him.

"She touched me!" Ian exclaimed. "I probably got dirty! Great!"

"You folk seem to have a certain talent with children," Mercury said. "You have cheered them as I could not." He slid back into the water and swam away.

They walked on. They might have cheered the children, but they were no closer to solving their own problem.

They encountered a man walking the opposite way. "Hello," Jumper said.

The man paused. "I never met a big talking spider before," he remarked.

"I was given the gift of tongues," Jumper explained. "Otherwise all you would hear would be mandible clicks. Do you have a talent?"

"I do indeed," the man said proudly. "I can transform my arms into anything." He demonstrated by changing them into wings, then giant claws, then longer arms, and finally into lengths of rope. "I can do just about anything I want to."

"Can you help us get across the moat?" Jumper asked.

"Well, I can form paddles." He did so. "But the moat monster and those piranha fish would eat me up, and anyone with me. So I don't think I can help you there."

That had been Jumper's impression. "Thank you."

The man moved on, and so did they. Soon they encountered another man. He had large insect eyes. "Hello," Jumper said.

"I see you are a transformed spider with the gift of tongues," the man said. "That's interesting."

"How do you know all that?" Jumper asked.

"I am Todd. I have the Eye of the Bee-holder. I can see things from more than one angle. You are obviously a normal spider, except for your size, and I see a bit of the tongues plant in the corner of your mouth."

Jumper was impressed. "Do you see a way for us to cross over the moat?"

Todd shook his head. "I see no way for you to do that. I'm sorry."

"Thank you," Jumper said regretfully. For a moment he had had hope.

They moved on. "There are people with many talents here," Olive remarked. "But none of them seem to relate well."

"Maybe that's the problem," Haughty said. "Somewhere here there's one who can help us, but we can't find him or her in this welter of irrelevant talents."

"That must be it," Jumper agreed.

They approached a man who was sitting at a table, looking unhappy. "What is your problem?" Olive inquired.

"I have a useless talent," he replied. "I can turn gold into lead."

"But have you tried reverse wood?" she asked, evidently remembering her prior success with the girl who turned wine to water.

"Yes, and it enables me to turn lead into gold. But nobody wants either gold or lead anymore; they have all they want from the Gold Coast, and they tell me to get the lead out. So what use is my talent?"

That stumped them. "We don't know," Olive said.

They came next to a woman sitting in a deck chair. She looked ordinary, and not satisfied, though she had very nice legs. "What is your talent?" Olive asked.

"I have freak-out knees," the woman said. "But they work only on men. I want to freak out women too."

That explained why they hadn't noticed, as they were a party of five females and a spider. Actually she did have very shapely knees, for a human, with good flesh and bone, surely quite tasty. But Jumper did not normally freak out at the sight of edible joints.

"It occurs to me," Phanta remarked as they moved on, "that some folk don't appreciate what they have. They are unhappy because they want more."

"Like us?" Wenda asked.

That made them pause. "Are we missing something obvious?" Haughty asked. "Something these other folk are showing us?"

"We must be," Olive said. "As bold smart querists we aren't much."

"Querists? You used that term before. I don't know it."

"People who ask questions," Maeve translated. "Inquirers."

"Let's keep pondering it as we go," Jumper suggested. "Something may occur to us."

The next person they encountered was a woman who seemed ordinary. "Hello," Olive said. "I am—"

"Don't get too close to me," the woman said, making a face. "I'm about to—ahh, ahh—"

"I'm sorry," Olive said, stepping back. "We don't mean to intrude."

Then the woman sneezed. "CHOO!" It was a hard sneeze. In fact, her whole head flew off, bounced on the ground, and rolled into the brush. Her body was left wandering aimlessly.

"Here!" the head called. "I'm over here!" But the body had no eyes or ears, so it could neither see nor hear.

Jumper reached down to pick up the head, carefully. He brought it to the body and set it on the neck.

"Thank you," the restored woman said. "I am Miss Gesundheit. It is my curse to sneeze my head off."

"We noticed," Jumper said. "That must be inconvenient."

"It's awful. That's what brought me here to see the Good Magician. He's going to glue my head on more securely, after I complete my Service."

This did not seem promising either. They moved on.

Then next was another woman, this one older. She looked really down.

Olive approached her. "Hello. We—"

"Don't touch me!" the woman said. "It's contagious."

Again, Olive stepped back, cautioned by their experience with the last woman. "What do you have?"

"I am Auntie Depressant. Touch me and you will feel better, but then much worse when the effect wears off. It is better simply to stay clear."

That seemed like good advice. They moved on, and came to half a crowd of people having a party.

A man staggered toward them. "Welcome to the Cate Family picnic," he said. "I am Intoxi Cate, who makes revelers happy. This is my brother Impli, who is a lawyer for the offense, and my other brother Vindi, who is a lawyer for the defense. And here is Recipro, always quick to return a favor. Things are always interesting here."

"Thank you," Olive said smoothly. "But we're just passing through."

The next group was no better. This was the Burr Family, with Tim who could make wood appear from nowhere, but was always falling over. Lim made things limber, but at the moment he was experimenting with cheese, and it stank. Slum made folk sleepy. Num could always make the right number needed. Encum tended to weigh things down. Har made good places for boats. Em made hot coals.

Unfortunately these were not the talents the group needed. They moved on, and encountered the Tard Family. Pe Tard knew all about green, black-eyed, and chickpeas. Mus Tard tended to make a hot tasting mess of things. Bus Tard was a big black and yellow bird capable of carrying 66 passengers.

That interested them. "Could you carry five winsome maidens and a large spider across the moat?" Olive asked.

"I could," Bus agreed.

Wenda pounced. "Wood you?"

"I would."

They seemed to have solved their problem. They got on Bus's back, where there were convenient seats. "We're ready," Olive said.

But the big bird didn't move.

"What's the matter?" Olive asked.

"I will get around to it in due course," Bus replied. "I never hurry."

Uh-oh. "When?"

"Maybe in three days."

"That translates to tardy," Maeve said. "It figures."

"We don't have three days," Olive protested.

"Or longer," the bird said lackadaisically. "I never arrive on time. It's a matter of principle."

They got off, realizing that this was after all a false lead. They huddled together for a conference. "I suspect all the remaining people will be similarly useless," Jumper said. "Those that could help us probably won't."

"But then how can we get across?" Phanta asked. "We don't seem to have a ghost of a chance."

The others smiled. Phanta knew about ghosts. But she was right: they were getting nowhere.

"There must be a way," Olive said. "Something we have overlooked. But if any who can help won't, the way Bus Tard won't, we're still stuck. Unless . . ." She paused as a bulb flashed over her head.

"Unless what, you perverse t**se?" Haughty demanded.

"I don't think tease is a bad word," Maeve murmured.

"It depends who you are teasing, with what," Phanta said. Jumper remembered how she had teased the innkeeper, and decided to untease him.

"Unless someone doesn't know he can help," Olive said. "And maybe could be persuaded to help without knowing."

"He?" Haughty asked. "Who?"

"Ian. The boy with the talent of pushing water away from his body."

"What good is that? He surely couldn't push the whole moat out of its basin."

"He doesn't need to. Let me talk to him."

But something was bothering Jumper. "It took two of us to get through the first Challenge. Maeve to distract the goblins, and Wenda to recognize and hurl the stink horn. If that's a pattern, it will take two to get across the moat, and two more to handle the third Challenge. If Olive has figured out the key, we still need to select another person to work with the boy."

"Haughty," Olive said promptly. "He likes her."

"Well I don't like brat boys," Haughty said. "Maybe we should wait until night and let Hottie tackle him."

"I think not," Phanta said. "The Adult Conspiracy prevents."

"Oh, p**s on the Adult Conspiracy!"

"Puns," Maeve translated. "A truly vile concept."

Jumper wondered, as he had before, whether her translations were completely accurate. But probably it didn't matter. It was the sentiment that counted.

Haughty let her feathers settle back in place. "Exactly what do you have in mind, Olive?"

"If he can repel water from his body, what would happen if he jumped in the moat?"

"He would make a dent in it," Haughty said. "So what?"

"Suppose he walked through it?"

"A traveling dent."

"Suppose he walked across it?"

"It's too deep in the center. The water would close over his head, forming a bubble."

"Or a tunnel, if the effect lingered," Olive said. "One we might use."

Haughty reluctantly nodded. "But what could I do?"

"You could charm him into doing it. He doesn't need to know where he is going; you could encourage him step by step."

"But I don't even like him!" Haughty protested. "I don't like any boy."

"You don't need to. What counts is that he likes you, and maybe will listen to you."

"I'd rather p**p on his head!"

"Pulp," Maeve murmured.

"Try to restrain yourself," Olive said, smiling. "You must be the sweetest, nicest, most encouraging harpy ever."

"Gah!"

But the others were starting to see it. "It just might work," Phanta said. "If the boy doesn't know what we're doing, he can't be tardy or balky. If Haughty truly charms him."

They all looked at Haughty, who withered. "All *right,* d**n it! I'll do it. But you'll have to tell me how. It's bad enough just looking nice, let alone acting nice. To a boy, yet."

They worked on it. "Smile at him every time you speak," Phanta said. "Pretend you are absolutely fascinated by his every word."

"Keep facing him, and inhale often," Wenda said. "Boys are knot supposed to notice, but they dew."

"When you feel like cursing, change to its opposite," Maeve said.

"And kiss him on the cheek, not the top of the head," Olive said.

"But mainly, express interest in his talent," Jumper said. "Say you want to find out just how strong it is, because you're sure it is better than he thinks it is, and maybe the two of you can prove it."

Haughty practiced smiling and reversing bleeps. "But I want you to know, this is very un-harpy," she grumbled.

"Remember," Jumper said, "if this works, you will get the solution to your problem with Hottie. So it should be worth being un-harpy for a while, just as Maeve has to try to be un-maenad and I have to ignore how delicious all of you look, even when I'm hungry."

"Oh, I'll do it," she agreed. "But I don't bl**ping like it."

"Nuh-uh," Olive said. "You don't *sweetly* like it."

"Lovely," Haughty snapped, the word sounding like its opposite.

They walked back to where the boy, Ian, still sat disconsolately, alone. Haughty visibly nerved herself and approached him. "Hello, Ian," she said nicely.

"The harpy!" he exclaimed gladly.

"I have been thinking about your talent. I think it is better than you think. It could be really useful, when properly applied."

"You really believe that?"

"Yes, I do."

"You're lying. You're a true harpy. I love that."

That seemed to set her back half a moment, but she rallied. "Actually we were discussing it, and figured out a way it might be used. Do you want to try it?"

"Try what?" he asked, looking at her front. Jumper realized that Wenda was right about what boys noticed.

"Bl**p!" she exclaimed impatiently. "I mean, very good. Let's see what your wonderful talent can do." She forced a smile.

"Was that a cuss word?" he asked eagerly.

"No! The bl**ping Adult Conspiracy says I can't cuss in your presence."

"That's why you have those stars in it," he said, catching on. "So I won't know you really said bleep."

"That's why," she agreed, kissing him on the cheek.

He looked pleasantly faint. "Can children freak out?" he asked. "Because I think I almost did."

"No, they can't freak out, because they don't know the real words."

"When you kissed me."

"You still can't freak out. I'll prove it." She kissed him directly on the mouth.

He freaked out.

"Oh, to h**l and d**nation!" she swore. "I blew it!"

Ian burst out laughing, unfreaked. "No, you didn't. I just pretended. But I bet if I were older, I would freak out."

"Let's test your talent," Haughty said, discomfited. She obviously wasn't used to dealing with boys.

She went to the moat, and the boy followed, sneaking more peeks at her front. The other members of the party remained in the background, letting her handle it.

"See if you can step in the water," Haughty said.

"But the piranha fish will bite me."

Haughty put her face down near the surface. "If you fish mess with us, I'll make a face like this," she said. Then she made a harpy face that curdled the nearest water. The fish fled.

"Say, you're good," Ian said.

"Harpies are mean birds," Haughty said with satisfaction.

Ian put his left foot to the water. It recoiled. He stepped on the sand below the water, and a depression formed around his foot. "See? I drive it away. I can't even drink unless I capture some in a cup so it can't escape. What use is that?"

"I'm not sure. But let's see how far you can take this. Wade out into the moat."

"I don't know. I never tried that before."

"I'll make a face like this," she said, repeating the one that had scared away the fish.

"Great!" he said, charmed. He waded into the water.

The water withdrew from him, leaving a dry trench behind.

"Great!" Olive echoed quietly.

Haughty followed in that trench. "Can you continue?" she asked. "This is so wonderful!"

"I guess," Ian agreed, flattered. He walked farther into the moat.

The water continued to avoid him, making a deeper trench.

"This is amazing!" Haughty said. "There seems to be no limit to your power."

Ian paused, glancing back at her. "You're just saying that."

"Well, maybe I'm exaggerating slightly. But it *is* a great talent. Can you go deeper?"

Ian walked deeper. The sides of the trench rose up until they were over his head. Then they curved inward until he was walking in a tunnel.

"My friends will never believe this," Haughty said. "May I bring them in so they know I'm not lying?"

"Sure." Her constant flattery was evidently shoring up his confidence.

"Hey, you characters!" Haughty called. "Come here!"

They came, following her into the trench. "Now do you believe it?"

"We believe you," Olive said. "This is terrific."

"But I doubt he could make it all the way across the moat," Phanta said. "There's just too much water."

"I'll show you," Ian said with another fresh burst of confidence. He strode forward.

The tunnel formed with him. Haughty followed him, expressing increasing amazement, and the others followed her. The adult humans had to bow their heads to fit within the tunnel, and Jumper had to scoot along on halfway-folded legs, but they all made it.

They walked along the bottom of the moat. The piranhas swam close, eyeing them, but couldn't reach them, and when Haughty looked, they quickly retreated. Even the moat monster took a look, but let the tunnel be.

The tunnel started angling up. Then it reached the other side, and opened into a trench again. They followed it all the way out of the moat.

"You did it!" Haughty exclaimed, kissing Ian again. "It's such a great talent! You can go anywhere you want to, and no river, lake or sea can stop you. You can even take your friends with you. What could be better than that?"

"I guess it is pretty good," Ian agreed in wonder.

"It certainly is," she agreed, and kissed him again on the mouth.

He froze. The trench and tunnel collapsed. The way across the moat was gone. But all of them were across.

"But he didn't freak out before," Haughty said.

"You didn't mean the kiss, before," Olive said.

"Oh, bl**p! I'm sorry."

"Just snap your fingers, and he'll snap out of it," Olive said.

"I don't have any fingers," Haughty said. "Just wings."

"Oh. Sorry." Olive snapped her fingers.

Ian snapped out of it. He found himself standing waist deep in water. "What happened?"

"I kissed you and you freaked out," Haughty said. "I'm sorry."

"Wow! I thought I was dreaming." Now that he had recovered, the water drew away from him, forming a waist-deep depression.

"We have to go now," Haughty told him. "But now you know how you can use your wonderful talent. You could even be an underwater tour guide."

"I guess I could," Ian said, beginning to appreciate the possibilities. "Thanks."

"And you're a wonderful boy. I'm glad I met you."

"Wow," he said, blushing. He stared after them as long as they were in sight.

"You're some actress," Olive murmured to the harpy.

"Who was acting? It *is* a great talent."

This time the circling glance included Jumper. It seemed the cynical harpy had become a believer.

And they had navigated the second Challenge. "One to go," Olive said grimly.

They faced the blank wall of the castle. There were no doors, windows, gates or apertures; it was solid stone throughout.

"There has to be a way in," Olive said. "And I think Jumper and Phanta have to find it."

Because Maeve and Wenda had handled the first Challenge, and Olive and Haughty had handled the second. It made sense that they all be tested.

Jumper exchanged a glance with Phanta, two eyes apiece. It was plain that she had no more idea how to proceed than he did.

"Maybe we should just follow it around and see what offers," he said, feeling inadequate.

"And try to recognize the key when we see it," she agreed.

They walked. Soon they came to what looked like a bear, but on closer inspection it turned out to be made entirely from rings. "What are you?" Jumper asked, curious.

"I'm a ring bear," it replied. "I commonly hang out at weddings, where they need rings."

Jumper tried to figure out a way that this could help them get past the wall, but his mind was blank. "Thank you."

"If you ever get married, remember me," the bear said, rattling its rings.

"Spiders don't marry," Jumper said. "At least, not the way human people do. But thank you."

They moved on. They came to a low hedge. But when they got closer, it turned out to be a very furry pig. In fact, it seemed to become a mass of foliage at its top, a veritable garden of shrubbery. "What are you?" Phanta asked it.

"I am a hedge hog, of course," the pig replied.

Jumper lacked the groaning reflex that human folk had, but he suspected he might be learning it. Another pun!

"Thank you," Phanta said politely, with only the ghost of a smile.

Next was a pine tree that was shaped somewhat like a fat pig, with needlelike hairs standing out from its body. "What are you?" Phanta inquired.

"I am a porky pine," the tree responded.

This time it was Haughty who groaned. "Porcupine, with quills," she said.

Maeve plucked a thick quill and put it to her mouth. "Pork rind," she said.

"Evidently this is not a guessing game," Maeve said.

"But what kind of game is it?" Wenda asked.

"We did not have to guess the names or talent of the folk in the second Challenge," Jumper said. "We just had to figure out how to use one to get across the moat. This must be similar."

"That's odd," Olive said. "Normally all three Challenges are quite different."

"This time it's not the Challenges, but the people who are different," Phanta said.

That seemed to be it. They moved on.

They came to a donkey who was busy counting things. When it saw them, it counted them. "Five maidens and a big spider," it said. "So it shall be noted."

"What are you?" Phanta asked.

"A census burro, of course."

Now there was more than one groan.

They came to a clumsy bird flapping around at the edge of the moat. "What are you?" Phanta asked.

"Awk!" the bird exclaimed.

"I asked, what kind of creature are you?" Phanta repeated.

"And I told you," the bird said. "I am an awkward."

"A clumsy auk," Maeve said, making a face.

They didn't seem to be getting anywhere. None of these creatures seemed likely to help them get beyond the wall.

An odd metal craft floated by on the moat. It lifted a metal arm to wave. "He-low, strangers," it called metallically.

"Oh, for bl**p's sake," Haughty said, disgusted. "It's a ro-boat, a floating robot. It could have carried us across."

"Had we just found it," Olive agreed.

"But it won't help us with the wall," Phanta said.

"We can spot puns forever," Wenda said. "But my suspicion is growing that knot one of them wood help."

"What are you saying?" Maeve asked.

"That we need to try something else."

Then a bulb flashed over Phanta's head. "Maybe we need to change the rules."

"And what are *yew* saying?" Wenda demanded.

"I am saying that maybe we should stop finding puns we encounter, and start defining puns we can use. Ones that will help us."

"Like what?"

"I do not know," the ghost woman confessed. "But there must be something."

That gave Jumper an idea. "Could there be a wall pun? Like a wall flower, or—" A lightbulb flashed over his head.

"What is it?" Phanta asked.

Jumper passed two of his legs across the surface of the wall. He found a shape. "A wall-rus!" he exclaimed.

The wall made a honking sound. A shape came out of it, a massive creature with flippers, a fishy tail, and two huge tusks. It plunged into the water. The wall-rus.

And it left a wall-rus–shaped hole in the wall, big enough for them to pass through. They had found the key.

They stepped through the gap. Jumper was the last. He was larger than the hole, but as a spider he was malleable, and he was able to squeeze through without discomfort.

They stood inside the wall, and inside the Good Magician's Castle. They had navigated the third Challenge.

4
MISSION

H ello, friends." It was a woman they had not seen before, standing in shadows.

"Hello," Jumper replied politely. "We have come to see the Good Magician."

"Of course. I am Wira, his daughter-in-law. I will take you to him now." She turned and led the way farther into the castle.

Just like that, they were succeeding.

"Don't you want to know who we are?" Olive asked somewhat plaintively.

"I already know you, Olive Hue. You and your friends have been expected."

This ruffled Haughty. "Then why did you put us through those bl**ping Challenges?"

"This is protocol, Haughty," Wira replied mildly. "The Good Magician needed to be sure your group had the required qualities for the mission he has in mind. Had you been balked, or given up, he would have known you were not."

"Guessing stupid puns?" Phanta demanded.

"Assessing a situation and discovering its solution, Phanta," Wira said. "We regret that more varied Challenges were not available at this time; the Magician has to make do with what he has on hand. The querists largely select themselves, you see, as you did."

"We just want to get our separate problems dealt with," Maeve said. "It's largely by accident that we formed a group."

"So it seems, Maeve. But perhaps it was fate. I wonder whether the fact that you are five winsome females and one rough male is really co-incidence."

"Yew can wonder, but we wood knot believe it."

"Perhaps you will, in time, Wenda." They entered a nicely lit room. "Here is Humfrey's Designated Wife, MareAnn."

"Half Wife," the woman said. She was about twenty-five and looked vaguely like a horse lover.

"Actually I'm 166, the same age as Magician Humfrey," she said. "Don't look startled, Jumper; I'm not a mind reader. It's just that I get this reaction a lot. We wives are spelled to maintain our ideal ages. In real life we'd all be long since dead. It's a perquisite of working with the Magician of Information."

"Yew dew knot look like half a woman," Wenda said. "*I* look like that."

"I am a half wife, not a half woman," MareAnn said. "I was Hum-frey's first love, but for reasons which seem trivial in retrospect I elected not to marry him until much later, by which time his quota was almost used up. I take my full month's turn, as do the other wives. That spreads out the burden."

"Burden?" Olive asked.

"He is not the easiest man to live with. He does get grumpy."

"I wood settle for a grumpy man, if he loved me," Wenda said wist-fully.

"Perhaps that will be the case," MareAnn said. "Have some horse chestnuts." She proffered a plate.

"They won't make us hoarse?" Phanta asked.

MareAnn laughed. "No, these are merely nuts in the shape of horses, from my chest of nuts."

They nibbled on nuts, making small to middle-sized talk. Wira had disappeared.

Then Wira reappeared. "The Good Magician will see you now," she said. "In the courtyard."

"Knot in his office?" Wenda asked.

"The party wouldn't fit. The courtyard is much nicer anyway. This way, please."

They followed her there. She was right: the courtyard was pleasant, with paths winding through flower gardens. "The Magician must like flowers," Wenda said appreciatively.

"He hardly notices them," Wira said. "The wives and I like flowers."

"Wives and querists can be a pain in the *," a gnomish little old man grumped, appearing ahead of them.

"In the what?" Olive asked.

"Asterisk," Maeve murmured. "Emphasis on the donkey."

"Good Magician, meet Maeve Maenad," Wira said.

"A maenad with a mind?" Humfrey asked. "Ludicrous."

"See, he likes you already," Wira murmured, preempting Maeve's furious retort.

"Well, I'm not sure I like *him*. He—"

"What is your problem, maenad?" Humfrey demanded.

Maeve opened her mouth. A wisp of steam came out and her wax teeth started to melt. She had learned to talk with them in, but there were limits.

"He means what brought you here," Wira said. "Your Question."

Oh. "I need to escape the stork. I was tricked into sending a signal, and—"

"And yours, woodwife?" he asked curtly.

"I want to bee a whole woman, so I can have a normal—"

"Yours?" he asked Haughty.

"I need to get rid of my nightly alter ego, Hottie."

The Magician turned to Olive. "Yours?"

"I want to be able to keep my imaginary friends."

He turned to Phanta. "Yours?"

"To be able to control my ghostly state."

"And yours, spider?"

"I want to go home."

"All will be granted. There will be a price."

"A year's service," Olive said.

"A mission. All of you will participate. Agreed?"

"H**l no!" Haughty said. "I have other business to attend to."

"So do I," Phanta said. "These are nice people, but this is a temporary association."

"Ad hoc," Olive agreed.

"For this purpose only," Maeve translated. "Getting to this castle."

"But we have to serve for the Answer, or he might knot solve our problems," Wenda reminded them. "We might as well serve together."

"First we need to know the mission," Jumper said.

"Background," the Magician said grumpily. "The Demon Pluto lost a Demon bet and lost so much status he was reduced to a Dwarf Demon, no longer considered parallel to the others. He was so angry that he hurled himself madly about and crashed into the cable connecting the Mundane Internet with the magical Outernet, severing it. Now there is no contact between the two, and folk are getting annoyed. It is imperative that it be restored. But it will not be easy to repair. Only someone with the ability to span both magical and mundane realms can do it, by first drawing the several portions together, then reconnecting them. That is you, Jumper."

Jumper jumped, surprised. "Me!"

"Half your legs are positive, and half are negative, so you can straddle the Internet and Outernet without getting fried. That is why you must do this job. When you accomplish it, the flux that hooked you out of your realm will be abated, and you will be able return to it at will."

"That makes sense," Jumper said.

"But what about us?" Haughty demanded. "We're not spiders, and we have nothing to do with Demons, whether dwarf or otherwise. In fact, it might be dangerous to mess with one." The others nodded in agreement.

"More background," the Magician grumped. "There is a suspicion that the crash into the cable was not entirely accidental. Pluto may have taken it out in a fit of rage, or worse, cunning."

"Cunning?" Haughty asked.

"He may have been embarrassed by his demotion, so he severed the cable to prevent news from circulating. It is already known in Mundania, but not yet in Xanth. He is pretending to remain a full-status Demon. Repairing the cable would enable the news of his humiliation to get through to Xanth. So he may wish to prevent the cable from being repaired."

"And he'll chew up anyone who tries," Maeve said, picking right up on the violent aspect.

"And even a Dwarf Demon is still a lot more than any mortal creature can handle," Olive said. "So it will be dangerous."

"All the more reason for us knot to participate," Wenda said.

"Jumper will not be able to do it alone," the Magician said. "That is why he will need a supportive group."

"But we're no such group!" Phanta protested. "We're just innocent helpless maidens."

"With your help, it is possible," the Magician said.

"How do you know this?" Maeve demanded.

The Magician looked down his nose at her. This was a nice effect, because the maenad stood half again as tall as the gnome. "I am the Magician of Information."

"But you're up against a Demon," Olive said cannily. "They don't follow mortal rules."

"Precisely, maiden. Therefore I rely on the Prophecy that covers this situation."

"Prophecy?"

"The one Jumper carries with him. I believe it implies that he should emulate the Ogre."

"It doesn't say that," Jumper protested.

"It says in part, 'Like the ogre.' Because there is Demon involvement I am not sure, but resembling the ogre seems indicated."

"I'm a spider, not an ogre!"

"You can, however, emulate his situation or action."

"What kind of a Prophecy is that?" Maeve demanded. "It's just confusing advice. We don't even know which ogre."

"There is only one ogre who ever did anything notable," the Magician said. "Because ogres are justly proud of their strength, ugliness, and stupidity. That is Smash Ogre, who through a fluke of parentage was not sufficiently stupid, and thus managed to accomplish something. He actually won the respect of the Night Stallion, the lord of the dream realm. He has to be the one."

"I've heard of him," Olive said. "But he's old."

"He is sixty-five years old," the Magician agreed. "But still alive. Your first step will be to visit him and find out what to emulate. Then do so. This will enable the group of you to accomplish the mission."

"If we survive the Demon," Olive said. "It's not worth it."

"You will have a basis to judge whether it is worth it," the Magician said. "I have arranged for the temporary solutions." He lifted a box containing six small vials. "Each of you will drink one potion, and your problems will be solved for the duration of the mission. When you accomplish it, the solutions may become permanent. If you do not, they will dissipate, and you will face the same fates you do at present."

"You are saying," Haughty said, canny in her turn, "that we can start the mission, but opt out any time if we change our minds?"

"I am saying that," the Magician agreed. "However—"

"There's always a however," Olive murmured.

"—not only will you lose your solution, you will cause the others to lose theirs, because only the complete party can accomplish the mission."

"The others wood knot like that," Wenda said.

"What could they do about it?" Phanta asked.

"We could tear you apart," Maeve said, removing her wax teeth to show her points.

"Not if I turned ghostly," Phanta said.

"Not if I flew away," Haughty said.

"Not if I bit your head off," Jumper said.

"Not if I imagined a dragon friend to protect me," Olive said.

Wenda was troubled. "I dew knot want to dew any of those things. I just want to bee a real woman instead of a hollow shell."

There was a brief embarrassed silence. "We were just discussing it," Olive said after half a moment. "We're not thinking of doing it."

"Then it seems the mission is on," Jumper said.

"Take your solutions," the Magician said. "Then I will fill you in on the details."

"Details?" Haughty asked suspiciously. "I don't trust this."

"Mainly that there will be two additions to your group, to match the number in the ogre's original group, in case that is the nature of the emulation. You must maintain that number throughout, because the auspices indicate that only the complete group of eight can succeed in accomplishing the mission." The Magician frowned. "I repeat: it is imperative that the mission be accomplished."

"Additions?" Olive asked.

"Two more girls."

A glance circled around one and a half times. "Girls are harmless," Phanta said.

"As long as they do their part," Olive said.

Maeve cut to the chase. "Who?"

"They are sisters, age nineteen. Nice girls. Their names are Dawn and Eve."

"Why them?" Wenda asked.

"They became too competitive about a prospective boyfriend, so their parents grounded them until they sort it out. This mission will accomplish that."

This time a shrug went around the group. They could get along with two nice girls. Especially typical boy-crazy teens. They would not have much else on their limited minds, so they could surely be managed.

The Magician passed out the vials, and each drank the solution. The effect was immediate.

Wenda's stuffed clothing fell off and she stood nude, her back side as plump and rounded as her front side, her head solid. She was as pretty as any nymph. She gazed at herself in a pool, amazed and gratified. "Oh, I wood give anything to bee like this always!" she exclaimed. "And my circuitry is no longer all in my shell, so Com Pewter can knot use me now."

Maeve did not change visibly, but something about her did. Jumper knew that the stork had been banished from her vicinity; she no longer needed to hide. She was so relieved she was positively pretty.

Haughty also did not change visibly, but her manner did. "I feel it! I have control over my state. Hottie can appear only at my bl**ping behest." Hottie appeared for a moment, frowning, then faded. She had been leashed.

Phanta also remained the same yet changed. "I'm no longer wary of the dark," she said. "I won't ghost unless I choose to, day or night, eyes open or closed." For a good moment and a half she became ghostly, then returned to her solid state. "Glorious!"

Olive summoned an imaginary friend, a phenomenally beautiful woman. "This is Angie Ina," Olive said. "As a child she was a heartthrob. Now as a woman she is drop-dead gorgeous. Can you stay awhile, Angie?"

"I believe I can," Angie agreed. "As long as there are no young men present."

"Only a spider and an old man," Olive said. "Neither will drop dead looking at you."

"Well, when you need a young man to drop dead, just let me know," Angie said, smiling.

Jumper was a spider, but even he felt the power of that smile. His multiple knees weakened, and he had to stiffen them lest he drop. A real human man would have been dead already.

"Why don't you take a walk around, Angie," Olive said. "Just don't show yourself to any young men."

"I will try not to," Angie agreed, and walked away. Even her walk was knee-weakening; there was a certain swing to her hips that attracted all of Jumper's eyes on that side of his head. Yes, she looked delicious, but it seemed to be more than his appreciation of prospective food.

"The thing is to verify that she can continue existence when out of my sight and mind," Olive explained. "I want her to exist until I send her back to vacant imagination."

"You will, however, be able to summon only one friend at a time," Humfrey said. "It is a limitation of the spell."

"I can live with that," Olive said.

Jumper hesitated with his own vial. It was translucent, containing reddish fluid. "Unless this sends me home, why should I take it?" he asked reasonably.

"Yours isn't quite the same," the Magician said. "It won't send you home; that will be enabled when you reconnect the cable. But because there is likely to be some opposition, and perhaps danger, all of you will need to be able to work closely together. In addition, a group with a giant spider will be perhaps too obvious, so you will need to have the ability to mask it. This potion will enable both."

Now Jumper was suspicious. "How?"

"By enabling you to turn human."

Jumper was revolted. "I don't want to be human!"

"Temporarily. The potion is effective until nullified by the counterpotion." The Magician held up a vial with a bluish liquid. "You will not be trapped in a foreign form."

"I don't want to be in it even temporarily," Jumper said.

"Jumper, I hate to say it, but he is making sense," Wenda said. "Suppose the Demon is looking for a party with a big spider? He will know exactly which it is, and we wood knot bee able to hide from him. But a human man might fool him. Yew should try it."

"And get some practice on two legs," Maeve agreed.

"And let us get to recognize your human form," Olive said.

They did have some points. Jumper nerved himself, then gulped down the solution.

Immediately his body began to change. It started shrinking. His four front legs merged into two, and so did his four rear legs. His round body shrank into an oblong torso. And worst of all, his eight eyes clustered together to form only two. He could no longer see in all directions simultaneously. He could no longer maintain his balance by having a leg at every point. He tilted, and started to fall.

Wenda and Maeve caught his arms on either side, supporting him. Still he wobbled, and they had to jam close to his sides to support him more firmly, keeping him upright. Olive and Phanta came up in front and behind, helping. He was surrounded on four sides by human damsels.

He kept his feet, thanks to their help. But there were other oddities.

All four maidens were remarkably soft, and the way they pressed against him felt odd but good. Remarkably good.

"Put some clothes on him," Haughty called. "At least some shorts."

"Clothes?" Jumper asked. "Spiders don't wear clothes."

"You're not a spider anymore," Haughty reminded him.

Wira hurried up with a pair of boxer shorts. They looked ready to punch someone out, but she reproved them and they settled down. "Lift one foot," she said to Jumper.

He tried, but with his legs bound together in pairs he couldn't. Instead he tried to fall over again, and would have succeeded if the four girls had not held him firmly in place. Very softly and firmly.

Wira knelt down and put a hand on one of his thick-legged feet. "This one."

Aided by her touch, he lifted two of his hind legs. They came up together, and she put one loop of the shorts over the foot. Then she had him put that foot down and lift the other so she could fit the other loop over it. Finally she hauled the shorts up until they reached the top of his legs and fit around his middle, covering the accessories there.

"That's better," Haughty said. "Naked men aren't necessarily very aesthetic."

"Actually he is handsome enough," MareAnn said. "Not as well-endowed as a horse, but then, what else is? He could make some girl a fine companion."

"Very fine," Phanta agreed, patting Jumper's rear side. "Too bad he had to cover it up."

For some reason the others laughed. But Jumper couldn't focus on that now. He was too busy trying to get his balance. Not only had he been reduced from eight legs to four, two of them were up in the air, not touching the ground. This made it just about impossible to remain vertical. He would have fallen, were it not for the continuing support of the four girls.

"I don't think this can work," he said. "I must get all four limbs on the ground, to maintain my balance."

"Not so, Jumper," Wira said. "You will get the hang of it soon. It's a perpetual balancing act, but it can be done."

"Meanwhile, we wood knot let yew fall," Wenda said, clinging closely to his left side. She seemed unusually soft her entire length. Perhaps because she was no longer made of wood.

"Definitely not," Olive agreed, remaining plastered to his front side. She was not only soft, she was obscurely exciting in a way he had not noticed before.

"Get away from him, you flirts," Haughty said. "Let him find his own balance."

Flirts? They were merely holding him up. Still, there was something remarkably interesting about them. He might have figured out what, if he wasn't having so much trouble staying upright.

"Here is a walker," Wira said. Sure enough, a metallic framework was walking behind her. "Put your hands on its rails; it will support you while you learn."

The walker came to stand before him. Jumper got his arms loose from the grips of Wenda and Maeve and put his new hands on the bars.

"You too, Olive," the harpy cried. "And you, Phanta."

"Oh," Olive said, as if just now realizing that she was standing mostly between Jumper and the walker. She squeezed around it and got out of his way.

"Ditto," Phanta said, stepping back from his hindside.

Now he was nervously alone, but the walker did help to keep him upright. He hauled one foot forward, then the other, taking his first steps.

"A few days should do it," Wira said. "Then you won't need the walker."

"A few days!" he exclaimed. "I thought this was for just an hour."

"It is until you learn how to manage your human form," Wira said. "You can't afford to be clumsy when you invoke it on an emergency basis. I'm sure the girls will help you cope."

"I'm sure I can learn to walk faster than that," he said desperately.

"But you will also need to learn the nuances of human behavior. Such as not going around naked."

"What's wrong with being natural?" he demanded.

"Humans aren't natural. They are girt about by all manner of conventions. It will take time for you to catch up with them all."

"I'd rather stay a spider."

Wira shrugged. "Maybe your friends can persuade you otherwise."

"First dibs!" Phanta said. A frown circulated among the others, but they did not protest openly.

"What are you talking about?" Jumper asked.

"Persuasion," Phanta said. "Here is one reason for you to remain human for a while." She stepped close, ghosted through the walker, and stood immediately before him. She put her arms around his body and hugged him close. Then she put her mouth up to his and kissed him.

It was like getting smacked by a warm living pillow. Little stars and planets radiated outward from the contact and orbited his head. Suddenly she was not only warm and soft, she was lovable. He seemed to float halfway out of his body and to peer down from above, seeing the two of them standing there, his hands on the bars of the walker, her arms wrapped around him, their two faces connected.

Then everything whited out and he saw nothing.

Until something snapped near his human ear. He opened his eyes. Phanta was gone and he was standing alone again. "What happened?" he asked, still halfway reeling.

"You freaked out," Haughty said. "She kissed you, and you flipped. That means you're sufficiently human."

"Now do you know why you should remain human for a time?" Olive asked.

"To do that again?" he asked.

"To know how to handle it," Wira said.

He had not wanted to remain any longer in this odd clumsy body. Now it seemed there could be some reason: to avoid being vulnerable to freaking out, which might incapacitate him at a bad time. "Yes, I must learn," he agreed. "Maybe I need to kiss her again."

"After you learn to walk," Wira said. "And then it will be someone else's turn. To assist you."

Oh. He had taken a sudden, surprising liking to Phanta. He had not liked or disliked any of the girls before, apart from the pleasant camaraderie of friendship. It wasn't the kind of thing spiders did. Perhaps it was coincidental. But he probably needed to understand it.

He practiced walking with the walker, and began to develop the skill. His body had relevant reflexes, when he let them operate, constantly correcting his balance. Finally he put aside the walker and walked alone without falling.

The girls applauded. He had learned something useful.

Then they dressed him. Wira brought male human clothing, and the girls showed him how to put it on. There were trousers that were similar to the trunks, only larger. One foot at a time, and draw them up as far as they would go, then fasten the belt to anchor them there. A shirt, that went on over the arms and back, then buttoned up the front. Shoes.

"What?" he demanded. "Spiders don't wear anything on their feet! It would mess up webcasting."

"You don't have web in human form," Wira said.

So he reluctantly submitted to donning socks and shoes. They seemed unbearably clumsy at first, but soon he got used to them.

Then he became uncomfortable. "I need to—" He hesitated, because he had learned that the related terms were seldom if ever spoken in public.

It was Haughty who caught on. "You need to p**p," she said. "And I don't mean pulp."

"Yes. But this clothing—"

"I'll handle this," Haughty told the others. "Harpies have gutter experience." She looked at Wira. "Where is the chamber?"

"This way," Wira said.

Soon Jumper and Haughty were in the chamber. There was a bench with the center of its seat cut out, leaving a hole. "Take down your pants," she said. "Your shorts too. Then sit on the hole."

Mystified, he did so. "Now p**s," she said. "P**p."

He caught her meaning despite the asterisks. "But there's no ground here."

"It's below the hole."

Oh. It seemed that for some reason humans covered up the ground, so they could use it for this purpose without going outside the building. He realized that this must be why the girls had gone into a special little chamber on occasion at rest stops: to p**s and p**p. He concentrated on the business at hand, though it wasn't exactly his hand he was using. The clumsy anatomy seemed to be working.

In due course they returned to the others, mission accomplished. Jumper now knew how the human body functioned in this respect, and how to handle the problem of clothing.

Next they went for a human dinner. There wasn't a fat bug anywhere in it, just vegetables, fruits, breads, drinks, and other things. Olive guided him in human manners, it being her turn. He had to learn how to use odd little utensils instead of just picking things up and chomping them. It was ludicrously inconvenient, but possible. At least the drink wasn't rhed whine; none of them wanted that.

Then it was time to rest for the night. He had to learn how to use a bed. This was a frightfully inconvenient device, with a distastefully soft mattress, and cloth sheets that seemed to be designed for tangling limbs. But Olive insisted it was necessary, because it was the human way. She tucked him in, kissed him, and by the time his freakout ended she was gone. There was nothing to do but sleep through the night.

"I wouldn't say that," a soft voice said.

He recognized it. His merely human eyes were unable to penetrate the darkness, but his ears worked well enough. "Angie Ina! Olive's imaginary friend. What are you doing here?"

"I think Olive forgot about me," Angie said, coming to sit on the bed beside him. "But with the Good Magician's spell, I can remain in existence longer than her limited attention span. So I am exploring my own independent parameters." Her hand found his right ankle. "It seems you have assumed human form, Jumper."

"Yes, I am practicing for when I may need it. So as not to be ignorant and clumsy. But I would much prefer to be in my natural form."

"There may be compensations."

"The others seem to think so."

"Perhaps we can do each other some good," Angie said as her hand massaged his leg in an alarmingly evocative manner. "I want to garner some independent individual experience, and I think you need it too. What was it like when you first changed form?"

"The girls had to prop me up on four sides, lest I fall. They were remarkably soft."

"Soft like this?" she inquired, finding his right hand. She lifted it and carried it to her chest.

The scene seemed to jump, though the darkness prevented any scene from showing. "What happened?" Jumper asked, dazed.

"You freaked out, as I rather suspected you would."

"Why did I freak out? I can't see anything to make me do that."

"Because touch can do it too, when the man is fresh, new, and innocent. I put your hand on my breast."

"Is that what Haughty would pronounce br**st?"

"Exactly. Had I done that in daylight, you would have dropped dead. As it was you merely freaked out. We shall have to work on that."

"Work on what?"

"Your innocence. You will have trouble completing your mission if any woman can nullify you so simply."

"I don't know how to fix my innocence."

"Fortunately, I do. I will educate you so that by morning only the very most potent panties will freak you out, and then only briefly. Thus will I accomplish my bit for the mission."

"You can do that?" he asked, amazed.

"Oh, yes, Jumper. I must say it is a pleasure being able to relate in this manner without killing my lover."

"Your what?"

"I think we have talked enough," she said, pulling the sheet off his body. She stretched out beside him. "We will start with kissing, and go on from there. I think the bird will not notice, because you're really a spider and I'm imaginary. I trust you have the wit to keep a secret; I would prefer that my friend Olive not know immediately."

"I don't understand."

That was all he managed to say before she kissed him. The rest of the night was a melange of freak-outs, but she was correct: by morning nothing she could do made him freak, though she did bring him more pleasure than he had imagined a single body of any type could experience. His greatest pleasure before had been biting the heads off juicy fat bugs; this was an order of magnitude greater.

Then she left him floating in the darkness, obsessed with the sheer wonder of it all. He didn't even get to bid her farewell. But he did remember that this was supposed to be a secret. He would certainly honor that, partly in the hope that he would see—rather, feel—Angie again.

In the morning it was Phanta who got him up. "But isn't it one of the others' turn to help me?" he asked.

"Wenda is a woodwife, with no indoor experience before this mission," she explained. "Maeve is a maenad, ditto. We had to educate them similarly at the Bra & Girll. So it is up to Olive and me, because we have experience."

"There is something else," he said as he dressed. "When you kissed me, I freaked out. Why did that happen, and what is it?" Actually, he now had half a notion, but the other half still perplexed him.

"It is a power human women have over human men," she said seriously. "They can flash their panties, or sometimes their bras, and the men freak out. Inexperienced men can be freaked out by kisses. You are thoroughly inexperienced. It relates to stork summoning."

"Stork summoning," he repeated, a fair light dawning. That was the bird Angie had referred to! "That's what got Maeve into trouble."

"Yes. So it's not something carelessly done."

No? His dawning understanding made him question that. "But you— with Crater—"

"Sometimes it is possible to go through the motions without actually signaling the stork. If a girl knows how. I did it with him, then turned ghost, which nullified anything he had given me. But other girls can't do that. So as a general rule, you don't want to go through those motions unless you are serious about the relationship."

He knew of another girl who could do it, though. Those had been phenomenal motions! The kind he would have been glad to do with Phanta, had she cared to go that route. But he wanted the final confirmation. "With you—when you—I felt—what was that?"

"I vamped you, as I did Crater. To show you that there are potential rewards to being human. But you know I have no serious interest in you, because you're really a spider. A nice guy, but a spider." She paused. "If you should decide to remain human permanently, I might reconsider. But first we have a mission to accomplish."

"We do," he agreed, satisfied to end their discussion of this subject.

Phanta made sure he was ready for public display. Then they went to join the others for breakfast. They were all there, with Haughty on a perch at the end of the table. Jumper was seated at the other end, facing her, with the four maidens at the sides.

"How was your night?" Olive inquired.

"It was a surprisingly pleasant night," he said. "I would be satisfied to have every night like that." He hoped Angie was listening.

"That's good," Wenda said. "We feared you wood have trouble sleeping in the human form. I did; I kept rolling on my backside and waking up startled. I never had a backside before."

"I had to adjust to back side and front side," Jumper said. "Both could be quite remarkable." He hoped they didn't realize he wasn't talking about his own sides. "As well as arms, legs, and face." Though he had night experience with only one woman, he was sure she was utterly remarkable.

"I slept very well," Maeve said. "For the first time in days, I did not have to worry about being found by the stork."

Jumper smiled with his human mouth. He was learning facial expressions too. "I did not worry about the stork either."

They all laughed, assuming he was joking.

After the meal they went to the courtyard and trained him some more, teaching him minor human nuances like nodding politely when someone said or did something stupid, and not scratching his backside when anyone was watching.

Then they got serious. "You need not to freak out when any girl touches you or flashes you," Olive said.

"Flash?" he asked.

"I mentioned it this morning. Remember? Panties." She turned around, hoisted her skirt, and showed him. He got a flash of olive-drab green. He blinked, keeping his feet.

"He barely freaked, if at all," Phanta said. "Maybe he didn't catch enough of a glimpse."

Jumper had glimpsed them well enough, but was now almost immune, thanks to Angie. He nodded politely.

"Try again," Phanta said.

Olive tried again. First she made sure he was looking, then she bent over and threw her skirt up over her back. Jumper got a full in-his-face sight of well-filled panty.

The impact knocked him back, but he retained consciousness. "Very nice," he said.

"You just don't have it," Haughty cackled.

Olive glanced down at herself, evidently suppressing surprise and anger with a tinge of wonder. "Then let someone else try it."

"Gladly." Phanta stood before Jumper and flounced her skirt. Again he felt the impact, but it simply wasn't enough to freak him out.

Then Maeve tried it, and also failed.

Finally Wenda tried it. At that moment Angie Ina appeared in a shadowed alcove beyond her and simply turned to face away from him, not even lifting her skirt.

Jumper found himself lying on his back staring up at the sky, where an afterimage of Angie's backside lingered.

"Wenda did it!" Olive exclaimed as they helped him back to his feet. "Her panties freaked him out!"

"Who would have thought it," Phanta said, not seeming entirely pleased. "The woodwife."

"Maybe it's because my backside is new," Wenda said, surprised.

Wira entered the courtyard, conducting two more maidens. One was fair as the morning sunlight, with bright red hair and green eyes, the other dark as the close of day, with black hair and eyes. Both were strikingly beautiful.

"Please meet the final two members of your party," Wira said. "The Princesses Dawn and Eve."

"P-p-princesses?" Olive stuttered.

"We thought they were ordinary girls," Phanta said.

"We are ordinary girls at heart," Dawn said, with a smile that brightened the courtyard.

"Who happen to be Sorceresses," Eve said with a frown that darkened the courtyard again. "Grounded for the duration for no particular reason."

"Well, if you hadn't tried to steal my boyfriend—" Dawn flashed.

"*Your* boyfriend?" Eve retorted darkly. "*My* boyfriend. You're always stealing mine."

"Can I help it if they prefer sweetness to gloom?"

"Sickly sweetness!"

"They're right," Olive murmured. "They are typical teens, quarreling over boyfriends."

"Not for much longer," Dawn said brightly. "We're nineteen. Soon we'll be out of the teens."

"And ungroundable," Eve agreed darkly.

"And these are the other members of the mission," Wira said firmly. "No need to introduce them."

No need? What was this?

Dawn stepped forward to shake hands with Olive. "Olive Hue," she said. "Whose talent is to generate imaginary friends, one of whom is watching us now."

"Oh!" Olive said, chagrined. "I forgot to terminate Angie!" She looked around. "Where are you, Angie?"

But Angie did not answer.

"I can't do it until I touch her," Olive explained. "She must be out of hearing."

"Or maybe doesn't want to be terminated," Phanta said. Jumper was sure that was the case. How could Angie explore her life if it abruptly ended? He was glad she would remain, especially if she came to him again at night.

Dawn shook hands with Phanta. "Phanta, whose talent is to become a ghost," she said.

"How did you know that?" Phanta asked.

"It is my talent," Dawn replied. "I know anything about any living thing I touch."

"And I know anything about any inanimate thing I touch," Eve said. "We have complementary talents."

"You didn't seem to be complimenting each other just now," Olive said.

"ComplEmentary," Dawn said, capitalizing the E.

"They fill each other out," Eve said.

"You are both well filled out," Olive agreed, her mouth quirking. Jumper suspected he was missing something, again.

Dawn went on to Maeve. "Maeve Maenad!" she exclaimed, surprised. "I took you for a girl!"

"I'm a fake girl," Maeve said.

"To escape the stork," Dawn agreed. "That's unusual. But of course that scoundrel tricked you. In fact he raped you."

"He what?" Jumper asked.

"He tricked her into a love spring, then had his way with her. That was rape, because it was fraudulent."

"I wish I could chomp him," Maeve agreed.

"And Wenda Woodwife, another surprise," Dawn said, shaking hands with the next. "Well rounded."

"I wanted a rounded backside," Wenda confessed. "Men like it."

"They certainly do," Eve agreed. "It is the foundation for effective panties."

"And Haughty Harpy," Dawn concluded, touching a talon. "Together with Hottie Harpie."

She had proven her talent: she did know everything about anyone she touched.

Now Dawn came to Jumper. She took his hand, then her pretty mouth rounded with surprise. "You're a spider in human form!" she exclaimed. "Distant descendant of the Jumper who traveled with Grandpa Prince Dor to ancient Castle Roogna. An honorable lineage!"

Jumper was taken aback. "Thank you. I just want to return to my form and my realm."

She laughed. "Not entirely. I will keep your secret."

She knew about his liaison with Angie! "Thank you."

"For one thing, it gives you reason to complete this mission, doesn't it? The secret pleasures along the way."

"Yes," he admitted.

"Are you two princesses really going to travel with us?" Olive asked.

"Yes we are," Eve said. "It's our folks' way of getting back at us for fighting over a man."

"You can't share him?"

Dawn shook her head, her hair flouncing brightly. "We are princesses. We don't understand sharing."

"Couldn't he choose one of you?" Phanta asked.

"He's making *us* choose," Eve said darkly.

"But you're princesses and Sorceresses," Olive protested. "How can he make you do anything?"

"We wonder about that ourselves," Dawn said.

"But if you can touch him and know all about him," Phanta said, "then you surely know how to handle him."

"We both touched him and still couldn't tell," Eve said. "We're not sure whether he's alive or dead."

"This is weird!" Olive said.

"Yes," Dawn agreed. "But he's some man."

They let that be, and went back to training Jumper. By the end of the day he was almost sharp enough to fool anyone who wasn't a Sorceress.

"Tomorrow you should be able to revert to your own form," Wira said. "Then the group of you can start your mission."

"That will be a relief," Jumper said.

Dawn shot a sidelong glance at him. She knew he was hoping for another night with Angie.

And when he was alone in the dark, Angie came. "Thank you for keeping my secret," she said.

"Princess Dawn fathomed it. She said she would keep it too."

"She must have fathomed many secrets, so has become tolerant." She joined him on the bed and soon made him float in ecstasy. It was another great night.

"Will I see—I mean, meet you again?" he asked as the night weakened. She kissed him. "I think not."

"But you're so much fun to be with! If I have annoyed you in any way—"

"No, Jumper. It has been wonderful with you. You truly appreciate me, and I have enjoyed showing you how not to freak when you are near a woman. But my time in this realm must be limited. Olive can't summon another imaginary friend until I fade, and your party will surely need other friends."

"The sight of panties still freaks me some," he said desperately.

"You just want me to stay with you longer."

"Yes," he said, doing a human blush in the darkness.

"You're so sweet. But you need a real woman, not an imaginary one. So let's see if I can shore you up against panties, and then I really must go."

"Yes, shore me up," he agreed. He had discovered that freaking out, or coming close to it, was actually a pleasant experience.

"You understand, whatever you do with me is not really real," she said. "It's like a dream: it may seem real, but it's imaginary, because I am imaginary."

"It does seem real," he agreed eagerly.

"However, imaginary actions can have real effects. Your education is real, and your growing immunity to freaking is real. Even if our relationship is unreal."

"I hate to think of it that way."

A pale ray of moonlight was coming in a window. Angie went to stand in it, in her underwear. When the light struck her panties, Jumper almost freaked, but managed to hang on to consciousness.

"You are doing well," she said. "Maybe your spider nature helps shore up your immunity."

Then she lighted a candle and tried it again. This time he did freak, but recovered fairly quickly. They ran through it again, and again, until he was able to look at her and retain his composure, though severely buffeted.

"If you can handle my panties, you can handle any panties," she said. "I suggest that you conceal your ability, however."

"Conceal it?"

"Fake freaking out. That way no one will know you have become relatively immune. It could save your life or sanity, if a hostile nymph vamped you."

"Wenda and Maeve aren't hostile nymphs," he protested.

"True. But if you ever encounter another maenad, she may try to nullify you long enough for her to get within tearing and biting range. If you fake it, then you can bite off her head when she attacks you."

He nodded in the human manner. "I could do that."

"You are ready, Jumper."

He feared she was right. "Could we pretend I'm not, one more time?" he asked timidly.

"Ah, Jumper, you are miscast as a spider! You could make some lucky woman a marvelously submissive human husband." But she came to him, and they made love one more time, in the flickering candlelight. It might not be real, but it was delightful.

Then she dressed and went to the door, and he knew he would not see her again. "Thank you, thank you, Angie Ina," he called after her. "You truly make my heart throb."

"Welcome, Jumper. It's nice to be so sincerely appreciated." She was gone, leaving him both fulfilled and desolate.

Jumper got up, cleaned, dressed, and was ready when Olive came to fetch him. "You'll never believe what happened," she said. "I found my imaginary friend Angie Ina. It seems she had gotten lost. Now she's back in my mind where she belongs."

"I do believe," he said, with mixed feelings.

At breakfast Princess Dawn took one look at him. "You are ready," she said. "So it's time to start the mission."

"It is time," he agreed, slightly sadly.

"Where dew we start?" Wenda asked.

"Well, the Magician says to emulate the ogre," Olive said. "So maybe we had better consult with the ogre. Ogres are justifiably proud of their stupidity, but he might know something."

The others nodded. It was time to see the ogre.

5
OGRE

For a good two and a half moments it felt weird being a spider again, with eight eyes and eight legs and no concern for panties. Then Jumper settled comfortably back into his natural role.

Except in one respect: he discovered that he retained his memory of, and appreciation for, certain manform activities. He *did* now have an interest in panties, and in the activity they suggested. Angie had left her mark on him.

"It's good to have yew back, Jumper," Wenda said.

"Thank you, Wenda. But I was always Jumper, and value your friendship whatever my form of the moment." More than that: he now could see that in her filled-out form she was a luscious nymph, one who would be pleasant to hold and kiss. But for at least two and a half reasons he could not say that.

In fact, all six and a half of the girlform companions were appealing individuals. The half, of course, was Haughty, who lacked the human lower portion.

The Good Magician painted a compass on Olive's wrist that pointed toward the Ogre residence, and she checked it every so often. The first part of the trip was on an enchanted path, so they had no concern about safety. They walked along in a loose group, still getting to know each other.

Dawn fell in beside Jumper, who was at the rear. He was able to travel much faster than the humans, so was not setting the pace. "That was smart of Angie," she murmured. "To immunize you against panties."

"She said it could save my life or sanity."

"She's right. Also it makes sense. You're immune as a spider, so this extends it to your human form."

"I won't assume human form unless I have to," he said. "I have many potions and counterpotions, but I don't want to waste them."

"That, too, makes sense." She paused. "Are you really immune in this form?"

"Yes," he said, glancing at her with two or three eyes. It wasn't a lie, because he was immune in both human and spider forms, thanks to Angie.

And paused himself, for she was wearing only bra and panties. She was very pretty, for a human, and the items were nicely filled. But they affected mainly his memory: he would have loved to see them when in human form, when it might have been possible to do something with them. As it was, they were interesting but hardly freaking. As a spider he was limited to looking, not touching.

"Just testing," she said, and in half a moment she was fully dressed again.

He had heard from one of the other girls that Dawn and Eve were two of the naughtiest princesses extant. He was beginning to believe it. They were both Sorceresses, but would they really help the mission?

They encountered a man walking in the other direction. "Well, hello, lovely maidens," he said jovially. "And hello, huge ugly spider."

"He is Jumper, and he is knot ugly for his kind," Wenda said firmly. Her flesh was much firmer now, instead of wooden; perhaps it contributed to her dialogue.

"I apologize," the man said. "I am Michael, and my talent is to touch a picture, or draw one, and be transported to that scene. So I travel a lot, and see many interesting things, and tend to speak my mind openly."

The girls introduced themselves. "Could you draw a picture of the Ogre's Den and enable us to go there instantly?" Haughty asked.

Michael shook his head. "Sorry. It works only for me."

"Ah, well," Haughty said, disappointed.

"I don't suppose one of you lovely creatures would care to—" Michael began.

"No," they chorused.

"In that case I'll be on my way." He sketched a picture in the dirt with one finger, stepped on it, and vanished.

They resumed their trek.

A peculiarly shaped mountain loomed ahead of them. It resembled two enormous wheels connected to each other by rods. What did this portend, if anything?

"Found something," Olive called from ahead. "Not sure what it is."

The others caught up to her. It was a small corral with several wheeled frameworks in it. Jumper had never seen anything like it, but of course this wasn't his realm. The other did not recognize it either. Yet it was right beside the enchanted path, within its protection, so must be useful in some way.

Eve touched one of the contraptions. "It's a bicycle," she announced, using her talent to know about anything inanimate. "Made in Mundania for human transportation by a company named Playing Card."

"But doesn't look anything like a playing card," Olive said. "It's not flat, and has no hearts or diamonds or whatever."

"They don't care about what makes sense in Mundania," Eve said. "This can efficiently carry a person along a flat path."

"I wood like that," Wenda said. "I'm knot used to so much walking."

"That is surely true for most of us," Olive said. "But this doesn't look much like a magic carpet, either. How does it work?"

"You sit on its seat and push on the pedals with your feet," Eve said. "I think I grasp the principle."

"*We* don't," Phanta said. "What good would pedal pushing do?"

"Maybe I can demonstrate," Eve said. She put her hands one one of the bicycles and wheeled it out onto the path. Then she put one leg over it, grasped the handles with her hands, set her feet on the pedals, and pushed.

They stood amazed as the bicycle rolled forward, carrying her along. "See?" she called, turning her head to look back at them. "It's easy!"

But the bicycle, not correctly steered during her distraction, veered into a tree trunk. Eve crashed, and fell to the ground, her feet over her head. She wore black panties, matching her hair. Jumper clamped down on his freak reaction, thankful again for Angie's training. As it was, he needed all eight feet on the ground to maintain his balance.

"Ouch!" she exclaimed, scrambling to her feet. She had bruises and scrapes on her arms and legs.

"I have a friend!" Olive exclaimed. "A nurse."

Her friend appeared, dressed in a white uniform with a cute white cap. She hurried to Eve and quickly applied salve on the hurts. Soon the injuries faded; the salve was magically healing.

"Thank you, nurse," Eve said, flexing her limbs. "I'm feeling much better now."

"It's my job," the nurse said, and faded out.

It occurred to Jumper that Olive's talent was more useful than he had thought. It had provided entertainment, education, and now healing.

Eve returned to business. "Of course you have to look where you're going," she said. "I'll try this again."

She did, and this time rode the bicycle along the path without crashing. She stopped, turned it around, and rode back. It looked remarkably smooth. Jumper felt guilty for his continuing fascination with her briefly exposed panties. He wished he were a true human, and that he could be with her and—but he had to stifle that. He had no right to harbor such a desire. Angie had taught him not to freak out, but had not taught him not to desire.

"That could bee useful," Wenda said.

She was right. Jumper, observing carefully, judged that the girls could travel forward about three times as efficiently on bicycles as on foot, and faster.

"That's the mountain!" Maeve exclaimed. "It is shaped like a bicycle."

"It's a Mountain Bike," Eve agreed. "That's why the bicycles are here: they are a gift of the mountain."

The others decided to try it. They got bicycles and tried riding them.

There were many false starts and several falls, but in due course all of them managed it.

They rode on, and now were able to keep Jumper's pace. They moved rapidly along the path.

Until Olive's compass indicated that they had to diverge from the enchanted path. The bicycles needed smooth land for their wheels; they could not be used in the rough forest.

They parked them regretfully in another corral and resumed footing it, following the compass. Now they would have to be on guard, because their safety was no longer assured.

They set off afoot, with the two princesses leading the way so they could spot anything dangerous, alive or not. Jumper brought up the rear, again, to make sure no predator attacked them from behind. Haughty was tired, having kept up with the bicycles well enough, but at the expense of her energy, so she perched on Jumper's back.

"I never would have thought I'd ever be friends with a spider," she remarked. "But you're satisfactory, Jumper. When you were in manform you were positively handsome."

"I wouldn't know."

"Well, *now* you know. That's why the girls have been eager to help you adjust. I daresay one would have joined you in your bed at night, if you had asked her."

"I wouldn't ask."

"Maybe one invited herself."

What was she after? "Why do you think so?"

"Because someone pretty thoroughly defused your freak index. That surely didn't happen on its own."

Now he knew: she was after his night secret. "Why do you think so?" he repeated.

"Because when Eve crashed on the bicycle and upended, you didn't freak. She's a princess, a Sorceress, and a d**ned pretty young woman. Any man should have freaked, yet you didn't. You saw the color of her panties and took it in stride."

"Black," he admitted. "Matching her hair. Most appealing. Perhaps it was fortunate I was not in human form."

"Don't give me that, you sn**k. Once a man, always a man. I'm a harpy; I know base motives."

"I have no base motives." Base desires, certainly, but not base motives.

She dismissed that with a laugh. "Was it Olive? She took a shine to you the moment you assumed manform."

"No!"

"Phanta? She's a willing wench."

"No."

"Maeve? She certainly knows what it's all about, having run afoul of the stork."

"No. You are insulting these fine maidens."

"Then it must have been Wenda. Woodwives are notorious, and now she is fully fleshed. She must have been eager to try out her new backside."

"No!" he said, disgusted.

"Now this intrigues me. You have just eliminated all the prime suspects, because the princesses weren't on the scene then. Yet I don't think it would have been Wira, and I strongly doubt it would be Mare-Ann. Are you trying to deceive me, Jumper?"

"It was Angie Ina," he snapped. Then realized that he had given it away just when he had her stymied. She had halfway tricked him into revealing it. It seemed that harpies were good at that sort of thing.

"The imaginary doll," she said musingly. "That was dangerous and irresponsible of her. You could have dropped dead."

"She was careful. It was something I needed to learn. Please don't tell the others."

"Dawn surely already knows. You can't keep anything from her."

"She knows," he agreed. "But I promised Angie to keep the secret."

"And Olive knows," she continued inexorably. "Because Angie was a creature of her imagination, and whatever she learned would have reverted to Olive once they reunited."

He hadn't thought of that. "Maybe she does. Still, it's supposed to be secret."

"When three of the seven know it? Jumper, they're *women*. The others will fathom it by osmosis."

"But at least I would not have betrayed my trust."

Haughty shook her head. "A spider with honor. Well, in that case I'll let it be."

"Thank you."

The folk ahead had paused, and Jumper caught up to them. They were gathered around an old woman working with a huge pot on a low fire. The pot was bubbling vigorously. "That looks good," Olive said. "Is it some sort of soup or stew?"

"Not at all," the woman replied, dumping an armful of foliage in. The broth bubbled up, absorbing it.

"Because if it is, we might like to share it with you. We are travelers, and it is about lunchtime. Is there anything we might trade for it?" Actually they had small backpacks with sandwiches and tsoda pop provided by MareAnn for their journey, but it made sense to forage when they could, extending their supplies. It might be a long journey.

"Nothing," the woman said, tossing in a few mossy stones.

"Exactly what are you cooking, then?" Phanta asked.

"I am cooking up a storm," the old woman said with half a cackle. "You had better get under cover soon. It's going to be a drenchpour."

At which point a huge puff of steam rose from the pot and floated toward the sky. Little jags of lightning flashed from it, followed by burps of thunder. It was indeed a forming storm.

"D**t!" Haughty said. "It was bad enough when Fracto chased us."

"That piker?" the woman asked. "He has no taste at all. I brew superior storms. Mine are boiling hot, of course."

It certainly seemed to be threatening. "Is there anywhere we can seek temporary shelter?" Jumper asked.

The woman glanced at him. "My, you're big for a spider! You might try for the old abandoned music shop. It's right down the path. But beware of the luters."

Jumper would have liked to learn more about the luters, but fat drops of hot rain were starting to fall and they had to hurry. They ran on down the path, and soon did spy the shop. Its front sign said YE OLD ABANDONED MUSIC SHOPPE.

The door was unlocked, and they piled in just as the boiling rain got serious.

"It might be abandoned," Olive said, "but its wares remain." Indeed, there were all manner of musical instruments laid out on shelves. There were drums, violins, flutes, brass instruments, harps, and many others.

"A harp!" Haughty exclaimed. She fluttered to the nearest, set herself at it, and drew her legs forward to touch the strings. The tips of her talons plucked at the individual strings. Lovely music sounded.

The others stared, amazed. It had never occurred to any of them that harpies had anything to do with harps.

"Well, we don't advertise it," Haughty said, picking up on their reaction. "Bad for our reputation as totally gross creatures. But I couldn't resist." She finished the melody and stepped away from the instrument.

"We will keep your secret," Dawn said with a halfway obscure smile. The others laughed.

"What are these luters we were warned about?" Phanta asked.

"Maybe I can fathom it," Eve said. She put her hand on a wall, paused, looked surprised, then spoke. "This is one of those private minor tragedies that needs to be corrected. The shop proprietors were called away several years ago on a family emergency, putting a spell on the shop to protect it from theft. But they never returned, and the spell is wearing thin. Soon it won't be effective anymore, and then everything will be stolen."

"But that's not about the luters," Phanta said.

"I'm getting to that. The luters are neighboring folk who aren't very honest. In fact they are thieves; they steal anything they can. The first night the proprietors left, the luters came and stole everything. The protective spell is passive; it won't take direct action. That's because the proprietors are pacifists; they don't like violence. So the robbers aren't hindered. But when morning comes, it draws the instruments back to their places in the shop. So the luters come again in the night to steal them again. This has been happening for three years."

"How much longer can the spell do that?" Phanta asked.

"Maybe another month. The luters know that, so they keep stealing, wearing it out, knowing that eventually they'll get to keep and sell their ill-gotten gains. By the time the proprietors return, the shop will be empty."

"This is a nice shop," Haughty said. "It is giving us shelter from the hot rain. We need to help it." She glared around, but no one disagreed.

"Then we'll need a plan," Dawn said. "And a leader to implement it. Anyone volunteer?"

The girls sent a glance ricocheting around their faces. It caromed back and forth, split into fragments, and finally caught seven of Jumper's eight eyes, beating him back half blinded. "Ungh!" he exclaimed.

"Very good," Eve said. "Jumper has volunteered." She turned to face him with a smile that looked disarming from one angle, and somewhat predatory from another. Highlights reflected from her dark eyes, in the shape of panties. She knew he had seen!

What could he do? "Uh, okay."

"And what is your plan?" Dawn inquired sweetly. Her eyes reflected the shape of bras. It seemed she was the higher twin, while Eve was the lower. But both knew his secret, and were threatening to reveal it if he did not cooperate. They were Sorceresses, and acted with the assurance their powers gave them. He should have done what Haughty recommended, and come clean about his liaisons with Angie. Now he had to come through.

Then a bulb flashed. It illuminated the entire plan. He scrambled mentally to collect all the details before the light faded. "We will stay the night. We will ambush the luters when they come, and scare them so badly they will never return. Then they won't steal the instruments, and the spell won't have to work so hard to protect the shop until the proprietors return."

"Brilliant!" Wenda said, and kissed him on the carapace. He was ashamed to admit how much he liked that. She was the first friend he had made in this realm, and the most innocent, and in that sense was his favorite.

"We don't want to actually hurt anyone," he continued, "because the shop proprietors don't want that. But the luters won't know that. So I will threaten to bite the head off one, and Maeve can threaten to chew the hands off another, and Haughty can threaten to p**p on the face of another. Phanta can turn ghost and scare the s**t out of others. Olive can summon a friend, maybe Angie, to threaten to make them drop dead. Wenda can ask them what kind of wood they'd prefer to have jammed up their backsides. And the princesses . . ." Here he faltered. He hadn't quite secured their roles before his bulb faded.

"We are Sorceresses of Information rather than action," Dawn said. "And we prefer to be anonymous to outsiders. But I can touch the luters and find out what will scare them most, so that you can assign the most effective threat to each one."

"And I can touch their clothing and find out more about them," Eve said. "Between us, we should know their names, homes, friends, and possessions. That may help lend verisimilitude to the threats."

"Lend what?" Wenda asked, perplexed.

"Make it all seem realistic," Eve clarified. "That counts, if we want the scare to last."

"Very good," Jumper said, pleased. "Now we should eat, and rest, and perhaps sleep, so as to be wide-awake when night falls."

The girls agreed. They ate their sandwiches, drank their tsoda, and lay down on the chairs and floor to sleep. Haughty, tired, found a canvas form to lie down on. Then she screeched.

"What's the matter?" Olive asked, startled.

"This thing—it's stretching me!"

They all looked. Sure enough, the harpy was stuck to it, and was getting elongated. Her head and wings were at one end, while her tail and legs were at the other.

Eve touched it. "No wonder! It's a stretcher!"

"A what?" Olive asked.

"A stretcher. It stretches anyone who lies on it."

"Just get me off it!" Haughty cried.

Eve touched it again, to discover that. Jumper noticed that the harpy's body was coming to resemble that of a winged nymph, with more fully fleshed legs and fully formed midsection. But she was a harpy, and did not want that.

"Say the magic word 'contraction,' " Eve said.

"Contraction?" And the stretcher shrank back to its former dimensions and unstuck her. Haughty hopped off and found a perch by a window. She was back to her natural form, but seemed somewhat wrung out.

Jumper threw a web up to stick to the ceiling, spun a quick hammock, and swung from it for his rest.

"Jumper."

He looked down. It was Wenda. "Yes?"

"That looks so cozy. Wood yew make one for me too?"

Surprised, he agreed. Soon she was slung beside him in her own cocoon. The more he thought about it, the more he liked her request. She was a true woodland creature, uncomfortable inside a house.

But he had hardly relaxed before he heard something. It wasn't yet night, but someone was approaching the house. So Jumper got down quietly and went to the door, just to make sure it wasn't a sneak attack. He opened the door half a crack.

A woman stood there in the limited shelter of the arch over the doorway, dripping wet from the rain. "Hello," she said. "I am young Chelsea, seeking shelter from the storm."

Was this a ruse by the luters, to get someone inside to open the door for the main attack? Jumper did not trust this. "This is not a good place," he said.

"Oh, is it happening with places too, now?"

Had he misheard? "Is what happening?"

"I am cursed to fall in love only with folk who are already committed to others. I invariably befriend them, and they return my interest, but of course we can never be together. I need to find a way to break the curse. If now I am also finding nice places of refuge that won't work out, it's getting worse."

This certainly did not sound like a ruse. Jumper found that he believed her. "Wait one moment," he said. He went inside and sought Dawn, who had awakened and was alert. "I need to verify the validity of a person at the door."

"Got it," she said, and went to the door. She returned in little more than a moment. "She's as she says; she's not a luter. But that curse—"

"Do you think Olive has a friend?"

She pursed her lips, nodding. "You're pretty smart, for a spider." She went and fetched Olive. "Have you a friend who can nullify a curse?"

"That depends on the curse," Olive said.

"A curse of misguided emotions."

"I do have a friend for that. His curse is to destroy love. He's not very popular. But he might cancel hers out."

A scowling man appeared. "I smell someone in love," he said. "I hate that." He walked to the door and poked his hand out. "Not any-more," he said with grim satisfaction, and faded out.

Was that really a cure? Jumper wasn't sure. He went to the door, but young Chelsea was gone. So he returned to his cocoon; what else was there to do? He hoped he had done the girl some good.

In the early evening they set up for the luters' raid. Dawn and Eve stood on each side of the doorway, ready to touch the luters as they entered, and the others hung back, waiting to have their victims identified.

They arrived on schedule. The door flung open and a typical village lout barged in.

Dawn touched him. "Hugh Mann, who can change the shade, color, tone, type, description or manner of anything he touches," she announced. "That's a good talent; I don't know why he is a luter."

Hugh glanced at her. "Because I want more," he said. "I don't want just to change things, I want to have more of them. I'll never be satisfied."

Angie Ina appeared, summoned by Olive. "Your greed will be the death of you," she said.

Hugh stared at her. His heart throbbed violently. He dropped to the floor.

"Remember, next time you get greedy," Angie said, and faded out.

The next lout entered. He saw Hugh and paused. "Huh?" he asked in lout language.

Dawn touched him. "Really dull. Terrified of spiders."

Jumper's turn. "I'm going to bite off your stupid head," he said, clashing his mandibles. "After I finish with your friend."

The lout turned and fled back out the door. "I'll be lurking for you, right here," Jumper called after him.

The third lout came in, tripped over the body, and fell onto the stretcher. "Ooooww!" he howled as he got stretched. Then he somehow managed to turn over, get his feet under him, and dive out the window, the stretcher still fastened to his back.

"Let him go," Olive said. "He won't be back."

They went through about six men in all. They had been effectively demoted from luters to louts. When no more came, Jumper hauled the first one out and left him in front of the shop as a warning to others. He wasn't dead, because Angie had turned down the heat just enough, but he had suffered a severe heart throb that he would surely remember.

They had done it. They had scared off the luters. The music shop would be safe from robbery for some time.

"Now we can sleep the rest of the night," Olive said. "Mission accomplished."

"Those hammocks," Phanta said. "They look more comfortable than the floor. Can you make them for the rest of us, Jumper?"

So he spun more hammocks, and soon all of them were hanging, even Haughty. They had found a better way to camp out.

In the morning they finished off their sandwiches and tsoda, girded themselves, and resumed their journey.

Olive's compass guided them accurately, and by noon they knew they were coming into ogre country. The trunks of trees were twisted into pretzels, the mirror surfaces of ponds were cracked from ugliness overload, and small dragons were furtive.

Something rattled, startling them. It looked like a snake, with a bulbous tail. This was what was rattling.

"Oh, that's just a rattler," Wenda said. "A baby ogre's first toy."

"That's a relief," Phanta said as it slithered away.

Then in the jungle rose a crudely twisted wickerwork mansion formed from woven trees. From its vicinity came odd sounds, as if several bovine creatures were being tortured. They approached somewhat nervously, and Haughty flew up to take an advance look.

"No problem," she reported. "It's just moosic."

"Are yew parodying my pronunciation?" Wenda demanded.

"Not at all, blockhead. They're cows."

They came to an outdoor theater where a grizzled ogre and a fading nymph were seated on pulped boulders, listening to the serenade. A cow was singing an aria, accompanied by a small orchestra of little crabs. They had tiny violins and bows and played very well, though the cow's voice tended to drown them out. Then five other cows joined in for the refrain, and the crabs were completely submerged. They accepted it with poor grace; in fact they were crabby.

The serenade ended and cows and crabs departed. Now the nymph turned and saw the visitors. "Oh!" she exclaimed. "Seven lovely nymphly damsels to see me, and a gross ugly spider to see you, Smash."

"Me see," the ogre agreed. He was wearing some kind of white stuff on his head.

"Will you girls join me for a jelly sandwich? The bread is from a nice breadfruit tree, and the jelly from the finest jellyfish. I am Tandy, Smash's wife. That's an ice cap on his head; it helps keep it cool when he tries to think, which isn't often, fortunately. We don't get many visitors in our dotage."

The girls introduced themselves to Tandy, while Jumper approached the ogre. "I am Jumper Spider. I—"

"He wend, Dor's friend!" Smash exclaimed.

"Uh, no. He's my distant ancestor. But I know he thought highly of you, Smash. You helped Prince Dor when he was young, and Jumper appreciated that."

"He talk, me balk." He meant that Jumper was talking, but Smash wasn't impressed.

"Come off the two-bit doggerel, ogre," Jumper snapped, clicking his mandibles. "I know you can talk as well as I can, and you don't need a gift of tongues. I'm just about as strong and ugly as you are, and probably not as smart. Ogres may be justly proud of their stupidity, but you're only half ogre, thanks to your father Crunch's dalliance with a Curse Fiend. We have serious business to discuss."

"Oh, you know," Smash said, not annoyed. "That's different. Why are you here?"

"The Good Magician mentioned a Prophecy that sounds more like advice: emulate the ogre. At least that was the way he translated part of it. We think you must be the ogre, so we need to know what to emulate."

Smash scratched his head, concentrating. The ice cap melted, and several fleas leaped off as his brain heated. "I don't know that Prophecy. I just did what I had to do."

"You accompanied and protected seven assorted maidens, and married one of them. I have seven maidens, but doubt I'll marry any. You impressed the Night Stallion. I doubt I could do that. You were true to your mission, whatever it was. I will try to emulate that. Do you have any advice or insights I lack?"

Smash shook his head, and more fleas were flung off. "I can't think of any. But maybe Tandy can." He called to his wife, who was sharing T & jelly with the others. "Hey, girl! Give whirl."

"Don't let him bullspit you, Smash," Tandy called back. "You helped all seven maidens achieve good lives. You explored the gourd realm, spooking the horrors, and when the Night Stallion tempted you to take over as the Night Ogre, you turned him down. You're the most constant creature imaginable, and I love you." She returned to her dialogue with the girls.

"That's a good recommendation," Jumper acknowledged.

"But I can't think what aspect of it applies to you," Smash said. "Exactly what is your mission?"

"To repair the broken cable that connects the Mundane Internet with the magic Outernet. It seems the Dwarf Demon Pluto severed it, and may not want it restored. So we anticipate some interference. But that does not seem very similar to your experience."

"True," Smash agreed. "I never went up against a Demon, not even a dwarf one. I fear your mission is hopeless."

"I can't accept that," Jumper said. "I just need to find the way to complete it, so I can go home."

"You're ogre-headed!" Smash exclaimed, pleased.

"I suppose I am. But does that fulfill the Prophecy?"

Smash shook his shaggy head. "Maybe so. No know. I've been too distracted by another riddle."

"Another?"

"I will quote it: How much okra would an ocher ogre ogle if an ocher ogre could ogle okra?"

Jumper shrugged with all eight limbs, and answered off the top, and a bit to the side, of his head. "I would say that an ocher ogre would ogle what an ocher ogre could ogle if an ocher ogre could ogle okra."

"That's it!" Smash exclaimed, astonished. "But of course I can't ogle Okra Ogre because my wife would get jealous."

"Okra is an ogre?" Jumper asked, surprised.

"Yes. She married Smithereen Ogre."

This was crazier than Jumper had realized. "I assumed okra was a vegetable."

"That too," Smash agreed.

"Alert!" Haughty called from above. "Something's coming." She glided back to the ground.

They looked. A flock of ten birds was approaching. Or were they? Jumper oriented several eyes on them and got a clearer picture. "Those are not birds. They are winged humans. No, they have dragon heads."

"Drakin!" Dawn said. "Humanoid dragons. All they do is hunt and fight. This can't be a friendly visit."

"Who would dare raid an ogre's den?" Eve asked.

"I think we don't have time to discuss it," Tandy said. "Let's hope they are friendly. If not, we'll have to stop them."

Jumper was still focusing on them. "They are watching us," he said. "One of them is focusing on each of us. That is, one on me, one on Smash, one on Haughty, and so on. They are breathing fire."

"That's war," Dawn said. "Dragons who come in peace keep their fire, smoke or steam suppressed. It's protocol."

"Then we had better organize," Jumper said grimly. "Form partnerships: one strong person with one weak one, to protect her." He glanced around. "Wenda—to me."

The woodwife didn't question it. As a fully fleshed nymph she wasn't strong, and even as a wood nymph she might have caught fire. She ran to join Jumper, her hair flinging back.

Then the first of the drakin arrived. The dragon-headed winged man folded his wings, which seemed to grow smaller, and dived at Jumper.

Jumper spun, formed, and threw a loop of webbing. It circled the drakin's head and drew tight around his neck. Jumper jerked, and the drakin fell out of the air, his jet of fire going astray. Jumper threw three more sticky strands over him and trussed him up with a few expert twitches of his legs. This one was finished.

But another was still closing on Wenda, dragon mouth opening. "Dodge!" Jumper said. She did, and the blast of flame missed. Jumper threw a loop about his neck, hauled him down, and in half a moment had him similarly trussed up and helpless. Two down.

Meanwhile another eye was covering Smash and Tandy. Two drakins were revving up, about to send out blasts of flame. Smash simply picked up a head-sized rock and hurled it with such force it knocked his drakin out of the sky before it got close. It landed on its back, its fire going poof and expiring. Tandy made a throwing motion, but there was nothing there. Yet her drakin reacted as if struck by something, and also fell out of the sky, its fire making crazy patterns in the air. What had happened?

Then Jumper remembered: Tandy's talent was throwing a tantrum. She must have thrown one at the drakin, and it had scored, taking it out.

Another eye saw Haughty and Phanta team up. They conferred hastily, then Haughty hopped onto Phanta's cupped hands and deposited—an egg! Phanta took that egg and threw it at one of the two drakins approaching. It struck and exploded, blowing one more creature out of the sky. An explosive egg! Jumper had not realized the harpies could do that.

The other drakin smacked right into Phanta—and passed through her. She had ghosted, giving it no substance to strike. It crashed into the ground, where Haughty pounced, clamping her sharp dirty claws on its head. "Move, and I squeeze," she said. The drakin had the sense not to move.

The next team was Olive and Maeve. Olive summoned an imaginary friend who turned out to be something like a demoness, remarkably shapely. "I am C Duce the cemoness," she announced. "Not an amoness, bemoness, demoness, or eemoness, but a cemoness. Look on my works, yet mighty, and despair." She inhaled as she turned, her clothing puffing into vapor.

The drakin's eyeballs glazed, blinding it. It lost direction and plowed into a tree trunk. The trunk, annoyed, swung open a lid, took the drakin in, and slammed closed. The creature was now securely locked in the trunk. C Duce had seduced it into oblivion.

Maeve was somewhat less subtle. She leaped to intercept the drakin before it oriented its fire. She caught hold of its head and put her mouth to its snout as though about to kiss it. But she didn't kiss, she bit. In fact she chomped a jagged piece out of its face. Its fire exploded within its head, almost blowing it apart. The head ballooned, then snapped back together—just in time for the maenad to take another bite. The drakin jerked back, leaving a smoldering chunk of flesh behind, and fled.

That left the two princesses. Jumper suspected they could handle themselves. Indeed they did: as the two drakins charged, Dawn ripped open her shirt to flash her bra, and Eve hoisted her skirt to flash her panties. The two drakins froze in midair, freaked out. They were, after all, humanoid males.

As suddenly as it had begun, the battle was done. All the drakins had been nullified.

Now they had time to reflect. "Why did they attack us?" Jumper asked. "We were no threat to them. All they needed to do was leave us alone."

"And it was too easy a victory," Tandy said. "None of us were hurt, though they are dangerous creatures. Surely they could have scorched a few of us."

"This bears investigation," Dawn said. She approached the one she had stunned with her bra, reaching out to touch its hide. In half a moment she would know all about it.

But the drakin puffed into smoke and dissipated before she made contact. So did its companion, stunned by Eve.

"I have two trussed up," Jumper said.

"Thank you." Dawn approached them. But they too puffed away before she could touch them.

"This becomes curious," Olive remarked to no one in particular.

"I've got one," Haughty said. But then hers too dissipated, leaving her clutching the head of nothing.

"We have one locked in a trunk," Olive said. But even as she spoke, they saw a wisp of mist seep out of a crack in the wood. That one, too, had vaporized.

"I have a chunk in my mouth," Maeve said, taking it out. But as she did so, it faded and vanished.

"It seems they weren't made to last," Phanta said.

"Or to be questioned," Wenda said. "Even magically."

"It is most curious," Haughty said. "They seemed so vicious, with each one attacking one of us, but none of them actually hurting us. Had they ganged up on any one or two of us, they could have taken us out before we could stop them. So this wasn't a very good plan of attack."

"It had more drama than substance," Eve agreed.

They looked at the ogre, who hadn't spoken. "He scare, beware," he said in stupid ogre talk.

Or was it stupid? "It was meant to scare us, not to hurt us," Jumper said. "To warn us."

"Warn us about what?" Tandy asked.

"About our mission. This has to be from Demon Pluto. To stop us from pursuing our mission. The Good Magician warned us about that."

"But a foreign demon can't interfere in Demon Xanth's territory," Tandy protested. "It's against Demon protocol."

"Not directly," Princess Dawn said. "But the Demons aren't bound by mortal ethics. They interfere in each other's business all the time, surreptitiously. Then when they get caught, they suffer loss of status."

"Which Pluto already has suffered," Eve said. "So maybe he doesn't have much to lose. But he can do a lot indirectly. Like persuading the drakin to raid us. He wanted us to catch on, and to be wary, because next time the attack might not be token but real."

"It can't be real," Olive said. "That would violate the Demon pact. He can scare us or trick us, but not actually hurt us."

"Unless he is desperate enough to cheat," Haughty pointed out.

"That does make me nervous," Phanta confessed. "But not nervous enough to quit. I like having my imaginary friends be as durable as I choose."

"And I like having a full body," Wenda said. "In my natural state I

can knot freak any man out with my panties, because I dew knot have a
bottom to mount them on."

"And I still want to get home," Jumper said. "Still, it would not be
fair to make people participate where there is serious risk."

"We all have to do it, or none of us can," Dawn reminded them.

"So let's vote," Eve said. "Who wants to quit?"

There was a silence.

"Does this mean that all of you want to continue with the mission?"
Jumper asked.

"Yes," they chorused.

"Then it seems we are united," Olive said.

"But we still don't understand the Prophecy," Jumper reminded
them. "Even the Good Magician had to guess, because of the Demon involvement. We don't even know what we need to learn from the ogre."

"Yes, you do," Tandy said. "That you are oink-headed enough to keep
going despite a clear warning. That's the way Smash is, bless him." She
kissed Smash on his hairy ear.

That, it seemed, would have to do.

6
LOST THINGS

"What's next?" Wenda asked. "I wood like to relax after that scare."

Jumper consulted the Prophecy. " 'Like the Ogre beware rogue her; With heart and mind, but be not blind.' That makes no more sense to me than it did before."

"Let me touch the original paper," Eve said.

Jumper held it out, and she touched it. "Oho! There's a hidden subtext between the lines: 'Risk the wrath of the Lost Path. You'll be unbound when what's Lost is Found.' "

"The Lost Path is in the gourd!" Wenda protested.

"Where?" Jumper asked.

"The dream realm," Olive explained.

"It does make some faint sense," Dawn said. "When you enter the gourd realm, you are blind to the regular realm. We may find out how the rest relates when we go there."

"What about getting unbound?" Phanta asked. "Who is bound?"

"We are all bound to our mission," Eve said. "It may be an oblique way of saying that there is something lost that we must find if we want to complete our quest."

"How do we go there?" Jumper asked.

"We fetch hypno gourds and peer into their peepholes. But we'll need a safe place to do it, because our bodies will be vulnerable."

"Here in the Ogre's Den," Tandy said immediately. "There's nowhere safer."

"Oh, we couldn't impose," Olive said.

"No, I'm serious. Smash explored the gourd realm long ago. He knows how it is. He'll be glad to protect your bodies."

Jumper glanced at the ogre with several eyes. "True?"

"Me see," Smash agreed. He continued to use ogre talk in public, and Jumper didn't question it.

So they marched into the Ogre's Den, which turned out to be surprisingly spacious and well kept inside. That would be Tandy's doing. Smash went out to harvest a basket of gourds while Tandy fed them and set them up on comfortable mats. "You will be going in together," she said. "But we will need to know when to bring you out, so you need to assign one person we can wake periodically."

"Me," Haughty said. "I distrust the gourd the most."

"And we will need to find the Lost Path," Olive said.

"But you said it was in the dream realm," Jumper said.

"Yes. But the dream realm is huge. Bigger than reality, actually. The Lost Path is lost somewhere within it. So entering the dream realm is only the first step. We will need an adequate strategy to find it."

"Who can find something that is lost by definition?" Haughty asked.

A dim bulb flashed over Smash's head. "Damme, Sammy."

"What? Who?" Jumper asked.

"It's the ogre way of saying d**n me," Haughty explained.

"No, the other."

Tandy smiled. "That's Jenny Elf's cat, Sammy. He can find anything except home."

"Anything? Even the Lost Path?"

There was half a silence as the realization sank in. "We need Sammy Cat," Olive said.

"And how do we find Sammy?" Haughty asked.

"We may just have to trek to where Jenny lives," Jumper said.

"That will be a whole 'nother adventure," Haughty warned. "She's across Xanth from here."

"Then why does the Prophecy list the Lost Path now?"

"There must be a reason," Tandy said. "Prophecies may be opaque and confusing, but they don't waste space."

Now a bulb flashed over Phanta's head. "Olive! Conjure Jenny as a friend."

"But she's not my friend. I don't even know her. I'm sure she's a nice person, but we've never met."

"Your imaginary friend."

"But she's not imaginary."

Phanta spelled it out. "Jenny is real. You don't know her, so your friendship with her is imaginary. Conjure her as your imaginary friend."

Olive's mouth fell open. "Could I do that?"

"You can try it, certainly," Phanta said.

"Well, then, I will."

"Not yet!" Phanta said. "Wait till we're in the dream realm. Then conjure her, and have her bring her cat."

Olive looked at the others. They were surprised too, but it did seem worth a try.

"One other thing," Jumper said. "Exactly what are we looking for on the Lost Path? The Prophecy doesn't seem to say."

"Yes it does, in its fashion," Eve said. "We'll be unbound when what's Lost is Found. We already figured that out."

"But hundreds of things could be lost. That's not much help. What specific thing do we need?"

"Prophecies specialize in obscurity," Eve said. "That's because they are prone to paradox. If we understood perfectly what is going to happen, and didn't like it, we would act to change it, so then the Prophecy would no longer be true. So the words have to just nudge us in the right direction without providing the whole answer until it is too late to change it."

A small silence circulated. Finally Olive shrugged. "Maybe Jenny will know."

Jumper was not entirely satisfied with that either, but had no better suggestion.

They made themselves comfortable on their mats. "Now we want to bee together," Wenda said. "Otherwise we'll find ourselves in different areas and wood really bee lost. We dew knot want that. So we need to touch each other as we peek, at least to start."

Jumper moved his mat to the center. He settled down and extended seven legs to touch each of the others. He used the eighth leg to orient his gourd.

"Are we ready?" Wenda asked. "Then on the count of three. One. Two. Peek."

Jumper tuned out seven eyes and put the eighth to the peephole of the gourd. He knew the others were doing the same thing with their fewer eyes.

He found himself in a region of circles. The seven maidens were in a circle around him, of course, but there were also patterns of circles painted on the floor. Beyond these were a number of men who seemed to be idle.

One approached him. "Hello, giant spider. What tangled web have you woven to get caught in this circumference? Did you bring your succulent captives here so you can suck out their juices in peace?"

"No, no!" Jumper exclaimed, startled. "These are not captives! They are friends. We are here on business. I am Jumper Spider."

"I am Sir Vice. I am here to help. What can I do for you?"

"It would help to know the nature of this place."

"This is the home of Sir Cumstance, where idle sirs gather. Both spiders and maidens seem out of place here, being animal and female."

"We do find ourselves in an unusual circumstance," Jumper agreed. "We are looking for the Lost Path."

"I have no idea where that would be; it was lost eons ago and never found. But perhaps Sir Vey would know; he lists and itemizes many things." He made a hand signal. "Sir Vey!"

Sir Vey came forward. But it turned out that he did not know the location of the Lost Path either. "That is the one that doesn't make the listings," he explained. Neither did the obsequious Sir Vant, or the crazy Sir

Tified, or the doctor Sir Junn. "We don't get around much," Sir Culation said. "We stay close to the ground," the snakelike Sir Pent explained. "But we are very sure it isn't here," Sir Tain said. "We simply do what we need to endure," Sir Vivor said.

So it seemed. "Then we shall summon another friend, and move on," Jumper said. "Thank you for your help, sirs."

"We are amazed you can handle it," Sir Prize said.

They huddled in a private circle, and Olive concentrated on Jenny Elf, her imaginary friend, together with her cat Sammy. Would it work?

A woman formed. She looked fairly ordinary, but was somewhat smaller than average human size, and had pointed ears and only four fingers on each hand. That had to be Jenny Elf.

"Well, hello, Olive," Jenny said. "It has been so long I must have forgotten we were friends." She went to hug Olive. "But I don't think I know your other friends."

Olive quickly introduced them, starting with Jumper, and summarized their situation. "So we are hoping Sammy can find the Lost Path for us," she concluded.

"Surely he can," Jenny agreed. "He can find anything but home, so I try to keep him fairly close. But Claire has good sense, and fathoms things Sammy doesn't, so he doesn't really get lost anymore." She lifted her voice. "Sammy! Where are you?"

An orange fluffball of a cat appeared. "This is Sammy," Jenny said. He settled down into speed-bump mode, in no hurry about anything.

Then beside him appeared a sleek female cat, looking at Jumper and the others alertly. "Claire Voyant," Jenny said.

And an odd little cat. "And Kitten Kaboodle," Jenny said. "She has nine tails. One for each of her lives, each a different story."

This was somewhat more than Jumper had anticipated. "They are welcome, especially if they have any idea what we are looking for. We just hope Sammy can find the Lost Path."

Claire arched her back and gave Jenny a look. "She says you are looking for the Found Cabin."

"I don't understand."

"She says you will when you get there."

At least now they had half a notion where they were headed. "Then let's find the Lost Path," Jumper said.

Suddenly Sammy was up and running. "Wait for us!" Jenny cried, running after him. The rest of them followed her, except for Claire, who paralleled him, seeming to know where he was going.

There was a blur of dream realm settings: a horror house, walking skeletons, moving buildings, and several sets where creatures with cameras were recording bad dreams for deserving sleepers. Jumper was surprised that some scenes they passed through were quite pleasant; they weren't all scary. Then he realized that dreams could be good as well as bad. Also, a seemingly nice dream could have a savage under-current. It all depended on the dreamer.

Then, abruptly, they were on a winding path, vaguely similar to the enchanted paths they had traveled on. But this one was littered with lost things: lamps, pictures, coins, shoes, pencils, half-eaten sandwiches, homework papers, and many odd socks. There were two roughly human bodies with heads that seem to sit crosswise on their necks. He did not understand them at all.

"Headphones," Eve explained. "Pick one up and hold it to an ear."

Jumper did so. Eve picked up the other. "Hello," she said into one end of it. "Hello," her voice said in his phone.

"Hello," he replied, startled. At least now he understood: these heads could talk to each other.

They put the heads back on their necks and checked other lost things. Some were vague blobs. "Causes," Jenny murmured. "Nonphysical things can also get lost, especially when a person is distracted by greed or love."

One lost thing was a man. "Don't come near me," he said, cringing.

But they had to pass near him to follow the path. "Why?" Haughty asked. "We mean you no harm."

"Because I am José," he said. "My talent is Empathy. I feel whatever others are feeling."

"But that's a good talent," Dawn said. "Akin in a manner to mine. I am Dawn, and I know all about any living thing I touch." She touched him in midcringe. "Ouch! Now I understand! You can't tune it out."

"That's right," José said. "I feel your pain, joy, confusion, anger, guilt—everything. And I can't turn it off. I have little chance to be my-self except when I'm alone. So please leave me alone."

Dawn turned to the others. "We need to get past this man as quickly as possible, so he won't suffer all our feelings."

"Then we had better run," Eve said. She led the way, running past José. The others followed, and soon they were clear, while the poor man recovered from their feelings.

Jumper realized that this was truly an unusual region. He really had no idea how they had found it, or how to leave it. "What do we do now?" he asked.

"We follow the Lost Path to its end," Jenny said.

"That must be where the Found Cabin is," Olive said.

"Whatever would we want with a cabin?" Haughty asked.

"Only the Prophecy knows," Phanta said with a pained laugh.

They followed the path, increasingly tuning out the litter of lost things strewn along it, though Jumper was surprised by some. What was a haunted sailboat doing here, or a yellow submarine, or a set of carved stone tablets? There was even a town whose inhabitants didn't seem to know they were lost. And countless lost opportunities. Those seemed especially sad.

Then at last they reached the Found Cabin. It was perfectly ordi-nary, nestled in a scenic valley. It was overgrown with weeds; no one had been here in a long time.

They entered it and looked around. Dust covered everything. Wenda and Olive got busy with broom and dust cloth to clean things off, and soon they were revealed. And what things they were!

There was a shining sword. Maeve picked it up and flourished it, and it moved and glinted marvelously. On its steel side was printed the word COURAGE. "I could really use this weapon," she said. "It's magic; it fits my hand perfectly, though it was surely made for a man, and is feather-light, though I'm sure its real weight is heavy."

"Test it," Olive suggested.

Maeve set a heavy bolt of wood from the rack beside the fireplace on a chair, and swung the sword at it. The wood flew into two sections as if made of jelly. "It's solid," she announced unnecessarily.

Eve came forward to touch it. "You can't keep it," she said. "It's not really a sword. It's a symbol. It's a man's lost courage. It needs to be returned to him."

"Then I will help return it," Maeve said regretfully. "It is far too fine a thing to allow to remain lost, whether real or symbolic." She returned the sword to its resting place.

There was a large red heart. Wenda picked it up, pressed it against her chest, and almost dropped it. "It's beating!"

So it was. Dawn came to touch it. "This is another symbol," she said. "It is the lost love of a man or woman, who is slowly dying for lack of it."

"Then it must bee returned," Wenda said. "Though for a moment I felt so gloriously in love I could hardly stand it. I wish I could find a love of my own like that."

Another was a statue of a human head. Olive picked it up—and she too almost dropped it. "It's alive!"

Indeed, the head's eyes were blinking, and its mouth was twitching. But it looked confused.

Dawn touched it. "This is the symbol of a lost mind," she said. "Someone is going crazy without it."

"It must be returned," Olive said, setting it back down. "Though for a moment I felt so much more intelligent."

Phanta picked up a small tombstone. On it were engraved the words WHAT'S THE POINT?

Eve touched it. "Symbol for the lost will to live," she said. "He is very unhappy, and will die if he doesn't recover this in time."

Phanta put it back. "He will be a ghost."

Two objects were left: a model of a human hand, and a statue of a unicorn. The two princesses exchanged most of a look. "These must be for us to return," Dawn said.

Eve picked up the hand. "Yes. This is the symbol for honor. Someone has lost his honor, and is most unhappy."

Dawn picked up the last. "Oh, it is alive, but not happy. This is the symbol for innocence. A girl has lost her innocence."

"You can't return that," Haughty said.

"We have to," Jumper said. "The Prophecy says we won't get what we must have until we return everything. At least, I think that's what it implies." That necessary obscurity was most frustrating.

"But innocence, once lost, is irredeemable," the harpy said. "That's the tragedy of all girls."

"There must be a way," Jumper said. "Otherwise we have no hope of completing our mission."

"Well then, let's get to it," Maeve said, picking up the sword again. "I'll return this, and use it along the way. Where should I take it?"

Eve touched it again. "It was lost by Warren Warrior, a mercenary. He is out of business now, because he lacks the courage to fight. Sammy can find him."

"You can't go alone," Jumper said. "I'll go with you."

Maeve send a sidelong glance his way. "Do you think I need protection?"

"Yes. From your own violent nature. Someone has to keep you acting like a woman. You have been very good with us, but out on your own you are bound to revert. They'll never let a maenad pass among them without a noxious commotion."

"You have a point," she agreed reluctantly. "But do you think those folk are any more likely to accept a giant spider?"

"Oh, bleep!" he swore. "You mean I have to act human too?"

"By your own logic," she said sweetly, her teeth glinting.

Jumper's eyes caught those of the other members of the party. They all agreed. He wasn't clear how their eyes conveyed the sentiment, but they did.

"I will have to do it," he said.

"You will have to go with each of us in turn, as we return the symbols," Eve said. "Because according to the implication of that Prophecy, one of us will discover something you must have to complete the mission."

She was right, though he was not entirely certain of her motive. There were dark recesses to her personality, contrasting with the bright surfaces of Dawn's.

"I will support and guard each of you," he agreed. "Because you are all delicate, innocent, helpless maidens." Irony did not come naturally to him, but he was learning.

Haughty choked with a swallowed snort of laughter, and all but Wenda smiled knowingly. "We are maidens," Haughty said. "Let's leave it at that."

"I will even let you carry the sword," Maeve said. "You may need it, because in manform you won't be able to bite the heads off miscreants."

"I understand that some things are different in the dream realm," Jenny said. "That a person's basic nature remains despite transformations. So Jumper might retain his spider strength. And of course you can't be killed. You'd just wake up."

"But we're in the gourd," Olive said. "We can't break eye contact with the peephole on our own."

"Then I'm not sure what would happen," Jenny said. "Maybe you'd just lose consciousness until the peephole contact was broken. But there's no sense in being careless."

"No sense at all," Olive agreed.

Jumper brought out one of his collection of vials. He emptied it into his mouth. He shrank into manform. Naturally he had no clothes.

"Well, now," Dawn said brightly, flashing her bra.

"Indeed," Eve agreed, flashing her panties.

Jumper did not freak out, thanks to the training Angie Ina had given him. But he did react. He couldn't help it. The two princesses were double-teaming him, feeding illicit images into both of his human eyes at once, and they were extremely attractive girls.

Then he became aware of the others. Olive was looking faint, while Phanta's gaze was narrowing assessingly. Those were definitely not good signs.

"Oh, for s**t's sake," Haughty said. Considering how calloused she was as a harpy, that was alarming.

"Oh, my," Jenny said, blushing. Taking into account that she was married to a virile werewolf, that suggested the magnitude of the problem.

Wenda, womanfully averting her direct gaze, hurried to him with lost clothing she had found. "Yew wood knot want to go naked," she said, sending a wooden glare at the two princesses, who were giggling naughtily. She helped him put the pants on, so that his reaction was suitably covered up.

Dawn and Eve might be Sorceresses, but they were also mischievous teens. Yet the others did not seem to be entirely dismayed, again except for Wenda.

Fortunately Haughty changed the subject. "If Sammy's guiding you there, what about Claire and Kitten Kaboodle?"

"They're staying with us," Olive said, stroking Claire.

"We like them," Phanta agreed, cuddling Kaboodle.

"And we have notes to compare with Jenny Elf," Dawn said. "It has been some time since we last visited with her."

"Yes, we want to know what married life is like," Eve said. "Once we settle which of us gets the man."

"There's something else, maybe irrelevant," Jenny said. "I was reminded of it by Jumper's, um, display."

"You didn't get enough of a look?" Haughty inquired, as Jumper fidgeted, embarrassed.

"I got more than enough. It's that what happens in the dream realm, isn't necessarily real in the real realm. So some things that happen are more apparent than real."

"It was quite apparent," Haughty said.

"I dew knot understand," Wenda said.

"Try a specific," Olive suggested, beginning to catch on.

Jenny flushed faintly. "Well, for example, if a boy were to kiss a girl in a dream, that wouldn't be the same as kissing her in waking life. She might not even know about it, if it was only his dream."

"Suppose she did know about it?" Maeve asked. "Maybe even dream the same dream?"

"That would be more of a mutual experience," Jenny agreed. "But still not the same as doing it solidly."

"How about a communal dream, like this one?" Dawn asked brightly.

"That would be real on one level. They would be sharing their affection. But still not, well—"

"Out with it, moons girl!" Haughty snapped.

Jenny visibly braced herself. "If they summoned the stork, the signal wouldn't go out. Because that requires a, um, physical interaction. Not a dreamed one. It's in the big book of stork rules."

"No signal?" Maeve asked, more interested than was perhaps seemly.

"Oho!" Haughty exclaimed. "A license to f**k!"

"Or at least to be a bit freer than usual," Phanta said thoughtfully. "A girl might have more fun than she would care to risk in real life."

"Knot that she wood," Wenda said primly.

"Not that she would," Phanta agreed. But she did not seem to have a full measure of sincerity.

They seemed to be well settled in for the duration. "We shouldn't be long," Jumper said, taking the sword from Maeve. It immediately strengthened his arm and body, making him feel bold. It might be a symbol, but it was a powerful one.

"Sammy, find the man this belongs to," Maeve told the cat.

Sammy had been snoozing, but now he took off. "Wait for us!" Maeve cried, but the cat never paused. They scrambled desperately to keep up with him.

There followed another melange of images as they plowed through the dream sets. Jumper hadn't thought to ask whether the deliveries had to be made inside or outside of the dream realm, but since they were locked in until they were let out from outside, they must be within.

Then Sammy drew up at a small castle. Its drawbridge was up, and its walls were blocked with stones. Only a wisp of smoke from a high chimney suggested that anyone was inside.

Jumper and Maeve drew up beside the cat, panting. It had been quite a run. "This is where he is?" Jumper gasped.

Sammy lay down and licked his paw. That seemed to be answer enough.

"How are we going to get in to see him?" Maeve asked. She was still breathing hard, and Jumper couldn't help noticing that despite the human clothing, this did intriguing things for her body.

"I suppose we can knock on the door."

Then came a distraction. A birdlike creature came flying around the castle, orienting on them. "What is that?" Jumper asked.

"I don't know. It's not a dragon or a griffin."

The creature landed before them. "I am Fletcher Flion. A winged lion who can speak your stupid dialect."

"Nice to meet you," Jumper said, remembering the human convention. "I am Jumper, and this is Maeve. We are here to deliver something to Warren Warrior."

"Too bad. No one interacts with that coward until I do, and thereafter it will be too late, because he will be dead."

"Listen, animal—" Maeve started, but Jumper cautioned her with what would have been a sharp glance from his upper right eye. In this body that turned out to be his right ear, but it had the same effect. She did not want to give away her nature.

"I am afraid we must insist," Jumper said. "We are going in to see him."

"And I must insist: you shall not. I have challenged Warren to come out and meet me in fair combat, and I am laying siege to the castle until he does so."

This time Jumper remembered to use his human eye to exchange a glance with Maeve. "You take the sword inside," he said, "while I deal with this balky creature." He handed the sword to her.

"You shall not," the flion said. "My minions will stop you." He made a roar, and two more flions appeared from behind the castle, flying rapidly in.

They came to land before Jumper and Maeve, two sleek females. "I am Sharon," one said.

"I am Sharoff," the other said.

Shar On and Shar Off. Jumper was coming to appreciate why some folk groaned at puns.

Fletcher took off and resumed circling the castle, screaming challenges to the warrior inside, leaving the dirty work to the females. Flions, it seemed, were like that.

"All we want to do," Jumper said, "is make a delivery inside that castle. Why do you oppose this?"

"Fletcher has a grudge," Sharon said.

"And we do what Fletcher says," Sharoff said.

"So you won't let us pass in peace?"

"We won't let you pass at all," Sharon said.

"Then it must be war," Jumper said with regret.

"But you have only one sword," Sharoff said. "We will dispatch the unarmed one first, than gang up on the other."

Maeve smiled. "We will make it easy for you. Neither has the sword." She plunged it into the ground between them.

"Then you are even bigger fools than you look," Sharon said.

"And you both look quite fleshy and tasty," Sharoff said. "As does your cat."

Sammy remained where he was, unconcerned.

"Give us a moment to strip," Jumper said. "We don't want to mess up our clothes." He started undressing, while keeping a wary eye on the flions.

Maeve, thus given leave, stripped also. She finished by removing her wax teeth. She stood revealed as a maenad.

"This grows interesting," Sharon said, gazing at Jumper's body. "I will enjoy chewing on that meat." He wasn't sure exactly what part of him she was looking at.

"I've always wanted to devour a maenad," Sharoff said.

Then the two of them charged.

Jumper stood his ground. He reached out with his two strong human hands and caught the flion by her front shoulders. Jenny was right: he had retained his spider strength. He heaved Sharon into the air so that she was standing on her hind legs, facing him. Her leonine head was unable to strike at him. "Now we can do this the hard way or the easy way," he said.

She didn't flinch. "What is the hard way?"

"I let go of you and you fly away, leaving us alone."

"That's too hard for me. What is the easy way?"

"I bite off your head." Too late he remembered that he wasn't a spider at the moment. Part of his strength was because his two human arms were actually four spider legs, doubling their effect.

Meanwhile Maeve had evidently retained her own strength and

viciousness. She was clawing with sharp nails and biting with pointed teeth, having abandoned any pretense of feminine gentleness. The flion was hard pressed.

Sharon shifted in his grasp. Her body thinned down. Her head lost its mane and shrank into a small one. Her wings disappeared. She was now a lovely human woman. "Yes, I am a shape changer," she said. "Now bite my head off, big man."

His bluff had been called. Jumper opened his mouth wide. And discovered that it wasn't only his spider strength he retained. His mouth opened wider than his face. He *could* engulf her head.

"You seem to have defeated me," she murmured, unalarmed. It was almost as if she wasn't serious about the fight. "Postpone your bite for a while, and use me for my obvious purpose." She inhaled, making her bare chest swell. It was a most remarkable effect. "If I do not please you, *then* you can bite off my head."

The oddest thing was that he was tempted. Angie had shown him what fun a willing woman could be.

"Beware," Maeve murmured.

Jumper glanced at her. She had overpowered Sharoff and had a haunch ready for chomping.

That reminded Jumper that Sharon was not really a lovely woman. Maeve was that. Sharon was a shape-shifted lioness. If he spared her even a moment, she would likely turn on him and rend him limb from limb.

"Sorry," he said, and opened his mouth again.

"Bleep," she swore, and shifted into a sinuous snake that slipped from his grasp and slithered away. She had taken the hard way.

At that point Sharoff also changed to a snake and slithered away, leaving Maeve with her mouth open, her bite of flesh gone before she could savor it.

"Well, at least we won," she said, halfway philosophically. She pulled the unused sword out of the ground and carried it in one hand.

They put their clothing back on and went to the castle gate. It was a portcullis whose iron bars were set too closely together for the flions to pass, but not too tight for the two of them. They wedged through, walked to the wooden door, opened it, and entered the castle proper. Sammy Cat went on ahead.

But something was bothering Jumper, and in no more than three-quarters of a moment he got it. "The flions are shape changers. Why didn't they change to humans or snakes to get between the bars and inside?"

That perplexed Maeve too. "Maybe they didn't think of it. Or maybe there are traps, so they need to fight Warren outside."

That made some sense. "We had better be alert for those traps."

She nodded. "I'm a maenad; I can smell trouble. You're a spider; you should be able to smell it too."

They sniffed together. There were some crude traps, which they had no trouble avoiding. They made their way through the castle, which seemed to be empty.

"So where is Warren?" Jumper asked, frustrated.

Then they spied Sammy, who was snoozing before a bedroom closet door. He had led them to Warren; they simply hadn't been paying attention.

Maeve went up to the door and tried the knob. It did not turn; the door was locked. "Warren, come out!" she called. When there was no answer, she struck at the door with the sword. It clove asunder and the two halves fell away on either side.

There, huddled in a dark corner behind hanging clothing, was the figure of a man. That had to be Warren.

"We have a delivery for you," Maeve said.

"Don't hurt me!" the man moaned, huddling lower.

"You sniveling freak!" Maeve cried, outraged. She smote him on the top of the head with the flat of the sword. And stood amazed.

The sword did not strike with a satisfying clonk. Instead it sank right through his head and into his body, disappearing. The hilt dissolved, so that Maeve was left holding nothing. She stepped back, dismayed. What devious magic was this?

The man unwound. He got to his feet in the closet, knocking aside clothing. "My courage!" he cried. "You brought back my courage!"

"That was our delivery, yes," Maeve agreed.

"I love you!" He leaped out of the closet and swept her into his embrace. He kissed her firmly on the mouth.

"Mmmph! Mmmph!" she protested, trying vainly to push him away. Finally she took two handfuls of his hair and wrenched his face away from hers. "Get away from me, you miserable coward!"

"Coward no more, thanks to you," he said. "You beautiful creature. I'm going to marry you."

"I'm a *maenad*!" she shouted.

He took a better look at her. "Why, so you are, you luscious thing." He drew her in close again, one hand on her pert bottom. "My ideal soul mate."

"If you don't unhand me instantly, I'll chomp your face off!" she threatened.

Warren smiled. "And you've got the lovely sharp teeth to do it, don't you, my love. But you know you can't scare me; I've got my courage back. So bite me; I dare you." And he drew her in for another kiss.

Jumper, expecting mayhem, was about to step in to separate them. But Maeve, to his surprise, submitted to the kiss, and did not chomp his face off. It seemed he had called her bluff. Except that Jumper doubted it had been a bluff. Why had she changed her mind?

After a good two and a half moments they came up for air. Maeve looked flushed. Had she been overtaken by a sudden illness?

Then she spoke, carefully. "If you really have your courage back, Warren, why don't you go out and fight that flion?"

"Then will you marry me, you captivating damsel?"

"Maybe. If you live."

So that was it: she was getting rid of Warren without getting his blood on her own hands. She was really angry.

"Immediately." Warren's sword appeared in his hand. He strode out of the bedroom, down the stairs, and out of the castle. They followed, bemused.

"Fletcher!" Warren bawled. "You sniveling cur! Get your mangy tail over here so I can cut it off!"

The flion appeared, circling around the castle. He came to land before them. "So you have come to face the inevitable at last, you miserable man-thing."

"I have my courage back, you winged kitten. You stole it and lost it, but this marvelous creature found it and returned it to me." He sent a loving glance at Maeve.

"She's a maenad! A wild woman!"

Warren stared down his aristocratic nose. "And what is your point, hairball? Was there ever a more fitting match for a warrior?"

"Well, you won't live long enough to enjoy the moment. En garde!" Fletcher leaped.

Warren swung his sword in a short arc as he stepped to one side. The flion's head went sailing from his body. "Oh, you got me!" he said as it landed and bounced. "Lucky blow." It rolled into the moat with a splash.

"You should have known better than to challenge a warrior," Warren said, pushing the rest of the body into the moat.

That seemed to be the case. Jumper was impressed with the change in the man. Courage made all the difference.

"What now?" Maeve asked, taking stock.

"Now we can marry," Warren said, turning to her. "First we have a glorious session on the bed. Then we'll set off for adventures galore, wreaking havoc wherever we go."

But Maeve hesitated, evidently remembering her situation with the stork. "I have a mission to accomplish first."

That certainly did not sound like a no. It seemed the warrior had impressed the bloodthirsty maiden.

Warren sighed. "Then accept this token of my desire," he said, producing a miniature sword hung on a string. He put the string over Maeve's head so that it circled her neck, with the sword resting against her chest. "Merely invoke it at any time, and it will bring you to me for an hour. What joy we might accomplish in that hour!"

"I'll think about it," Maeve agreed. "Now we have to go."

"Sammy," Jumper called. "We need to find the Found Cabin."

The cat took off, and they followed, barely keeping up. In due course they reached the Found Cabin. Sammy went to snooze by Jenny's feet. He couldn't find home, but fortunately this wasn't home.

The others were eating bread with conjured grape jam, while playing two rounds of drawbridge. It seemed they had found a card game by that name, that consisted of a pack of fifty-two thin bridges with assorted numberings, which consisted of bidding for particular ones. It seemed complicated, but of course he was only a spider. Still, the cat Claire Voyant was their eighth player, and she seemed to be at no disadvantage.

"So what happened?" Olive asked. It seemed she was the "dummy," which did not appear to relate to intelligence, so wasn't focusing on the game at the moment.

"I . . ." Maeve stalled out. "You tell them, Jumper."

He told them. In half a moment the two card games dissolved and all of them were paying close attention. "So Maeve returned the Sword of Courage," he concluded, "and Warren Warrior kissed her and—"

"He *what*?" Olive and Phanta asked together.

"And she did knot chomp off his face?" Wenda asked.

"She must be in love," Haughty said smugly.

Maeve merely stood there, blushing. That was impossibly unusual for a maenad.

"He wanted to marry her, but she said she has to complete the mission first," Jumper said.

"And get rid of that pesky stork," Dawn said.

"That too," Maeve agreed, finding her voice.

"How could you do such a thing?" Olive demanded. "Maenads want only one thing from a man, and that's a pound of his flesh freshly ripped out of his body. They don't fall in love."

"Maybe it's not love," Maeve said. "He gave me an amulet. He wants me to visit, for an hour, for a glorious session on his bed."

"That's stork signaling!" Haughty said. "That's mischief."

"I know," Maeve said. "But this time I think I want to do it. It's not as if the storks will know. Not if the signal doesn't go out."

"Disgusting," the harpy said. But she did not seem fully serious.

"We can be free here," Phanta said. "Free in a manner we can't—or shouldn't be—outside. In a way it makes us equal with men."

"They have little if any responsibility," Eve said. "A little less for us would serve them right."

Several others nodded thoughtfully. Jumper wondered what was going through their minds. How could diminished responsibility benefit anyone?

"And we still have five symbols to return," Olive said. "Who is next?"

There was half a silence. Jumper broke it. "Let's relax tonight, and decide tomorrow morning. We have had enough adventure for today."

"Yes, it's been quite a game of drawbridge," Phanta said, laughing.

Then Haughty vanished. "What happened?" Jumper asked, alarmed.

"Oh, she's just popping out to verify the waking world," Olive explained. "She does that every few hours. Don't you remember?"

Now he did remember. "We have been dreaming for some time. We probably need to take a break."

Haughty reappeared. "Food, sleep, and p**p," she announced. "Are you ready?"

"We can return to this same place?" Jumper asked.

"You can't avoid it. That's the way the gourd is."

"Then take us out," Jumper agreed.

Haughty vanished again. After a scant two moments, so did the rest of them, one by one: Maeve, Wenda, Olive, Phanta, and Dawn. When Olive went, so did Jenny and the cats, because they had been conjured by Olive.

"It's just you and me," Eve said. She turned and flashed her panties. Then she vanished.

Jumper, caught off guard, was half freaked. That d**ned tease!

Then he blinked. He was lying on the mat, and Tandy's hand was before his face, intercepting his connection to the gourd's peephole. "Welcome back, Jumper," she said, smiling. "You must have seen something interesting, just now; your face went slack."

"Nothing important," he said, knowing that the truth would only make everyone laugh. Eve had had her little joke.

But he knew he would have to maintain a better guard, because those panties certainly were potent.

7
HEART AND MIND

I n the morning, refreshed, they returned to the dream realm. When Jumper put one eye to the peephole he found himself in the Found Cabin, right where he had left it. All of them were there, appearing one by one.

"I will summon my imaginary friend Jenny," Olive said. She concentrated, and in hardly more than a moment Jenny appeared, along with Sammy, Claire, and Kaboodle, swishing her nine tails.

"Whose turn is it?" Jenny inquired.

"Mine, I think," Wenda said. "I was the second one to pick up a symbol. The Heart of Love."

"That's odd," Maeve said.

"Odd?"

"The way mine changed from Courage to Love. I picked up the Sword of Courage, but then Warren said he loves me. Who could ever love a maenad?"

"A bloodthirsty warrior," Haughty said. "But you don't need to guess, girl. Invoke your amulet. Go see him for an hour. Then you'll know for sure."

"But that might be only passion, not love."

Haughty laughed. "Much the same thing, for a man. Go. They don't need you here for that time."

Maeve looked around somewhat helplessly. "Is that true?" She seemed pitifully eager yet doubtful.

"True enough," Olive said.

"Well, if it's really all right . . ."

The others nodded. Maeve lifted the little sword. "Take me to your master," she said. And vanished.

"She's used to making love, not war," Phanta said.

"I think that's actually one lucky warrior," Eve murmured.

Jumper found he agreed. Maeve was one taut, pretty, shapely female, trying to learn how to be a woman instead of a vicious creature. She would surely give the warrior a lot of pleasure as she learned the nature of his interest.

Which reminded him of Sharon, in her brief woman phase. Of course she had merely been trying to trick him. But in that moment she had been a most tempting morsel. Not that he had any business noticing.

"I hope mine works out as well," Wenda said, picking up the heart. She glanced at Jumper. "Are yew coming with me?"

Oh. He was still in spider form. "Yes. Let me change." He took a vial, sipped it, and became the naked man.

Wenda was already there with clothing for him. Dawn and Eve mischievously flashed their undies, but too late to embarrass him. Even so, he blinked. They had reversed it, with Dawn showing her bright white panties, and Eve her dark bra. Both were as well filled as their prior examples, and did momentarily stun him. The others didn't notice that they were showing anything, but of course they were showing it only to Jumper. It was highly selective naughtiness.

Wenda held up the heart. "Sammy, find who this belongs to," she said.

Sammy went from midcatnap to midair without any intervening stage. He was on his way.

"Wait for us!" Wenda cried belatedly, running after him. But of course he didn't wait.

They charged through the dream sets again, in a blur. One was an ocean, but somehow they crossed the water without sinking in. They came to a shore, and then to a palace.

Then they were in a royal bedroom. A maid was combing the hair of a handsome prince; their identities were clear because she wore a cloth headband, and he a sparkling golden crown. Sammy was snoozing at their feet.

"Well, now," the woman said, spying Sammy. "I think we have found a cat."

"No, yew did knot," Wenda said, arriving on the scene, followed by Jumper. How they had gotten there without passing through doors or walls Jumper wasn't sure. "Sammy Cat found yew."

The maid's eyes widened. "Is this *the* Sammy Cat? Princess Jenny's friend?"

"Yes," Wenda said. "And I am Wenda Woodwife, and this is Jumper Spider, who is guarding me. We have come to—"

"Prince Charming!" the woman exclaimed. "We have remarkable visitors!"

"Charmed, I'm sure, if you say so, Mercy," the prince said, evidently bored.

"I brought the lost Heart of Love," Wenda said. "To which of yew does it belong? I wood knot want to make a mistake."

The maid, Mercy, looked stricken.

"It is yewrs?" Wenda asked alertly.

"No," Mercy said, but she had paled dangerously.

"Sammy led us here to the two of yew. If it's knot yours, it must bee the prince's."

"Well, I have lost my love," Prince Charming said. "But I don't think any change of heart on my part will solve that problem. My wife just dumped me for a richer king. I am quite out of sorts. If it weren't for Mercy and my sister Sharon, I'd throw myself into the sea."

Wenda exchanged a confused glance with Jumper. The prince had a point. How could the heart help him? Yet it seemed that Mercy knew something she didn't want to speak of. And what a coincidence that

Charming's sister should be named Sharon, the same as the flion who had briefly vamped him.

"Maybe your sister will have a thought on the matter," Jumper said, hardly daring to guess what to expect in such a woman.

"Maybe," Charming agreed. He heaved his voice up by its bootstraps. "Sharon! I need your input."

In barely half a moment she appeared: a lovely dark-haired creature of a woman with eyes that fairly glinted with illicit comprehension. It *was* her!

"What is it, Charming?" Sharon asked, her voice compellingly dulcet.

"This nymph found a lost Heart of Love, and thinks it's mine. But I don't need to love, I need to get my lost love back. So what's with the heart?"

Sharon pursed her lush red lips. "Perhaps my art will fathom it," she agreed. Then she turned, leaned forward just enough to proffer half a glimpse inside her curvaceous décolletage, and smiled. The air around Jumper warmed perceptibly. "So nice to see you again, Jumper. And who is your friend?"

"Wenda," Wenda said quickly.

"Clearly not a maenad," Sharon said. "How did a forest creature like you come by the heart?"

Sharon was making Jumper increasingly nervous. She knew too much, and obviously remembered him from their encounter in the other venue. He had had no idea she was really a princess!

"It was in the Found Cabin," Wenda said. "I am trying to return it to its owner. But—"

Sharon nodded. "But there seems to be a confusion, yes. It does seem to be symbolic of my brother's loss, but such a magic artifact should represent the solution to a problem, rather than a complication of it."

"Yes," Wenda agreed, disgruntled.

Sharon's eye speared the maid. "And what do you know of this matter, Mercy?"

Mercy burst into tears.

Sharon's gaze hardened. "Do I have your permission to fathom your part in this?"

Jumper did not know a great deal about human interactions, but strongly suspected that a maidservant could give a princess only one answer to such a request: yes.

"Then here is my fathoming," Sharon said. She moved her hands in a magical pattern, and a scintillating cloud formed around Mercy. The scene changed around her.

In fact it became a view of the depths of the ocean. There was Mercy, nude and lovely, swimming blithely along, propelled by her fish tail.

Her *what*? Jumper blinked both his human eyes, but the sight didn't change. Mercy was a mermaid.

"Fascinating," Sharon breathed.

Mercy swam toward a commotion on the surface of the sea. There was a storm there, attacking a wooden ship. It blew so hard a man was swept into the water.

He was Prince Charming.

"This becomes intriguing," Sharon said.

Charming tried to swim in the rough seas, but he was evidently better as a man on the water than under it, and soon he was on the verge of drowning. At this point Mercy reached him. She wrapped her arms about him and propelled him to the surface so he could breathe again. When he didn't, she squeezed him hard so that the water in him spewed out. Then she put her mouth to his and blew air into him, forcing him to breathe again.

He choked and coughed, but remained unconscious. So she bore him to the nearest shore, a sandy beach, and heaved him onto it. She hauled herself out just far enough to give him one more kiss of life, then slipped back into the water.

As Charming recovered consciousness, a princess happened to come along the beach, collecting shells. She spied Charming and ran to him. She tried to lift him up, but was not strong enough and fell onto him. As his eyes opened, she was the one he saw, there in his arms. "You saved me!" he exclaimed, knowing nothing of the true situation.

Mercy saw this happen from the water. She was clearly happy that

Charming had been rescued, but had another problem: she had hugged him and kissed him, and fallen in love with him. That was made clear by the little hearts that hovered around her head when she gazed in his direction. But there was nothing she could do. Her tears were lost in the sea as the vision faded.

"You!" Charming said. "*You* saved me, not the princess!"

"I couldn't let you drown," Mercy said.

"But what are you doing here? You have legs now."

"I got a spell," she said. "To convert my nether portion. I went on land, but it took me time to learn the language and make my way as a two-leg, and by that time you were married. So I applied for a position as a maidservant."

"And for the past decade you have loyally served me," he said. "I never suspected."

"I did not want to interfere in your life. I just wanted to be close to you."

"Mercy Mermaid is a better woman than your wife was," Sharon murmured.

"*You* are my lost love," he said. "So far and yet so near. Give me that heart!"

"No!" Mercy cried.

Too late. He had already taken the heart from Wenda and clasped it to his chest. It sank in and disappeared. "Now I love you," he said. "You are a better woman than the princess ever was. Now I will marry you and live happily ever after."

"No," Mercy repeated tearfully.

"What? One does not say no to a prince."

Mercy was clearly uncomfortable. "I would not hurt you for the world, Charming. But I can't marry you."

"I don't understand."

She burst into tears again.

"This too, I think I fathom," Sharon said. "For a decade Mercy has been your loyal servant. She has combed your hair, made your bed, helped you dress, done all the little personal things you required. While you loved another woman. She came to know you quite well. Now she faces the prospect of doing all these things for you for the rest of her life, *plus* serving your pleasure in bed. It is too much. She is a creature of the sea, and she has been long away from it. She wants to return to her natural environment."

"Yes," Mercy said. "I thought I loved you, Charming, but that wore thin as I washed your stinky socks and scrubbed your messy chamber pot. I must go home."

"But I love you!" Charming protested.

"I would only leave you, as your wife did. The call of the sea is too strong."

"But I absorbed the heart!"

"I tried to prevent you."

It occurred to Jumper that there was a certain poetic justice here. Mercy had loved the prince, unrequited; now he loved her, unrequited.

"But where will I go, what will I do?"

"You will surely find another woman to love." Mercy fled the scene, and in three and a half moments they heard the splash as she dived into the ocean. She was definitely gone.

"But perhaps I can help answer your question," Sharon said. "Have you considered the one who returned your lost love to you? Perhaps this was not coincidental."

"The one who . . . ?" he repeated, perplexed. Then his eye fell on Wenda.

"Now wait an instant," Wenda said, alarmed.

"I'm on one bleep of a rebound at the moment," Charming said. "I need a pretty, innocent, loyal woman to console me."

"But I wood knot bee that to yew!" Wenda protested.

"I love the way you express yourself. You're a forest nymph. You'll never jump into the sea."

Sharon caught Jumper's eye and held it relentlessly. "Let's give them some privacy to work this out," she said. "Come to my chambers with me."

"But I can't do that! I have a mission."

"To which you will return in due course. What are you going to do, bite off my head? Right this way, you intriguing man."

"I'm not a man," he said as she led him away. "I'm a spider."

"Oh, another shape changer? I like you better than ever."

"Not exactly. I just—"

She gave him a gentle push, and he found himself lying on her soft bed. She was right there with him. "We're not in combat mode now, Jumper. Let's see what we can do with each other."

"No! This isn't—"

She cut him off with a kiss.

Still, he did not trust this. "Who are you, really? What are you?"

"If I answer you, will you let me have my way with you?"

He was thoroughly nonplussed. "What way is that?"

"It goes something like this. First we kiss." She kissed him again, and his smooched face radiated guilty pleasure into his body. "Then we remove our clothing." Her hands were already busy. In a mere fragment of a moment they were both deliciously bare. She was trying to freak him out with bra and panties, except that she wore none. "Then we—"

"No!"

She drew herself close to him. "I don't think I heard you, Jumper."

"I said no!" He struggled weakly to escape.

"You say no, but it sounds like yes."

"No!"

"Do you mean it doesn't sound like yes?"

"Yes!"

"Ah, you agree to the deal at last."

He opened his mouth, but she stifled it with another kiss. Her body reminded him forcefully of Angie. But he dredged up another fading effort. "No."

"Exactly what are you afraid of, Jumper?"

That set him back. She wasn't asking him to leave his mission or commit to anything. In that respect, she was just like Angie, and excruciatingly tempting. "Just answer my question."

"Gladly. I am Sharon, sister of Charming, who in real life is not a prince but a lesser Demon, Charon, who associates with the Dwarf Demon Pluto."

"Pluto!"

"Yes, the one you are opposing. I represent the enemy, in that respect. It is my mission to divert you from your mission."

This was amazing candor. "Are you a Demon too?" That would explain how she could shape change and do fathoming magic; Demons weren't limited to single talents the way mortals were.

"A very minor one, Jumper, hardly worthy of the capital. Barely above the uncapped demons common in Xanth."

"But any Demon is way beyond the comprehension of mortals."

"Not necessarily. I am close enough to mortality to share some of its passions. Such as this one." She kissed him again, and stroked him with her hands. "Now I have honestly answered your question, Jumper, and I expect you to do your part."

"But I'm not going to give up my mission!"

"I have not asked you to."

"But—"

"I told you that my mission is to stop yours. But that is not our deal of the moment. I have established truth between us, so that we can enjoy our fling. I'll try to stop your mission another time."

"You're not—?"

"Not," she agreed.

That seemed sufficient. After that a ferocious ellipsis encompassed them. Sharon was every bit the woman Angie was. Of course, somewhere in the back of his awareness, behind a thick cloaking mental curtain, was the awareness that neither was a real woman. One was imaginary, the other a Demoness. That did not hinder his passion of the moment, but it did make him doubt that there was any real future here, even for a real man, which he wasn't. Even had it not all been part of a dream.

Then they were returning to the other room. "We really must do this again some time, Jumper," Sharon murmured.

He could only agree. The long-term future was dubious, but what a present!

Wenda was just getting her own clothing back on. The prince was sound asleep on the bed. Jumper decided not to ask her how she had put him to sleep; he had half a notion.

"He's some man," she said as they followed Sammy back. "He gave me a magic ring to invoke, when—"

"I understand." All too well.

"But we are going to complete our mission," she said firmly.

"Yes," he agreed. But he was beginning to wonder: if Sharon worked for Pluto, who did Charming work for? Surely he was another agent determined to stop their mission. They were entering treacherous waters.

"I really dew like him," Wenda said, oblivious to Jumper's own situation. "He treats me like a complete woman. There are worse things than being a princess."

Treacherous indeed.

They reached the Found Cabin. The girls were playing cards again. Maeve was back. She was the first to spy their return. "You found someone!" she exclaimed. "Both of you!"

Jumper froze. Wenda blushed so deeply that the others laughed. She was able to blush quite well, now that she was soft flesh instead of hard wood.

"You really must tell us," Jenny said. "We're women; curiosity is our nature."

"Yew tell them," Wenda squeezed out through her blush.

So Jumper tackled it. "We found the Little Mermaid. She—"

"The Little Mermaid!" Haughty exclaimed. "She's from a bl**ping different story."

"So am I," Jenny reminded her. "Anything can appear in Xanth, and more so in the dream realm."

"That's right; I forgot. Carry on."

"It seems she saved a drowning prince, and fell in love with him," Jumper said. "But then he married someone else, a princess. So Mercy—that's her name, Mercy Mermaid—went to work as his servant. But the princess dumped him, and the Heart of Love made him love Mercy instead, but she decided to return to the sea. So now he's interested in Wenda."

"And she's interested in him," Maeve said shrewdly. "The same way I'm interested in Warren."

"Exactly the same," Wenda agreed, her blush making a valiant effort to intensify. "Prince Charming treats me like a complete woman."

"You signaled the stork!" Eve said darkly.

Wenda's blush threatened to stain the air around her. "Several times," she confessed. "He—the Heart—rebound—he's a virile man."

"I know exactly how it is," Maeve said. "Now I know how much fun a man can be, when he tries. Did he give you an amulet?"

"This ring," Wenda said, showing her hand.

"That's a wedding ring!" Dawn said brightly. "On the wedding finger. You married him."

"Oh! I didn't know!" Wenda's blush finally overcame her, and she swooned.

"She's besotted," Haughty said. "It's a wonder she returned for the mission."

"She is loyal to the mission," Jumper said. "But when it is done . . ." He didn't finish, because his own situation was disastrously similar.

"And you," Maeve said to him. "Was it that shape-changing wench?"

"Sharon," he agreed. "She—"

"Seduced you," Eve said, quick to fathom secrets.

"Yes. But that's not the worst."

"There is worse?" Olive asked with mock shock.

"She's Charon's sister, and Charon is the Demon Pluto's friend. They are trying to distract us from our mission."

"How do you know this?" Eve asked dourly.

"She told me."

"Before or after she seduced you?" Dawn asked brilliantly.

"Before."

There was half a silence.

"But I told her we would continue the mission," Jumper said before the silence could be completed.

"Well, now we know Pluto's strategy," Haughty said. "He's trying to distract us, one at a time, by offering us romantic men. Or a sexy wench for Jumper. Can we handle it?"

Phanta looked at the blissfully unconscious woodwife. "I suspect we'll have to. Maeve and Wenda are loyal, and Jumper, but the rest of us have not yet been tested."

"If any one of us deserts the mission," Eve said gloomily, "it will be lost."

"That's the h**l of it," Haughty agreed. "But what can we do but continue, hoping to be steadfast?"

"Who's up next?" Phanta asked.

"I believe I am," Olive said. "With the Head of Mind."

"Then go to it, girl," Haughty said. "We have time for one more scene before we have to break for food and p**p."

Olive picked up the head. "I feel so much saner. I'm sure I'll be objective."

"Until you deliver the symbol," Eve said sinisterly. "Then you'll be your usual ordinary self again."

"And that's when some handsome man will court you and try to corrupt you," Dawn said dexterously.

"I know. But if Maeve and Wenda can be true, so can I." She turned to the black cat, who was of course asleep. "Sammy, take us to who needs this."

The orange doormat became a streak of fur. They were on their way.

After the usual melange of impressions, they came to a really odd region. It seemed to be a castle, but instead of being mounted atop a mountain, it was sunk into a sizable chasm, so that its highest turret barely projected above the ground. Sammy was snoozing at the brink of the cavity. Obviously he could not take them the rest of the way without a disastrous fall.

"I think we must be looking for the man in the low castle," Olive said. "Though this does seem like a crazy scene."

"Crazy," Jumper echoed. "The man has lost his mind."

"Oh, yes! And I am about to return it to him. If I can reach him."

A weird notion occurred to him. "Is it possible that he doesn't want his sanity returned?"

"Ludicrous! Who would ever want to be crazy if he could be sane?"

She had to be correct. "Then we must find a way past this crazy barrier." Jumper studied it. "The way the castle rises from the depths, it's almost as if it is surrounded by a moat."

"Beware the moat monster," Olive agreed.

They inspected the gulf that surrounded the castle. The moment he got close, Jumper's head spun with the weirdness of it. Craziness was in the very air.

"I wonder," Olive said. "Could you fling a web across it? Lasso a turret, so we could swing across to the top of the castle?"

"I can try," Jumper agreed. He spun a line, whirled it around—and fell to the ground, dizzy.

"The craziness is getting to you," she said. "Too bad."

"Could you summon an imaginary friend who could help us cross?"

"Great idea!" She concentrated, and a woman appeared.

"Don't touch me!" the woman warned. "I'm Anna Phylactic; I'll shock you with allergy."

"You're not the friend I tried to summon," Olive said, taken aback.

"You'd have to be crazy to summon me," Anna said.

"Crazy," Jumper said, seeing it. "It's affecting you too."

"You're right," Olive agreed. Her allergy-inciting friend faded out. "So it seems we can't use our talents for this purpose. It's like the Good Magician's Castle."

"If it is, there must be a way."

"A crazy way," she agreed. "Let's look around."

"Maybe there's a stink horn."

She laughed. "You made a funny. You're getting more human, Jumper. Did that wench really seduce you?"

"Yes," he agreed, embarrassed. That was another human trait. "I couldn't resist her."

"Was she as good as Angie?"

So she did know. "Yes."

"But you remain true to the mission."

"Yes. Of course I'm not really human, so maybe it's easier for me."

She glanced sidelong at him. "Perhaps."

They looked around, but all they saw was a loose piece of paper weighted down by a broken piece of chalk. Jumper picked both up. "We should find a place to dispose of this litter."

"You don't think it's a stink horn?"

That was irony or humor, which were more human traits. What she meant was, could this be some devious key to entering the castle? Obviously not.

Then he saw the words, which his human eyes were able to read: DRAW BRIDGE.

A crazily variegated bulb flashed over his head. "I think this *is* a stink horn!"

"How so?"

"I mean it's a pun, maybe, or literal. We should draw a bridge."

"But we need more than a picture."

"Let's see." He braced the clear side of the paper against a flat stone and used the chalk to draw a crude picture of a bridge.

"Oh my goodness," Olive breathed.

Jumper glanced up from the paper. His crude bridge was forming between the brink of the chasm and the castle. The chalk, or paper, or both were magic.

He completed his drawing, and the bridge was complete. It wasn't handsome or particularly sturdy, but it was there. The crazy device had worked, in this crazy scene.

Sammy came to life. He bounded across the bridge to the castle. Jumper and Olive followed, and soon they stepped onto an upper turret. "Stink horn," Olive murmured, and kissed him on the cheek.

A winding stair took them into the depths of the castle. Jumper was no expert on castles, but even he could appreciate the weirdness of this one. It had clearly been constructed by a madman.

Sammy led them to a crowded little den. There was a wild-eyed man scribbling on more magic paper. Word-filled scrolls surrounded him, piling up on the floor. This must be the one who had lost his mind. The man in the low castle.

"Hello," Olive said tentatively.

The man looked up. "We can remember it for you retail," he said.

Olive was taken aback. "Remember what?"

"The three stigmata."

"The three whats?"

"You don't remember? Too bad. I have total recall."

"He's mad," Jumper whispered, reminding her.

"Oh. Yes." She advanced on the man. "Take this, please." She shoved it at him.

The statue's head collided with the man's head, and sank in, disappearing.

The man paused, astonished. "Suddenly I am sane!"

"Yes," Olive said. "You lost your mind, so we returned it to you."

"This is disaster!"

They stared at him, uncomprehending.

There were footsteps in the hall. Sharon appeared, taking in the scene at a glance. "What have you done to my crazy brother?" she demanded, appalled.

"We returned his mind," Jumper said. She was another man's sister?

Sharon rushed to the man. "Oh, Dick, I'm so sorry!" She turned on Jumper and Olive. "You should be ashamed of yourselves. Look at the harm you've done."

"Harm?" Jumper asked numbly. "All we did was restore his sanity."

"Exactly. This is Dick Philip, the infamous writer. How can he write his wild books now? His mad genius is gone, thanks to your meddling."

"I—I'm sorry," Olive said. "I thought—"

"Try not to think, doxie. It's dangerous."

"Maybe I can help," Olive said. "I have some pretty wild friends. For example here are two writers, Robert Hindsight and Isaac Azimuth. They're very good at seeing future history and new directions in science."

Whereupon two demented-looking young characters appeared. "Hi," the boy said. "I'm Willie."

"And I'm Nillie," the girl said.

"Apart we're reasonably well behaved," Willie said, pushing a chair into the wall, denting one or the other.

"But together we're sheer mischief," Nillie said zestfully, her elbow knocking over Dick's mug of boot rear so that it sent several scrolls flying.

"Oh, bleep!" Olive swore. "I forgot the madness of the environment. I can't summon the right friends." The figures faded out.

"Just a moment," Dick said. "That's your talent? Conjuring people?"

"Imaginary friends," Olive agreed. "I'm Olive Hue."

"I love you too," he said, sweeping her into his embrace.

"I didn't say—" she protested.

"The madness made it sound like 'I love you,'" Jumper said.

"Well, it does, but that doesn't mean to take it literally."

"However, I choose to do so," Dick said, kissing her soundly. "You are exactly what I need now, Olive Hue."

"This is crazy!" she protested weakly. It was obvious that the crazy kiss had considerable impact; two and a half little hearts were orbiting her head.

"On the contrary," Dick said. "It is completely rational. Deprived of my own creative madness, I need yours. With you by my side, I may yet achieve notoriety if not greatness. Perhaps they will even film truly bad dreams from my ideas."

Sharon nodded. "You broke it, you bought it, doxie."

Olive looked wildly about. "I—I—" Then she made half a decision. "I need to consider further. Kiss me again."

He did. This time six little hearts and a planet swirled around her head.

"Let's give them time to consider," Sharon murmured, catching Jumper by the hand. Such was his bemusement, he allowed her to lead him to a separate chamber.

"Are you going to seduce me again?" he asked, trying to put up at least a show of resistance as she set his hands on her plush bottom. He could feel the intoxicating outline of panties under her skirt.

"Of course. Do you object?"

"Well—"

She kissed him on the mouth. "You were saying?"

"Nothing."

Her hands were busy with his clothing. "What, not even how you still expect to complete your mission?"

"Oh. Yes."

"You drive a hard bargain. I have no choice but to accede." She drew him down on the bed with her, flattened her bare body against him, and stroked him somewhere exciting. Then the ellipsis caught them both and flung them madly about before wearing them pleasantly out.

After a reckless time they returned to the writer's den. "If you must go, at least carry this with you," Dick was saying as Olive tucked her blouse back in. He proffered a tiny model pen.

"What is it?" she asked as she combed out her storm-tossed hair.

"An amulet that will conjure you to me for an hour at a time. So I can glean inspiration from your wild imagination."

"Is that all?" she asked archly.

"Yes, in the five minutes remaining of the hour after our phenomenal passion is expended."

She nodded. "Ah. Very well, then." She took the pen.

"I believe they have worked it out," Sharon murmured.

"So it seems," Jumper agreed.

It was time to return to the others. Sammy led them there.

This time the girls were engrossed in a new game, and did not notice the return of the two. "That looks like Nineteen Questions," Olive whispered, cautioning him to silence. "They must have gotten tired of cards." So he was quiet, not sure what this was about.

Wenda was in the center, while the others sat in a circle around her. "My turn to ask," Dawn was saying. "If you had a nice man, and could make him do anything you wanted, for one minute, what would it be?"

The woodwife was silent. "That's the game," Olive whispered. "She must answer only yes or no, truthfully."

After a pause to let Wenda think about it, Dawn asked "Kiss your mouth?"

Wenda shook her head, no.

"Kiss your hand?"

No.

"Your foot?"

No.

"The further it goes, the worse it gets," Olive whispered. "By the time it gets to the nineteenth question, a person can be reduced to a quivering mass of mortification."

"Your chest?"

Wenda blushed, but shook her head.

"Your newly rounded bottom?"

Wenda's blush was burning. She did not want to answer. Then she spied her salvation. "They're here!" she exclaimed, having a legitimate way to change the subject. "Did yew—?"

There was a muted sigh among the others. The game had just been getting interesting. Jumper had found it so, also. Why should a girl want a man to kiss her bottom? But, thinking as a man, he realized that this might indeed be fun, for no sensible reason he could fathom.

Olive held up the pen. "Yes, he gave me an amulet. He is one crazy lover, even if he is now utterly sane."

"Maeve and I know how that is," Wenda said, her blush fading. "But yew did knot—?"

"I didn't quit the mission. I made that clear. So even if he is an agent of Pluto, all he's getting is me."

"And you?" Maeve asked Jumper.

"She was there again," he agreed. "Posing as his sister."

"You're becoming fascinated with her," Dawn said, touching his hand. "That's dangerous."

"I know. But I am true to my mission, and I know there's no future in that relationship. I'm a spider."

"And she's a shape changer. She could assume spider form, if she wanted to."

"There's the thing," he said glumly. "She won't want to. Once we complete the mission, she'll disappear, angry. So my only chance with her is now."

"I'm afraid you're right," she said sympathetically. "You deserve better, Jumper."

What would be better, regardless what he deserved? He changed the subject. "It must be time to get out of the gourd."

"It is," Haughty said. "Are we all ready?"

"But we didn't finish the game," Phanta protested.

"You don't need to," Haughty said. She disappeared.

Then they started disappearing, one by one, as before. This time the last one left before Jumper was Dawn. "I'll bet you think I'm going to flash you," she said.

"Well, Eve did, and you seem similar in your mischief."

"Jumper, we both enjoy incidental naughtiness. But there is more to it than that. Sharon is trying to win your love so she can demand that you quit the mission. We're trying to remind you that there are other women who have what she has. You don't have to be with her to get it."

What was she driving at? "I don't think I understand."

"Don't let her corrupt you from the mission. We don't want to have to step in to salvage it."

"I'm not going to quit the mission!"

"Because Eve and I are prepared to do what we have to do to keep you on track. We need you, Jumper."

What they had to do? "I still don't think I understand."

"Have fun with her, but never lose your larger perspective. The welfare of Xanth depends on it. That Internet–Outernet connection is the only remaining reliable link to Mundania. If we lose that, it could be centuries before any similar link is reestablished."

She was serious. Obviously the two Sorceresses were not here incidentally. "And I thought you were just going to flash me."

Dawn smiled. "That too." She opened her shirt, revealing her outstanding bra. "We will go as far as we need to, to salvage the mission. We hope we don't have to."

Then at last she vanished, leaving Jumper half stunned. Half of that was from her full bra, which really did have eye-glazing magic. The other half was from her words. Was she implying that she and Eve would take their flashing to the next level and actually seduce him, to counter Sharon's influence?

Dawn must have arranged to have this time with him. This was no irresponsible teen girl; this was a cynical Sorceress with her own agenda.

What had he gotten into?

8
LIFE AND HONOR

Next day they were back in the Found Cabin, ready for the next scene. This time it was Phanta with the Tombstone of Death, or at least the lost will to live.

"We see a certain formula," Eve said. "Sharon caters to Jumper, getting him out of the way so a handsome man can seduce whichever girl brings the symbol. Every one of us will be under siege by the minions of Pluto. He may be reduced to a Dwarf Demon, but he remains far more than any of us can handle directly. His main constraint is that one Demon can't directly interfere in the territory of another. So he's trying to seduce us away from our mission, literally. Those men are crafted to be highly appealing. But we can be sure they'll all dump us the moment they are sure they can't corrupt us. So play along, but not too far."

"Why is Pluto so determined to prevent the cable from being repaired?" Phanta asked. "Surely he can't be that thin-skinned about his demotion."

"We don't know," Eve said. "Maybe there's a Demon bet involved. Whether he can prevent the repair. One that might restore his status if he wins."

"In that case, he has just begun to fight," Haughty said.

"Yes. But that's not our concern. We just need to get that break repaired."

"That's all," Jumper agreed, realizing that it was likely to be a considerably greater challenge than they had thought.

"After we discover what we're looking for in dreamland," Dawn said.

Phanta lifted the tombstone. "What's the point?" she asked, then was flustered. "Oops, I was reading it. I mean, Sammy, lead us to the one this belongs to."

The cat was off like an orange flash. Jumper and Phanta followed as well as they could.

This time they found themselves in the horror territory. Walking skeletons were rising out of graveyards, ghosts flitted in the windows, and an impressive haunted house loomed against the pale light of a gibbous moon. At this point Sammy faltered. He settled on the ground, but no one was there.

"What, lost, Sammy?" Phanta asked. "Do you want me to ask directions?"

How could he be lost? Jumper wondered. Sammy could find anything. But Phanta was already ghosting.

She floated up to a window and broached a ghost, who looked taken aback. Maybe it wasn't accustomed to dreamers assuming its own nature.

After a moment and a half she returned, to both Jumper and physical form. "He says the cat is not lost, he just ran afoul of a patch of catnap." She went to Sammy, reached down, and pulled up a clump of herbs that were under Sammy's nose.

The moment the catnap was clear, Sammy resumed motion, apparently not realizing that there had been an interruption. "Thanks, ghost!" Phanta called, blowing the ghost a kiss. The ghost reeled and floated away, blissfully freaked out.

Sammy ran to the dark garden beyond the haunted house, where scary statues lurked. But he didn't stop there. He ran on by, past a field of grazing sheep, to a nearby barn. And by it, to some sort of grim building. And inside it.

Now the true horror of this setting became evident. The stink of death suffused it. Blood was splashed around, as if some maniacal murderer had gone berserk.

A man appeared. "Hey, this area is restricted. No visitors."

Sammy settled down at his feet.

Jumper faded into the woodwork. This was Phanta's mission, to handle as she saw fit.

She did. "Did you lose your will to live?"

The man paused. "How could you know that, stranger?"

"I am Phanta, here to return what you lost." She showed the tombstone.

The man shook his head. "I can't accept that."

"Why not? Isn't it yours?"

"You would not like my explanation."

Phanta studied him. He was a handsome man. Jumper had discovered that that sort of thing could influence a woman. "Try me," she said.

He sighed. "Very well. I am Shepherd, guardian of the sheep."

"We saw them grazing outside," she said.

"Yes. They trust me. That's why I don't want to live."

"I don't understand."

"You would hate me if you did."

This was becoming curious. What was on the man's mind?

"Try me," Phanta repeated.

Shepherd looked at her. She was a pretty woman. Jumper knew from personal experience that that sort of thing could influence a man. "Are you sure?"

"I promise not to hate you."

Encouraged, Shepherd continued his explanation. "I guide my flock, and protect them from the big bad wolf. They know they are safe with me. But I am cursed to betray them."

"Cursed?"

"By the Night Stallion. I once made a joke about a horse of a different choler, and someone snitched, and he cursed me. I can't escape until rescued by a fair maiden or a horrendous monster, and none of them come to this dull setting. I am doomed."

"How do you betray them?" Phanta asked.

"I slaughter them. This is the slaughterhouse."

That explained the blood.

"But you don't have to do that," Phanta said, appalled.

"Yes, I do. That's the curse. Each day I must summon ten of them here single file, and club them to death and butcher them as they come. The curse compels me. I hate it, and I wish I could die."

"But aren't the sheep innocent?" Phanta asked.

"Yes. That's part of the hell of it. They are all innocent ewes. I am monstrously guilty. Yet they die, and I survive. In another hour I must do it again."

This was too much for Phanta. "Jumper!" she called. "I need your help!"

Jumper came out of the woodwork to join them. "I don't know what I can do," he said. "A curse is a curse."

"Who are you?" Shepherd asked suspiciously.

"I am Jumper Spider, locked into clumsy human form for the moment."

"So you are cursed too! You're really a monster."

"In a manner," Jumper agreed.

"You two—a fair maiden and a monster," Shepherd said, a lightbulb flashing over his head. "You have come to rescue me!"

"Yes, if we can figure out how," Jumper agreed. "But we're not authorities on curses."

"But we can try," Phanta said.

They tried. "Couldn't you just walk away?" Jumper asked.

"And desert my loyal sheep? I couldn't do that. They'd soon lose their way and starve, suffering a crueler extinction than what my curse provides them."

He had a point. Except that the tombstone asked "What's the point?" Maybe that was the real question.

"Why should we bring you your will to live, if you hate your job so much you don't want to live?" Phanta asked.

"I don't know. It's this job, this curse, that's destroying me. Each time I kill a loyal sheep, I die a little myself."

"We have to get you out of that job," Jumper said.

"But the curse—"

"F**k the curse!" Phanta exclaimed. "Oops, I'm imitating Haughty."

But Jumper was getting a glimmer. "You are bound by the curse. What are the sheep bound by?"

"They go where I guide them," Shepherd repeated with forced patience. "They trust me."

"Suppose you told them the truth?"

"I couldn't do that!"

"Why not?"

"The curse prevents me."

"Suppose someone else told them?"

"They wouldn't listen. They don't trust strangers."

"Maybe they would, if we did it correctly."

"Are you daft? The language doesn't matter. They heed only me."

"I think Jumper is on to something," Phanta said. "I could tell them."

"Haven't you been paying attention? They won't heed you. They're *sheep*."

"Let's give it a try anyway."

"No, this won't—"

She stepped into him and kissed him hard on the mouth. He fell back, three-quarters stunned. "You don't object, do you?" she inquired.

Shepherd opened his mouth. Phanta opened her blouse. That increased the dose of stun, and he couldn't speak. There was a certain private satisfaction watching a woman herd a man, when Jumper himself was not the victim.

"This way," Jumper said, moving to the corral outside.

Phanta took Shepherd by the hand and led him out. He tried again to protest, but she used her free hand to flick up her skirt for half a flash, and he was silenced. She did know how to use what she had.

There were the sheep, milling about. "Hey, ewes," Phanta called loudly. "Shepherd has an announcement to make."

They continued to mill, ignoring her.

"This is important," she said, annoyed. "In fact it's a matter of life and death. Yours."

Not one sheep paid attention.

They were getting nowhere. Shepherd was right: the sheep paid attention only to him, and he was mute, thanks to Phanta's kiss and underwear.

"Do you have a stupid death wish?" Phanta demanded, beginning to get angry.

Then a really bright bulb flashed over Jumper's head. "The tombstone," he said. "Try it on *them*."

"But it's for him."

"Yes. But maybe not directly. Heave it into their midst."

"I think you're crazy," she muttered. But she lifted the tombstone and hurled it into the center of the flock.

It puffed into dark vapor and settled among the sheep. Immediately their attitude changed. They stopped milling and gazed at Shepherd as if seeking his guidance.

"*Now* tell the sheep," Jumper said. "Speaking for him. Keep him quiet."

"Now I get ewe," she said with two-fifths of a smile. Then she stood directly in front of Shepherd, facing the sheep. "Listen, ewes," she said. "I have a message for you from Shepherd. He has an indisposition at the moment and can't speak for himself, but you can see he agrees."

Shepherd opened his mouth again. Without even looking, Phanta twitched her skirt up, flashing more panty, and he was instantly stifled.

"Shepherd is a good man," she continued, "but he is under a curse. He must kill you, ten by ten, every day. He hates it, because he loves you, but he has no choice."

The sheep listened. They looked at Shepherd, who struggled again to speak, but only succeeded in seeming to agree. Phanta had him under control.

"So what does he want you to do about it?" Phanta asked rhetorically. Then she looked blank. She had run out of ideas.

"Revolt," Jumper said. "Break out. Then he *can't* kill them."

"He wants you to revolt," Phanta said. "To break out of here. So he can't kill you."

Their expressions changed. Understanding was coming. But they still didn't know what to do.

"I'll show them," Jumper said.

"My friend Jumper will show you how," Phanta said. "Follow him."

The sheep looked again at Shepherd. He tried yet again to protest, compelled by the curse, but once more was stifled by a flash of panty. Panty magic might not be stronger than the curse, overall, but Phanta was close while the curse was general, so she was able to block it long enough.

Jumper went out. He gazed at the wall of the corral. Then he nerved himself and charged headfirst into it.

The impact was stunning in a way that panties weren't, and the fence held after denting only a little.

But the sheep understood. They might be innocent ewes, but they knew how to butt. They charged at the fence, heads down.

The fence might have held against a single sheep, or several sheep. But it was battered by a hundred sheep. It was stretched and fractured, and in moments it fell flat and the sheep charged over its supine boards. They had done it!

But then they milled about again, not knowing what to do next. They needed new guidance.

"Organize them," Jumper told Phanta as he got back to his feet.

"You need to organize," Phanta cried. "Elect a leader. Follow him." She paused. "I mean, her. She'll tell you what to think, what to do. The ewe tube."

But the sheep didn't understand about elections. They just looked at Phanta and Shepherd.

In desperation, Phanta turned to Shepherd. "We've done it. The sheep revolted and broke out. You can't kill them outside of the corral, can you?"

"No," he said, surprised. "The curse doesn't reach out here."

"Tell them how to hold an election. To organize," she said.

"Yes, I can do that, now."

"Nothing can stop you," Phanta said.

A woman appeared, running from the broken corral. "Shepherd!" she cried. "What are you doing?"

"It's my sister Sharon," he said. "She's cursed too. She'll stop me."

"This is my job," Jumper said. He jumped out to intercept the woman.

"Get out of my way," she exclaimed. "I have to stop my brother from—"

Jumper silenced her with a firm kiss. Turnabout was fair play, he had heard somewhere. Now he was taking her out of the scene, so that Phanta could complete her mission. Because it would not be finished until Shepherd had thoroughly broken the curse.

Sharon jerked her head back. "You don't understand! I have to—"

This time not only did he kiss her, he took two handfuls of her filled panty.

She pulled back again, less violently. "Are you going to keep doing this?"

"Yes."

"Why?"

"Because you're such a fetching creature I just can't keep my hands off you."

"Bleep!"

"Of course. But first we must get private."

She laughed. "How can I resist such a sweet invitation?"

Soon they were in the building, on a bed of straw, nonsummoning the stork.

"You're a good learner," she remarked.

"You're a perfect accomplice."

"I meant about how to foil a curse."

"That too," he agreed.

"I wouldn't do this if I didn't like you," she said, doing it enthusiastically.

"Of course. How else can you corrupt me?"

"Maybe too good a learner," she muttered.

In due course they returned to the field outside the corral. The sheep appeared to have been organized.

"They are holding their election," Phanta said. "Once they have their chosen leader to follow, he can lead them away from here, and our job will be done."

"The curse will have nothing to enforce," Shepherd agreed. "I will be out of a job. I won't be sorry to see the slaughter stop, but I will miss the sheep. They're nice folk."

"Who will no longer be ewesed," Phanta said with a smile.

"I will be alone."

"You will surely manage."

He considered. Then a faint bulb flashed. "I will have nothing to do except court you."

"What?" she asked, surprised.

"Your underwear fascinates me. I want to get closer to it. And you. I love your kisses."

"But I was just distracting you from the curse so that we could save the sheep."

"You did a most effective job. I hope you will continue distracting me forever."

Phanta looked at Jumper. "What do I do now?"

Sharon answered instead. "You made your bed. Now lie in it."

"Yes!" Shepherd agreed.

"I don't know."

Then Shepherd took hold of her and kissed her. Little hearts swirled.

"Well, maybe," she said breathlessly.

The sheep alleviated their huddle. A ewe approached Shepherd.

"You have chosen?" he asked.

"Ewe," she bleated.

"Yes, you are all ewes," he agreed. "You're a selected flock. But who did you choose to lead you far from here?"

"Ewe," she repeated.

"We've just been over that. I know your nature. I just want to know your new leader."

Then Jumper caught on. "This is how she says 'you.' They have chosen you to be their leader."

Shepherd's jaw dropped half a measure. "But I betrayed you! I was killing you! You don't want to have anything more to do with me."

"Ewe."

Shepherd shook his head, dismayed. "But why?"

The sheep formed part of a smile. "Ewe're cute."

"I'm a murderer!"

"Ewe've changed. We want ewe."

"It seems you have a job after all," Phanta said. "*You* can lead them to perpetual safety."

"But I'm a cursed depressive!"

"We gave your will to live to the sheep," Phanta said. "Now they want to live. If you are with their flock, you'll share it. You won't be depressive any more."

He considered. "That may be. But now I realize that there must be more to life than just leading sheep around. I need a woman to fulfill me. You."

"But—"

He kissed her again. This time there was a small explosion of hearts.

Phanta turned to Jumper. "Excuse us, please. Why don't you two go back to the barn for a while?"

"But—"

"This way," Sharon said, leading him there.

Jumper realized that once more the man of the scene had impressed the woman of the scene. It was, after all, the dream realm. He allowed himself to be led. It wasn't as if he didn't want to go.

After another ellipsis-battering bout in the stall, Jumper became reflective. "In time we'll complete our mission. Then you won't need to distract me anymore. Will I ever see you again?"

"Do you feel ewesed?" she asked.

"Yes."

"In time, when you fail to complete your mission, and you admit your defeat, will you want anything to do with me?"

"Well, I'm a spider. So I will have no reason to remain here."

"None?"

"Oh, Sharon, I know you're the enemy. But I wish—"

She kissed him. "So do I. But of course our relationship is doomed."

"Of course," he agreed sadly.

They returned to the field. Shepherd and Phanta seemed to have worked things out. "He gave me an amulet, so I can visit him," she said, holding up a miniature shepherd's crook.

"Do it soon," Shepherd said. Then he went to lead the sheep to salvation, and Sammy led Jumper and Phanta back to the Found Cabin.

The others knew the situation at a glance. "Yew, too," Wenda said. "I mean, ewe. Yew dew look sheepish."

"I, too," Phanta agreed, showing her little crook.

"Sooner or later, one of you will be corrupted," Haughty said. "Then we'll lose the mission."

"But those men are so handsome," Maeve said.

"And they make us feel so beautiful," Olive agreed.

"And Jumper's no better," Haughty said. "Someone really worked him over this time."

"Let's get on with the next scene," Jumper said.

"My turn," Eve said, picking up the Hand of Honor. "Sammy?"

The cat was on the way again, and they chased after him through the usual array of settings. This time they wended south, all the way to Centaur Isle, to an enormous edifice. It might be Xanth's fanciest stall. Sammy settled on a small bed of straw.

There was a handsome male centaur, pondering a pile of papers. He looked up as they arrived. "Ah, you must be the human assistants I summoned. Are you good at paperwork?"

"No," Eve said. "I'm nobody's assistant. I came to return your lost honor."

"What would I want with that? It took me years to scheme my way to the top, and honor had nothing to do with it."

"Then you really need this." She pushed the hand at him.

He raised a hand to ward it off. That was his mistake. The two hands met, and the symbol sank into the living one. "Oh, no!"

"Mission accomplished," Eve said, satisfied.

"The bleep it is," the centaur snapped. "You have dumped me into an awful mess. You'll have to stay and help me get out of it."

"You don't know who you're talking to, horsefoot," Eve said. "You can't tell me to do anything."

"And you don't know whom you are addressing, hominid wench," the centaur said. "I will tell you exactly what to do."

Eve glared at him, sparks flashing from her eyes. "Really?"

He glared back, his own eyes sparking. "Really."

"I am Princess Eve, the Sorceress of the inanimate."

"I am King Clark Centaur, whose talent is to compel others to do my will."

"Impossible. That talent has been used before."

"Not in a centaur."

"Centaurs don't have talents."

"We do. We just did not admit it before."

They glared at each other, the imperious human princess and the imperious centaur king, more sparks coruscating halfway between them where the glares collided.

Jumper realized that he would have to mediate. But he had no idea how. Then he got an idea. "Sharon," he said. "Where are you?"

"Who calls me?" her voice came. Then she stepped into view. She was a lovely female centaur.

Jumper took a flying guess about her identity in this scene. "Your brother has a quarrel with Princess Eve. I may be able to calm her if you can calm him."

She nodded. "Clark, she doesn't know any better. She's *human.*"

"Eve, we need to see this through and wrap it up," Jumper reminded her.

It worked, to an extent. "That's right," Clark said. "We have to make allowances for inferior species."

"Inferior species!" Eve repeated, outraged. "Look who's talking, horserear!"

"Clark, they don't see themselves that way," Sharon said. "You should apologize, as a matter of expediency. We try to get along with humans."

"You're right," he said reluctantly. "I'll apologize."

"And you need to accept it," Jumper said. "For expediency."

"Oh, all right," Eve said ungraciously.

Clark stepped toward her. "I apologize, gourd fashion." He put his hands on her hips, lifted her into the air, and kissed her soundly on the mouth.

Eve, caught by surprise, started to protest. Then the kiss sank in, and she stopped resisting. Then she started kissing back. She wrapped her arms about his upper body and drew herself closer.

Jumper and Sharon stared as a little heart formed over their heads. "Oh, no," Sharon murmured.

"Why is he kissing her?" Jumper asked.

"It's a gourd-style apology. Traditionally it gets more intimate until the apology is accepted."

They were still kissing. "That looks like more than an apology to me," Jumper said.

"They're taken with each other. Oh, the scandal!"

"Scandal?"

"Centaurs don't have miscegenational relationships."

"Do humans?"

"Sometimes. There are a number of variants, like ogres, elves, goblins, and gnomes that interact on occasion. But centaurs have a higher standard."

"What about spiders and shape shifters?"

Now she smiled. "Sometimes."

The long kiss finally broke, and Clark set Eve down. "Accepted," she breathed.

Clark seemed a bit unsteady on his four feet, but he spoke firmly enough. "However, you know you have complicated my situation."

"I didn't mean to. I was just returning your lost honor."

"That's the complication. I have schemed ruthlessly to eliminate competition and rise to the centaur throne. The sudden return of my honor will make it difficult for me to retain it."

"I thought governing was an honorable thing."

"Ideally it is. But politics is seldom ideal."

"And I didn't know centaurs had kings."

"They didn't, until I arranged it to consolidate my power."

"Well, maybe you should give it up."

He shook his head. "It is hardly feasible. The vacuum would be filled by anarchy, unless the least scrupulous centaur seized power and slaughtered his competition. The resulting chaos would be my fault. I can't in honor allow that to happen."

"You've got a problem," she agreed.

"A problem you brought."

Eve started to huff up again, but this time Jumper intercepted her. "You can be very persuasive, when you try," he murmured. "Why don't you consider it a challenge? To develop the talent of centaur persuasion."

"I don't have that talent!"

"But maybe you could adapt your considerable abilities as princess, Sorceress, and lovely woman, and persuade him to accept his honor and do the right thing."

She considered. "You're no slouch at persuasion yourself, you know. I'll try it, just as a challenge."

"Thank you." Jumper retreated.

Meanwhile Clark had been pondering, and came up with an idea. "You're a princess. Maybe you can help. Have you had experience governing?"

"No. But I am a Sorceress. If you need to know about inanimate things, then I can help."

"It's the animate centaurs I need to know about."

"Then maybe the one you want is my sister Dawn."

"The one I want is you."

"How do you mean that?" she demanded, bridling.

"Eve," Jumper murmured. "Persuasion."

She reoriented, and took a more positive tack. "But we have no future, Clark. We're not physically compatible."

"An accommodation spell would fix that."

"Accommodation to *what*?"

"Eve," Jumper repeated.

She nodded, mentally removing her bridle. "So it would." She sighed. "We should not have kissed. It started something we shouldn't finish."

"I apologize."

"That's not sufficient."

"I know. But what else can I do?"

"You can apologize the gourd way. Pick me up."

"But—"

"Are you slow on the uptake?"

He paused, then picked her and kissed her again. Several more hearts appeared.

The persuasion was starting.

"They're right," Sharon murmured. "They should not have kissed the first time. Now they're stuck in a descending spiral."

"Descending?"

"The gourd-style apology leads to more of what they are apologizing for. Obviously they both want it."

"Why don't they just stop?"

"I'll show you." She put her hands on his elbows, heaved him up, and kissed him.

Jumper felt half a slew of hearts radiating out. Her new form didn't matter; her kiss was as potent as ever.

After a deliciously long moment she drew her face back a little. "I shouldn't have done that, so I'll apologize." She drew him in and kissed him again. More hearts appeared.

After another timeless instant she drew back again. "And I shouldn't have done that either," she said. "So I must apologize again." This time her kiss caused the hearts to tumble over each other, forming an expanding cloud.

Jumper was beginning to understand. But he was more interested in kissing her. Which was, of course, the descending spiral.

"You mentioned an accommodation spell," he gasped at the next break. "I'm not sure exactly how that works."

"We don't need it. Get on my back." She set him down, and he walked around her to climb onto her back. Then she carried him to another stall.

"Why don't we need it?" he asked. "Isn't it magic to enable two dissimilar creatures to—to get together?"

"You'll see."

When they were private, she changed to human form and embraced him. Oh. He had forgotten about her shape-changing. It occurred to him that it might be fortunate that dream romances did not alert the storks. What kind of baby would a Demon/human/spider crossbreed be?

In due course, exhausted for the moment, they agreed to give it a rest. She returned to centaur form and carried him back to the king's stall.

Eve and Clark seemed to have settled their relationship, one way or another, and were now concentrating on the piled papers. Eve picked up one and commented on it. "This is made by a totally honest scribe," she said. "I suspect from what it has seen and overheard while in his company that he does not approve of you, but he's not a politician and prefers to keep his mouth shut."

"Then he should be ideal to research and make quality appointments," Clark said. "His opinion of me may improve when he learns that I have recovered my honor."

"Yes." Then she looked up and saw Jumper and Sharon. "We're searching out the best possible appointments, so that he can be the best possible king. He may have achieved the office by illicit means, but now he will fulfill it with honor, so that the centaurs will prosper better than before. I may serve as liaison to the human court. Humans and centaurs can do each other much good, if they care to try."

"Makes sense to me," Jumper said, gratified that things were working out. "How about you, Sharon?"

"I support my brother in whatever he does. An honestly run kingdom makes sense."

"How does this forward your agenda?"

"If she marries him, she'll desert your mission."

"I'm not going to do either, of course," Eve said. "The mission is first. Then, if Clark is still interested, we'll consider a royal liaison complete with accommodation spell."

"But if his talent is to make people do his will, he may make you quit the mission."

"Newfound honor prevents me," Clark said. "Besides, that might annoy her, and I don't want her annoyed at me."

"You bet you don't, horsetail," Eve agreed. But now the name was an endearment rather than an insult. She picked up another paper. "This one was handled by an utter scoundrel. You can't trust him farther than you can see him."

"But he's one of my most loyal assistants!"

"He is also pretty good at fooling people. But this paper has seen how he is when not observed, and it's quite different. He is loyal only until it will pay him to betray you."

"This is hard to believe."

Eve's lips quirked. "Believe me, or believe him."

"I believe you," he said immediately. "And it is apparent that I need you. We must go through all of these papers."

"Yes, we must." She glanced again at Jumper. "This will be quite dull for you. Why don't you go for a ride in the park, or something? We have a kingdom to organize."

Jumper looked at Sharon. "Certainly," she said. "Hop on."

He did, and she carried him out into the surrounding countryside. It was lovely, with centaurs working everywhere. "They are very industrious," she remarked. "Good workers."

"I'm sure. Do you actually care about the centaurs?"

"No. But what I said about my 'brother' is true: I serve his purpose. He wants Clark and Eve to get to know each other. Actually a human/centaur liaison would indeed be beneficial to both."

"So far you have tried to corrupt five girls and me. I don't think you have succeeded with any."

"We have only begun to corrupt. You have not yet seen the second act."

Jumper made a human shrug. "I can't wait."

"Fortunately, we can." She entered another private stall, and was instantly all human. "And you will have trouble living without me, by the time I'm through with you. Once any male has tasted the wares of a Demoness, no mortal female can fully satisfy him."

Jumper feared she was speaking literally. But he couldn't resist her warm embrace.

In due course they returned to the palace stall. Clark and Eve were wrapping up. "I think you are well on the way to establishing an honorable kingdom," she told him.

"Here is an amulet," he said, giving her a tiny silver horseshoe. "When you are interested—"

"When you have that accommodation spell. It is too complicated without it."

"Tomorrow."

"Tomorrow."

Sammy Cat had been napping throughout. Now he was in motion, leading their way.

Soon enough they were back at the Found Cabin.

"Yew too!" Wenda exclaimed.

"Well, it's all in the dream realm," Eve said. "I surely wouldn't do this in real life."

"Dew what?"

Eve laughed, showing the horseshoe. Then everyone laughed. Jumper suspected that Clark might already have found the accommodation spell.

"But we are going to complete the mission," Haughty said severely.

"Oh, yes," Eve agreed. "Fun is fun, but the mission comes first."

Jumper hoped that really was the case. Sharon seemed too confident, and the girls were too willing. But all he could do was carry on and hope for the best.

Haughty vanished, then returned. "Time for the break," she said.

One by one they disappeared. This time Dawn was the final one. "Tomorrow it is you and I," she said, and opened her shirt, flashing him with her bra. "Do you know what this is?"

"Your upper undergarment," he said, not freaking. He had seen too much recently to be seriously affected, though it did, as always, stir his illicit desire.

"My booby trap," she said, and vanished.

Oh, ugh! What an uncouth pun. That, rather than the bra, was on the verge of freaking him out.

Then he was back with the others in the Ogre's Den. Another day was done, but they still had not found what they needed from the dream realm. Suppose they completed the final delivery, and still didn't find it? Would that mean that Pluto had succeeded in stopping them after all, while diverting them with these spot scenes? But he did not voice this doubt.

"You look worn," Tandy said. "Too much time in the gourd can do that."

"Tomorrow it will be finished," Jumper said. And hoped that it was.

9
INNOCENCE

Next morning they gathered again in the Found Cabin. It was Princess Dawn's turn, and she was ready with the little silver unicorn symbol. But Jumper was nervous. He paused before taking his dose of conversion elixir.

"In each case, there has been a man in trouble, and his sister Sharon has been there with him," he said. "This is scripted material, and we have been playing right into the script. I think that is dangerous for the success of our mission."

"It surely is," Haughty agreed. "But how else can we fulfill the Prophecy?"

"I don't know. But I am beginning to wonder about the validity of the Prophecy. We have taken it on faith. Suppose it, too, is crafted by Pluto?"

That made them pause. "How *do* we know?" Haughty asked. "We never questioned it."

"Neither did the Good Magician," Dawn pointed out.

"But neither did he exactly endorse it," Eve said. "He's letting us figure it out for ourselves. Maybe what we have to figure out is that it's fake."

"That is my concern," Jumper said. "If so, we are wasting our time here in the dream realm."

"But we have met some really handsome men," Phanta said.

"Which may be the idea," Olive said. "To distract us so we don't question the larger picture."

"And now we face a challenge of Innocence," Dawn said. "Could it be our own innocence at stake?"

"We're knot very innocent after what we did with those men," Wenda said.

"This is the dream realm," Eve reminded her. "We may be deluded about what stork summoning actually entails. Have any of us done it in the real realm?"

"Yes, I have," Phanta said. "But I ghosted out the stork aspect."

"And I," Maeve said. "It got the stork after me."

"I haven't done it directly," Olive said. "But a number of my imaginary friends have, so I think I have a fair notion." She glanced passingly at Jumper.

"So have I," Jumper said, taking his cue. "But that was with an imaginary woman, so maybe it doesn't count."

"How does your experience here in the dream compare?" Eve asked.

"It's much better in the dream," Phanta said. "The man is paying more attention, catering to you, loving you. In the real realm, once he gets what he wants he either goes away or falls asleep. It's not nearly so much fun."

"He went away," Maeve agreed ruefully. "Leaving me to deal with the stork alone."

"That's the risk the girl takes," Olive said. "My friends are mostly disgusted. They thought he liked them for themselves, and it turned out that once he sent the signal he hardly cared about anything else."

They glanced at Jumper. "I guess I did that," he confessed, embarrassed. "I was interested in just the one thing. She didn't complain. But she was teaching me."

"She liked interacting with a man who didn't drop dead at the sight of her," Olive said. "Your spider heart didn't pain you the way a human heart would have."

"Still, I was being a typical thoughtless man. You girls encountered much better men."

"Knot better, just different," Wenda said. "Yew wood listen to us, and beecome a satisfactory lover, woodn't yew?"

"I would try," Jumper said humbly. "Knot that—I mean, not that I wood ever, would ever—"

"We know," she said, squeezing a foreleg.

He hoped they *didn't* know how attractive he found them, regardless of his form. He had never known human beings before, and was increasingly impressed. Sharon was compelling, and he truly enjoyed his time with her, but he also enjoyed his time with the girls, in a different way. One huge difference was that he trusted them in a way he did not trust Sharon. They were his honest friends, not his deceptive enemy. But it wasn't entirely platonic, as Dawn and Eve demonstrated when they teasingly flashed him. And that hint Dawn had dropped about going beyond teasing . . .

"So we're experiencing idealized relationships," Eve said. "With men who have an agenda: to corrupt us."

"Scripted," Jumper agreed.

"Those are not to be trusted," Dawn said. "We should not allow those men to seduce us."

"How fortunate that you now have the chance to show the way," Eve said sweetly. "When that handsome, sweet-talking man comes at you, you just tell him to disappear."

"Exactly as you told that centaur king," Dawn shot back.

"Listen, you bra-brained, morning-air-headed—"

"Look who's talking, you panty-pooping, night-stalking—"

"I think it's time for us to get moving," Jumper said hastily, gulping down the vial he had been holding.

And of course both girls flashed him simultaneously, only worse: Dawn's bra and Eve's panties were missing. And he reacted, causing the others to laugh appreciatively before Wenda could cover him up. He had fallen for their little trap, and embarrassed himself. Again.

Dawn, fully clothed, addressed the cat. "Sammy, this time let's try the scenic route, so that our approach is not so obvious. Maybe we can surprise them."

Sammy was off in his usual manner. Did he understand? They would just have to follow and hope for the best.

This time their route led to a Playing Card bicycle stand. It seemed these existed in the dream realm too. So Jumper and Dawn mounted and rode after Sammy as he bounded along the path. It wound through field and forest, o'er hill and dale, and past appealing lakes. He did indeed seem to be taking the scenic route.

Jumper glanced down at the front of his cycle, and saw a little sign he hadn't noticed before: PA CHINE. What did that mean? He glanced across at Dawn's cycle, and saw that its sign said MA CHINE. Oh—they were male and female machines, for male and female riders.

The path darkened; a storm seemed to be brewing. Jumper hoped it wasn't another sadistic tantrum by Fracto, the nasty cloud. Just the darkening was a nuisance, as they were passing through a forest, so that the shade of the trees intensified. These human eyes did not see as well as spider eyes; there were too few of them, and they tended to focus straight ahead, instead of all around. He was afraid he would steer into stone or pit.

Dawn picked up on his concern, her talent seeming to work without her actually needing to touch him. "Try these," she said, passing him something from her backpack as she cycled beside him. Which surprised him; he hadn't noticed the pack before. Had it even been there?

He looked at the object. It was some sort of small folded framework, with circles of glass in the middle. He could not make tail or head of it; in fact, it seemed to have neither.

"Oh, I forget," she said. "You don't know much about human things. Halt, and I'll show you."

He brought the bike to a halt. She stopped beside him, then laid down her machine and stood before him. She took the object from his hand, held it aloft, leaned forward, and kissed him. Then, as he stood slightly stunned, she set the contraption on his face. "What?" he asked, uncertain whether he was questioning her about the kiss or the object.

"They're sun glasses," she said. "You'll see."

He looked through the lenses, which were now in front of his eyes.

The dark shadows were gone; it was now bright as full noonday. In fact, a patch of sunlight seemed to be hovering before him, illuminating the region and Dawn. "What?" he repeated, feeling even less certain.

"Sun glasses," she explained. "They can be useful when the view is gloomy. Let me adjust them." She leaned forward, and he saw right down inside her shirt and bra. That slightly stunned him again. He wasn't freaking out, but the impact did shake him.

When he recovered, she was back on her cycle. "Now we can move at speed," she said. "You can see everything." She pedaled her pedals and rode ahead of him.

She was wrong: he didn't see everything, only a portion of her white panty where her shirt did not quite tuck in to her skirt. That set him back yet again, but he focused with determination and managed to get his cycle moving, following hers. Was she doing it on purpose?

"Of course," she said with satisfaction. "It's called flirting."

"But you know I'm really a spider!"

"That's what makes it a challenge. Eve and I can freak out any normal man without effort, but it's much harder to do it to you. So we rise to the occasion."

But then something went wrong. Dawn veered off the path and had to stop, looking faint.

"What's the matter?" Jumper asked, concerned, though part of him suspected it was another flirting ploy.

"I don't know. Suddenly I'm out of energy."

Then Jumper felt it too. Something was draining him. He looked around, trying to figure it out, and saw a sign: PARA SITE.

He put the words together, as he had with the bicycles, and made sense of it: parasite. Something that leeched energy from a person. "We must get away from here," he said urgently.

But Dawn was already sinking to the ground. She couldn't walk, let alone ride. She was barely conscious. The same fate might soon overtake him.

Desperate, Jumper did something he feared he might later regret: he took the transformation antidote, returning to his natural form. Then, as a big spider, he picked up the two bicycles with two legs, Dawn with a third, and hobbled five-legged on along the path, away from the awful site.

As he went, his weakness diminished and he made better progress. He was escaping the site. But Dawn was still largely out of it, so he continued carrying her.

He saw a shelter ahead, perched by a lake. He went to it, and set the bikes and Dawn down before it. Then he put a leg in the lake and splashed water on Dawn. He meant to catch her face, but it soaked the rest of her body. He was messing up his rescue effort.

"Oh!" she exclaimed, waking. "You naughty boy!"

"I'm sorry. I just wanted to wake you."

She put out a hand to touch his leg, immediately fathoming everything. "Now I understand. You rescued me from the para site. Thank you, Jumper."

"That's all right. Why did you call me naughty?"

She glanced down at herself. "You soaked me, so that my clothing is glued to my body. A man would have done that so he could see everything without actually undressing me."

"Oh. I should have been more careful."

"You were tired too. That's why you missed my face. We had better stay here the night and recover."

"But Sammy has gone on ahead."

"He'll surely find us." She smiled. "This is the scenic route. Now you will see some real scenery. I must wash myself, and dry my clothes. Fortunately you have reverted to spider form, so you won't get any ideas."

"I wouldn't—" But he couldn't finish, because he had a notion what she meant, and was already guilty.

She touched his leg again. "I know, Jumper. But stay in that form for the night, and we'll pretend that you are completely indifferent. Sometimes these little white lies are necessary for social purposes."

Lies had sizes and colors? Jumper was still learning things about human culture. A white lie, it seemed, was a good, or at least necessary one. That suggested that a black lie would be bad or unnecessary. He wondered what green, yellow, blue, red, or striped lies would be.

"Oh, I like you, Jumper!" she said, still fathoming his thoughts. "But to answer your question, no lie is good, and there are no colors. A white lie is one made to make a person feel better. So when I flash you, and we pretend it has no effect, we are making ourselves feel more comfortable about spending the night together without clothing. I am supposed to be innocent, and you are supposed to be indifferent, so it's all right. The lie protects our reputations."

"Reputations are important," he said, getting it straight.

"Especially for princesses and heroes."

"Heroes?"

"You're the hero of this tale, Jumper. Didn't you know?"

"No."

"Well, the protagonist, or viewpoint character, which is much the same thing. The rest of us are merely supporting characters."

"But I'm not special!"

She brought his foot to her face and kissed it. "Yes, you are, Jumper."

Then she efficiently stripped off her clothing, stood gloriously bare, and jumped into the lake. Rather than continue being slightly stunned, Jumper turned away. There would be food to gather, assuming they could eat it in the dream state. If not, he would find some other chore to take up his attention. Rather than live a white lie.

He saw Dawn's wet clothing lying in a pile on the ground. It occurred to him that it would dry better if he hung it up, so he spread it across some nearby bushes. But it was now shady evening, with no sunlight to speed the drying.

Then he got an idea. He fetched his sun glasses, which were dangling by a loop of his silk, and put them on. The glare of their sun bathed the clothes, heating them so that they steamed and dried.

"Beautiful, Jumper," Dawn said from the water. "Maybe I won't have to sleep nude after all. I'm disappointed."

"I did wrong?" he asked, dismayed.

"By no means. It's humor, with a tinge of truth." Then she glanced down at herself and screamed.

Jumper was alarmed. "Is there a water predator?"

"No! Look at me! I'm fat!"

He looked. So she was. How had this happened?

Then he saw the sign they had missed before. FAT FARM. He went to read the fine print: "Beside the Fat River, growing Trans Fats. Beware. Just looking at them puts ten pounds on a girl." And Dawn had done more than look; she had plunged in. She had become one bulging blubber of a girl.

"What's that?" Dawn called from the water.

"You're in the Fat River, not a lake," he called back.

"Eeeeeeek!" she screamed, putting seven E's into it. That was surely a scream for the record books. "*Do* something!"

Jumper read the finer print. "Antidote: visit Bare Lake, adjacent." He looked, and on the other side of the path was another lake. "You have to skinny dip in the other lake," he called, gesturing.

Dawn didn't argue. She hauled her massive body out and lumbered across the path to cannonball into the other lake. The splash was so great it soaked everything around it, including Jumper. Fortunately he wasn't a girl, so it didn't affect him.

The skinny dip worked. In half a moment Dawn was her original self again, slender everywhere except here and there. She hauled herself out immediately and grabbed a towel from a towel bush and swiftly dried herself off. "Thank you, Jumper. You saved me, again." Now that she was herself, physically, she was calm once more.

"But why didn't it affect you when I splashed you?"

"I think it did. But it wasn't enough water to put on more than a few pounds, so I didn't notice."

He realized that was possible. The sign's warning about just looking at a trans fat making a girl gain ten pounds was an exaggeration. It took full immersion to have full effect.

She lifted the white panties and held them closer to the glasses. They had no freak power, oddly, in this state.

Dawn smiled. "Here's a secret, Jumper. Bras and panties have no freak power by themselves. It is only when they are in contact with warm flesh that the magic manifests. I'll show you."

She lifted one bare leg, and then the other, putting the panties on. As she did, there was a powerful burst of freak power. Then she pulled the panties tight on her and turned around, showing her backside, and the freak almost knocked him over. He was not as immune as he had supposed, despite Angie's lessons. "Just be thankful for two things, Jumper," she said. "First, that I'm not my sister, so lack the panty power she has; I'm more of a bra' bonnie girl. And second, that you *are* a spider, so have considerable natural immunity."

"I'm thankful," he said. But secretly he almost wished he could have been a real man, and that she was not teasing.

And again, his thoughts were not secret from her, embarrassingly. She gazed at him, her own thoughts masked. "Actually, a girl could do worse," she murmured.

"I don't understand."

She changed the subject. "Oh, there's Sammy!"

Indeed, the cat had returned, and was now snoozing in the shelter. He must have discovered that they were no longer following.

"I think my bra is dry now," Dawn said. "Watch if you dare." She brought it to her front.

Jumper didn't dare, knowing better than to try to defy her area of strength. He turned away.

"But the rest of my clothing will take longer to dry," she said. "So let's eat something and turn in."

He had located a pie plant that included a shoe-fly pie, so he had the fly from that while Dawn ate a cherry pie. She seemed to find both pies funny, for some reason, but did not explain. Sammy woke long enough to lap up a milkweed pod. Then they settled down together under the shelter, Jumper folding his legs under him, Dawn lying on a pile of straw. "I don't think this is a fully enchanted path," she said. "So there could be danger. But you should be able to handle it, especially if it's anything living that I can identify." Then she closed her eyes and went to sleep.

This, too, bothered him. How could a person sleep when already in the dream realm? But in two and a half moments he closed six of his eyes, leaving only two alert, and slept.

They woke to an astonishing sound. Dawn leaped up in her bra and panty. "What is that?"

"I think it's music," Jumper said.

She went outside, and he followed, glad again, to an extent, that he was not a human man. She really needed to put on more clothing.

In Bare Lake was a fish quartet: 1st Tuna, 2nd Tuna, Barracuda, and Bass. They were singing in the new day. With them was a dancing fin, cutting intricate patterns in the surface of the water.

Jumper and Dawn watched and listened, entranced. When the song finished, the fish sank back under the water, and the fin angled to the bank. Now it could be seen that it was part of a big doll: a doll fin. The doll emerged from the water and walked on surprisingly little feet to meet them. She was not affected by the water's skinny property, perhaps because she *was* a doll.

"Greetings this fine morning," she said. "I am Little Foot. I wanted to be a marine biologist, but dancing is more fun. I hope you enjoyed our show."

"We did," Dawn said. "I am Dawn, and this is Jumper."

"You have a very nice bra."

"Thank you. I try to keep it well filled."

Little Foot looked at Jumper. "We don't see many spiders your size around here. Are you on leave from a scary dream?"

"No, merely on a mission," Jumper said.

"Oh? What are you looking for?"

"Innocence," Dawn said.

Little Foot laughed. "I don't think you'll find it in that outfit." She returned to the water, and soon was nothing but a departing fin.

"She's right," Dawn said. Her clothing was dry, and she put it on. "Maybe now we can complete our mission."

They got on their bicycles and rode after Sammy, who was bounding along at his usual pace.

Until they came to another lake. The path stopped at its bank, and so did the cat.

There was an island in the center, bearing a looming castle. That must be their destination.

"What do we do now?" Dawn asked, abruptly uncertain.

"We cross to the island," Jumper said.

"I don't think we want to swim. There might be loan sharks, water dragons, or worse. You can never tell when a dream will turn bad."

"I think I can manage." Jumper spun a mass of silk, formed it into a mat, and spread the mat on the water. He stepped onto it, his weight making it dent but not sink, and spun some more. He laid another mat ahead, and moved onto it.

"Suddenly I appreciate your ability," Dawn said, stepping gingerly onto the first mat. Sammy joined her.

They proceeded on across, slowly. Jumper took up the mat behind them and set it in front, so as not to waste silk.

A prettily colored fish swam up, gazing curiously at them. Jumper looked at it with several eyes, and it immediately blushed and turned away.

"That was a coy Koi," Dawn said. "A harmless creature."

Oh. Jumper continued with the silk matting, and in due course got them most of the way across to the island.

Then several colored fins cut toward them. "Beware," Dawn said, alarmed. "Those are loan sharks. They'll take an arm and a leg if you let them."

Jumper was not about to let them. He needed all eight legs for his present task. So he spun a lasso and whirled it around. When a fin came close, he lassoed it and gave it a good yank. Part of the shark was jerked out of the water. The thing threshed its tail and escaped, fleeing the area.

The other sharks considered. Then they too departed the scene. They were interested only in easy marks.

"You're really some creature," Dawn said.

Jumper continued, and soon they were at the island shore. They stepped onto it and looked around.

It seemed to be a complete little land in itself, with fields and forests and even a trickling stream coming from the hill on which the castle perched. The path picked up where it had left off, wending its way toward the castle.

"Uh, Jumper," Dawn said. "Maybe for our purpose you should turn human again. Whoever this innocence is for, I suspect he or she would not properly appreciate your natural form."

She was being diplomatic, which was another human quality. She was reminding him that he needed to set up for the standard white lie of his humanity. She was surely correct. A truly innocent human person could freak out at the sight of a giant spider.

He took a vial and gulped down the elixir. In barely a moment he was human.

And there was a girl. "Hello, visitors," she said brightly, "I am Sati Sfaction, here to welcome you to Dust Isle. We have a feast in preparation for you."

Dawn stepped forward to give the girl a friendly hug. Jumper knew Dawn was actually seeking physical contact so she could learn everything about her. Such as whether she was really friend or foe. "I am Dawn, and this is my friend Jumper."

The girl looked directly at Jumper for the first time. "Ek," she screamed faintly, blushing, not even managing to squeeze out two E's. Then she swooned.

For Jumper was naked. In the distraction of the island, in the absence of Wenda, they had forgotten to put clothing on him.

"Quick, spin yourself some clothing," Dawn said. "Not that it really matters."

This made him pause. "What?"

"Sati isn't really an innocent girl. She's something else. I can't tell what."

He spun silk and quickly wove it into a pair of shorts, which he donned. "But you can tell anything about any living thing."

"Yes. She's not a living thing. Not exactly."

"Then what is she?"

"The minor Demoness Sharon," the girl said, sitting up. Obviously she had not freaked out, and had faked her swoon. "We are neither living nor dead; we're eternal entities."

"Sharon!" he exclaimed, now seeing the resemblance. "You always appear as someone's sister."

"This time I'm someone's daughter. I have a role to fulfill, so for now I'm Sati. I can sense ghosts, and even lend them a physical body, for a while."

"You would like our friend Phanta," Jumper said.

"A role?" Dawn asked suspiciously. "You're Pluto's minion, trying to mess up our mission."

"Yes. But there are parameters."

"There are whats?"

"Parameters. Variable guidelines that shift with the situation. I am confined to limited devices of corruption."

"Such as?"

"Such as making Jumper fall in love with me, so that he will give up the mission in order to win my return love."

That put it out into the open. "But demons, capped or uncapped, have no souls," Dawn said. "They can't love."

"But we can make deals," Sharon said. "If Jumper makes the deal, I will put on such an emulation of love that he won't be able to tell the difference."

Which meant that he could not afford to love her. She needed to be limited to a stork object. "Let's get on with the delivery," he said gruffly.

Sammy had been loitering. Now he moved smartly along the path toward the castle, and they followed.

"To do that," Sharon said, "you will have to play the part." Her countenance changed subtly, and she was the girl Sati Sfaction again.

"I'll play my part," Jumper said impatiently. He was annoyed with himself because he still hoped for a session alone with her, corrupting as it might be.

"Then I must introduce you to my father, King Belial," Sati said. "I love him, of course, but he's a domineering man who constantly spies on me. He has the talent of creating, controlling and banishing creatures of dust."

"Dust devils," Dawn said.

"Sort of. These aren't real ones, just his artificial ones. But you can't tell their nature from seeing them."

"I can tell dust from a living creature," Dawn said.

"Can you? What about that?"

They looked. A fat piglike creature was coming toward them, bearing an array of sharp quills. It emitted an odor of pine trees. "That's a porkypine," Dawn said. "A cross between a pig and a pine tree. They're rare."

Then the porkypine dissolved into a cloud of dust and fell apart.

"One of Belial's dust creatures," Sati said, having made her point. "He uses them to watch me. He's afraid I might meet someone manly and do something I shouldn't."

"Would you?" Dawn asked.

"Of course. I'm a naughty girl."

"Well, we have our own chore to complete, regardless," Dawn said. "We have to restore a girl's lost innocence."

Sati laughed somewhat harder than strictly necessary. "Lotsa luck!"

"It does seem unlikely," Dawn agreed. "Nevertheless, that's our mission."

"I think it's impossible. Apart from that, I'm the only woman in the castle who is even theoretically innocent, and no spell will restore me to my pristine state, if it ever existed."

"Maybe it's for a man," Jumper said.

"Such as my father Belial? Forget it. You have a bum lead this time."

"Sammy doesn't think so," Dawn said, evidently nettled. Indeed, the cat was still sedately leading the way.

Sati shrugged. "Well, what will be, will be."

They came to the castle gate. Sammy went right on in, and they followed. He led the way up a huge winding stone stairway. A mouse peeked at them from a crevice, then dissolved into dust. The proprietor was watching them.

"I am getting curiouser and curiouser," Sati said. "This is where my father's bedroom is. There's been no one innocent there in generations."

The cat drew up at a massive closed wooden door. "What we want must be beyond that door," Dawn said.

"Then you want my father." Sati knocked.

In half a moment it opened. There stood a solid but still handsome older man. This was obviously King Belial. "The feast is downstairs," he said gruffly.

But Sammy walked right by him, and up to a closed closet door. He sat again, waiting.

"That closet is private," Belial said.

"But that's where we have to go," Jumper said.

"Too bad. The door is locked, and only I know the magic password to open it. Go down to the banquet hall, feast, spend the night if you wish, then go home. There's nothing for you here."

"You can't—" Jumper started.

But Dawn put a hand on his arm. "Why don't you let Sati give you a tour of the grounds while I reason with Belial? Perhaps I can persuade him of the logic of our case."

Jumper was about to protest, uncertain what kind of persuasion she had in mind. But Sati took his arm. "This seems reasonable," she murmured. "We have marvelous sights to show off." She guided him out the bedroom door.

Jumper glanced back. That was one of the awkward things about this human form: he couldn't see behind him without turning his head, so that everyone knew what he was looking at. Dawn was also taking the king by the arm and guiding him toward the bed. She was going to show him her bra, or worse!

Sati didn't take Jumper outside, but to her own bedroom suite. "You know I can't let you go without indulging in some intimate dialogue," she said, closing the door behind them.

"But we aren't even at our destination," he protested. "This is just a stop along the way."

"A pleasant stop," she agreed, stepping out of her clothes.

Which was surely what Dawn was doing with the king. Well, when push came to shove, he realized that Dawn was a princess, and of an age to do what she liked. She wanted to have her share of the free fun the dream realm offered, if only to match what her sister had done.

"You pause to think too much," Sharon said, pulling him close to her. "It slows the narrative." He discovered that his silk shorts were off; she must have removed them during his distraction. They landed together on her bed.

Then the rest of the dream realm faded out of his awareness as he became lost in the ever new and exciting wonder of her eager body. How he wished that such an affair could be real, instead of just a diversion to prevent him from completing his mission! She was such a fine woman, even if she wasn't really a woman, but a Demoness. She had said that she wanted to make him fall in love with her, so that he would give up the mission to win her return love. But a Demoness couldn't truly love, so his wish was foolish. Even so, he was well on the way to that folly.

"A punny for your thoughts," she said as they lay surfeit for the moment.

"What?"

"Did you hear the one about the quarter pounder? It's a sledgehammer used to pound quarters."

"Who would want to pound residential quarters?" he asked, perplexed.

She laughed. "Oh, Dawn is right! You are such a delight."

Then he realized that it was her pun. He had walked right into it, and now was required to share his thoughts.

He sighed. The human form was good for that. "I was wishing for the impossible."

"That I would love you for real, instead of in pretense?"

"Yes."

"Let me tell you something, Jumper. There are fundamental laws of magic that apply even to Demons. One is the rule of marriage. When a mortal marries a D/demon—that is, capped or not—half the mortal's soul goes to the demon. That changes the nature of the demon so that she develops a conscience, and is capable of love."

He stared at her. "If you married me—"

"My love for you would become real. I would be constrained by the same ethical guidelines as a mortal woman, though I would remain immortal. Your wish would be granted."

He was amazed. "Then—"

"All you need to do is marry me."

Then he saw the catch. "But of course you would never do that. It would be too limiting for you."

"Jumper, if that's what it takes to stop your mission, I'll do it. All you have to do is ask me."

"Ask you?"

"To marry you. In return for abandoning your mission."

"I can't do that!"

"Too bad. If you married me, not only would I be perpetually loyal to you, I'd do it with you every day. Every hour, if you chose."

"Do it?" he asked blankly.

"This." She took hold of him and led him into another fantastic sequence of lovemaking.

"But I'm a spider!" he protested when he recovered his breath after the siege.

"And I'm a shape changer." Suddenly she was a giant spider. "I am your best match, Jumper. For a price."

She was indeed. But he refused to pay her price. "I won't ask you," he said.

She reverted to sexy human form. "You don't know what you're missing."

"I do have half a notion," he said with deep regret. "But I made a deal, and I will honor it."

"You and that stupid ogre," she said. "Chained by your souls. Now that I think of it, I would really hate to be bound by honor. It leads only to mischief."

"Yes." He got off the bed and put his silk shorts back on. It was time to see what kind of a deal Dawn was fending off.

"You should dress better than that," she said. "The servants would freak out if you attended the banquet in that." She got lithely up and went to a closet. In half a moment she brought out a nice human suit. "Don this."

He didn't question how it was she had a male suit in her bedroom closet. This was, after all, the dream realm. He donned it, and it fit perfectly.

They returned to the king's bedroom. Belial lay exhausted on the bed, while Dawn was just snapping her bra back together. There was no need to inquire as to the nature of her reasoning with the man.

"But our mission—" Jumper said, afraid she had made the same deal he had turned down.

"Continues," she said. She walked to the closet and put a key to the lock.

"Oh, bleep," Sharon said. "You sold it for the key."

"He couldn't resist the deal," Dawn agreed. "He's a man. You know how it is."

"And you're a woman," Sharon agreed. "You know how to use it."

Jumper realized that Belial was supposed to tempt Dawn from the mission. Instead she had tempted him from his key. She was a princess and a Sorceress, but also some woman.

Dawn turned the key. The lock clicked. The door opened. Beyond it was a swirling blankness.

"I'll be d**ned," Dawn breathed, emulating the harpy's word blotting.

"Yes, it's a secret portal to Mundania," Sharon said. "Your mission evidently takes you there."

Sammy got up and walked into the swirl.

"Let's go," Dawn said, grasping Jumper's hand.

They followed the cat into the unknown.

And landed in the room of a young Mundane girl. She was sitting on her bed, sobbing piteously. Beside her sat an ornate little box. Sammy settled down by her feet for a nap. This was definitely the person they were looking for.

"Uh, hello," Jumper said.

The girl looked up. Her face was streaked with tears. "Who are you?"

"I am Jumper, and this is Dawn. And that's Sammy Cat. We're from the Land of Xanth. We're here to restore your lost innocence."

The girl burst into renewed tears. "No one can do that!" she cried. "I am Dora, beset by the Drums of Dole, and have fallen into a Blue Funk. There is no hope for me."

Dawn approached her, extending the Unicorn Symbol, but it shied away. Something was preventing the restoration of her innocence.

Dawn touched Dora's head. "You need to visit Xanth," she said, fathoming more about the girl. Jumper realized that Dawn now knew how Dora had lost her innocence, and what to do about it.

"Where?"

"Come with us. And bring your box." She took Dora's hand and led her to the closet.

Jumper and Sammy followed, trusting Dawn to know what she was doing.

They passed through the blank swirl and emerged in King Belial's bedroom. Belial and Sati/Sharon were standing there, still surprised by the party's passage through the portal.

"This is Dora," Dawn said. "Short for Pandora. She opened her box, when she shouldn't have, and all the evils of Mundania were loosed, making it a horrible place. Those evils cost her her innocence. But Xanth is new to her, so she can start over, with renewed innocence."

Dawn extended the unicorn symbol again. This time it sank into the girl. "Oh!" she cried with innocent delight.

"Now open the box again," Dawn said.

Dora did. Something flew out, swirled around the room, touched Jumper, then sailed on out the window.

Jumper's eyes and mouth opened in awe. "Suddenly I have Hope!" he said. "Hope to complete our mission despite the barriers yet to be overcome."

"Yes, the one thing left in the box was Hope," Dawn said. "It seems that was what you needed, Jumper. Now it is loose in Xanth, so any-body will be able to share it."

"But what about me?" Dora asked.

"You have a private portal to Xanth," Dawn said. "You will be able to visit here whenever you want to. I'm sure these nice people will help you start your innocent exploration of it."

"Why should we do that?" Sharon demanded.

"Because if you don't, you will anger Jumper and me," Dawn said decisively. "Then you will have absolutely no hope of achieving *your* mission. You can't afford the risk."

Sharon exchanged a glance with Belial. Then she extended her hand to Dora. "We'll start with our magic gardens," she said. "They have wonders galore."

"Time to return," Dawn said. She addressed the cat. "Sammy, this time show us the direct route, not the scenic route."

Sammy was up and in the air, leaping out the window. Jumper hesitated, but Dawn didn't; she scrambled out after the cat. So Jumper did also, though hardly sanguine about it.

He found himself suspended from a hook that somehow caught the back of his neck without hurting him. He saw that Dawn was similarly hooked, and holding Sammy in her arms.

"These are not narrative hooks," Jumper said.

"We have hooked up," she explained. "These will transport us where we are going."

Oh. There were still surprises in this larger realm.

But as they swung along below an invisible line, proceeding rapidly across the variegated terrain of dreamland, Jumper saw that Dawn was pensive. "Is there something wrong?" he asked, concerned.

"There is," she agreed. "Maybe you will be able to figure out a way to handle it."

"I will try."

"You know how these dream episodes have seemed scripted? We figured out that Demon Pluto was involved, using his minion Sharon to distract you while the men charmed our girls."

"Including you?" he asked.

"Including me. King Belial turned out to be quite a man. I must confess I loved being with him as we seduced each other. But did you wonder why I was so eager to do it? It wasn't just to win the key to the portal."

"The other girls had their turns; you wanted yours."

"Yes. But more than that, I wanted to get close to one of those men so I could use my talent to really study him, to fathom the riddle of these settings. To ascertain exactly how Pluto plans to balk us, even if we don't get corrupted. Because I was sure it couldn't be as simple as just charming us, or you."

"But isn't Belial a minor Demon too, like Sharon? So you can't truly fathom him?"

"Yes. But I am after all a Sorceress, and my power goes beyond the ordinary. Those men may be dream emulations of living men, but that emulation enabled me to pick up some information. Being as close to

Belial as I was, for as long as I was, I was able to glean a fair amount of information. And that's the problem."

"You learned more? But that's good!"

"That's better than ignorance, yes. But not good. I learned that we have understood only the upper layer of the deception. The next layer down is worse."

"Whatever it is, we'll tackle it together," Jumper said. "Now that we have a fair Hope of success."

"Maybe. The top layer was the series of lost things to be returned. That Challenge was all scripted by Pluto. The next layer will challenge our unity as a team. That may be more difficult."

"I think I am not properly understanding you."

"Here is what I found: those were not six different men employed by Pluto. They *are* Pluto."

"Pluto himself?" Jumper said, surprised.

"Pluto himself, playing six different roles. Seducing six different girls. Including me."

"But then—"

"We are in competition with each other for his attention. Because we are all fairly smitten with him. The nice men we have loved do not exist. The privacy we thought we had was nonexistent. We have all been scr**ed. I am personally furious. How do you think the others will feel?"

"They'll be spitting fire."

"And how do we tell them?"

"I have no idea." But he knew he would have to get an idea soon, because already the Found Cabin was coming into view ahead.

10
D*MSEL FURY

W hat happened?" Wenda asked. "Did yew prevail?"

"In a manner," Dawn said. "We were able to gain Hope for the success of the mission."

"Why do I suspect that's not all?" Haughty asked rhetorically.

"Jumper will explain. After we leave the dream realm. How did the rest of you fare, these past two days?"

"Two days?" Phanta asked. "Two hours."

"But we were gone a day and a night and another day," Dawn protested.

"In your dream," Eve said, laughing.

Jumper exchanged a glance with Dawn. Could this be true?

"Believe it," Maeve said. "We had some good card games, but only two hours' worth."

"I suppose time is different, in dreams," Jumper said. "But we are ready to return to our waking state."

"Then I think you won't be needing us anymore," Jenny said. "It has been nice knowing all of you. You really must come visit me in waking life, at Werewolf Island."

"We'll try to," Olive said. "Sammy has been a big help."

"He always is," Jenny agreed, picking up her cat. "Fare well, all." Then she and the cats faded out.

"We need to wake also," Jumper said.

"I'll let the ogres know," Haughty said, and disappeared.

Then Jumper thought of something. "I thought Olive was limited to one imaginary friend at a time. How could she summon Jenny, then summon others elsewhere?"

"This is a communal dream," Olive reminded him. "The rules are more liberal. We can all do things in dreams we can't do in real life."

"Like wildly making out with men we hardly know," Phanta said. "Because we know it's only partly real."

Then the others started disappearing too, one by one. This time Eve was the last to go. "You spent a night with my sister? What did you do with her?"

She was surely teasing him, so he teased her back. "Nothing I wouldn't do with you," Jumper said. "Especially in a dream."

"That's entirely too much." She hoisted her skirt, but disappeared before any panty showed. She had mistimed it, this time. That was just as well. What would she do when she learned that her centaur king was really the Demon Pluto?

Jumper found himself back in the Ogre's Den. "You must be tired," Tandy said. "Maybe you should rest and sleep before you move on."

Jumper realized that he was indeed tired. Also, that would postpone his explanation about Pluto. "Yes." He reverted with relief to his natural spider form; somehow the change he had made in the dream had held in the waking state.

First they had a simple meal. Then they found nooks and crannies and settled down to sleep. Wenda came to join him, as she had before. He truly appreciated her trust and support. She was their group's most innocent member, but also the most sensitive one.

"Whatever is on yewr mind is pretty heavy," she murmured. "Even in yewr spider form."

"It is," he agreed.

To his relief, she did not press him further. She was really a nice girl.

In the morning they organized and set off early on the path to Castle Roogna, the next address in the Prophecy. Because that was where Button Ghost resided. They were no longer sure the Prophecy was valid, but it was their only guide.

They found bicycles again, and rode them, making good time. Jumper remained in spider form, preferring to bound along rather than struggle with the wheeled machine. It was not an enchanted path, but no monsters threatened them. Maybe the monsters didn't care to tackle a giant spider. Or maybe the monsters just hadn't yet roused themselves.

They halted a couple hours out at a wayside shelter, where they foraged for breakfast. Then they gathered for the inevitable. The girls had not forgotten Jumper's promise to explain what had happened in their two days/two hours excursion. This was what he dreaded.

"Dawn and I learned something on the way to discovering and releasing Hope," he said. "You aren't going to like it."

They waited, not interrupting him, unfortunately.

"In the dream missions, each of you except Haughty encountered a man," he continued. "We suspected that these men had been disposed by the Demon Pluto to distract you, just as Sharon was distracting me. First they tried to delay us. Then they tried to make us love them, so that we would heed their pleas to abandon our mission. This did not work."

"If they still like us after we complete the mission," Olive said, "then we'll certainly be interested."

"Because then we'll know they like us for ourselves," Phanta said. "And are not faking it."

"A girl needs that reassurance," Maeve agreed.

And they were not going to get it. "What we learned is that those were not men influenced by Pluto," he said. "They *were* Pluto."

There was half a silence. They were not getting it.

Dawn stepped in. "Pluto assumed their forms."

An indefinable but not pretty expression hovered in the vicinity of Eve's face. "We were all making out with the same man?"

There it was. "Yes," Jumper said.

"I fathomed it," Dawn said. "My talent is to know anything about anything I touch that is alive, and the Demon Pluto is not exactly alive, but I got close enough to him long enough to pick up on it."

"I'll bet you did, you sneak," Eve snapped. "You're trying to steal my man again."

"I'm no more thrilled than you are," Dawn said. "I thought I had a handsome king to myself."

"My courageous warrior?" Maeve asked.

"My jilted lovesick prince?" Wenda asked.

"My crazy genius writer?" Olive asked.

"My remorseful slaughterhouse shepherd?" Phanta asked.

"My honorable centaur king?" Eve asked.

"My dust-creature king," Dawn said regretfully. "All the same." She frowned, an unusual expression for her. "That's not even the worst of it."

"There's more?" Eve asked.

"That mysterious man we were competing for before—the reason why we were banished to this mission—he's Pluto too."

Sudden fury shook Eve. "Him too!"

"Him too," Dawn agreed, for an instant mirroring her sister's expression. "He was corrupting us before we even knew there was a mission."

"He has gone too far," Eve said grimly.

"And my minor Demoness Sharon," Jumper concluded. "Not Pluto, but definitely Pluto's minion. She offered to marry me if I would quit the mission."

"Suddenly I'm glad I had to sit out those incidents," Haughty said.

Dawn oriented on Jumper, frowning. "You mean to say that while I was charming the key to the portal to Mundania from King Belial, you were considering marrying his accomplice, Sati Sfaction?"

"Satisfaction!" Eve exclaimed. "You fell for a pun, Jumper! You've got dust in your head."

"And you were making out with a centaur," Haughty said to Eve. "I'd hate to say what *you* got in your pants."

"I turned her down," Jumper said quickly, before the imperious females could come to claws.

Now both princesses focused on him. "Why did Sharon think you would be interested?" Eve asked.

"Well, she's a very seductive creature."

"All of Pluto's forms and minions are seductive," Dawn said. "You practiced to resist that, and she knows it. So why did she think you might take it to the next level?"

This was awkward, but he had to answer. "She said that when mortals marry demons, the demons get half their souls and become halfway moral. So then I would be able to trust her, and she would really love me, instead of faking it."

"And that tempted you?" Eve asked.

He hated this. "Yes. She's a lot of woman, and a shape changer, so she could be a spider with me. She said that once a man has relations with a Demoness, no mortal woman will satisfy him. I fear she is right. I don't think I could find a better match. If only I could trust her."

"Then you do understand our position," Dawn said.

"I surely do," he agreed.

"So you know why we are angry," Eve said.

"Well, that's not quite the same. My girlfriend isn't the same as all your boyfriends. I don't feel betrayed in the same way."

"But maybe close enough," Dawn said.

Jumper was confused. "What are you leading up to?"

"We will need your cooperation," Eve said.

"My cooperation for what?"

"For our practice for what we have to achieve," Dawn said brightly.

"What is that?"

"Vengeance," Eve said darkly.

"I don't understand."

"Because you're not a woman," Dawn said.

"Who has discovered that her wonderful boyfriend has been six-timing her," Eve said.

Oh. "I think I do share your distress, to the extent I am able," Jumper said. "Of course this was all in the dream, so I know I didn't really do with her what it seemed I was doing. But I understand that imaginary interactions can have real effects."

"You do seem to grasp the situation," Dawn said.

"So that underlying your imaginary experience is a certain burning rage," Eve said.

"Yes. What do you want me to do?"

Dawn looked around the group. "Just resume manform and tell us what is most effective."

"Most effective?"

"So we will know how to turn the tables on Pluto," Eve said. "Next time we encounter him, in any guise."

Jumper still did not really understand, but he gulped a vial and assumed manform. He looked around for clothing, and Wenda brought him a pair of shorts. "Thank you." He put them on. At least this time Dawn and Eve had not flashed him. Their mutual anger at Pluto must have distracted them.

Wenda took his hand. "Let's forage for something to eat, deer," she said.

"Deer?" he asked, astonished. "Wenda—"

She laughed. "Yew really dew knot understand, dew yew! We're practicing to seduce yew and win yewr love, the same way those aspects of Pluto did with us. We need to know what works."

"But I'm not Pluto! I'm not even a real man."

"So yew should bee a tougher sell than Pluto," she agreed. "What works on yew should work on him."

"This seems crazy! I never thought of any of you as girlfriends." Though his most secret guilty fancy would have liked to have any of them that way.

"We're knot," Wenda said. "But we need to learn to put on a good enough act. Yew need to play along, so we can get it right. Yew must resist our efforts to the best of yewr ability."

"But how can I play along and resist at the same time?"

"That is the art of it. Yew must pretend to bee interested, but never actually signal the stork."

"I suppose," he agreed dubiously. Pretense was another human trait he was struggling to learn.

"That's wonderful!" She wrapped her arms about him and kissed him.

Suddenly he was intensely aware of her as a living, fully-formed woman. She was very nice to hold and kiss. "That's effective," he said faintly.

"Make a note," Wenda said to the others. " 'Deer' did knot work, but a kiss did."

"Noted," Haughty said. "But it might be that 'dear' would have worked."

"That's the way she says it," Phanta reminded her. "Any word that has a forest homonym. It's her nature. He knew what she meant."

That was true. Wenda had been expressing special affection for him. "But I gather I am not to believe any expression of romantic interest."

"That is true," Maeve said. "So if any of us can seduce you when you *know* we don't mean it, that will be the technique we want."

They really were practicing for seduction, and this was no longer the dream realm. Jumper wasn't sure how he felt about that.

They found a pie tree, and harvested an assortment to take back to the others. Jumper found a crabapple tree with several ripe crabs, which he collected for eating when he was back in spider form.

"Yew're so smart," Wenda said, smiling.

This bothered Jumper. "You're such a nice girl, and I love to see you smile, but paying me fake compliments turns me off," he said. "I like you best when you're being natural."

She clouded over. "I'm sorry."

"And don't pretend tears, either," he said, irritated.

"Of course knot," she agreed. But her face was wet.

That was when he realized she wasn't faking the tears. She really was a relatively innocent girl, with feelings that could be hurt. He had blown it.

"Wenda, I apologize," he said. "I thought—never mind what I thought. I'm sorry."

She turned away. "I'm knot good at this. I will never bee able to fool Pluto."

He set down his armful of pies and put his arms around her. "Wenda, please. You are my first friend in this world. I do like you. If things weren't so complicated, I'd like to be with you. You're a natural woodlands creature, and a sensitive sweet girl. But I'm not really a man, and we have the mission."

She rested her head on his shoulder and sobbed. "I dew like yew too, Jumper. I wish there was knot any mission."

There it was. The mission was a burden on them both. But what could they do but continue?

After a time they separated. Wenda wiped her face clear and Jumper picked up the pies again. They returned to the others.

"I dew knot want to dew this anymore," Wenda said.

Olive objected. "But we have to find out how to—"

"I dew knot want to fake liking a person I already like," Wenda said simply.

There was half a silence. Then Maeve stepped forward. "Then I will take over. I have a more vicious nature." She glanced at Jumper. "You know I'd as soon tear off your foot as kiss you."

"Yes," Jumper agreed, though he doubted it. He liked Maeve too, and believed she liked him despite her truly vicious underlying nature.

"So this is sheer fakery." She hugged him and kissed him. She must have learned how to do it, because it was one savagely effective smooch.

He fell back, a quarter stunned. "Fakery," he agreed.

They exchanged a glance, neither fooled. If Wenda was adorable because of her simple innocence, Maeve was attractive because of her fierce passion. She should certainly be able to fake it, when the time came.

There was a horrendous steamy grinding sound. They all jumped up, alert.

It burst into view. It was a small bird.

They stared. How could all this sound be coming from such a small creature?

The bird saw them and paused. "Hello," he said. "I am Roger Road-runner." Then he ran on, and the sounds followed him. It was a hard blacktop road that formed in Roger's wake.

"Well, it's going our way," Dawn said. "It will make it easier to cycle on."

They ate the pies and resumed riding their bicycles, this time on the newly paved road. It did seem to be easier for the girls. Maeve rode beside Jumper, and he couldn't help noticing the way her nice legs flexed when pedaling, and how her nice bosom accented itself because of her forward-leaning position. It didn't help that he was sure she was making sure he noticed. She was practicing a silent seduction, and it was uncomfortably effective. He felt both guilty and embarrassed: guilty for the stirring desire, and embarrassed that the girls could so readily invoke it.

"Make a note," he said to Haughty as she flew by.

"Noted," she agreed, needing no explanation.

They made good progress, until they encountered the dragon.

It was a smoker standing on the path facing them. "Beware," Dawn murmured. "Folk fear fire breathers, but steamers and smokers are just as dangerous. We don't want to mess with it." She had surely encountered dragons before, and so knew all about them.

"Pluto must've sent it to block our route to Castle Roogna," Haughty said. "We don't need a long detour."

"So it is my job to deal with it," Jumper said. "I'll need to change form, so I can use my silk."

"Don't bother," Haughty said. "I know a better way." She flew forward, right up to the dragon, changing to Hottie Harpie in midair. Before it could exhale a cloud of suffocating smoke, she kissed it smack on the snoot.

The dragon was so surprised and perhaps dismayed that its charge of smoke backfired. Its snoot swelled up like a balloon, its eyeballs bulged, and smoke leaked out of its ears. Then it exploded. Foul smoke roiled in a giant ball, polluting the entire path.

The party backed up as the smoke surged toward them. Haughty remanifested and flew, barely escaping it. "Contamination!" she screeched.

"She's right," Eve said darkly. "There are trace elements that will get in our lungs, blood, and bones, making our lives miserable. We don't want to touch that cloud."

"So we have to detour after all," Jumper said.

"Yes," Dawn agreed. "That dragon was obviously sent by Pluto to prevent us from reaching Castle Roogna. It was a Demonic trap: either the dragon balked us directly, or the toxic cloud formed by its destruction balked us."

"So if we detour, won't he send another monster to balk us again?" Haughty asked.

"Yes," Eve said. "But now we have been warned. We can try to be better prepared for the next."

Jumper made a human sigh. They would have to try a new route.

They turned their bikes around and retraced their route until they came to a crossing of paths. "Which one do we take?" Jumper asked.

"The one leading to the right," Eve said after touching it. "It loops about wastefully, but does eventually lead to Castle Roogna. We can still make it by tonight if we ride swiftly."

They took the right path, and rode swiftly along. Sure enough, it looped freely, turning in great circles to cross over or under itself. They couldn't avoid the loops without getting off their cycles and climbing up or down to the continuation, which would have taken more time than simply cycling on. So they kept going, not completely pleased.

They paused for a rest and snack at a wayside stop. Maeve stayed with Jumper as they foraged. "Actually I do like you," she murmured. "You're another predator. I would be happy to practice my loving on you, because it's something I want to know quite apart from vengeance on that wretched Pluto. But we're in such a hurry now, thanks to the detour, that there's no time. Unless we have to spend another night on the road."

"With fortune we'll make it by nightfall," he said. But privately he almost hoped there would be another delay.

"That's nice," she said, catching him for a kiss.

"But I didn't say anything."

"A girl knows. Even a bloodthirsty predator like me. I didn't really mean what I said about eating your foot."

"I suspected," he said.

"I didn't even have to suppress my urge to bite your mouth when I kissed you."

"Thank you. You certainly emulate a normal girl well. It's a good act."

She kissed him again. "Are you sure it's an act?"

"No."

"Then you're right: it's effective."

So it really was an act. He knew that shouldn't disturb him, but it did. "Yes."

She put her hand on his. "It's not an act."

"Thank you," he said, relieved.

"Who do you like better: Wenda or me?"

"Will you eat my foot if I answer honestly?"

She laughed, showing her pointed teeth. "Not this time."

"I like you both, in different ways. She because she is an innocent forest creature, and you because you understand about biting heads off prey."

"I do indeed! I would do it myself, but my mouth isn't big enough. But if you had to choose whom to be with, for a night alone together, which of us would you want?"

"I would want both of you, for your different qualities. I respect you both."

She tried again. "I think we are talking at cross purposes. Which one would you choose to summon the stork with, if you remained in human form?"

Oh. "I still would want you both. You are both quite well formed for your species."

"I think we do have time for this." She kissed him again. This time she put her whole body into it, pressing those well-formations on her front tightly against him. He couldn't help reacting, and knew she knew it. "Now what do you say?"

"Please don't do that, if you want to save time. You make me want to—to get even closer."

"Closer than to Wenda?"

"No. I'd like to be with her too."

She shook her head. "Either you are being diplomatic, or I simply don't have what it takes to be fully alluring. I haven't had much practice at this, having usually eaten anything I got that close to."

"You're alluring," Jumper said. "When you rode beside me on the bicycles, I wished I could hold you."

"Or you're hopelessly male, wanting more than you can have."

"I'm hopelessly male," he agreed.

They rejoined the others. "Close kisses work," she reported. "But not completely. He still has control of himself."

"So noted," Haughty said.

She had been trying to make him lose control? In the guise of practicing her technique? He would have to be more wary than he had been. After all, that wasn't the kind of relationship he had with these women.

"My turn," Olive said.

They resumed traveling, and now Olive rode beside him. "I could summon Angie," she murmured.

"Is that considered fair play?"

"No, bleep it. I have to figure it out by myself."

That seemed just as well.

They were making good progress, until they encountered a grazing animal whose dull gray bulk somehow filled the path so that they couldn't pass. It had four column-like feet, a mobile trunk at one end, enormous floppy ears, and a small tail at the other end. They drew up, got off their bikes, and tried to walk around one side, then the other, but somehow the creature was always in the way despite not seeming to notice them.

"What is it?" Maeve asked, irritated.

Dawn stepped up to touch the huge flank. "It's an irrelevant," she reported. "Generally harmless, it doesn't matter to anyone, but somehow it's always in the way."

"Well, we need to pass," Phanta said. "We don't have all day, or even an hour, to spare."

"Maybe we can encourage it to clear the path," Haughty said. She flew up to its head. "Get your fat rear out of here!" she screeched in one ear. But the irrelevant ignored her.

"Nothing bothers an irrelevant," Dawn said. "It's proof against logic or threatening. It ignores everything. Nothing disperses it."

"Nothing?" Olive asked. "How about this?" And beside her appeared a fiery dragon.

"Not even that," Dawn said.

The dragon issued a blast of fire to toast the animal's vast flank. But the irrelevant seemed not even to notice. It continued grazing, ignoring them all.

"Bleep," Olive swore as the dragon faded.

"Maybe this," Phanta said. Suddenly she was a big fearsome ghost. She floated up to hover before the creature's small eye. "Booo!"

The irrelevant continued grazing, ignoring her.

"So it's like that is it?" Phanta-ghost asked. "Well how do you like this, you big ignorant mass of nothing?" Her ghost form flattened out into a sheet, which draped itself over the irrelevant's head so that it could not see, hear, or breathe.

The creature melted, becoming a big mound of vile goo that spread all the way across the path and into the forest beyond. A ripening stench rose from it.

"Oh, for pity's sake!" Phanta exclaimed, floating clear and returning to her human form. "Now it's polluted the whole region."

"You can't get rid of an irrelevant," Dawn said. "You can only avoid it."

So it seemed. Highly annoyed, they turned around and rode back along the path. They would not be reaching Castle Roogna today.

They drew up at a wayside stop, foraged for supper, washed, and settled in for the night. Jumper and Olive, it turned out, had a shelter to themselves.

She doffed her clothes and snuggled up to him under the blanket. "I just want to sleep," he said quickly.

"No one's stopping you. Just ignore me."

But when he closed his eyes and tried to relax, she set the full length of her bare softness against him. "Admit it," she murmured. "Wouldn't you like to do something with me?"

"I'd like to sleep with you."

There was half a pause. "You were speaking literally," she said then.

"Yes. We surely have a hard day's travel tomorrow, and we all need our rest."

She wrapped her arms and legs about him. "In a moment," she said.

But he suspected she had more than a moment in mind, and if this continued longer, he would surely succumb. He was supposed to resist as well as he could. So, with a certain regret, he drank a vial, and returned to spider form.

"Bleep," she said. "I got too obvious, and blew it." But now she went to sleep.

In the morning Haughty made another note. "Naked seduction is not sufficient."

They organized and took another path. Jumper resumed human form, so he could ride a bicycle; that actually was easier now than keeping up on spider legs. This time it was Eve who rode beside him.

"What are you girls really up to?" he asked her.

"You already know, so your question is rhetorical," she said. "We need to find out what makes a girl irresistible to a man. Nothing less will suffice to spring the trap on Pluto."

She was right, but he remained disturbed. "But I'm not Pluto! I'm just Jumper, trying to be friends with all of you."

"And succeeding beautifully," Eve agreed. "So if one of us can seduce you despite your determination to remain neutral, we will know we have found the secret."

"I just want to accomplish my mission, so I can return to my own realm."

"And to do that, we will need to neutralize Pluto. Somehow. Reversing his own ploy seems our most promising approach."

The newest path meandered uncertainly, but Eve assured them that it did eventually lead to Castle Roogna. A path, as an inanimate thing, fell within her purview.

"Do you know, I am coming to like cycling," Eve remarked. "But I'm getting tired of constantly leaning forward."

Jumper glanced across at her. She was indeed leaning forward, and her blouse fell open so that he could see inside. Whereupon he crashed into the brush.

She dismounted and came to help him up. In the process she leaned even farther forward. He felt his eyes glazing over. "Are you all right?" she asked, putting her hands on his human shoulders. That gave him the most awesome view yet.

"Oh, stop it!" Dawn snapped. "Try this instead."

That was when Jumper realized that none of Eve's exposure had been accidental. She had been showing him ever-deeper visions of her unbound breasts, though they were not her specialty. "Make a note," he gasped. "Accidental partial exposure is more effective than full nudity. Even if it's not accidental."

"So noted," Haughty said.

Now he saw that Dawn had found another kind of cycle. This one was low set, with the pedals in the front, so that the rider lay on her back to make it move. That would mean that Eve's blouse would remain completely closed.

But she seemed undismayed. "A recumbent bike," Eve said, touching it. "This should be interesting." She got on it and pedaled.

And her knees lifted as her legs moved, showing everything under her skirt in shifting flashes. This *was* her specialty. Jumper came perilously close to freaking out once more. Angie had not prepared him for this approach.

"Noted again," Haughty said. "I think we have something here. Partial exposure, by seeming coincidence."

"But we do need to keep moving," Dawn said sharply.

They found a pair of slacks for Eve, and she cycled in them. That enabled Jumper to focus on his own riding. But whenever he blinked, he saw those animated bare legs. Had it not been for the obstruction of the bicycles, and their need to keep traveling, Eve could have seduced him right then.

Would it work on Pluto? Jumper thought it should. Pluto obviously liked women, and Eve was the hottest girl yet.

"Oh, there's a cocoa nut tree," Wenda called. She was always the first to spy woodland artifacts.

They drew up at the tree, and had hot cocoa from its sturdy nuts. It was a nice refreshment.

A man appeared, walking along the path. He paused when he saw the girls. "Hello."

"Have some cocoa," Maeve said, bringing him a cup.

"Thank you. I am Zach. I have a problem."

Maeve stepped close to him. Jumper realized that she was practicing her seduction technique, seeing whether she could fool this stranger into believing she was a normal girl. "I am Maeve. Can I help?"

Zach glanced down as he accepted the hot cup, and blinked as he saw into her décolletage. The cocoa started to slop. "Uh—"

"He's freaking out," Eve murmured. "Decrease the view."

Maeve, pleased, closed her neckline with one hand. Zach recovered. "I am cursed to be unable to settle down until I solve a riddle," he said, unaware of his pause.

"A riddle?" Maeve breathed.

"Any law has an exception. I have to find one that *is* the exception. That is, that has no exception. So far I have been stymied, and so I can't settle down."

This was obviously beyond Maeve's intellectual expertise. Her eyes flicked to Jumper in mute appeal.

It was beyond his expertise too, but he had to try to help. So he said the first thing that came into his mind, irrelevant as it might be. "I think, therefore I exist."

Zach stared at him. "That's it! How can there be any exception to that? Nobody can think without existing."

"Yes," Maeve agreed, relieved.

"Now I can settle down!" His gaze embraced Maeve. "Would you—"

"Sorry," she said quickly. "I'm a maenad." She removed her wax teeth and showed her points.

Zach backed away so quickly he almost fell. "Thank you! Adieu!" He fled.

"Well, at least you solved his problem," Eve remarked.

"Jumper did," Maeve said.

"But he lacks the décolletage," Eve said. "Well played, Maeve. You freaked him out without even trying."

"I *was* trying. I just didn't think it would work."

The others laughed appreciatively. This was progress.

Then they resumed traveling—and encountered a chasm that severed the path. It dropped way deep into darkness, and was about fifty feet across. "It's a new offshoot from the Gap Chasm," Eve said after touching her finger to its brink. "Fostered by Pluto to balk us. No way around it. We'll have to cross it." Then she paled.

"What's the problem?" Haughty asked.

"I just remembered," Eve said. "I'm afraid of heights."

"But this isn't a height," the harpy said. "It's a depth."

"Not exactly. Crossing it by means of a bridge or floating means I'll see the bottom far below. That will freak me out, and I don't mean pantywise."

"She's right," Dawn said. "I'm afraid of depths. We discovered it in the past couple of years. We simply can't go some places."

"For p*ty's sake," Haughty said. "We'll lose at least another day if we have to detour again."

"We may have to anyway," Olive said. "I can ghost over, Haughty can fly over, but how will the rest of you cross?"

"There's a way," Jumper said. He swallowed a vial and assumed his natural form. "I will spin a stout line, which you can carry across, Haughty, and anchor on the far side. Then we'll be able to ferry the others across."

"Go without me," Eve said, looking faint.

"But we need our whole party," Jumper reminded her. "According to the Prophecy, the loss of any member will prevent us from completing the mission. I can carry you across."

"I'd go crazy wild and cause us both to drop into the void. I'm not being coy; I can't do it."

"I'll make a cocoon."

"I tell you, I can't—" She paused. "A cocoon?"

"You won't be able to see the gulf at all."

"Let's do it," Haughty said.

They did it. Jumper spun his stout line, Haughty carried it across the chasm and tied it around a stout ironwood tree, and he anchored it around another tree on the near side. Then he spun a basket, and a smaller line. He fastened the line to the basket, and hung the basket over that main line. Then he clambered along the line himself, needing no basket, carrying the light cord.

"Someone get in the basket," he called.

Wenda got in. "Dew knot drop me," she said, smiling. Then Jumper pulled on the thin line, hauling the basket along while the harpy hovered beside it.

"Ooo, fun!" Wenda cried, thrilled. "I wood like to travel this way all the time."

Soon she reached the brink, and Jumper helped her out of the basket. "Yew are wonderful!" she exclaimed, kissing him.

"Honest appreciation," Jumper said to Haughty. "Make a note."

"Noted," Haughty agreed.

"Yew mean that works better than all my effort before?" Wenda asked.

"Yes. Your impulsive emotion makes me want to kiss you back. Because it wasn't calculated."

"Why knot try a calculated one, to compare?"

Oh. He embraced her and kissed her. It was wonderful. So did that mean it didn't have to be impulsive? No, it was because he knew she really liked him.

Then Jumper moved back across, carrying the empty basket. One by one he hauled them across, until only Eve was left.

"I don't know," she said. "I may go wild anyway."

"It won't matter. The cocoon will be tight, except porous so that air can pass through. You can be as wild as you want." He got busy spinning it.

When it was done, it was a thimble-shaped bag with a flap on the top. Eve got in, and he drew the flap over and sealed it closed. Then he picked up the cocoon and set it in the basket, sticking it in place.

He went across the gulf, and hauled the basket along as before. There was no sound from it; Eve had not gone wild. He brought it to the brink and lifted the cocoon and basket clear, setting them beside the tree. He opened the flap.

Eve was there, unconscious. She had made it, but freaked out in her fashion.

"Kiss her," Haughty said, laughing.

Of course Jumper was in spider form. They all laughed, mostly with relief.

Jumper returned to manform. Then he did kiss her. Eve revived in midkiss, and kissed him back. "Thank you," she murmured. "Let's not do that again."

Now Jumper resumed spider form and swung back across the line with the basket. He packed two bicycles into it and hauled them across. He continued until all of them were recovered. Only then did he cross one more time, sever the line, and swing back across the gulf while the girls watched nervously. There was half a scream, no more than two E's in the eek. He struck the wall, then clambered up it to the surface.

"We forgot yew were a spider," Wenda said apologetically.

He returned to manform. "I am glad to be useful."

They mounted their cycles. This time Dawn accompanied him. "I think we're making progress," she said. "We are finding ways to seduce you despite your resistance. I think this will help us achieve our goal."

"To complete the mission?"

She smiled. "That too. I was thinking of vengeance. We remain six very angry females."

"But what will you accomplish by seducing Pluto? He should be happy to have any of you."

"Seduction is only the first step. We want to win his love, then force him to give up his opposition. Turn his own fell ploy against him."

"Wouldn't it be easier just to get to the cable and fix it?"

"If he lets us."

And that of course was the challenge. Pluto was not going to let them.

This time there was no further mischief, and soon the high turrets of Castle Roogna came into sight. They had achieved one more spot objective.

But Jumper knew there would more mischief soon enough.

11
BUTTON

They arrived at Castle Roogna not long before nightfall. It was an impressive edifice, with massive walls and high towers rising above the surrounding trees and fields.

They rounded a turn, and there were three chubby men blocking the way. Jumper managed to come to a halt before crashing into them. "Uh, hello," he said uncertainly.

One of the men spoke up. He vaguely resembled a plank across a thick wooden door. "We are Lock, Stock, and Barrel. When we join hands we can shoot things, or even blow them up completely."

Jumper looked at the second man, who resembled the base of some pointed instrument, then at the third, who was like the trunk of a beer-barrel tree. "I see," he said. "We are just passing through."

"Then you will have to pay a toll," the second man said.

"A what?"

"A toll, troll," the third man said. "Or we'll blow you up."

Then Dawn drew up on her bicycle. "Uh-oh," Lock said. The three men sidled quickly off the path.

"There was a holdup?" Dawn asked.

"Three men, Lock, Stock, and Barrel. But they left as you arrived."

She frowned. "I see. That alerts us."

"Alerts us to what?"

"To triple brat mischief. Don't be concerned; I'll handle it." She did not clarify it further.

They resumed riding. As they entered the orchard, a teen princess appeared before them. Jumper knew she was a princess because of her cute little crown. She wore a green dress, had greenish-blond hair, blue eyes, and an impertinent look. "Who are you?" she demanded of Jumper, who was leading the party.

Princess Dawn surged forward on her bicycle as Jumper stopped. "Never mind, Melody, you little twerp," she snapped brightly. "We're on business."

"Dawn!"

"And Eve," Eve added darkly, arriving on the scene.

Suddenly two more teen princesses appeared, garbed in brown and red. "What naughty business are you two up to this time?" the brown-dressed one demanded.

"Not your business, Harmony," Dawn said.

"Sure it is," the red-dressed one said. "The adults are away at the moment, leaving us in charge."

"Not in charge of us, Rhythm," Eve said. "Now let us by; we've had a hard trip and we don't need your meddling."

The three little princesses considered. Obviously the two big princesses were not about to tolerate mischief. "At least introduce us," Melody said.

"And your friends," Harmony added.

Dawn sighed. "Group, these are the three little princesses Melody, Harmony, and Rhythm, who sing and play the harmonica and drum to generate their general-purpose mischief—I mean magic. They are comparatively innocent—"

"Ahem," Rhythm said.

"Except for Rhythm, who is taking naughtiness to a new level with the aid of an aging spell and a captive humanoid cyborg," Dawn concluded. "Though it is true that the three of them did help save Xanth from Ragna Roc, so they are not entirely superfluous."

"And these are Jumper Spider," Eve said. "Wenda Woodwife, Maeve

Maenad, Haughty Harpy, Olive Hue, and Phanta. We're on a special mission we don't care to elucidate. Now leave us alone."

It occurred to Jumper that there might be some rivalry between princesses. Then he caught on: Lock, Stock, and Barrel had been an early manifestation of the three little princesses. They had hid when they saw Dawn, because she would have penetrated their ruse instantly. In fact she must have guessed it from Jumper's description. No wonder she had been impatient.

"A spider?" Melody asked. "He looks like a man."

"In temporary manform," Jumper said.

"A woodwife?" Harmony added. "She looks like a nymph."

"I filled out," Wenda said.

"A maenad?" Rhythm asked. "In clothing, with regular teeth?"

"I don't like it any better than you do," Maeve said.

"Well, don't mess up the castle," Melody said.

"Or the orchard," Harmony added.

"Or the zombie graveyard," Rhythm concluded.

The three vanished.

"They seem juvenile," Jumper remarked.

"Actually, they are powerful Sorceresses, and they did save Xanth," Dawn said. "Not that we'd say it to the brats' faces."

Melody popped into view. "We heard that!" She vanished.

"Stop snooping," Eve snapped.

"Awww," Harmony said, appearing briefly.

"What is this naughtiness with Rhythm?" Olive asked.

Rhythm appeared. "I invoked a spell to age me ten years for an hour, and hauled him into a love spring. If only I could remember the details!" She faded.

Olive nodded. "That's naughty, all right. I suspect she remembers some of the details despite her denial. The Adult Conspiracy must be quivering with rage."

"Adult Conspiracy?" Jumper asked.

"To Keep Interesting Things from Children," Dawn said. "Children are not supposed to find out how to signal the stork until they are at least eighteen years old. That prevents them from staging a revolution and cutting the adults out of the process."

"Eighteen years?" Jumper asked.

"You have a problem with that?" Eve asked.

"Yes. I am only four months old."

A silence landed on them with an inaudible thud. Then Dawn laughed. "What is that in human terms?"

"About twenty-four years, I think."

"So nobody's been abusing you," Eve said.

"It hasn't seemed abusive," he agreed.

A cloud of smoke appeared. "What's this about contumely?"

"About what?" Jumper asked, surprised.

"Maltreatment, insult, vilification, discourtesy, misuse—"

"We already said it, Metria," Dawn said. "Abuse. Now go away."

"Metria?" Jumper asked.

"A mischievous demoness, little d," Eve said. "She's always sticking her nose in other people's business. Ignore her."

The cloud expanded and shaped into a sultry human female form. "Yes, ignore me, you handsome hunk. Why haven't I seen you around before?" The form's clothing slid down slightly, baring the upper surface of her curvaceous chest.

"I haven't been here before," Jumper said.

"That's no excuse." The décolletage dropped farther.

Actually, it was interesting, but Jumper was tired and wanted to get a decent night's rest before the rigors of the next day. "Maybe we can meet more formally sometime," he said, and started his bicycle.

All of the demoness's clothing vanished, and she floated nude before him. "How's that again?"

Unfortunately for her, deliberate full nudity was not the freak-out that accidental partial exposure was. He rode right past her, and the girls followed. "That showed her," Dawn murmured approvingly. "She'll suffer Xanth's most humongous snit."

"I heard that, little Miss Sunshine!" Metria's voice came. The thing about demons, big or little D, was that it was impossible to be certain they were really gone.

They rode up to the castle moat, and to the drawbridge, which was down. "Hi, Sesame!" Eve called. "It's just us."

The monster nodded, recognizing her, and sank back under the water.

They parked their bicycles at the portcullis and entered Castle Roogna. Jumper was impressed; the castle was large, far more massive than the Good Magician's Castle, with a strong wall inside the moat. It was also a palace, and the interior was girt by colonnades, lovely carpets on walls and floors, ornate furniture, and spacious chambers. It was also well kept; evidently there were servants who maintained it in royal style. There were many healthy plants; he understood from what the Princesses had said in idle moments that Queen Irene's talent was growing plants, and it showed. The girls seemed similarly impressed, apart from the two princesses, who evidently took it for granted.

"I am knot at home in buildings," Wenda said. "But I wood almost bee comfortable here." That was a considerable compliment to the castle.

"Thank you," a tile on the floor said.

Maeve, Wenda, and Phanta stared. "Oh, I remember," Olive said. "King Dor's talent is talking to the inanimate, and it talks back. He's here so much that some of the magic lingers even when he's not here."

"You've got it," Dawn agreed. "But objects tend not to be very smart."

"Oh, yeah, flamebrain?" the tile retorted. "I can see up your legs, and that's not all."

Dawn stamped warningly on the floor right beside it, and the tile shut up.

"We don't take any guff from smart-bottomed objects," Eve said. "Don't let them get to you."

"You're welcome," Wenda murmured to the tile, in answer to its thank-you.

"You can step on me anytime, nymph," it said appreciatively.

The two princesses led them to a suite of rooms they could use for the night. They were well appointed, with beds and bathrooms. But

Jumper was uneasy, not feeling comfortable in human paraphernalia. "Maybe I could resume spider form and sleep outside."

Dawn laughed. "No such luck, Jumper. Tonight you are with me. I will show you all the ropes."

That was part of what he feared. The twin princesses had his number, as someone had remarked, and he would be powerless against any serious move either of them made. Worse, they knew it.

But after they had supper, which was brought to them by quiet servants, and went to their rooms for the night, Dawn's attitude changed. "You're a good creature, Jumper; I would have known it even if my talent didn't tell me. Change form and hang out the window for the night; I won't tell."

"Thank you," he said, truly appreciating it. So he did, and she covered for him. Except that Haughty flew by.

"What's this?" the harpy demanded, hovering.

"Make a note," he told her. "Dawn could seduce me, in appreciation for her kindness. Instead she's letting me be comfortable."

"Noted," Haughty said, and flew on.

Now that he had time to reflect, Jumper remembered the concluding line of the Prophecy: "And Button Ghost unmasks the Host." That had to signal the key to the completion of their mission, but what did it mean? It simply did not seem like enough. For one thing, it didn't even mention the cable they had to repair.

Well, if the Host were a person, maybe he would know. But why would he be masked?

Jumper fell asleep without untangling the tangled silk of the Prophecy. The whole thing, from the narrative hook on, was a frustrating mystery. Only the support of the girls made it worthwhile. Wenda, Maeve, the princesses . . .

In the morning they had breakfast served, then gathered for their next effort.

"Now we want to contact Button Ghost," Dawn said. "Eve and I have seen him on occasion, but he has never spoken to us; we think he's mute."

"But maybe another ghost could converse with him," Eve said.

There was only a quarter pause before Phanta spoke. "Then it is my turn. If you can bring him here, I'll try."

Dawn put her hands to her mouth. "Button!" she called. "We have something you may like."

A faint form shimmered before them. It resembled a child, a little boy, perhaps six years old. He made no sound.

Phanta shifted into ghost form. She approached the boy. He drifted back uncertainly. She gestured, evidently saying something in ghost talk. He listened. She indicated the other girls one by one, introducing them, and then Jumper.

Button became excited. He smiled and floated across the floor. Phanta followed, turning back to beckon the others. The ghost was leading them somewhere.

They followed the ghosts through several halls until they came to a stone staircase, and up it several stories. Then along another hall to a separate section of the castle. This one had a spiral stairway leading up to a high isolated turret. Jumper looked out the windows as they ascended, and saw that they were now far above the moat. Eve, nervous about heights, kept her eyes fixed on the stairs, not looking.

At the topmost chamber, barely big enough for them to jam into, they stopped. Phanta turned physical. "Button indicates that there is a way to what we seek," she said. "It's not quite clear, because he can't speak, but he seems to know why we're here. So I think we should follow him further."

"What *dew* we seek?" Wenda asked.

"The conclusion to the Prophecy," Eve said. "Trusting that it relates to the success of our mission."

"So we follow," Maeve agreed.

Button floated up to a panel set in the wall. Eve touched it. "This is a doorway we never knew about," she said. "And we thought we knew this castle inside out."

"Trust a ghost to have secrets even from us," Dawn agreed. "We thought this turret was an empty storage chamber. We weren't interested in storage."

"We were interested in fun, mischief, and boys," Eve said. "Not necessarily in that order."

"We preferred them combined," Dawn agreed.

"Past tense?" Haughty inquired.

Both princesses laughed. Jumper agreed. Their mischievous male
interest was definitely still present tense.

Eve touched a mark on the panel, and it swung open. There was a
dark space.

"That's not big enough for much storage," Olive said.

"It's a chute," Eve said, "leading down to the dungeon."

"The dungeon!" Dawn said. "I can't go there! It's too dark and deep,
with all the castle looming over it."

Jumper remembered that Dawn was afraid of depths. "Why don't
you stay here, and we'll go down and let you know what we find. It's
best to have someone behind, in case there's an accident, so she can
bring help."

Dawn kissed him, causing him to wobble on his feet. "She agrees,"
Eve said as the others laughed.

Button jumped into the chute and disappeared. Phanta followed, disappearing similarly. Then the others did the same, silently vanishing
into the darkness.

Only Jumper and Dawn were left. "I don't know how long this will
be," he said. "If we're not back by nightfall, seek help."

"I will," she said. "Be careful, Jumper."

He jumped into the chute. In a fraction of a moment—no more than
a tenth—he was sliding down through the darkness. He wished he had
thought to change back to spider form so that he could have better seen
where he was going; these human eyes were simply inadequate. Also so
that he could snag some sticky silk on a wall and slow his descent. But
he could tell that he was spiraling down and down.

Then at last there was a bit of light ahead. He shot into it, found
himself in midair, and landed on a soft bed of blue moss. The chute ex-
ited from the ground behind him, as if it had ascended from the depths.
That was curious.

Jumper looked around. There were the six girls, standing in a disheveled circle, waiting for him to get his bearings. He made the effort, but the bearings were elusive.

"If yew had followed faster, yew could have caught us with our panties showing," Wenda reproved him. "We landed every which way."

"I regret my tardiness already," he said gallantly. Then he remembered: "Our party has to be complete, or our mission will fail. We need Dawn with us."

Then he saw Button Ghost hovering nearby. The child shook his head.

"Or maybe we need us all only committed," he said. "Dawn is still with us, guarding our rear."

"That must be it," Eve agreed. "Still, she could function here, if she could get here. It's not oppressive at all."

Jumper looked around more widely, and was surprised. This was no dungeon! It was an open land, with a deep red sky, white ground, and blue plants. In the near distance was a nice yellow lake. "It's different, though," he said.

"It is a Demon landscape," Eve said. "With aspects tending to be inverted. So down seems up, and colors are opposite."

"How does this relate to the resolution of the Prophecy?"

"That is obscure," Eve said. "My talent does not fathom it. Maybe because the Prophecy is not an inanimate object, but a concept."

"But Button Ghost can lead us to the answer?"

"That seems to be our best guess."

Jumper looked at Phanta. "He's mute. But he can understand what we say?"

"Yes. And he can respond. He just can't say anything."

"Then can you play that naughty game, where one person asks questions, and the other nods yes or no?"

Phanta's mouth fell open. "Out of the mouths of bugs and spiders comes wisdom we never thought of!" She faced the ghost. "Button, do you know the game of Nineteen Questions?"

The ghost nodded. It seemed she didn't even have to turn ghost for this.

"Do you know about the Prophecy?"

He nodded yes.

"Do you know it's incomplete?"

Yes.

Jumper was impressed. She had made a wild guess, and gotten confirmation. An incomplete Prophecy.

"Who made it?"

Button just floated there.

"Oops," Phanta said. "Wrong phrasing. Do you know who made it?"

Yes.

"Was it a Magician?"

No.

"A Sorceress?"

No.

"A mortal person?"

No.

Phanta paused, uncertain what to ask next.

"A Demon?" Eve asked.

Yes.

That set them all back. "The Demon Pluto?" Phanta asked.

No.

"Some other Demon?"

Yes.

"A full Demon?"

No.

"A Dwarf Demon?"

Yes.

"One we know of?"

No.

Phanta paused again. "We can't go beyond nineteen questions," she said. "It stops working after that. I've asked twelve. We don't want to waste any."

A bulb flashed over Eve's head. "Did he lose a Demon bet?"

Yes.

"Did he get demoted?"

Yes.

"And confined?"

Yes.

"And can he be redeemed only if something special happens?"

Yes.

"Only three questions left," Phanta reminded her worriedly.

"I know how these things work," Eve said. She turned to Button. "Such as marrying a mortal princess?"

Yes.

"What are you saying?" Jumper demanded.

Eve smiled grimly. "Not me. I'm thinking of my sister. She could bring brightness into anyone's life."

"But she's not here to defend herself!"

"Precisely."

He gazed at her, appalled. She met his look for a moment and an instant, then laughed. "There are other princesses, you know. I'm sure one would be interested. We'll have to meet the Demon and discuss it."

"Meet him? But look at all the trouble Pluto has made. We don't want to make things even worse."

"Not even if we manage to enlist a Demon on our side?"

Jumper looked at the others. Maybe this was feasible. Maybe this was the way they could complete their mission. "See if he can take us to that Demon."

"Can you, Button?" Eve asked.

Yes.

"Made it with one to spare," Eve said.

Jumper addressed the ghost. There was still a lot more he would have preferred to know, but this was definitely progress. "Then lead on, Button."

Button floated across the white landscape. They followed.

Until they came to a goblin hill. Jumper recognized it, because he had seen one in his original life. It looked like a pockmarked blister on the ground. Button skirted it, but the green goblins poured out like vengeful ants. "Oh, I wish Dawn were along," Eve said. "She would be able to identify them."

Then Button zipped back to them. Phanta turned ghost and signaled to him. He made a violently negative gesture.

Phanta turned mortal. "Don't let them touch you, any of you. Those are hemo-goblins. They will give you a rare blood disease."

"But they're already surrounding us!"

In was unfortunately true. The goblins had formed a three-quarter circle, so that only an ugly white patch of plants remained unblocked. Worse, Button was leading their way right through it.

"Deter gent!" Wenda exclaimed. "Plants that clean men so thoroughly they can knot stand it! That's what we want."

"It is?" Jumper asked uncertainly.

She considered. "Maybee the others had better carry yew across the patch, so yewr posterior does knot get cleaned." She considered, smiling. "That wood knot bee fun for yew. I understand men dew knot like getting their rears reamed."

"We can do that," Maeve said.

"Ream my rear?" Jumper asked, alarmed.

"Carry you across," Maeve clarified. She seemed to find the matter humorous.

So while Wenda went to make a rearguard, holding an armful of deters, Maeve, Olive, Phanta and Eve hauled Jumper up by his arms and legs and carried him through the patch. The plants tried to reach him, but only managed to brush his skin, leaving itchingly clean streaks. This was certainly a deterrence. He was glad that none of them got near his rear.

Meanwhile Wenda stood before the goblins, threatening them with the plants. The hemo-goblins clearly understood the danger, and stayed carefully out of reach. Their rears were probably almost as filthy as their mouths, both of which would get reamed. But the moment Wenda left, they would surely find a way to use tools to push aside the plants so they could charge through and catch the travelers. The patch extended to the walls of a steep canyon, so there was no way around it.

"Yew go on!" Wenda called. "I will knot let these gents pass!"

"We can't do that!" Jumper said.

The girls set him down beyond the patch. "We have no choice," Eve said. "The mission demands it. We'll pick her up on the return trip."

"But—"

"Dew it!" Wenda called. "But dew knot bee too long about it!"

Jumper realized they were right. It was best to do what they had to do quickly, so they could return to rescue Wenda from the siege of the goblins. They would surely not treat her kindly, once they overwhelmed her.

Button resumed floating. The path wended onward. Now their party was down to six, having lost two members. Jumper hoped there would not be further problems.

That hope was in vain. The canyon walls drew together to make a narrow path, and in that path was a pile of sticks blocking the way. Jumper went to clear them out, but had a problem. The first one stretched rather than separated from the ground; he couldn't pull it free.

Eve touched it. "No wonder. That's a pla stick. It's so supple you can't clear it out." She looked at the others. "And that's an ela stick, even worse; it will stretch farther than you can haul it. And that one's a spa. Don't touch it!"

"But we need to get through, and they are in the way."

"Not by hauling on them," she said firmly.

"I could jump over them, in my natural form," he said. "I could carry you across one by one."

"No good; they'll move to get in our way again. They don't like getting passed over."

"Maybe I can help," Maeve said. "I've had some experience with balky things." She stripped away her false wax teeth, stepped out of her clothing, and faced the sticks. "I am a ferocious stick-thirsty maenad. I am going to chomp anything that gets in my way," she announced.

Button's eyes bulged, but he didn't freak out. He was, after all, a child, who must have seen bare girls in Castle Roogna. So he was naughtily amazed, but as a ghost he didn't count as being in violation of the Adult Conspiracy. Technically.

A pla got in Maeve's way. She chomped it, biting a ragged chunk out of it. The stick retreated, hurt. The others kept their distance.

"You folk go on," Maeve said, spitting out the chunk. "I will anchor them here. I'll chomp any that try to move."

Again, they had to accede. They moved on, following Button, while Maeve glowered at the sticks, cowing them. Jumper even thought he heard a faint moo.

The walls closed in until there was hardly any path left. Then it plunged into a deep pool.

"Well, we can swim," Eve said, stepping out of her clothing. Olive and Phanta did the same. Button's eyes bulged again as he floated over the water, but they ignored that. So Jumper had to strip also, though he felt awkward.

"It isn't as if we're showing anything we haven't all seen before," Eve said, and jumped into the pool. The others followed, except for Haughty, who flew above the surface.

The water flowed out the other side, through a small round hole. Button floated there, indicating it as their route. But there was a creature in the water. It was sleek and fat, with broad flippers.

"That's a seal," Haughty said. "It seals things off."

"What if it seals the exit?" Jumper asked. "How will we return?"

"I'll stop it," Haughty said. "If it comes near the hole, I'll kiss it on the snoot and stun it for a time."

Jumper remembered how she had kissed the smoker dragon on the snoot and caused it to backfire. Kisses seemed to be remarkably effective against monsters. "Don't overdo it," he said. "We don't want to get that poor seal unstuck."

Olive, Eve, and Phanta laughed. They remembered too.

They swam for the exit. The seal zoomed in to seal it off. Haughty swooped down to intercept it. She metamorphosed to Hottie and planted a smoldering kiss on the seal's nose. Sure enough, it froze in the water, stunned.

"Keep your distance," Hottie screeched as she hovered between the seal and the exit. "There's more where that came from."

The remaining four of them followed Button through the hole.

Jumper found himself sliding along a watery channel slanting down through a cavern. The water came to a metallic mesh and sank through it, leaving the four of them sitting on the mesh. Three lovely bare girls and Jumper, all being ogled by the ghost.

Jumper found this quite awkward, because every movement the girls made jiggled their flesh in assorted places. He couldn't help reacting as they got to their feet and shook themselves dry.

"Oddest thing," Eve remarked with a third of a smile. "I seem to have tuned out every detail of my companions below their faces. Does anyone have a problem with that?"

"No," Olive said with another third of the smile. "In fact, I seem to have the same condition."

"So do I," Phanta said with the final third, completing the smile.

Jumper realized that they were sparing him some of his embarrassment. "Thank you." He got up, his concern fading. They really were nice girls. Of course he could have changed to spider form, but he hadn't thought of it in time.

They followed the ghost on along the passage.

But now metal hands reached out from the walls to take things. When there were no objects to take, the hands took liberties instead. "Hey!" Olive protested as one groped for her bottom. She might have tuned out some detail visually, but this was actually touching.

They drew back to consider. Button floated on through the passage, but he was not physical so the hands did not grab his parts. However, the rest of them had a problem.

Eve touched a hand. "This is steel," she said. "It will try to steel anything that passes through this avenue. It won't let anyone pass unless there's something to steel."

Jumper realized that this was similar to the way Wenda talked. The metal spelled it metal's way.

"What about our dignity?" Phanta asked. "I can turn ghost and pass through, but I resent the need to."

"And once that's taken," Olive said, "what about our return trip? We won't even have our dignity for it to steal. Will we be able to pass?"

"I doubt it," Eve said. "But I may have a way to balk it, because I understand it. I will steel myself against it."

"How will that help?" Jumper asked.

"Cancellation of puns," she explained. "It can't steel from me as long as I am steeled. But I will have to remain here to maintain that condition, because the same device won't work twice. The rest of you will have to go on without me."

"I hope there's someone left to deal with the Demon," Jumper said.

"The Prophecy took us to Button," she reminded him. "He is bound to take us to the Demon."

Jumper hoped that was really the case.

Eve steeled herself valiantly, and the steel hands were quiescent. The remaining three of them made it on through the passage unscathed.

But soon another obstacle appeared. This was an older man with a handlebar mustache. "Well, hello, people," he said, evidently noting the bareness of the girls.

"Hello," Jumper said, surprised. "We did not expect to meet anyone down here."

"Readily explained," the man said. "I am S R Shepherd, but just call me Shep. I was given a chance to come to Xanth, but am required to perform a service first. So I am here, performing it. I must admit it has been a lonely vigil, until now."

"I met a man named Shepherd," Phanta said, "but I doubt you are related." She frowned, evidently remembering how she had been fooled.

"I am Jumper," Jumper said. "And these are Olive Hue and Phanta. We had to swim through a pond, so we left our clothing behind. We are on a mission."

"Aren't we all," Shep agreed. "I was on a mission for many years in Mundania, as a letter carrier. It was a great way to meet people. I like people."

Jumper found himself liking this man. "We must seem like an odd collection."

"I love collections," Shep said. "Coins, stamps, other things—I'm just a natural collector. May I inquire about your mission?"

"We have to see a Demon," Jumper said.

Shep sighed. "I was afraid of that. You see, my assignment is to stop anyone from reaching that Demon. I don't know what he's done to deserve such imprisonment, if he deserves it at all, but if I don't do my job I won't be allowed to enter Xanth proper. So I can't let you pass, much as I would like to let handsome folk like you three do anything you wanted to." His eyes passed over the bodies of the girls with a certain merry appreciation.

"But we have to see him," Jumper said. "It's important."

"Please, return the way you came, or stay and chat; I'd love that. I don't wish you any harm. But I can't let you pass."

"How do you propose to stop us from passing?" Olive asked.

"I was given a magic talent for the duration," Shep said. "It is the ability to conjure a fragment of the Void. Do you understand what I'm saying?"

"The Void," Olive said, clearly awed. "That's the region of Xanth from which nothing returns."

"Yes," Shep agreed. "And a fragment of it is like a small black hole. It sucks anything in, permanently. So please, I beg of you, don't make me conjure it. Those things are dangerous."

"Dangerous? Can't you abolish them as well as conjure them?"

"Yes, but the first one I conjured got away from me and disappeared in the cavern system. I was inexperienced. I don't want to risk that again."

Olive shot a glance at Jumper and Phanta. She had something in mind. They both nodded, waiting to see what it was.

"You mentioned coin collecting," Olive said. "My talent is conjuring imaginary friends. I believe I have one who collects coins. Would you like to meet him?"

"Certainly!"

An old man appeared, carrying a heavy suitcase. "Hello. I am Coinroy," he said. "I am rather proud of my collection." He opened the suitcase, which turned out to be stuffed full of coins. Some fell on the ground.

Shep picked them up to return them to Coinray. But he paused, amazed, as he looked at them. "This is a Lydian gold coin—from the very dawn of the coin age!"

"I have been at it for a while," Coinroy agreed.

"But this is fabulously rare and valuable! You shouldn't carry it loose in a suitcase!"

"But sorting them all is so boring, I just never get around to it."

"Let me help you sort them. If this is typical—"

"Gladly." Coinroy poured out the suitcase on the floor. Coins of many sizes piled up, copper, silver, and gold.

"Ancient China!" Shep said. "And here's one from Tuscany, circa 500 BC! I never saw one of those before!"

"I'm sure I have some duplicates," Coinroy said. "You are welcome to them."

Jumper and Phanta sidled on by. Shep was completely entranced by the coin collection. Olive had found a really effective distraction. She remained there, in case another friend should be needed.

Now they were two: Jumper and Phanta. And Button Ghost, of course. They were following him down a widening passage. "I hope we don't encounter any more impediments," Jumper said.

"If it continues the way it has been going, I will have to nullify the next one, and you will have to meet the Demon alone."

"But if there are two more, what then?"

"Let's not think about that."

The passage opened out into a lovely cave chamber. Enormous stalactites hung from the ceiling, straining to reach similar stalagmites reaching up from the floor. It was almost as if they were in the mouth of a phenomenally toothed monster.

Then the jaws started closing. "Run!" Jumper cried.

They ran, but the myriad stone teeth were in the way. Jumper made it to a clear zone, but one caught in a tangle of Phanta's hair, hauling her up short. She struggled to free herself as the jaws slowly closed on her.

Then Jumper saw something else. It was a deep black blob floating in the chamber. Starlike lights coruscated within it. Ahead of it was a thick row of stalactites. Behind it was a clear passage. The thing seemed to be feeding on stalactites, and the coruscations were their remains as they crumbled into nothingness.

It was the lost fragment of Void! A small black hole, swallowing everything in its path. And it was drifting right for Phanta.

"Turn ghost!" Jumper cried. "Get out of there! Now!"

"What?" She was distracted by the caught knot in her hair, and didn't see the black hole.

He didn't have time to explain. He turned spider, rapidly spun a silk rope, and flung it between the stone columns to lasso her. He yanked her toward him, so hard that her hair snapped off the tip of the stalactite and brought it along.

"What?" she repeated, as she bumped past columns and finally landed at his feet.

"Look," he said. "The black hole."

She looked just in time to see the black blob swallow the place where she had been, broken stalactite and all.

"I would have been swallowed," she said, aghast. "You saved me, Jumper!"

"I'm sorry I was so rough," he said. "I just had to—"

"Oh, my goodness," she said. "I would have been dead, just like that!" Then she broke down into tears.

Jumper changed back to manform so he could comfort her. He put his arm around her. "You're safe now."

She turned into him. "Oh, Jumper! Thank you!"

"You're welcome, of cour—"

He was cut off by her fierce kiss. It was so passionate that it threatened to freak him out.

Phanta wrapped her arms and legs about him, still avidly kissing him. She was hot and soft and fantastically exciting.

Then something happened. Jumper wasn't sure exactly how, but the next thing he knew he was exploding in pleasure that radiated from his midsection throughout his body. Phanta was with him, sharing it, never relinquishing the kiss.

For a timeless yet eternal moment they clung together, immersed in the sheer delight of the experience. Then at last it faded, and they fell apart.

"What was that?" Jumper panted.

Phanta started laughing, helplessly. "Maybe you can guess!" she gasped.

Then he caught on. "The stork!"

"We signaled the stork," she agreed. "Not in imagination, not in a dream, but for real. Are you disappointed?"

"No! But I never meant to—"

She kissed him again, briefly, signaling affection rather than passion. "Jumper, you aren't experienced, but I am. You know that. I was so grateful for being rescued from doom that I forgot myself and seduced you. I apologize."

Now he had to laugh, weakly. "Where is Haughty, to make a note?"

"That a bad scare can tumble a person into seduction? We'll inform her in due course."

"We must marry," he said.

"What?"

"When a man has his way with a woman, he must marry her. Isn't that the human rule?"

She shook her head. "Oh, Jumper, you're so sweet! There's no such rule. It's just a convention in some circles. You are under no obligation to take it further."

"I'm not?"

"Not," she agreed.

"But I was supposed to resist. I got carried away."

"Jumper, Jumper, Jumper," she said fondly. "We both got carried away. Sheer emotion of the moment did it. But I don't know how emotional the Demon Pluto is. Still, I want to clarify this: I am one of six very angry girls, and I want to destroy Pluto for the mockery he made of my love. But I like you, Jumper, and don't mean you any harm. So this is only an incident, not meaning any romantic commitment. I'm glad to have given you a moment of pleasure, and now we must get on with the mission."

"The mission," he agreed, remembering. She had certainly set him straight. "So we remain . . . just friends?"

"Friends who shared an experience. We must put it behind us for now, without rejecting any part of the memory."

"Put it behind us? Why?"

"Because I think we are about to meet the Demon."

He followed her glance. Button was hovering near a large stone door, and the door was slowly swinging open.

12
DEMONESS

T he ghost floated through the doorway, and Jumper and
Phanta cautiously followed.

And paused. For there lay a lovely freezing world of
ice. There were mountains and valleys, plains and glaciers, crystalline
trees and houses.

And a handsome woman whose hair was a mane of ice fibers and
whose skin was glassy ice. "Welcome, travelers," she said.

"Uh, hello," Jumper said uncertainly. "We were looking for—that
is—"

"I am the Demon Eris," the woman said. "Or if you prefer, Demoness. Assuming roughly human form for your convenience. The seeming
ghost you followed was my trace spirit identity, the only aspect of me
able to escape confinement."

"Button wasn't really a ghost!" Phanta exclaimed. "Yet he seemed
like one."

"The ghost of the hope of redemption," Eris said. "Sent to lead someone to my prison."

Jumper was getting his bearings. They had assumed the Demon was
male, because Button was, but evidently they had been mistaken. It was

best to verify the rest. "Is it—is it true that you need to marry a mortal prince, or something, to escape?"

"It is true," the Demoness agreed. "It is a standard ploy in our Demon wagers, because mortal princes are not a dime a dozen, and not many of those who exist would care to make any such commitment." She glanced at Jumper. "You don't happen to be a prince, by any chance?"

He laughed, embarrassed. "No, I'm just an ordinary mortal male spider. But one of our party thought the Princess Dawn might be interested." Then he had to correct himself. "That is, we thought you might be male."

"Lovely creature," Eris agreed. "She could be a real asset when dealing with mortals, because of her understanding of living things."

"You know her?" Jumper asked, surprised.

"In a manner. My spirit wisp is familiar with all the denizens of Castle Roogna, having been there for a century. Dawn certainly would do, though her sinister sister Eve is more intriguing. But it has to be voluntary, and male, which complicates things."

"I suppose that would," Jumper agreed. "We came here in search of the origin and continuation of the Prophecy."

"Of course. Come into my parlor and I will clarify it."

Her parlor turned out to be an elaborate chamber in an ice palace, with ice couches that were surprisingly comfortable. Their cushions were made of snow, which was resilient, and somehow not cold. In fact he was not cold at all, and Phanta did not seem to be either. Jumper reminded himself that this was not an ordinary setting.

"Let me start closer to the beginning of this incident," the Demoness said as they relaxed with drinks of iced tea and cold cakes. "Approximately a century ago there came an opening for a promotion to full Demon status. In this region the main contenders were Pluto and me, both Dwarf Demons eager for advancement. So we gambled: the winner would get the promotion, while the loser would be relegated to oblivion. Since Demon wagers must depend on essentially random or nonsensical events, such as those determined by mortals, we set it up for a mortal decision: which of our planets would the mortals choose to recognize first? I believed I had the advantage, as my planet was larger than Pluto's, with a larger orbit. Obviously it was more important."

She paused. Phanta took advantage to insert a question. "Is your planet one we know about?"

"No. That relates to the history of this incident. At the time we made the wager, neither of our planets was known to the mortals. They were bound to discover them in time. That was the randomness of it: we could not know which one. Naturally I did not leave it purely to chance. I asked my girlfriend Sharon to intervene on Earth."

"Sharon!" Jumper exclaimed. "Your girlfriend?" This bothered him in more than one respect.

"Yes. She's actually quite a woman." Eris paused, contemplating him. "I see you are disturbed, so I will clarify that Demons are not bound by the rules of mortals, and we may associate with each other in ways not all mortals would approve. Yes, she was my girlfriend. Because she was not a primary in this wager, she could do what Pluto and I could not: influence the mortals. She agreed to visit Earth under cover and guide one of their primitive astronomers to search their sky in the right vicinity, so he would discover my planet. That would give me the victory. What I did not know then was that she was Charon's sister, and Charon was Pluto's minion. It was my foolish fault for not checking her background. So she influenced the mortal astronomer to search Pluto's area of sky, and his planet was discovered first."

"That must have ended your relationship," Jumper said, relieved in about one and a half ways.

She sighed. "It did. And thus did Pluto achieve promotion to full Demon status, while I was banished a century ago to this nether prison, to languish until rescued by a mortal prince. It was a foul deal, and I curse the memory of the Demoness who betrayed me."

A century! But of course time was different for Demons, who were eternal. "But wasn't she true to her brother?" Jumper asked, still not completely comfortable with this news.

"Yes. And to her true lover, Pluto. That, too, I did not know at the time. She deceived me, and caused me to lose. She is not to be trusted. Not that I will ever have anything to do with her again."

That was understandable. But it left a hole in Jumper's heart. He had somehow thought there could be something between Sharon and himself, maybe, possibly, if things worked out. Obviously he had been a fool. He was glad that he had never truly trusted her, yet grieved to have his cynicism vindicated.

"Now about the Prophecy," Eris said. "I knew that I would never be rescued if I did not help myself to whatever degree was feasible. So I sought a way to alert the mortals to my situation. I could not address them directly, because of my confinement, but I could do so indirectly. My spirit wisp went out to spy on human events at the castle, which was as far as he could reach without extraordinary effort. Thus I learned the mortal language, and crafted the Prophecy. It was designed to lead a mortal prince to me."

"But it was given to me!" Jumper protested.

"Not exactly. You see, I made many Prophecies. The problem was getting them to individuals who could or would act on them. I tried sealing them in bottles and floating them down the river, but the river emptied into an isolated nether sea no one visited, so they were lost. I tried blowing them out into the air, but these were mostly destroyed in storms. Thus for decades I got nowhere. Finally I managed to stick one to a narrative hook that was swinging randomly about. You, it seems, were the one the hook caught, and the sticky Prophecy transferred itself to you. It was intended for a prince, but it seems the hook acted indirectly. It got the Prophecy to the attention of two princesses, per- haps somehow assuming that this equated to one prince. Thus it finally brought you to me. But perhaps we can yet save the situation, if you notify Princess Dawn of its true nature so she can locate a suitable prince."

"But that Prophecy is guiding *me*!" Jumper insisted. "So I can repair the cable. That's the whole point of it."

"That may be the way you or your Good Magician interpreted it," Eris said. "That was not its original intent."

Phanta seemed to be no more pleased than Jumper. "You mean we have all been following a false Prophecy?"

"Not false," Eris said. "Merely irrelevant to your particular mission."

"Fighting monsters," Phanta continued. "Falling in love, struggling to win through to ultimate victory—when it didn't even apply to us?"

"That is the case," the Demoness agreed equably.

"It's an outrage!" Phanta flared.

"How so?" the Demoness asked.

"We were all betrayed by false love. Now we've been betrayed by the Prophecy itself. That's just as bad in its way. It leaves me seething."

"I don't understand."

Phanta looked fit to explode, so Jumper stepped in. "Demons don't have souls," he reminded her. "They don't have human emotions. All they care about is status among their own kind. You are being emotional. She is being rational, by her definition. The Prophecy accomplished her purpose, so she is satisfied. She doesn't care how it inconveniences eight mortals."

"You are marvelously understanding," Eris murmured. "I admire that."

For a moment it seemed Phanta was going to flare at Jumper, but she stifled it. "And do *you* care, Jumper?"

"Oh, yes! I really liked Sharon, and I still like the rest of you, and I hate to see you hurt. I am also frustrated by the problem of our mission. I don't see how we'll accomplish it now."

"You are halfway rational. Maybe that's best. Maybe we should address this rationally, the way Eris does."

"Yes, of course," Jumper agreed. "We should bargain with her. But I don't see what we can offer her to make her complete the Prophecy to address our mission."

"I do." Phanta turned to the Demoness, who was waiting with perfectly rational passivity. "You need to marry a mortal prince to abate your situation? It won't make you a full Demon, but will at least free you from your prison."

"Correct."

"And we have one or two princesses in our group who surely know some princes. Just one prince would suffice."

"Correct."

"And those princesses are just as angry at Pluto as I am, having suffered similarly."

Jumper began to see where she was leading, thanks to his ability to appreciate human emotion.

"Correct," the Demoness said.

"And they will be just as mad as I am when they learn about the irrelevant Prophecy."

"Correct."

"Then why the bleep should either of them want to help you?"

Eris was taken aback. "They would decline?"

"Yes. Their foolish irrational emotion would make them tell you to go to hell."

"Actually, Pluto governs Hell, or more properly, Hades," the Demoness said. "With his wife Persephone. I could not go there."

"It is an established principle that princesses do not marry men they are mad at, or help women they are mad at," Phanta continued inexorably. "So the rational approach is to make them un-mad."

"Correct. But what would un-madden them?"

"Gee, I don't know." Jumper recognized irony there, and kept silent. "But it might help if the girls got their dream men back, this time for real, and found a way to complete the mission. That might not make them eager to help anyone, but at least they wouldn't be as angry as before."

Eris turned to Jumper. "This seems to be manipulating emotional states. I do not understand emotion. Does this program make sense to you?"

"Yes," Jumper said simply.

"How might we achieve such details?"

"Maybe if we all met together and discussed it," Jumper said. "The girls are reasonably smart. One of them might come up with something feasible."

"Then let's meet, here and now."

"There's a problem," Jumper said. "The girls are stuck at various places along our route, protecting it so we can return safely."

"If we can negotiate a deal, and a princess finds a prince for me, I will no longer be confined, and the way will no longer be blocked. There will be no further need to guard it."

"That's rational," Jumper agreed. "I will go back and tell them to come here."

"There is no need. My ghost aspect can notify them and lead them in."

"They may not believe him," Jumper said. "Unless he carries a credible message."

"What would that message be?"

Jumper considered, but didn't think of one.

"Vengeance is ours," Phanta said. "Follow Button."

"But that's not true," Jumper said. "We haven't negotiated any deal yet, let alone achieved any revenge."

"We will," Phanta said. "Trust me."

So they made a printed sign with those words, and Phanta touched it, ghosting it, so that the ghost Button could carry it. He took it and flitted back the way they had come.

Belatedly Jumper thought of another complication. "Dawn—she's afraid of depths. She can't come here."

"There is a more direct route," the Demoness said. "One that lacks depths. Button knows that route."

Soon the girls started appearing, led in by Button Ghost. The first was Olive. "Coinroy is still marveling over Shep's fantastic coin collection. I doubt he even misses me. But what's this about?"

"We will be negotiating with the Demoness Eris," Phanta said. "For our mission, and the return of our dream men."

Olive made a moue. "Our phantom dream men? Tell me more." The two walked away, conversing.

"You associate with pretty girls," Eris remarked.

"Coincidence," Jumper said. "I did not choose them."

"The Prophecy did. I did not wish to be rescued by an ugly prince."

Jumper had to laugh. Then he had to try to explain why, because the Demoness did not understand laughter. It had not been all that long since Jumper learned it himself, but he made the attempt, and the Demoness seemed to be getting it. She seemed to be quite intelligent.

Eve appeared. "What a castle!" she exclaimed. "Of course it needs more carpets on the walls, so it won't look so cold."

Jumper introduced them. "This is the Princess Eve, a Sorceress. This is the Demoness Eris. As you surmised, she needs to marry a mortal prince."

"You are wondrously lovely," Eris said, surveying Eve's nude charms.

Eve paused part of a moment, amenable to flattery, then decided. "Sorry, I have another agenda."

Oops. Eve thought the Demoness was hinting at something else.

"But your sister?" Eris asked.

Eve's lips quirked. "Maybe. That is for her to say."

Jumper decided to keep his mouth shut.

"Still, let's look around your castle," Eve said. "It looks worthy." They walked off.

Jumper wondered what Eve's other agenda was. A Demoness would be a considerable catch, even for a prince.

Haughty Harpy arrived. "Who would have thunk it," she said, her gaze covering landscape and castle.

Jumper explained the situation.

Maeve appeared. They caught her up on things. "How about some clothing?" she asked.

They explored the bedroom area of the castle, and discovered a number of royal robes, evidently set up for the handsome prince the Demoness hoped some day to marry. Maeve tried one on, and it fit her perfectly, being gender neutral or, more likely, a magic gown. "I'm beautiful!" she exclaimed, surprised, as she gazed in a wall-sized mirror. She was correct.

Wenda came. "Ooo, I want one too!" she exclaimed when she saw Maeve, though she was clothed. "Have yew another?" Soon she too was breathtakingly lovely in a royal gown.

And finally Dawn appeared. She immediately knew the situation the moment she touched Jumper. "Well, we'll see," she said.

Soon they were all gathered in the castle's family room. The girls were richly garbed, stunningly fair, for they had not only dressed, they had washed their faces and done their hair. But Dawn was noticeably fairer than the others, including her sister. Jumper realized that this was not accidental. Dawn, not Eve, was the one who might have considered marrying the Demon. Except that it had turned out to be a Demoness. Jumper wasn't sure what was going on in either of their minds.

There was a silence. Jumper realized that someone had to conduct the negotiation, and he, being neither girl nor Demoness, seemed to be the one. He opened his mouth—and was overtaken by a pause.

For there before him stood Sharon. She was breathtakingly beautiful, fully equivalent to the others.

"What are you doing here?" Jumper demanded.

"I believe I belong in this number," she said. "And I may have something to contribute."

Now Eris showed some emotion. "You betrayed me, foul creature!"

"And was in turn betrayed," Sharon responded.

"That surely served you right."

"Aren't you curious about the details?"

"No." For she was a Demoness, and the details could not relate to any acquisition of power on her part.

"But we are," Haughty said. She too had donned a bit of costume: a scintillating tiara. "You have been serving Pluto. What could have changed your mind, you scheming h*ssy?"

"I am a schemer," Sharon agreed. "It comes with the condition of being female." She looked around, and only Wenda shook her head in denial. She had not yet had enough experience as a whole woman to properly develop that trait.

"Get on with it," Haughty snapped.

"I am Charon's sister, and was Pluto's lover. I did Pluto's bidding, in the hope that in time he would marry me. I enabled him to achieve promotion to full Demon status. But then he married that mortal upstart Persephone." She frowned. "A mortal! Can you believe it?"

"Actually, yes," Dawn said. "It seems Demons have a taste for mortal princesses."

"She was no princess!"

"She was the equivalent," Dawn said. "She was the daughter of a god, and beautiful. What more could any male ask?"

"A Demoness!"

"Are you, or have you ever been, innocent?"

"Of course not! No Demoness is or ever was."

"As a mortal Persephone surely was. That appeals also."

"Oh, damn, you're right," Sharon said, realizing. As an un-innocent Demoness she wasn't bound by limitations of vocabulary, and could utter uncensored words.

"But didn't that happen a century or more ago?" Jumper asked.

"Yes. She married him when he achieved full Demon status, and backdated the historic references. And I, fool that I was, helped him achieve it."

"You know," Haughty said, "Sharon has a case. She is a woman scorned, like the rest of you."

"But why did you help him against us?" Jumper demanded. "You should have been on our side."

"I should have been," she agreed. "Especially since I found another male I could respect. But I was in denial about Pluto. I clung to the illusion that if he ever tired of Persephone, he would take me. So I helped him again—or tried to." She shook her head. "How wrong I was!"

Jumper was stunned. She had found another male? Wasn't he the only new one she had met?

"Wrong?" Haughty asked.

"He didn't dump Persephone," Sharon said angrily. "*She* dumped *him.* When he was demoted back to Dwarf Demon status. And he still didn't take me. He has found another woman. Another mortal. Another princess. That's the final outrage. I'll never help him again."

"Who?" Haughty asked.

"I don't know. Only that it happened very recently. Someone he met in a dream."

Eve swooned. Fortunately Olive and Phanta, standing on either side of her, caught her before she hit the floor.

Only Dawn seemed not entirely surprised. "Snap out of it, you faker!

Why are you trying to promote my assistance to the Demoness Eris?" she demanded.

"So you wouldn't try to steal my boyfriend—again," Eve said, recovering swiftly. "Or at least, the one I'm interested in."

"And who is that?"

"The Demon Pluto."

"So *you're* the one!" Sharon said, outraged. "I should have suspected."

"I didn't think I had a chance," Eve confessed. "But I had to try."

"And it seems you succeeded," Dawn said. "That must have been some session with the Centaur King."

"It was."

"And you were pretending to be one of the Furious D*msels," Jumper said indignantly. "When you had already used your wiles to corrupt him."

"I didn't think I succeeded," Eve said. "So I was angry too."

"So there you have it," Sharon said. "I'm in the same corset the rest of you are. Except for her." She shot a venomous glance at Eve. Fortunately the venom froze, bounced off Eve's face, and dropped to the floor with a glasslike tinkle.

"So why should you help us?" Dawn asked.

"Two reasons. Vengeance. And vengeance."

"I think I get the first," Dawn said. "But I don't understand the second."

"The first is the why of it. The second is the how."

"The how?"

"Eve will see your mission through. That will thoroughly embarrass Pluto."

"But why?" Haughty asked. "Isn't Eve changing sides, which will ruin the mission?"

"Of course I'm not changing sides," Eve snapped. "I agreed to see the mission through, and I will do it. I will marry him only after the mission is complete."

"See?" Sharon asked. "She is going to bring him more pain than I ever could."

"But won't he dump her, then?" Jumper asked.

"It is a matter of dominance," Eve said. "I will marry him on my terms or not at all."

Sharon nodded. "I am almost beginning to like you, you shameless feminist."

"So what will you do?" Dawn asked Sharon.

"I have discovered my own mortal interest."

"Who?"

"Jumper."

Now Jumper almost swooned. She really did like him! But could he trust her? This could be another devious ploy.

Dawn shook her head. "If only we could trust Demons."

"You could if you married us."

"Not before the mission is complete."

"So let's get that mission completed," Eris said. "I have no interest there; I want only to escape confinement."

Dawn turned a meltingly brilliant smile on her. "You have only to finish the Prophecy so we can complete our mission. And resolve the situation of my companions. Then in gratitude I will bamboozle a prince to marry you and make your next half century miserable."

"You are making two demands?" Eris asked. "Mission and friends? You are entitled to only one."

"Really? I must have miscounted. In that case, I shall have to look for someone else to oblige." She turned as if about to depart, in the process showing a fine silhouette as her gown flared.

"She's good," Sharon murmured.

"Wait!" Eris said desperately. "I didn't say I wouldn't honor two."

"Oh?" Dawn turned back. This time her gown caught the light behind her, becoming halfway translucent, so that her bra and panties blurrily showed. Jumper's breath caught as he fought down a blurry freak, and Button Ghost, in the direct line of sight, froze in place for a full moment.

"Really good," Sharon said.

"What do your companions require?" Eris asked.

"Well, it seems they met their ideal men in a dream, and got really interested in them, even granting them favors they would not have in waking life, only to later discover that these were not individual men but aspects of the Demon Pluto. So their romances were fraudulent throughout. They are embarrassed, humiliated, and most annoyed."

"Why?"

"Once you get half a prince's soul, you won't have to ask that question. But for now I'll explain that girls prefer to lend their favors only to the men they truly respect or love, and betrayal feels to them a bit like losing a Demon bet."

Eris fell back as if suffering a severe jolt of pain. "Now I understand."

"Since it was a Demon who caused this outrage, we feel that it will require the power of another Demon to abate it."

"That is rational," Eris agreed. "How should it be accomplished?"

Dawn turned to Jumper. "I think this is your area of expertise. What program can you recommend?"

Jumper was set back almost as forcefully as he had been by her blurred silhouette flash. He had no idea how to fix false love. "Uh—"

"Do you want my help?" Sharon murmured.

She could help? "Yes!"

"What do you offer in return?"

"What do you want?"

"Forgiveness."

"For what?"

"For deceiving you before about my interest in you."

"Are you interested in me *now*?"

"Yes, as I said."

"I mean, why are you interested now, when you were faking it before?"

"When Pluto dumped me, I realized that he was a lying male who had played me along without ever intending to get serious. I also realized that you are an honest male. You would not lie to me. I can trust you. I like that. You have other qualities to recommend you, as did your ancestor Jumper, but that was the turning point."

"You trust him?" Eris asked, surprised.

"Yes. He's not like me."

"So it seems." Was Eris actually impressed? Why?

But Jumper had a more immediate question. "How can I believe you?"

"I said that before too: marry me."

"Not before I complete the mission."

She nodded. "You have always been open about that. So here's the deal. Marriage after. Forgiveness before."

That seemed to make sense. "I forgive you." And he did, for she was right about his weakness: he could not tell a lie. And he did like her, and wanted to be with her, despite her nature. Despite knowing better.

She kissed him on the cheek. Then she spoke in a low tone that only he could hear. "I happen to know something about the mechanism Pluto used to invoke those men. They are not pure inventions; he lacks the imagination. They are takes on living men whose details are as represented. They were put into sleep and summoned to the communal dream, where they interacted with your girls. I think the men are quite taken with the girls, but they believe they are merely dream girls."

Jumper looked at her. "Can we reach those men?"

"Eris can. She can trace the connections Pluto made, and locate them, and conjure them here. The rest would be up to your girls."

"They will be able to handle it," he said.

"But there needs to be a framework for interaction. It's the human way; I have observed it over the centuries. A ball, perhaps."

"They would play with a ball?"

She smiled. "A fancy dance. Dawn can surely organize that."

"Thank you."

"A kiss would convey the sentiment better."

Oh. He started to take her into his arms, awkwardly. Then it became supremely un-awkward as she melted into his embrace and kissed him with the kind of passion he had not experienced since—since Phanta, not long ago. She was being the woman she could be, and that was a great deal of woman.

After he caught his breath and equilibrium, he addressed Eris, who had waited with Demonic patience. "Trace down and conjure here the six—no, the five men who dated Wenda, Maeve, Olive, Phanta, and Eve in our dreams. Provide suitable clothing for them so they can attend the ball without embarrassment."

"Delete mine," Eve said. "My interest is not in the centaur, but in the one who governed him."

Oh. "The four."

"That will take four moments."

But in half a moment someone else appeared. This was an old, crooked, but still spry man carrying a long staff or pole.

"Charon!" Sharon exclaimed. "What are you doing here?"

"Fetching you away from here, little sister," Charon said. "You must not serve the interest of any Demon but Pluto."

"You can't tell me what to do!" Sharon protested.

"We shall see." Charon faced her, raising his staff. A horrible power emanated from it.

Sharon shrank back, evidently knowing and fearing that power. Jumper thought he should do something, but he had no idea what. If Pluto was a Dwarf Demon, Charon was a Mini-Demon, but still way beyond anything Jumper could handle.

Then Haughty flew across the chamber, converting to Hottie. She smacked into Charon, kiss first. It was so hot that wisps of steam curled up from the contact.

The Demon stepped back, but Hottie stayed with him, her kiss heating into smokiness. Little hearts . . . no, planets . . . no, coins orbited their heads.

Charon backed into an ice wall, which started to melt, but Hottie continued to kiss him. Jumper doubted he had been kissed so hotly in centuries.

Finally he managed to break it off. "All right!" he gasped. "You win." He cast aside his staff and transformed into a male harpy. It seemed he was another shape changer, like his sister.

The two harpies flew up to a rafter and perched. Then they settled into some serious necking, making feathers fly.

"She saved me," Sharon breathed. "He would have sent me across the Styx."

"His stick is on the floor," Jumper said. "Are there other sticks?"

She gazed at him. "And that is what I like most about you: your innocence. No, the Styx is the river that borders Hades, Pluto's domain. Now let's see to the ball."

They returned their attention to the preparations. The several moments had evidently passed, and there were four men standing in the hall, looking slightly baffled. Jumper recognized them: Warren Warrior, Prince Charming, Dick Philip, and Shepherd. Maeve was talking to Warren, Wenda to Charming, Olive to Dick Philip, and Phanta with Shepherd, explaining the situation. When the men started kissing the girls, Jumper knew it was working out. Eris had succeeded in meeting Eve's second demand.

Only Eve stood apart, lovely but alone.

One more man appeared, stout and strong with a vaguely doglike visage. "The Demon Pluto himself!" Sharon whispered nervously. "He can be a real canine when crossed."

"Who has interfered with my minion Charon?" Pluto growled peremptorily.

"I did, you t**d from h**l!" Haughty screeched from the rafter.

He whirled on her, sighting up as if aiming a rifle, not that such things existed in Xanth. "You, birdbrain?"

"Me, you s*n of a b**ch!" she screeched back. "He's not your minion anymore."

Pluto swelled up like a fire from the netherworld.

"Well, now, impostor," Eris said.

The fire evaporated. "You!"

"You have wandered into my temporary domain," Eris said. "You have no power here, traitor. Begone, like the treasonous cur you are."

Eve looked pained. "Please," she said.

Dawn picked up on it immediately. "Eris, for the sake of the deal we are making," she said. "Can't we have a truce, at least for the ball?"

Meanwhile Eve was taking Pluto's hand. "We are having a party here. I would appreciate it if you joined in. Please make a temporary truce with Eris."

Both Demons glowered. Both princesses smiled persuasively,

turning to display their charms. The Demon slowly melted, and the Demoness reluctantly yielded.

Now Jumper saw that there was nothing incidental in the way Eve addressed Pluto. When she moved, parts of her body showed, seemingly by accident, and her mannerisms were those of a girl desperately in love with the man she addressed. All the seductive devices the girls had discovered and practiced were being subtly focused on the Demon. Nothing was being wasted. What a display! She was absolutely lovely, and worse, sexy.

It was working too. Pluto was not freaking out, but his attention was riveted. Eve was Seduction Incarnate. No man could have withstood the sheer force of her appeal, and it seemed no Demon either. She was invoking his most ardent desire. A soulless Demon might not be capable of love, but he could be aroused. Pluto wanted her. Desperately.

"The girls are even better, working in tandem," Sharon murmured. "I never had much respect for mortal women, but I am learning it."

She did not know the half of it. "Mortal women have their points," Jumper agreed, remembering Phanta.

Sharon slapped him, not hard. Somehow she had fathomed his memory. "I can do better than that. Keep your wandering fancy on me."

"I will try," he agreed apologetically.

"That's better. Now let's join the dance."

For the chamber had metamorphosed into a gaudily decorated ballroom with colored lights and streamers. Music played from hidden recesses, and the partners were gliding out onto the central floor. The men were handsome in their newly crafted suits, and the girls were devastating in their flowing gowns. Dawn had evidently guided Eris well.

Eris and Dawn did the first dance, and it did not seem strange that both were female. They whirled around the floor, their feet stepping intricately, their motions perfectly coordinated. They made a marvelously handsome couple.

Then Pluto and Eve joined the dance, similarly smooth. It was hard to judge which Demon was more stately, or which princess was lovelier. But Jumper saw that Eve was still working on Pluto, now pressing against him, now whirling teasingly away, now catching him with a fleeting kiss.

She was turning his own ploy against him, as the six angry damsels had rehearsed.

And the others, though considerably less polished, made up for it with enthusiasm. Maeve with Warren Warrior, Wenda with Prince Charming, Olive with the crazy writer Dick Philip, and Phanta with Shepherd. Haughty and Charon flew down from the rafter to whirl together in the air.

And of course Sharon led Jumper into the dance. He knew nothing of dancing, but somehow she guided him through it so that he seemed competent. She was so light on her feet she seemed to float in his arms like a wisp of mist. In fact she *was* floating; her feet did not always touch the floor. Her hair sparkled as she turned, and her eyes held his. It was wonderful.

If he was not yet in abject love, he was being sorely besieged by the emotion. He knew this was not smart on his part, but Sharon was, almost literally, a dream come true. Only a faint warning awareness in the back of his mind restrained him.

Then Eris cut in, and Sharon grudgingly let him go. That spoiled the effect she had been making.

"Uh, why?" Jumper asked, bemused, as the Demoness guided him gracefully around the floor.

"I have long been alone, and you are a decent male," she replied candidly. "Too bad you're not a prince."

"Not only that, I'm not a man," he said. "I'm a spider."

"And I, like all Demons, am not bound by mortal limitations," she said. "Change forms, if you wish."

What was her point? He sipped a vial and reverted to his natural form.

And found himself opposite another big spider. She had changed with him.

Well, now. Jumper did his thing, which was to jump. She jumped with him, matching his effort perfectly. Soon they were in a marvelous spider dance, while the other dancers fell back to watch.

"Why?" he clicked in spider talk.

"I like you. If you were a prince I would marry you, and not just because it would enable me to escape."

Jumper found himself foolishly flattered. Meanwhile, he was absolutely loving this. Eris seemed to understand him in a way no other woman did. Certainly in a way no other spider would.

When the dance ended, they changed back to human form. "Thank you," Jumper said.

"It was a pleasure." She faded back, letting Sharon rejoin him. Somehow she impressed him less, not because she was less, but because Eris was more.

There were refreshments. They sat on the sideline, sipping boot rear, laughing at the boots. The scene seemed good. "I wish it could be like this always," Jumper said.

"Do not be deceived," Sharon said. "Until you accomplish your mission, nothing is decided. Not with the Demon, not with us."

"Nothing decided," he agreed with regret. She was a Demon, a very minor one, but a Demon nevertheless, without a soul, not to be trusted. Was she really interested in him, or was this merely another ploy to fascinate him so that he would have to do her bidding? No matter how many times he asked that question, he was never quite satisfied with the answer.

"But for the moment, we can enjoy ourselves." She touched his hand. And, oddly, that single little touch was more compelling than much of what else had passed.

Yet Eris lingered in his awareness. The thing about Eris was that he had no reason to doubt her. As far as he knew, he could trust her.

Then the music stopped. "It is time for the final negotiation," Sharon said. "This is the one that counts."

"Who has to do it?" he asked, fearing the answer.

"You, of course. You have a mission to complete." Exactly as he had feared.

What choice did he have? "It is my job to complete the mission of repairing the cable connecting the Internet to the Outernet," he said. "Demon Pluto wishes to prevent this. Demoness Eris wishes to escape confinement, which she can do if she marries a prince. So we suggest that if Eris finishes the Prophecy to enable us to complete our mission, and this is successful, Dawn will locate a suitable mortal prince to marry her."

"Agreed," Eris said.

"Agreed," Dawn said.

"And if I prevent it, I get Eve," Pluto said.

"You have it backward," Eve said. "If the mission is successful, I will marry you."

"This is the issue," Pluto said. "You have practiced your nefarious female arts on me, and compelled my fascination with your body, exactly as you planned. I want to win you without having to marry you. Then I will not inherit half your soul, and will not be governed by foolish scruples."

"Oh, really!" Eve exclaimed. "That's not *my* deal!"

"It seems to be the deal he proffers," Jumper said, realizing that the Demon had found a loophole. "Marriage would severely limit him, so he wants your love without marriage."

"Exactly," Pluto said.

"Why should I agree to that?" she demanded.

"To get him committed to a deal," Jumper said. "Demons are bound by nothing except the deals they make with other Demons. If Pluto has a chance to get you on his terms, he will make the deal."

Eve pursed her lips, considering. "If we complete our mission, Eris wins, and marries a prince and escapes. I will marry Pluto, and bind him with my half soul, so he will treat me better than he treated Sharon. And you, Jumper, can marry Sharon, making a decent female of her."

"That seems to be our offer," Jumper agreed, though he was no longer absolutely sure he wanted to marry Sharon.

"And if you do not complete your mission," Pluto said, "I will win. None of those three marriages will occur. I will have Eve to do with as I like, and Dawn will have no obligation to Eris, and Sharon will put a ring through Jumper's nose and make him wish he had remained a spider."

Jumper winced, knowing that none of the mortal participants were likely to enjoy that situation. "We need some limits on Pluto's interference with the mission."

"I will put five horrendous obstacles in your way," Pluto said. "Defeat them all, and victory is yours."

"One obstacle," Jumper said.

"Four."

"Two."

"Three."

Jumper looked around. Dawn and Eve exchanged a glance, and slowly nodded. This seemed to be a fair compromise.

"Those obstacles will be there before we depart here," Jumper said. "After they are placed, no Demon will interfere. It will be up to us."

Both Demons nodded.

"It must be possible for us to succeed," Jumper said. "If we do it correctly."

"Agreed," both Demons said together.

"Agreed," Jumper said.

Then he and the seven girls were back in the Castle Roogna turret. Demons and men were gone. The paper with the completed Prophecy was in Jumper's hand.

They were on their own, with three horrendous challenges to navigate. The stakes were divine and awful.

13
CABLE

N ot only that. It turned out to be morning—the same morning they had climbed to the turret. Their daylong adventure with the Demons seemed to have taken no time at all.

They compared notes. "Did we wend our way to the Demoness Eris's lair, and attend a ball, and make a deal?" Jumper inquired, nervous about the answer.

"We did dew that," Wenda agreed. "And I met Prince Charming in the wondrous flesh. He is a divine dancer. I wood like to have stayed a bit longer, like maybee forever."

"And I sat on a rafter with Charon," Haughty said. "He likes both me and Hottie. Me for intellect, her for making out. He has long been without a female; it seems that poling a raft to Hades turns off most of them. That sort of thing doesn't bother a harpy. I can have him all to myself, in whatever aspect. He has centuries of thwarted amour eager to be expressed."

"And I will be with Pluto," Eve said, "for better or worse, depending on the success of our mission. Either way, he's quite a man."

"So it seems it really happened," Jumper said.

"It really did," Phanta agreed. "As did our passing tryst."

The others looked at her. "Yew made it with him?" Wenda asked. "This is knot flirtatious humor?"

"Not," Phanta agreed. "He saved me from a small black hole. I was overcome by the moment."

"So that's the secret," Maeve said. "Small black holes."

"We must be sure to make note of that," Olive said.

"Noted," Haughty agreed.

The group looked as if it was making an effort to laugh, but it was unsuccessful.

"Meanwhile, we have three horrendous obstacles to overcome," Jumper said. "Or Eve and I will be enslaved by Demons."

"What of the rest of us?" Olive asked. "I don't remember us being mentioned in that Demon bet."

A pause circled around. "I don't think you were," Dawn said. "Not in the Demon negotiations. But you're definitely part of the mission."

"Surely so," Olive agreed. "But what is our fate if it succeeds—or fails?"

"My guess is that success will grant you permanent status as you are now," Eve said. "Full body, absence of stork, better control of imaginary friends, of ghostly form, and of harpy personality."

"And what of failure?" Phanta asked grimly.

"The loss of those things. Reversion to your prior status. Your men might not appreciate that."

"But the stork will catch me!" Maeve wailed.

"That's hardly as bad as what will catch *us*," Eve said. "I want to be Pluto's wife, not his plaything."

Jumper could only agree. He now knew enough of Demons to be assured that he needed the protection of half a soul in Sharon. She could be divine, but without that she would be, well, demonic.

Then he realized that he suffered from another complication. He had met the Dwarf Demoness Eris, and danced with her. He hardly knew her, but somehow that limited interaction had given him a foolish crush on her.

But it was Sharon who would claim him.

"So we simply must knot fail," Wenda said.

With that they heartily agreed.

"What of the Prophecy?" Haughty asked.

Jumper brought out the parchment, and discovered that it now had a continuation. "Go find the Cable, if you are able," he read. "You'll find it when, in the Ogre Fen."

"That almost makes sense," Dawn said. "We have to repair the broken cable."

"No it doesn't," Eve said. "The cable isn't in the Ogre-fen-Ogre Fen. It's between worlds."

"And what's this business about when?" Olive asked. "It should be where."

"That wood knot rhyme," Wenda pointed out.

"So this d**mn thing is just as confusingly obscure as it has been all along," Haughty said, disgusted.

"True to form," Jumper agreed.

"What about the rest of it?" Phanta asked.

Jumper focused on the parchment. "Let no maiden fair, Yield to despair."

"Who is it talking about?" Maeve demanded. "It's okay for ugly girls to give up?"

"You are all fair," Jumper said quickly.

"Oh?" Maeve asked. "Would you like to make out with any of the rest of us?"

"Yes. Any of you could have seduced me, in Phanta's place, after that black hole scare. You still could, if you really tried. You're all attractive, and you have all worked to be more so—the princesses especially. That's why Eve was able to win the interest of Pluto."

There was half a pause. "Noted," Haughty said. "So it is talking about us. We must not give up."

"What else is in the Prophecy?" Dawn asked.

Jumper read the last of it. "It will be nice, If you can splice."

"Splice the cable," Haughty said. "Of course that will be nice. That's our mission. Why is it saying the obvious?"

"Because it is unlikely to be obvious in practice," Eve said. "We knew this is not going to be easy. It has to be a Challenge whose outcome is uncertain, to be a fair Demon bet."

"And it surely is that," Jumper concluded.

They set out forthwith, fetching their bicycles and riding an enchanted path northward, because the Prophecy indicated that their first challenge was far north, at the Ogre-fen-Ogre Fen.

The path gradually curved to the right. "It's veering east," Eve noted. She stopped, got off her bike, and touched the path with one hand. "Oh—it's a detour. Complication of weather ahead, so it's taking a scenic route."

"Paths can do that?" Jumper asked, surprised.

"Magic paths can. They protect travelers not only by shielding them from hostile creatures, but by routing them compatibly. Don't be concerned; it will get us there."

The scenic route brought them to a lovely scene: a great valley with a winsome river winding lazily through it, with pretty foliage along its banks. "The Kiss Mee River," Eve said. "This should be fun."

They camped for the night at a shelter by the river. Brown plants grew beside it. Jumper and Dawn picked the pointed fruit of one. It smelled tasty, so they ate it. It was chocolate.

They turned to each other and kissed. That surprised Jumper, because he had not had any such thing in mind.

"Well," Dawn said. "You are growing bolder."

"I didn't do that," he protested. "You did."

Wenda came up. "Yew both did," she said. "Those are chocolate kisses. They grow all along the Kiss Mee River, of course."

Dawn laughed. "That's one on me! My sister would have recognized their nature instantly." She glanced sidelong at Jumper. "Shall we have another?"

"Uh, no," he said quickly, not sure what it might lead to.

"If yew want to make smarter decisions, try that plant," Wenda suggested, indicating one. "That is sage; it will make yew wise."

"Thank you, no," Jumper said, uncertain whether she was teasing him.

Unfortunately there was not a lot in this region that wasn't too sweet for their tastes, or that didn't threaten to make them more affectionate than they cared to be. That was the nature of the Kiss Mee valley. It was a region of love, not war.

Wenda dug up a sweet potato. "If we cook this, it will knot actually bee too sweet or friendly," she said.

"Then we'll have to make a fire, and find a pan," Dawn said.

But they found neither. "Can one of your friends help?" Jumper asked Olive without much hope.

"Certainly." A ten-year-old girl appeared beside her. She looked ordinary, but looked around, and became much sweeter. "Hello, Auspice," Olive said.

"Hello, Olive," the girl replied sweetly.

"Auspice is the daughter of Bink and Chameleon, after they were rejuvenated," Olive explained. "They were eighty-one and seventy-six, respectively, when they were youthened to twenty-one and sixteen, eleven years ago."

"Sixty years removed!" Jumper exclaimed.

"So they could be young again," Dawn agreed. "Hello, Auspice."

"Hello, great niece Dawn," the girl replied.

"What?" Jumper asked.

Dawn laughed. "Rejuvenation can do odd things. Eve and I are Bink and Chameleon's great-grandchildren, so Auspice is our great-aunt. Her talent is to change her nature involuntarily to match her surroundings in mood, attitude, appearance and abilities. That's why she became so sweet."

"That's nice," Jumper said. "But how does this help us cook a tuber?"

Auspice clapped her hands with girlish delight. "That's easy! I brought my cook book."

"But—"

The girl brought out a thick book she had somehow concealed on her person. She set it on the ground. "Where is your potato?" she asked.

Wenda gave it to her. Auspice set it on top of the book. There was a sizzle and the sweet potato softened visibly. It was cooking!

Then Jumper got it: a cook book was a book you cooked on. He had somehow thought it merely contained instructions for cooking.

They cooked several sweet potatoes, and had a nice meal washed down by water from the river. That of course led to a round of kisses. At least they knew it was not illicit passion. Then Auspice faded out, and the party settled down for the night.

Fortunately this time the girls allowed Jumper to sleep alone. They knew that it wasn't fair to douse him with Kiss Mee water and count it as any kind of seduction.

In the morning they washed up in very friendly fashion, ate some leftover potato, and mounted their bikes again.

They moved well, until they reached the huge Gap Chasm. This suddenly balked them, because the path led right up to the brink, and stopped.

"Not to worry," Dawn said. "My sister and I are long since familiar with this route. There's an invisible bridge."

"But Eve—" Jumper protested, remembering her fear of heights.

"You take the high route, I'll take the low route," Eve said.

"I don't understand," Jumper said. "I could revert to spider form and climb down the wall, with a safety line. But your magic does not relate."

"We'll show you," Dawn said. "Follow me, girls." She stepped out over the brink.

Jumper leaped to catch her before she plummeted to the depths— and crashed into an invisible barrier. He wrapped his inefficient human arms about it and hung on. "What?"

"Weren't you listening?" Dawn chided him gently. "It's the invisible bridge." She took another step out into midair, not falling.

So it seemed. Jumper hauled himself up onto it, then stepped back toward the brink—and abruptly fell. He barely caught the edge of the cliff in time.

"Oh, a detail I may have forgotten to mention," Dawn said. "It's a one-way bridge. You have to keep going the way you start across; you can't turn back. It doesn't exist behind you. Only for the next person."

Jumper scrambled back to land. "Thank you for that clarification."

"But now you can't use it," Eve said. "It no longer exists for you. You'll have to come with me."

"Gladly," Jumper said, disgruntled.

The four remaining girls started across, following Dawn, walking the bicycles, while Haughty spread her wings and flew along beside them. They walked out over the chasm, the breeze playing with their hair and skirts.

"This way," Eve said, and she too stepped over the brink.

This time Jumper did not leap after her. She obviously knew what she was doing. He hoped.

She disappeared into the gulf. Jumper went to the brink and looked down, almost afraid of what he might discover.

Eve was walking down the side. Her body was oriented vertical to the wall, horizontal to the ground. It was as though she were walking on level ground, only it was the sheer face of the cliff.

Jumper sipped a vial and assumed spider form. Then he stepped cautiously over the brink. It felt like level ground. Now he too was walking down the cliff without falling.

"It's a special path," Eve said. "It works for anyone. You just have to know about it."

Jumper looked around, not having to turn his head. Ahead of him was the distant depth of the chasm. Behind him was the lip of the gulf. He felt level, despite the confused orientation of the rest of the landscape.

He glanced at the girls on the invisible bridge. They were making good progress, their skirts flaring as the playful wind continued to tease them. Their legs showed to lesser or greater extent, and sometimes their panties flashed.

Jumper looked away. He wasn't freaking, but he was losing concentration at a time when he thought it best not to. His job at the moment was to get safely down to the bottom of the chasm. But they were nice legs, and nice panties.

In due course they reached the foot of the wall. They stepped out onto the roughly level bottom, and the world resumed its normal orientation. That had been an experience!

"Something else," Eve said. "We have a friend down here."

"A friend?"

"He's on his way now."

Jumper looked. There was a puffing cloud of steam whomping their way. In four and a half moments it manifested as a long, low, six-legged dragon blowing steam with each breath. "A dragon?" he asked, surprised.

"Stanley Steamer," she said. "Princess Ivy tamed him when she was a little girl, and we have been on good terms ever since." She lifted her voice. "Stanley! It's Eve! With a friend, Jumper Spider. Don't steam him."

The dragon drew up before them, eyeing Jumper as if not sure whether to take her at her word.

"We're on a mission," Eve said. "Can't linger here long. But it's nice to see you again, Stanley."

The dragon nodded, then went on its way. Jumper was impressed. The princess really did know the dragon.

"Look, there's a patch of little squirts," Eve remarked. "They protect themselves from the heat of the dragon by storing cool water. Some folk drink from them. You may want to collect a few."

"I may?"

"You never can tell when one might be useful."

So he collected a few. They were bulbs with thin necks pointing upward. They seemed satisfied to be harvested.

They crossed to the far wall, then walked up it in the same manner they had walked down the other. As they neared the top, there were the girls, having evidently dallied. They shook their skirts in unison, teasingly flashing Jumper.

"Dawn must have put them up to that," Eve muttered. "She's a naughty girl."

"And you aren't?"

She smiled obscurely. "I'm not up there."

Wenda was immediately above him. She jumped on the invisible bridge, making her skirt flare up to her waist. She wore a forest green panty. "Yew can knot touch me!" she teased.

Then Jumper realized what the little squirts were for. He aimed one and gave it a hard squeeze. A jet of cool water shot up and scored on the middle of the panty.

"Eeeeek!" she screamed, snapping her legs together. "Yew have a little squirt!" Of course she recognized the forest plant.

The other girls, catching on, broke out with a severe case of the giggles. Until Jumper squirted them too. Then the giggles became eekgles. They danced out of range, their motions showing even more naughty details.

At last they were all on level ground beyond the chasm, the girls still laughing helplessly. They were fortunate they had not dropped a bicycle into the chasm in their mirth. Somehow five of them had managed to wheel seven cycles across.

"We make a compatible group," Olive remarked.

"We do," Jumper agreed, not admitting that their nether displays had left panty-shaped spots floating before his eyes. They surely knew it anyway; their display had hardly been accidental. Yet now their teasing was friendly rather than seductive. They trusted him not to take advantage of them, and if he did, they wouldn't really mind.

Jumper changed back to manform so he could ride his bicycle. They mounted and cycled north.

Even traveling at speed, on the enchanted path, it took time, and as evening approached they pulled into a rest stop area near the Region of Fire. "There are five Regions," Dawn explained. "Air, Earth, Fire, Water, and the Void. They each have their typical climates, and it is best to avoid them unless you know what you're doing."

"Climates?" he asked.

"Air is stormy," Eve said. "Earth has volcanoes and earthquakes. Fire has fires sweeping across, burning everything up. Water is flooded with a few islands. And the Void is the original from which the black hole fragment came."

"Best avoided," Jumper agreed, shuddering.

Phanta came and kissed him. "From which you saved me. I will be forever grateful."

"Nu-uh," Olive said. "You had your turn, Phanta. Someone else can be grateful tonight."

The group laughed, but Jumper wasn't quite sure it was either jealousy or humor. Their relationship seemed to have entered a new phase.

Sure enough, when they settled down to sleep, Wenda and Maeve came to join him, lying close on either side. Again, he had the impression that neither would really object to anything he might choose to do with them, though they neither spoke nor acted seductively. They had their own boyfriends, and he had his girlfriend; this was something else. It was . . . friendship.

In the morning they discovered that two more people had come to the camp. A young man and a young woman, similar in appearance. They were just washing their faces and hands at the edge of the pond.

"Hi," the girl said. "I'm Gin. I'm very friendly. This is my brother Tonic; he's very active." Indeed, Tonic was already foraging for their breakfast.

Jumper introduced the members of their group. "We're looking for a cable, somewhere near the Ogre Fen."

"I know where there's a cable," Tonic said. He led the way to a steep hillside.

There was a metal vehicle on a track that led up the side of the hill. It was pulled by a metal cord attached to its front, so that it was moving rapidly up toward the top.

"That's a cable car," Eve said. "Not what we want."

"I know where there are several cables," Gin said. She led them to a house with a number of cords strung from its roof.

"That's a house of seven cables," Dawn said. "Not what we want."

Still, they checked with a woman who was sitting before the house, busily knitting. No, not sitting, hovering over the chair. She was short and thin, with small blue-green dragon's wings and blue-green wavy hair.

"Hello," Jumper said.

She dropped to the chair, and her wings folded, forming a cloak around her body. "Yes?"

"I am Jumper and my companions are at the shelter. We are looking for a cable, but I don't think it is of the type that festoons your house."

"I am Aura Dawn. I am knitting cable stitches for more festoons, but I could knit one for you if you need it. What will you use it for?"

"To repair the connection between the Internet and the Outernet."

Aura shook her head. "That's a much more complicated cable than I could ever knit. You will need the children's magic cable."

"The children's cable?"

"Five weirdly talented children. But you don't want to go near them. They are dangerous."

"If they have what we need, we may have to get it from them."

"Well, in that case, be very careful." Aura unfolded her cloak, reforming her wings, and flew back to her prior height. She resumed her cabling.

"Thank you," Jumper said, and returned to the shelter. "It seems that five talented children have the cable we need," he reported.

"Do we know where they are?" Haughty asked.

"No. I presume somewhere between here and the Ogre Fen."

"Could Dawn or Eve tell?" Phanta asked.

"No," Eve said. "We have to be close to a thing or creature to learn about it. We can't get close without knowing where."

"Or when," Jumper said, remembering the odd word in the Prophecy.

"Maybe I can find a friend who will be able to help," Olive said. She concentrated.

A woman appeared. She was shaped somewhat like a string bean, without curves. "Yes?"

"Oops," Olive said. "I was looking for a friend who could find things."

"I am she. I am Samantha. I can find flesh."

"I was thinking more of—"

"In fact I can find any flesh I need to make myself luscious," Samantha said. "Like this." She stroked her pipe-stem legs, and they became much thicker. She kneaded them into shape, and they became, indeed, luscious. Jumper couldn't help looking.

"Well, that's fine," Olive said. "But what I meant was—"

"Or like this," Samantha said, stroking her skinny arms. They thickened, and became firm and nice.

"Actually, we're looking for a—"

"Or this." Samantha cupped her chest with her hands, and mounds of flesh appeared. Soon she had amazingly sightly breasts. Jumper felt his eyes starting to glaze.

"Cable!" Olive cried.

"What?"

"We're looking for a section of cable, to do a repair."

"Why didn't you say so? I can't help you with that." Samantha faded out.

"Maybe we had better find it the old-fashioned way," Olive said, frustrated. "I usually just visit with my imaginary friends. Summoning them for particular tasks doesn't seem to work as well."

"Let's go on toward the Ogre Fen," Jumper suggested as his eyeballs slowly recovered. He suspected that their difficulty locating the cable was not coincidental; it was a Demon challenge they would have to struggle to overcome.

Jumper found himself riding beside Dawn. This was surely no coincidence. He wanted to talk to her, and chances were she knew it.

"Eve said you put the girls up to flashing their panties at me," he said. "Why?"

"A little friendly teasing isn't in order?"

"And then Wenda and Maeve slept beside me last night. I had the distinct impression they were offering me something."

"We are all your friends."

"Then *be* a friend. Answer my question. What is going on?"

She sighed. "You may not like the answer."

"I don't like the mystery. I want to be able to focus on the mission, not on the charms of my associates."

"Much is riding on our mission, for once no pun," she said, glancing down at her bicycle. "We don't know exactly why the Good Magician stressed its importance, but we believe him. Some of us now have our own personal stakes in it too. We know that if any member of it is lost, it will fail. So we have to handle not only the impediments, but our own unity. The one is as important as the other."

"Agreed. So why are they teasing me?"

"Eve and I are committed to the Demons, one way or another. We are, in effect, the prizes they can win for their victories: she for marriage, me to obtain a suitable prince."

"You should be able to find a prince. Eris is beautiful." He felt a foolish qualm as he spoke, because of his foolish crush on Eris.

"Not necessarily. Princes can be notoriously choosy, and there are not many available at present. If I am unable to deliver, I will have to sacrifice myself."

"Sacrifice?"

"There is a portal that changes the gender of any person who passes through it. I would become a prince, and marry her myself. To complete my commitment."

"Dawn!" he exclaimed, shocked.

"So you see, this is desperately serious business. We can handle it; we are Sorceresses, far more conversant with magic and the way of things than we normally pretend. We are not innocent."

"Agreed. The two of you are no longer teasing me. But I am committed too; I am bound to Sharon, one way or another."

"That's the problem."

"I am as committed to the mission as you are. If you make sacrifices, so will I."

"This is commendable," she agreed. "But you see, you *are* innocent. You are a spider, with no prior experience with human or Demon scheming. Your word is your bond, without nuances."

"Yes, of course."

"Sharon is a Demon, with all that implies. You are not in her league. Thus you are our most likely weak spot."

Jumper was hurt. "If she doesn't want me, of course I'll go away."

"She wants you. But we do not know her real commitment. If it is to Pluto, she will use you to achieve his ends. We need to see that you are not hopelessly helpless."

He had to concede that this was true. "I will try my best."

"We—that is, the girls—want you to know that there are alternatives. If one of them must go with you to protect you from Sharon, she will."

"Go with me?"

"Be your woman."

"But they have their own boyfriends."

"We discussed it, and they agreed: if any of them must protect you from Sharon, they will. Whichever one you prefer."

Jumper was having trouble getting his mind around this. "Like Phanta, that time?"

"Yes. They all like you, and are dedicated to the mission. It would not be too great a sacrifice. They will do what it takes to complete it."

"But I'm a spider!"

"In human form. If you chose one, she would seek a transformation spell so she could join you as a spider, if that is what you want."

Jumper shook his head. "You're right: I am innocent."

"In the interim, if you are inclined, take one of them temporarily. They are not as skilled as Sharon, but they can be trusted not to hurt or corrupt you. They are all worthy."

"I know it! I'm not sure *I* am worthy."

"You are, Jumper, you are. We are all in this together."

His emotions were mixed and confused. "I don't know."

She glanced at him sidelong. "That interim includes Eve and me. We can't commit to anything long-term, obviously, but during the mission we can be with you."

"This is awful! It tempts me. I hate that."

"Just keep it in mind."

Jumper was desperate to change the subject. "The cable—we have been asking strangers if they know where it is. We haven't gotten anywhere. Since we know that Pluto is trying to stop us, is there some sort of curse on the word?"

Eve made half a pause, surprised. "You know, there could be. Maybe we should not mention it. We can simply say we are in need of a piece of equipment."

"Let's do that."

Eve dropped back to notify the others, and Olive came up to ride beside him. "What she told you is true. We are interested in mortal men; you are interested in a Demoness. That's why we fear for you."

"But to—to—"

"It is not that much of a sacrifice, Jumper. We know you are worthy. We want you to keep your perspective."

"I will try to keep it without making demands on any of you."

"But if you do feel the need, and want the one who is most amenable, that would be Wenda. She is innocent too, and understands that aspect, and she does like you."

"Uh, thank you." He couldn't think of anything else to say. He found the commitment of the girls somewhat overwhelming. Despite their reassurances, he did not feel worthy.

Near dusk they reached the verge of the Ogre-fen-Ogre Fen. It was a huge flat bog girt with islands of trees, and devious paths made their way cautiously through it. How would they ever find the cable here?

They camped near a bit of open water and discussed the matter. "All we know is that we'll find it when, in the Ogre Fen," Jumper reminded them. "If we are able."

"We'll just have to ask around," Dawn said as they had supper. "I will know whether a person is telling the truth, though I won't know everything unless I touch him or her."

"We don't want to give away our identities," Eve reminded her. "Pluto may have sent out word to beware of two princesses."

"The rest of us can question them," Haughty said. "And Jumper will have to stay in manform, in case they are also alert for a big spider."

"And we should be wary of children," Olive said.

They washed, seemingly ignoring Jumper as they peeled naked and splashed in the shallow water, but he knew that this too was deliberate. They were demonstrating that they trusted him, while also reminding him that he did not need to be with Sharon to have access to a female body. His reactions remained mixed. He appreciated their attitude, but he did wish he could be with Sharon. Or, better, Eris.

When they settled down to sleep, Wenda joined him, alone. He took her hand, kissed it, and closed his eyes. After a time he was able to sleep.

In the morning they ranged out, looking for local people. There were several paths winding through the fen as if exploring it. They decided to go out in pairs. Jumper went out with Wenda, who just sort of stayed with him. They encountered a young man who was sitting by his fishing line.

"Hello. My name is Jumper, and this is my friend Wenda. I am looking for some equipment. Do you know where any is?" This seemed inane, yet how else were they to proceed?

"I have no idea," the man said, gazing at Wenda with perhaps a bit more than passing interest. "I am Ande. But I want your promise not to take our treasure."

"We're not looking for treasure, and if we were, we wouldn't take it from anyone else."

"So you promise?"

"Yes."

"Maybe my brother Bruce will know. He can see almost anything."

"Thank you. Where can I find him?"

"Just a bit farther along this path."

Wenda smiled at Ande, tacitly rewarding him for his assistance.

"Thank you," Jumper repeated, and they walked on.

Soon they came across a man carving a toy boat from wood. "Bruce?" Jumper asked.

The man looked up. His gaze fell on Wenda, and he paused, seeming slightly dazed. "Yes."

"I am Jumper, and this is Wenda. We are looking for some equipment. Your brother Ande said you might help."

"Well, I can help you look," Bruce said. He reached up and touched Jumper's forehead.

Suddenly there was something odd about Jumper's vision. He seemed to be seeing right through Bruce. "What is this?" he asked, alarmed.

"I just lent you my talent of seethrough," Bruce said. "Now for a while you can see through anything you wish to. Just focus carefully."

Jumper looked around uncertainly. He discovered that he could see right through trees when he tried, or not through them when he relaxed. He looked at Wenda, at first seeing through her, then curtailing the effect until he saw only through her outer clothing. There were her bra and panties, nicely filled. He blinked and moved on. Now he had a notion why Bruce had seemed dazed. He had been looking at Wenda's underwear.

"Uh, thank you," he said. "This should help my search."

"Maybe sister Clare will be able to help you," Bruce said as his gaze lingered on Wenda's skirt, or more likely through it. "She's not far beyond here."

"Thank you. We'll ask her." They walked on along the path.

"That man made me nervous," Wenda confided when they were alone. "The way he looked at me."

Should he tell her? He concluded that honesty was best. "He was looking through your clothing at your underwear."

"Oh!"

"I can see it too, for now. It's in good order." That was an understatement; the Good Magician had given her compelling flesh.

"Thank yew," she said, not perfectly reassured.

They came to a woman peeling potatoes. She was well formed under her clothing. "Clare?" Jumper asked. "I am Jumper and this is my friend Wenda. Your brother Bruce said you might be able to help us look for some equipment."

"Perhaps," Clare agreed. "Do you know anyone who knows where your equipment is?"

"No."

"Then I can't help. My talent is to tap into the memory of any creature, and then relive that memory. I can share that experience with another, just as Bruce can share his seethrough talent. Stop looking at my bra."

Jumper looked away, embarrassed. "I apologize."

She laughed. "Don't bother. Every man does, when he borrows that talent. He can't help himself. I was just letting you know I know."

"Yes," Jumper agreed weakly. "I think we should move on."

"So what do you think of it?"

Jumper hesitated. "Of what?"

"My bra, of course."

"It is spectacular."

She smiled. "Correct answer. So I'll tell you something. Beware of my sister Dele. She can change a person's age."

"You mean, make a person older?"

"Or younger. She may or may not elect to change that person back. So try not to annoy her."

"I will certainly try not to," Jumper agreed, shaken.

They walked on along the path. "I dew knot like these people," Wenda said. "There is something odd about them."

She was evidently more observant than he. "How so?"

"There is something false. I dew knot know exactly what, but they are knot exactly what they appear."

That made him nervous. "Should we break this off and seek elsewhere?"

"No. The cable might bee here. But we must bee careful."

"Agreed," he said, unsettled.

Dele was a fairly pretty young woman in a nice pink bra (he just couldn't help looking) sewing a blanket. "Hello, strangers," she called as they approached.

"You must be Dele," Jumper said. "Clare said you could change a person's age."

"Yes. Is there some age you would prefer to be?"

"We are satisfied as we are," Jumper said quickly. Now he was aware of the subtle wrongness about her. Wenda was right.

"Too bad. What brings you here?"

"We are looking for some equipment."

"You haven't seen enough?" she asked, inhaling.

Obviously she knew. "Apology," he said. "I'm not used to . . . I can't seem to help—"

Dele laughed. "Which is why Bruce lent you the talent. It is his idea of a joke. Clare and I are used to it."

"Thank you," he said uncomfortably.

"Can you describe this equipment?"

That was awkward. How could they keep it secret?

He concluded that they couldn't. They had been warned to beware of children, but these were adults, so maybe it was all right. "We are looking for a section of cable. We need it for a repair."

"Did you talk to Ande?"

"Yes. We promised him not to take your treasure."

"Then talk to Enze."

"Who?"

"Our fifth sibling, who guards our treasure."

"But that's not what we want."

"We'll see. Do you know the consequence of breaking a promise?"

"We're not going to break a promise," Jumper said.

"Enze can change a person's gender."

"We dew knot want to change," Wenda said.

"That's the least you will suffer if you break a promise to Ande. That's his talent: virtually unbreakable promises."

Another person appeared. Jumper wasn't sure whether this was male or female, and his view through the clothing didn't seem to help. So he thought of male, for want of certainty.

"Enze, show them our treasure," Dele said.

"This way." He led them to a house, and into it, to a curtained room. There was a single large chest. He lifted its lid.

Inside was a length of intricately wound metallic cable. Both its ends were torn and twisted, as if it had been ripped from a longer section. It must have been a considerable impact, because the cable was about a foot and a half thick.

"That's it!" Jumper exclaimed. "That's the section of the broken cable we need to repair the original cable."

"That is our treasure," Enzi said.

And they had promised not to take it.

Wenda was quicker on the uptake than Jumper. "Can we make a deal for it?"

"There is only one deal we want," Enze said. "To return to our youth."

"But you're not old," Jumper said.

Now the others appeared. "We are all children," Ande said. "But we were curious about the adult state, so Dele changed us all to young adults. It was a disappointment. Then we discovered that we couldn't change back."

"How did yew get the cable?" Wenda asked.

"We found it lying in the forest where it had landed. It has an aura of power about it, so we decided to keep it and trade it for our lost youth."

"We can't give you that," Jumper said regretfully. He thought of Olive and her imaginary friends, but suspected that none could duplicate the age-changing talent. Because this was supposed to be a difficult obstacle, and such a friend would make it too easy.

"Then go your way," Clare said.

What could they do? They left the house and cable. They couldn't take it, and couldn't trade for it.

"Does this mean we can knot complete our mission?" Wenda asked disconsolately as they returned to their base camp.

"I am afraid it does," Jumper said. "That has to be the missing section. Without it, we can't repair the main cable."

"The others will knot bee pleased."

He was sure she was right. "I am not pleased either. But I can't break my word. I don't care what horrendous penalties there may be; I wouldn't break it anyway."

"Beecause you're a good person," she said tearfully.

"I almost wish I weren't."

"I wood knot break it either."

He truly appreciated her support. "Wenda, I love you."

"I love yew," she repeated. "Dew yew want to take me?"

"No. I want you to be happy with your prince. But I want always to be your friend."

She was happy to accept that. "Then kiss me, and we will tell the others the bad news."

He kissed her, and she was wonderfully soft and sweet. But as his hands pressed against her back, he paused, startled. The back of her shirt was loose, covering nothing. "Wenda! Your back is gone!"

She felt behind her with her own hands. "Oh, no! I have reverted. Because it was only for the mission, and the mission has failed."

"I'm so sorry," he said.

"We will all be sorry," she said tearfully. "We will all lose what we borrowed."

They disengaged and trudged sorrowfully back toward the camp. Jumper realized that probably they would not have to tell the others; they would already know, because of the effects on them.

All because he refused to break his word. He was ashamed.

14
DESPAIR

They gathered at the camp. A cloud of gloom formed around them, blotting out the surroundings.

"I don't see what else you could have done," Olive said. "You made a promise. You were perhaps foolish not to verify its implication before making it, but any of us could have been caught similarly."

"Especially if Pluto set it up as a trap," Phanta said. "If Jumper hadn't made the promise, they might have hidden the cable, and if he had found it anyway, he still might not have wanted to take their treasure away from them. He's softhearted."

"That's one thing we like about him," Maeve said. "Some of us are with him because of it."

Dawn glanced across at Eve. "How are you feeling, sis?"

Eve grimaced. "About the way any princess would feel at the prospect of becoming the plaything of a rogue Dwarf Demon."

"Maybee he will marry yew anyway," Wenda said.

"Not if not compelled." Eve took a deep breath. "I gambled, I made a deal, I lost. I will pay the penalty."

"Well, let's pack up for the journey back to report to the Good Magician," Jumper said.

"No," Dawn said. "Let's stay here this afternoon and have a wild party, pretending we're happy. Tomorrow we can forge through the gloom."

They liked that idea. "There is a beerbarrel tree knot far away," Wenda said. "We can get disgustingly drunk."

"And gorge on sinfully fattening pies," Maeve said.

"And do things with Jumper that will embarrass him no end," Eve said darkly.

"A real orgy," Dawn agreed, brightening.

Jumper thought of protesting, but concluded that considering the circumstances, he would be satisfied to let them do those things. It might help take his mind off his failure.

They scattered and collected the makings of their party: a keg of ale rejected by a beerbarrel tree, super-sweet pies, several rich cheesecakes, and a crateful of bottles of tsoda pop. In the course of their scavenging they also collected a girl. Not an ordinary girl; her head, shoulders, arms, and torso seemed to float above her hips and legs, which were hardly more than bones.

She was Anne Orexic, impossibly thin, so it seemed appropriate to have her join the orgy, in the hope that she would gain some weight. In fact she hardly seemed to be together.

"How did yew get so thin?" Wenda asked. "Yew are even thinner than I am, in yewr fashion. Is yewr talent losing weight?"

"No, my talent is the four-letter word. I swam in Bare Lake so often I waisted away to almost nothing," Anne said, gobbling down a frothy scream pie. "So I lost my waist, and now my parts aren't really connected. I became a caution to other girls who wanted to skinny dip too much."

"Have some more pie," Wenda said, proffering a muscular piece of beefcake.

"What kind of four-letter words?" Haughty asked.

"They are commands. When I speak a four-letter word in a certain way, it happens. Such as 'Burn.'" She looked at the pile of sticks Jumper and Olive were making for a bonfire. "Burn," she repeated with emphasis.

Suddenly the pile was burning. Jumper stepped back, impressed. "Can you speak any others?" he asked.

"Sure. Boom."

"I DIDN'T HEAR ANYTHING," Jumper said. And paused, for his voice was booming.

The girls laughed—and their laughter boomed across the landscape and into the welkin. This was fun.

"OOPS," Maeve boomed. "WE FORGOT WATER. WE CAN'T CLEAN UP BEFORE WE EAT."

"WASH," Anne said. And water was flowing, forming a small stream beside their camp, washing on down into a nearby gully.

"Hey!" someone protested. It was not one of their group, because the voice didn't boom.

Jumper investigated. There in the gully was a small pool rapidly becoming a larger one, because of the stream of water. In it was a mermaid. She was of course bare, with a fish tail. The river was falling on her head, mussing her hair.

"We're sorry," he said. "We didn't know anyone was here when we conjured the water. I am Jumper."

"Oh, it's all right, I suppose," the mermaid said. "It just caught me by surprise. I am Oceana Rain Fields, the nymph of this pond." She moved out of the falling water and started brushing out her hair.

"Some of us want to wash up," Jumper said. "Do you mind if we use your pond?"

"Welcome," Oceana said. "I maintain it as a public service."

"Well, now," Phanta said, managing to get her voice down toward normal. "I was feeling grubby, so now I'll wash." She removed her clothing and started splashing in the water.

In half a moment the other girls were joining her. Jumper watched, bemused. They were lovely, sprightly, and sexy.

"Yew too," Wenda said, also managing not to boom. She came out to haul him into the throng. He had to get out of his clothes in a hurry to avoid getting them soaked. In another half moment the girls were happily scrubbing his back and other parts of him, heedless of any reaction he might have.

"You seem like such a happy group," Oceana said.

A glance ricocheted around before landing on Jumper. "We have our moments," he said carefully before getting dunked again.

In the midst of this melee, something approached. "OH, NO!" Maeve cried. "THE STORK!" Then she closed her mouth, embarrassed by more than the booming or her nakedness.

Before anyone else could act, the stork landed before Maeve. "Here is your bundle of joy," it said. "About time too." It turned, taxied, spread its wings, and took off.

They gazed at the bundle, not knowing what to do. The stork had struck the moment the way was clear, when none of them were on guard, and Maeve was stuck. She was a mother.

She looked around helplessly. Then she visibly nerved herself and reached into the basket. She picked up the baby. "She's a girl," she announced. "I will call her Mae. But I don't know what I'll ever do with her. I'm not cut out to be a mother."

Mae looked at her and cooed.

Maeve melted visibly. "She's so cute!"

The others exchanged some glances as they got out of the water and dried off, bidding farewell to the mermaid. The maenad was coming to terms with her situation.

Another figure appeared. It was a man. In fact it was Warren Warrior. "I have found you at last!" he exclaimed. "My fierce warrior woman!"

Maeve froze in place, naked, vulnerable, holding the baby, sheer horror spreading across her features.

"How did you find us?" Haughty demanded.

"We got wind of the Prophecy, so headed for the Ogre Fen and asked around," Warren said.

"We?" Olive asked.

"After that big dance, we men knew the score, so we left our day jobs and organized. We all have something on the line."

Maeve remained petrified.

"Uh," Jumper said. "There is something you should know, Warren. Her—our circumstance has changed. Maeve is no longer alone."

"Who took her?" Warren cried, grasping his sword. "I'll slay him forthwith!"

Wordlessly Maeve held up the baby.

Warren's mouth fell open. It seemed he had not picked up on that detail before. Then he poked a finger at Mae. She snapped at it, her little pointed teeth drawing blood before he tore it away.

"She bit me!" he exclaimed, staring at the wound. "She's a bloodthirsty little tyke."

Maeve winced, a tear trailing down her cheek. She was not about to give up her baby now, but what would it cost her?

"So you may not want to—" Jumper started.

"Fit to be a warrior's daughter," Warren said. "Come here, you beautiful little b**ch!" He picked Mae up and squeezed her to him. She gurgled and spit up on his shoulder. "See? She likes me too." He looked at Maeve. "How fast can we get married?"

Maeve came out of her stasis. "Soon," she said. "Am I dreaming?"

"Not anymore," Jumper said. "You've got a family."

"So receiving yew babee is knot so bad after all," Wenda said.

"Not so bad," Maeve echoed, looking awed.

"We wish you the best," Dawn said. "At least you have some joy of the occasion."

"I do," Maeve agreed. "I suppose there is no reason for us to stay here."

"No reason," Jumper agreed.

A woman appeared. "Will you be needing my service?" she asked Maeve.

Maeve looked at her perplexed. "Who are you?"

"I am Liz. I offer a diaper service. I bring piles of fresh clean diapers from a diaper tree, and return the soiled ones to the tree. Babies are nice, but they do soil diapers at a great rate. The trees love them; they feed on that soil. I know where all the diaper trees are, and can reach the nearest one quickly."

"We'll take it," Warren said, ineffectively wiping the spit-up from his shoulder.

Maeve nodded. The deal was made.

"I'll be right back with them," Liz said as she hurried away.

Maeve dressed, and she and Warren walked away with Mae.

"Well, we still have enough to party," Haughty said. Most of them were dressed now and having at the goodies. The girls were becoming more sociable as they swigged ale.

Another figure appeared. It was Prince Charming.

"Oh, I dew knot know what to dew," Wenda cried, suddenly appalled.

"There you are," Charming said. "Come here, you darling creature."

"But . . . but I'm only half here!" she wailed.

He swept her into his embrace and kissed her. "There's plenty left."

"But I'm hollow!"

Charming held her at arm's length and spoke carefully. "I was just dumped by a woman who was physically whole and luscious, but only half there in spirit. You are the opposite. I prefer your way."

She gazed at him, amazed. "Yew really dew knot mind?"

"Sure, I would prefer to have your backside too. But you're a wood-wife. It's you I love, not your back. We'll just have to get you some stuffing for appearances. Now can I get you alone, or must we marry first?"

Wenda looked halfway helplessly at Jumper. "Go with him," Jumper said. "You'll be a whole princess."

Charming hauled Wenda away. She went with only token reluctance.

Phanta wiped away a tear. "I get so sentimental when true love conquers," she said.

Now another man appeared. It was Dick Philip, the crazy writer. "Olive!" he exclaimed, advancing to kiss her passionately.

"But my imaginary friends won't endure beyond my attention span," she said.

"That's long enough. Now focus your attention on me. I'm going to write a fabulous weird story with you as the heroine."

They departed as he expounded on the story. But it was clear that he had more than a story on his mind.

"Well, we still have five of us for the party," Phanta said. She glanced at Anne. "I mean six."

Another man appeared. "Make that four," Shepherd said. "You're in my corral now." He kissed her. "The sheep are waiting."

"Sorry," Phanta said to the others as they departed. "Mustn't keep the sheep waiting."

But then a dark shadow fell on them, really a black blob, and it clung to Phanta. She couldn't help becoming a ghost, because the Good Magician's spell had dissipated.

"It's a darkness bomb," Eve said. "Clinging to her so she can't revert to her living state."

"Gheorge Ghost must have arranged it," Haughty said. "To trap her. She's helpless."

"We must help her!" Jumper said, bounding toward the blob.

"I don't think we can," Eve said.

Indeed, Jumper simply got lost in the darkness, and was unable to interact with the ghosts.

"The sheep will take care of it," Shepherd said, not seeming worried. "I came prepared."

"But she can't revert to her living state until she gets out of the darkness," Jumper said. "And Gheorge will never let her out."

"Watch. Listen."

"I can't see inside that blob, and I can't hear ghosts."

"Maybe I can help," Anne called. "Read!"

Something changed in the blob. It became translucent, so that figures could be seen within it. One was Phanta in ghost form. Another was a large menacing ghost: Gheorge. He was laying hands on her.

Printed words appeared. NOW I'VE GOT YOU, MY LUSCIOUS MORTAL CREATURE!

It was what Gheorge was saying, rendered into readable print. That was some talent Anne had!

The Phanta ghost tried to pull away. NO NO! I DON'T WANT TO BE WITH YOU! PLEASE LET ME GO!

But he held firm. NEVER, YOU SUCCULENT MORSEL. I WILL HAVE MY WILL OF YOU REPEATEDLY. THEN I WILL LOCK YOU UP IN DARKNESS AND SAVE YOU FOR MY NEXT FLING. HA HA HA HA!!

"He even managed two exclamation points," Haughty said, disgusted. "The unspeakable t**d."

"Watch," Shepherd repeated. "I did some research on ghosts, and made a deal. The sheep are coming."

Meanwhile Gheorge was hauling Phanta in for a smooch. EEEEK NO! she screamed. I WILL NEVER— But her protest was cut off by his fierce kiss.

RUMBLE. It was a sound signaled by the print. RUMBLE. It was growing in volume.

"What's that?" Jumper asked.

"The sheep," Shepherd said. "Thousands of ghost sheep I slaughtered, but they have forgiven me. I'm leading them to the Great Pasture in the sky where they can graze happily for eternity. But until they get there, we are together."

"But what can sheep do?" Dawn asked. "They're peaceful creatures, and Gheorge is a vicious ghost."

"The ewes are peaceful," Shepherd agreed. "Not so the rams."

Now the rumbling became a POUNDING as the herd of ghost sheep charged into view, led by an ornery looking ram.

"Gheorge," Shepherd said conversationally, "meet Ram Bunctious, the leader of the ghost flock."

WHAT THE BLEEP DO I CARE ABOUT A D*MN SHEEP? Gheorge demanded contemptuously.

BAM! George sailed into the air as the ram's butt caught his butt.

I WILL RAM MY HORN INTO EWE SO FAR IT WILL SPLIT YOUR GIZZARD! Bunctious bleated as he charged again.

I AM NOT A EWE, George protested as he stepped aside barely in time.

EWE WILL BE WHEN I'M THROUGH WITH EWE, Bunctious bleated as he spun about for another charge. His stout left horn oriented on Gheorge's midsection with disturbing accuracy.

Gheorge tried to run, but the ewes had formed a circle around them and wouldn't let him through.

Jumper began to catch on. "A ghost can't escape ghost sheep."

"Right," Shepherd agreed, satisfied.

Gheorge had had enough. He sailed up into the air, fleeing the flock.

Bunctious sailed right up after him. EWE CAN'T GET AWAY THAT WAY, EWE MISERABLE EXCUSE FOR A MAN. I WILL HAVE EWER DONKEY FOR A TROPHY, EWE SILLY BURRO.

The two disappeared into the sky, the ram in hot pursuit of the man. There was the titter of a stifled giggle among the remaining girls.

"I see what ewe mean, uh, what you mean," Jumper said, impressed. "Gheorge won't be bothering Phanta anymore."

The ghost Phanta emerged from the blob and became live Phanta. "Oh, Shep, that was beautiful!" she exclaimed, flinging her arms about him. "Your sheep saved me from a fate worse than death." She was speaking literally.

"You're part of the flock now," Shepherd said. "Of course the ghost ewes will expect some heavy petting. We still have a way to go before we reach the Pasture in the Sky."

"We'll get there," she said.

They moved on, surrounded by the ghost flock.

Jumper and the girls settled back into their party. But they were interrupted by another visitor.

"Charon!" Haughty said.

"I am not bound by the outcome of the Demon challenge," Charon said, assuming male harpy form. "You impressed me at the ball, and I want to see more of you. Will you come with me?"

"What do you offer?"

"A perch on my raft as I pole it across the River Styx with loads of souls going to Hades. A lot of smooching between shifts."

Haughty considered a fraction of a moment. "You know when night comes, I become Hottie. I can't help it."

"Two for the price of one. I am eager to associate with both of you."

Haughty looked at Jumper. "It seems like a fair offer to me," Jumper said. "If you like being at the fringe of Hades."

"Oh, I do," Haughty agreed. "It's a harpy's dream. Damned souls are fascinating."

"Then go. You too deserve happiness."

"Thank you." Then, to Charon. "Lead the way, O foul bird! We're going to H**l together."

They spread their wings and flew away.

"And now we are three," Dawn said. "Since the mission is lost anyway, I have another errand I would like to accomplish."

"Errand?" Jumper asked.

"To find a mortal prince for Eris."

"But that was only if we completed the mission."

"But I think it is not forbidden if we don't. Eris is deserving; I want to help her if I can."

"So do I," Jumper agreed.

She gazed at him, surprised. "Jumper! You've got a thing for her!"

He had to confess it. "Foolish, I know. But when she danced with me, spider style, I felt she really understood me. I know I'm destined to be Sharon's plaything, but if I had any choice in the matter, I'd be Eris's plaything instead."

"Then maybe you don't want me to find her a prince."

"No, do find her a prince, if you can do it without making your ultimate sacrifice. I couldn't help her anyway, and I want her to be happy. At least some good might come of this failure."

"You have a generous nature. So be it." Dawn nodded to her sister, and walked away.

"Ultimate sacrifice?" Eve asked.

"Dawn's ready to convert to male and be a prince, if that's the only way."

Eve was amazed. "I never suspected! My sister has more gumption than I thought."

Anne was finishing the last of the pies. "I don't know anything about it, but you folk seem to have had an interesting history," she said. "Thank you for the food. I think it is helping get me back into shape."

She was right: her upper and lower sections were now connected by a thin but feasible section of torso. It would take a lot more eating to restore her completely, but it was progress.

"We have indeed had an interesting mission," Eve agreed, "which is now winding down. Our party was not to celebrate so much as to have one last fling before we faced the fact of defeat."

"I'm sorry," Anne said. "I had better be moving on." She walked away.

"Now it's just the two of us," Eve said to Jumper. "Somehow neither the party nor the good fortune of the others managed to cheer me much."

"That's understandable," Jumper said. "You face an awful future."

"And you face failure to return to your natural sphere."

"Actually, this sphere has been more interesting than mine was. My time with the girls, and with Sharon, and with Eris . . ." He shrugged. "I would have been sorry to miss that."

"Something is bothering me," she said. "But I can't quite put my finger on it."

A dim light flashed over his head. "If the mission has failed, why hasn't Demon Pluto claimed you?"

"That's it," she agreed. "I know he is eager to despoil me."

"Yet you want to marry him?"

"It is heaven and hell," she said seriously. "He has wonderful qualities and awful qualities. If I marry him, the wonderful qualities will prevail and I will be a happy woman. But if he takes me without marriage, he won't get half my soul, his bad qualities will prevail, and I will be miserable."

"I take the point. It is somewhat the way I felt about Sharon."

"You really liked her. How is it that you suddenly got smitten with Eris?"

"I never could afford to trust Sharon. She fascinates me, but I don't know what side she's really on. I'm sure with Eris: she wants to marry a prince and escape confinement. That's understandable. So I think I can trust her, even though I know she is a Demon and I am purely incidental to her designs."

"And she danced with you in spider form."

"Yes. I really liked that. She seemed to understand me."

"The girls understood you."

"Yes, and I like all of them. Phanta seduced me, but any of them could have done so in similar circumstances. So I suppose I'm pretty fickle. I'm really not used to such human interactions."

"It is the nature of any human man to desire any attractive human woman he encounters," she said. "We all know that, and Dawn and I played on it, flashing you."

"Yes. But why? I was committed to the mission throughout; you didn't need to strengthen that."

"We thought we did, so that Sharon could not corrupt you away from it. We may have misjudged you."

"I don't know. I wish I knew why that cable is so important. I know Pluto doesn't want it restored, but why should the Good Magician care about it? Why should he assign two Sorceresses to help repair it?"

"It *is* important," she agreed. "But I don't know why. Now you have aroused my female curiosity. Why don't we complete our trek to it, so I can touch it, and learn all about it? Then at least we'll know."

"Done," he agreed. "But how can we find it?"

"I can find it," she said confidently. She touched a nearby stone. "Part of this stone's orientation is with respect to the rest of the terrain, and part of that terrain is the place where the cable reaches Xanth. This way." She set off on her bicycle.

He paced her on his. "It does seem slightly ridiculous, considering that we can't fix it anyway. But I really would like to know."

"Just as I would like to know why Pluto hasn't claimed me. That suggests that the mission has not yet officially failed. That maybe there is still a chance."

"If we can just figure it out," he agreed. "Maybe when you touch the cable, you will learn how it can be fixed without our full group. Because I thought that was the definition of our failure: if any one member was lost, the mission was forfeit."

"Apparently not." She paused, glancing at him. "Maybe it is you, Jumper. You are the one who can't be corrupted away from it. All the rest of us were just along to keep you on track."

He shook his head. "I don't see how I could be that important."

"These things aren't necessarily determined by personal importance. You are the one equipped to splice the cable back together. That makes you transcendentally important to this particular mission."

"Maybe so," he agreed dubiously.

"We can't reach the cable today. We'll have to spend another night on the road."

"There doesn't seem to be a time limit. I don't mind traveling with you."

"And you find me, also, attractive."

"I didn't mean that!"

"Unattractive?"

"No! I mean—"

She smiled. "Be at ease, Jumper. I'm teasing you. Do you think my panties would have made you react if I were unattractive to you?"

"No," he agreed, embarrassed.

"Let's make a night of it."

"That isn't called for."

"Let's face it, Jumper. I anticipate an eternity of being a Demon's plaything. I might as well have a session with someone I truly like and respect, before descending into that hell."

"Oh." What else could he say? "All right."

Then Sharon appeared. "So you're making out with her, you wretch! Why do I bother with you?"

Jumper was taken aback only half a moment. "Look who's talking! You're a Demoness, with no scruples. You've been playing me along so that I will do your will, whatever it is." He glared at her. "You can tell me now: what *is* your will?"

"I told you: I am mad at Pluto, so I want your mission to succeed."

"So you will have to marry me and become decent? That doesn't make sense to me."

"I am so mad at him that I am prepared to make even that sacrifice."

"If you really feel that way," Eve said evenly, "why don't you marry Jumper now? That will satisfy us that you truly are committed to our cause."

"You're impossible," Sharon huffed, and vanished.

"I really can't trust her," Jumper said. "But she does tempt me."

"Perhaps I can alleviate that. Kiss me."

"No, you don't!" Sharon said, reappearing.

Could Sharon actually be jealous of Eve? Or was she merely trying to wean him away from whatever remaining commitment to the mission he had? That suggested again that the mission was not yet completely lost, and that Eve's commitment bolstered his to make it possible. Yet he was unable to see how.

"I am curious," Eve said to Sharon. "If you are jealous of Pluto's interest in me, why are you trying to break up whatever interest Jumper has in me? If I have a night with Jumper, wouldn't that decrease my value to Pluto, and perhaps make it more likely that he would marry you after all?"

"You're impossible too," Sharon said, and vanished again.

"Something is operating here that we don't properly understand," Jumper said. "Now we can't be sure which of us she is trying to mess up. If she wants me, then she doesn't want me with you. If she wants Pluto, then she should want you with me."

"Which suggests that she wants you, not Pluto," she agreed. "Or that this is what she is trying to make us believe."

"So we still can't trust her," he said.

They came to a pathside campsite. They foraged for supper, then stripped and washed in the small lake. He had half forgotten how stunningly lovely Eve was, and seeing her bare again made him react.

"We could do it right here in the water," she murmured.

He was mightily tempted, but something stopped him. "No, with regret."

"Because of Sharon?" she asked.

"Because of Eris."

"Ah. I suspect you were ready to love Eris because she had the Demon qualities that attracted you to Sharon, and is more trustworthy."

"That may be it," he agreed. "I wish . . ." But he couldn't finish, knowing that Eris would have no such interest in him.

"We share a situation," she said. "We each want the Good Demon, and don't want the Bad Demon. Even though in my case the two overlap and your case seems hopeless."

"Yes."

"Yet it seems it is not yet finished, hopeless as it appears. There may be something we have overlooked. Maybe I'll discover it when I touch the broken cable."

"Maybe," he agreed.

They waded out of the water and dried, then went into the shelter for the night. Eve lay beside him, as lovely in repose as in activity. He regretted his decision to pass up her offer.

She opened an eye. "You sure?"

"No."

She laughed. "Let's compromise with a kiss."

"Yes."

They kissed, chastely, and she was wonderfully appealing.

"It's a good thing I'm not my sister. I would know what you are thinking."

"You know it anyway," he said.

"We are teasing each other without meaning to," she said. "So let's conclude this appropriately."

"I don't understand."

"The bleep you don't." She wrapped her arms about him, half rolled to be on top of him, pressed evocatively close, and kissed him again. This time there was nothing chaste about it. "Stop me when you've had enough."

He was silent.

There followed a sequence much like the one with Phanta, only more so. Eve clearly knew what she was doing, and had no regrets. "Thank you!" he gasped as it concluded.

"And I hope this spoils you for Sharon, and me for Pluto," she said, satisfied. "If we lose, they lose too."

"That's spiteful."

"Do you disagree?"

"No."

She laughed, kissed him again, then got up to clean up again. When she returned she asked, "Was it only for spite?"

"No."

"Agreed. *Now* we can sleep."

They did. But this time they held hands.

In the morning Jumper was pensive. "Are you sorry?" Eve asked.

"About last night? No. About today, yes. I fear we are about to confirm our failure."

"Which was one reason for last night."

"There were other reasons?"

"I really do like you, Jumper, as do all the girls. You are a genuinely decent person. None of us have any romantic future with you, but last night was friendship intensified. No one else needs to know, other than the Demons. I don't believe Eris would mind; she would understand. Accept it for what it was, and remember."

"I do. I will." It was all he could say, being overwhelmed by appreciation.

They set out on the bicycles, following the path to the cable. At one point there was another crack in the ground severing the path. But this time no harpy was along to carry across Jumper's silk cord.

"That's farther than I can jump," he said. "We'll have to climb down through it. I can make a web ladder. Or if a wind comes up, I can extend a kite thread and float us across."

"There's no wind. But I wonder . . . how far can you jump?"

"In my natural form, pretty far. That's my specialty. But there are limits."

"Try a practice jump."

"Very well." Jumper changed to spider form and jumped alongside the crevice.

And was amazed as he sailed high and far. "That's farther than I ever jumped before."

"I felt a certain vigor in my step," Eve said. "We seem to be gaining strength. I don't know why; I can't touch strength and know about it the way I can an object."

"This makes the difference. Now I know I can hurdle that crack. I will carry a line across, and come back for you and the bikes."

"I will need another cocoon."

He had forgotten her fear of heights. "Gladly." He spun one, she entered, and he sealed her in. Then he jumped across, toting a line, tacked it to a tree, returned, and carried Eve across. He let her out.

She kissed him. "At times like this, I really need to be with someone I can trust," she said shakily, kissing him on his mandibles.

"Welcome." He fetched the bicycles across, took up his line, and changed back to manform.

"Maybe the air here is invigorating, so we have more energy."

"Maybe," he agreed. He did feel light on his feet.

They continued on along the path. Around noon they reached the Xanth border. And paused, impressed.

For the forest and fields of Xanth abruptly quit. It was not a gulf or crevice; it was simply the end of it. Jumper was speechless.

"Xanth is its own world now," Eve said. "It happened two years ago, when a party of folk traveled the entire circuit of Ida's moons and corrected a glitch, separating Xanth from Mundania. So there is nowhere to go beyond Xanth."

"But we haven't found the broken cable!"

"We will." She glanced right and left. "That way," she said, pointing right.

They rode along the edge, beside the nothingness that was beyond the edge of the planet. Jumper hoped they wouldn't accidentally fall off. He had not thought about the shape of Xanth before, and never realized that it was essentially flat. A flat peninsula.

"No water?" he asked. "I thought there was sea beyond Xanth."

"There is around most of it. But the water has not yet filled in around the northern border, which once connected to the interface with Mundania. The sea will surely get here when it is ready."

"Oh." There didn't seem to be much else to say.

They came to a giant tree that spread half its foliage out beyond the edge. Its general outline was like a huge conical hat.

"Coven Tree," Eve explained. "Mundane witches used to meet here, absorbing some of the magic of Xanth. Now of course it is out of their reach."

"But how can they be witches without magic?"

"They have to fake it. Probably no one believes that they used to have real magic."

"That's too bad," Jumper said sympathetically.

They rode on. Soon they encountered a boy and girl arguing. "Mine is better," the boy said.

"No, mine is," the girl retorted.

Then the two spied Jumper and Eve. "Hey, you decide," the boy said. "My talent is conjuring things into bottles. My twin sister's talent is conjuring them out again. Which is better?"

Jumper exchanged a glance with Eve. He was learning the art of this, and she had a beautiful eye, so it was pleasant.

"Let's see a bottle," Jumper said as the two of them stopped their bicycles and got off.

The boy brought out a bottle. Inside it was a miniature woman screaming to get out. "You put living folk in?" Eve asked, concerned.

"Well, she annoyed me," the boy said defensively.

"Take her out," Eve said sternly to the girl.

The woman disappeared from the bottle and appeared full size outside it. "That impertinent rascal!" she exclaimed.

"They are arguing which talent is better," Jumper said. "Conjuring things in, or out. What do you say?"

"Out!" the woman said.

"There you are," Jumper said to the boy.

"Oh, yeah?" he said rebelliously. "So how's about I conjure you all into the bottle?"

Oops. Jumper grabbed the bottle and tossed it over the edge, into the void beyond Xanth. "You have the decision. Do not conjure any more people into bottles."

"Or what?" the boy demanded.

"Or I will use my talent," the woman said.

"Yeah? What's that?"

"I can make myself sick."

"So what?"

The woman's face turned greenish. "I'll vomit all over you." She heaved.

"Okay, okay!" the boy cried. "No more people."

Jumper and Eve walked on with the woman. "You bluffed him out," Eve said.

"Just as well," the woman said. "I could have made myself ill with a deadly contagious disease that would have taken him out. But then it might have spread."

"Just as well," Jumper agreed, relieved.

"Thank you for saving me from that bottle," the woman said to Eve.

"You're welcome," Eve said.

They mounted their bikes again and rode on, leaving the woman behind. "Why don't the people here seem to care about the edge of Xanth?" Jumper asked.

"They're used to it. They take it for granted."

"I don't think I could ever do that."

"Well, you're not human," she said. "I think that's part of what makes you so appealing."

"Thank you." He wasn't sure whether she was joking.

Finally they came to the cable.

The thick mass of wires descended from the sky beyond the edge of Xanth, and plunged into the ground, going where only it and perhaps Com Pewter knew. Up near a cloud it was torn, with a segment ripped out. The segment that had fallen into the possession of the talented children, who would not give it up.

Eve stepped up and touched it with one finger. "Oh, my," she breathed, clearly awed.

"Yes?"

"Now I know its purpose, and why it is so important that it be fixed."

He waited a full moment, knowing that the explanation would be impressive.

"It is a conduit," she said, "for an exchange with Mundania, which is now separated from Xanth by a virtually impassible gulf. A trading deal that both worlds need."

He waited another moment.

"We send Mundania magic for special effects," she continued, "such as rainbows, that can be seen only from one side. Perspective, in which distant things hurry to keep up with near things despite looking smaller. The way Earth's moon grows larger on romantic fall evenings. And of course the randomness that accounts for free will. Mundanians will really miss these things."

"But what is Mundania sending us?"

"Gravity."

"I don't understand."

"The magic of Demon Earth is Gravity. It holds all things to the surface of the planet so they don't float away and get lost. Without it, Mundanians would also float away. They wouldn't much like that."

"Of course. But what has that to do with us?"

"It is not our magic, so we import it from Mundania. It keeps our things, and us, from floating away. Now it is surely fading."

"The jumping!" he exclaimed. "That's why we're lighter. Less gravity."

"That would be it," she agreed. "Xanth really needs it."

"No wonder the Good Magician didn't tell us why the mission was so urgent. Xanth would panic if news leaked out."

"And we well might have let it slip," she agreed somberly.

"And if we don't repair the cable, gravity will fade entirely, and we'll all be lost," he said. "Now at last I understand why this mission was important enough to warrant two Sorceresses."

"As do I," she agreed. "Yet we seem to have failed. Pluto must just be waiting for us to admit it. Then by the terms of the Demon deal, he can pounce on me."

"And Sharon can pounce on me," he agreed.

"And we can't fix it," she said, stepping into his consoling embrace. This time it was nothing but mutual commiseration. "Oh, Jumper, is this the end?"

"It can't be," he said. But he feared it was.

15
SPLICE

Yet though failure stares us in the face, they have not pounced," Eve said. "What factor are we missing?"

"There must be a way to fix it, if only we can figure it out," Jumper said.

She touched the cable again. "There is some slack, because it curves while wending its way between realms. Enough to pull the ends together, despite the missing section, if we just had the strength to do it."

"I am strong, but not that strong," he said. "We would need considerable help."

"The other members of the mission," she said. "Maybe that's why all of them are needed. To pull it tight so you can splice it."

"They are girls, no offense. Are they strong enough?"

"No. It would take twice as much strength as they have. Maybe more."

"So there must be something else."

"Something else," she agreed. "But what?"

Jumper brought out the Prophecy. "Let no maiden fair, Yield to despair," he read. "It will be nice, If you can splice."

"It certainly will be," Eve agreed. "But the Prophecy didn't know that we wouldn't get that missing section of cable from the children."

"It didn't actually say we had to have it," Jumper said. "Just that we'd find it when, in the Ogre Fen. We did find it when we were there. We didn't get it, but the mission doesn't seem to have ended yet."

"We found it when we were in the Ogre Fen," she agreed. "But I'm afraid the maidens fair did yield to despair."

"Actually they all found happiness. But they wouldn't have left if they hadn't believed it was over."

"I just got a weird thought. We had to pass three bad obstacles. One was the challenge of getting the cable, after you promised not to take their treasure. Maybe the real test was of honor. We might have stolen their cable section, but none of us questioned the need to keep our promise. So maybe we passed that after all. Could another have been the belief that we had lost? So that we would give up when maybe we didn't need to?"

"That could be!" he agreed, surprised. "Demon bets can be devious, as we know. And the third is to splice the cable back together, if we can."

Two people approached. "How are yew?" one called.

"Wenda!" Jumper and Eve said together.

"I just could knot let yew go on alone," Wenda said as she came up. "So we came to help, if we can."

"Prince Charming too?" Jumper asked.

"I haven't done anything useful in a decade," Charming said. "Now Wenda has motivated me. How can I help?"

"Well, we will need to pull the two sections of the cable together," Jumper said, pointing to the gap. "If we can get enough people, maybe we can do it."

"Yew have the two of us," Wenda said.

Two more people appeared, one carrying a baby. "Halloo!" the woman called, her sharp teeth glinting in the sunlight.

"Maeve!" Eve said.

"I remembered that line in the Prophecy, about the maiden fair yielding to despair," Maeve said. "I refuse to be the one."

"Warren too?" Jumper asked.

"This is a kind of battle," Warren said. "Fit business for a warrior."

Eve caught Jumper's eye. "If this continues . . ."

"We might have enough people," Jumper agreed. "The girls are not yielding to despair."

Soon two more arrived: Olive Hue and Dick Philip. "We had this crazy notion that maybe it wasn't over," she said. "So we came to check."

And Phanta with Shepherd. "I had this ghost of a thought that maybe you could use some help."

A harpy flew in. It was Haughty. "Charon can't come; he has to stay out of it. But I told him I had to help my friends, and would return to him later. He couldn't stop me."

Finally Dawn reappeared. "Did you find a prince?" Eve asked.

"Not exactly. But I got a great idea."

"Oh?"

"I can't say what it is yet. But it will be perfect if it works out. Meanwhile I'm here to help."

Jumper looked at Eve. "Now we are twelve. Is that enough?"

"Just barely," she said. "We can haul the cable together, but there are a couple of caveats. I'm not sure what they are, but they need to be dealt with."

"Then let's get started," Jumper said. "We'll deal with them as they occur." He glanced at Olive. "It would help if you could summon a strong friend."

"I know just the person," she said. "Not strong, but with a relevant talent."

A woman appeared. "Hello, Olive," she said, looking around. "Who are your nonimaginary friends?"

"Hello, Leslie. This is a crew of us with a mission to re-connect two cables. I thought your talent would be ideal. You can put any two things together."

"Not exactly," Leslie said. "I can blend any two different objects, like a bottle and a stuffed animal to make a bottlemal, or even living and nonliving. Such as a man and a book, to make a manual. Or a woman and a mirror, which becomes a looking lass. But re-connecting two cables would be merging the same thing, and that's really fixing something broken, which is not my talent. So I can't help you there."

"Oh," Olive said. "Sorry. My mistake."

"Some other time, perhaps," Leslie said, and faded out.

"So this time I'll try strong," Olive said. "Hoping to get it right."

A huge shape appeared beside her. It was an ogre. He looked dully around. "Uh, duh?"

"Welcome to our mission," Olive said to him. Then to the others, "This is Online Ogre. He was really annoyed when the cable broke so he couldn't indulge his surfing passion."

Oho! "Yes, we can certainly use a motivated ogre," Jumper said. Because ogres were almost as strong as they were stupid, and they were exceedingly stupid. At least, that was how they preferred to seem; Smash Ogre had not been at all stupid once Jumper got to know him. Probably neither was Online, because it surely required some wit to surf, whatever that was.

They organized. Four people climbed to the far cable, including the ogre, using sticky web bits on their feet and silk web safety harnesses Jumper spun, and seven went to the near side. They took hold of the strong strands Jumper had attached loosely to the cables and hauled. Haughty was among them, using her claws and wings. So was Maeve, now with Baby Mae on her back in a makeshift carrier so she could keep her hands free. The two sections started coming together.

"Now I will need a pair of eyes to guide my connections," Jumper said. He was of course in spider form. "Because it will be all I can do to grasp the individual strands, and my color perception is not great. So you—"

He broke off, because Eve was looking pained. "I can't," she whispered.

He had forgotten her fear of heights! That was one of the caveats. But he had to have help.

"Maybe if I spin you a cocoon," he suggested doubtfully.

"Then I couldn't see to guide you."

There was no help for it. "I will do my best alone."

But then the two ends started separating. There was not enough strength in one team to maintain sufficient pull. They were losing it regardless.

Eve gulped. "If the mission fails because of me, then I am condemning myself to a lifetime of degradation. I might as well end it now."

"No, Eve! We'll manage somehow."

"No, you won't. Not without me." She closed her eyes, clenched her teeth, and took hold of the slanting cable. She started climbing.

And quickly let go, dropping back to the ground. "I can't," she said. Indeed, she looked as if she had aged three decades; her jaw was slack, her breathing shallow. She looked considerably less beautiful than usual.

Jumper hastily flung a safety harness about her. "If you lose your grip, you won't fall," he said. "You will merely hang below it."

"Thanks," she said through gritted teeth. But she still couldn't do it.

Jumper searched his mind desperately for something that might help. He came up with a faint notion. "You are close to your sister," he said. "You two argue, but you're close."

"Yes, we are twins," she agreed. "Almost identical."

"You might almost identify with her. That's why the two of you have quarreled about boyfriends. You have very similar tastes."

"Yes. She'll be wanting a Demon consort too." She smiled briefly through her pain. "Which she just might get, the hard way, by changing genders."

"In fact you are almost telepathic. You generally know where each of you are. That's why she returned."

"Yes, we relate."

"Can you put yourself in her frame of mind? Think of yourself as her?"

"I suppose. Sometimes when we were younger we switched clothing and fooled our parents, just for fun."

"She's afraid of depths. If you relate to her, maybe you can exchange fears. For a while."

She looked at him sharply. "I wonder."

"If you close your eyes and think Dawn thoughts, maybe you can get up that cable."

She kissed his mandible. "Maybe." Then she closed her eyes again and concentrated.

Her aspect subtly changed. Bright highlights seemed to appear in her hair, and she became almost fair. Then she smiled, and sunlight seemed to flash. "Who's afraid of the big bad sky?" she asked. She took hold of the cable. He could see that she was not quite convinced, but the mind change enabled her to fight off enough of the fear.

He watched as she climbed, eyes closed, to the end. Then, guided by the instructions of the others there, she caught hold of a strand and pulled. The cable ends started coming together again.

It was working!

But now he lacked a partner to guide his detail work. Could he manage to do it anyway?

He went up and tried. The torn ends had multicolored wires sticking out wildly in every direction. He simply could not tell them apart. The valiant effort of the girls and men was being wasted.

Sharon appeared. "So you are doing it," she said.

"Sharon! I need help! I can't see the fine wires well enough."

"Too bad," she said. "I suppose that means your mission will fail. Pluto will be pleased."

"Please! I can't do it without you."

She sighed. "If I do it, will you marry me?"

Jumper hesitated. He didn't want to marry her, but did he have a choice? "Yes."

"Exactly what is it you need?"

"The wires are of many colors. I need to match the colors from each cable, so I can tie them together correctly."

"Like this?" She reached out and found two yellow wires.

"Yes!" He reached for them.

She drew back, holding them just out of his reach. "These?"

"Sharon, this is no time for teasing," he said. "Give me the wires."

She let them go. "You fool! Did you really think I would help you, let alone marry you? You're a spider! I'm going to marry Pluto, and Eve will be my scullery maid."

"But you promised!"

"Funny thing about Demon promises," she remarked. "They don't mean anything unless couched as Demon bets or disciplined by half a soul. Deception is merely a means to an end. So long, sucker!" She vanished.

So she had betrayed him when it really counted. She was still Pluto's minion. Jumper was more disgusted than heartbroken. That was the second caveat: the help that could have made the difference, and chose not to.

Then another figure appeared. "Button Ghost!" Jumper exclaimed. "You can get this far from the castle?"

Button held up a ghostly sign. WHEN I HAVE TO. WHEN THERE IS SUFFICIENT MOTIVE. HOW CAN I HELP?

He was a ghost, without substance. But substance was not what Jumper needed at the moment. "Can you see fine detail? Colors?"

YES.

"Then you are what I need!"

Soon Jumper was connecting red to red, blue to blue, green to green, and the other colors that Button matched up. This was the job that only he could do, because the opposite charges of the wires of the two cable sections would electrocute any regular person. But his positive and negative leg charges could handle it. Strand by strand the cable was getting reconnected. As it was, the tension was taken up by the connections, and the men and girls were able to hold the ends in place more readily.

"Jumper." It was Haughty.

"Good work," he said, continuing to focus on the wires. About half the connections were made, and it was getting easier as it progressed. Success was coming into view.

"Jumper, we've got a problem," Haughty said urgently.

He glanced up at her. "No, it's doing well, thanks to you and the others."

"Look at the horizon."

He looked. There was a murderously black cloud rapidly expanding. "Uh-oh."

"That's Cumulo Fracto Nimbus, Fracto for short," she said. "Remember, we ran afoul of him before we started the mission."

"I remember. We had to get under cover."

"We can't do that this time. I think Demon Pluto put him up to it."

"But Pluto can't interfere directly."

"He could have set it up in advance, as part of the challenge. We can't prove otherwise."

She was right. It would be nice if they could splice, but this could be one reason they couldn't. They would have to deal with it.

"Girls," Jumper said. "And men."

The others looked at him, giving him their attention. Even Eve opened her eyes to look at him, saw the great open sky, shuddered, and clamped them shut again.

"What is it?" Olive asked.

"A storm is coming. Fracto. He's going to try to stop us from completing our work."

They looked around, spying the cloud. "Can we descend and wait him out?" Phanta asked.

"Not at our present stage. Only half the wires are connected. The storm will shake the cable, tearing the ends loose again unless we hold them. But that means—"

"That means we have to hold on," Maeve said. "Somehow."

"Oh," Eve said. "I—I don't think I can."

"I can tie us all on," Jumper said. "So no one can fall. But it won't be fun."

"Do it," Eve said grimly.

Jumper got to work spinning silk and casting lines. He wrapped them all in a kind of cocoon. They continued to grip the cable lines, so that the ends remained close enough together for him to connect.

He connected a few more. Then Fracto struck. First there was a powerful gust of wind. Then a burst of rain. Then lightning and thunder right next to them.

Most were doing all right, and Dick, the crazy writer, even seemed to be enjoying it. He was surely making mental notes for a terrific story about cables in the sky. But Eve's face was ashen beneath her wildly waving hair. She was not taking this well.

Jumper spun another cocoon, a thicker one, though he was running low on silk. He formed it about her body, shielding it from the rain. She would be in her own world, as she had been when crossing the gulf. "Thank you," she gasped as he closed the hood.

Now the storm worked into its main strength. The winds became gale force, then hurricane force. They whipped the cable back and forth like a plucked string. More lightning crackled. But it didn't strike the cable. Jumper realized that the cable must be protected by magic, so it couldn't be shorted out that way.

Hailstones pelted them. "Ooo, that smarts!" Dawn cried. But she ducked her head down and did not let go.

The storm shook them for what seemed like hours but was probably minutes. But it could not make them let go or give up. Finally it waned, as Fracto exhausted himself, and passed. They had outlasted it.

Jumper resumed work, with Button's assistance. The ghost had not been bothered by the storm, of course. The others remained as they were, holding the links in place. No one said anything. No one needed to.

At last it was done. Jumper wrapped a few more strands around the repair to secure it. The cable had been spliced. Victory!

There was no immediate effect. They descended to the ground, dripping wet but exultant. Online Ogre faded out, his job done. Jumper hauled Eve's cocoon down, and opened it.

"Did it hold?" Eve asked.

"Yes."

"Good." She fainted.

Dawn came to help her. "You did your part, sister dear," she said. "You helped us beat Pluto."

"And you conquered your fear, almost," Haughty said.

"Weird," Eve said, recovering. Girlish swoons seldom lasted long. "This is a really happy occasion. I mean, we have just saved Xanth from flying apart. Yet somehow I feel heavy."

A bulb flashed over Jumper's head. "That's it! Gravity is being restored. We were all getting lighter, but now we are getting heavier."

"That's it," she agreed. "So it's good news after all."

A figure appeared. It was Pluto. "Yes, good news for you," he agreed soberly. "Now I must marry Eve. It was the deal."

A male harpy appeared. "And I must marry Haughty," Charon said.

"We'll have a wedding," Dawn said. "As a princess I have the authority to perform it. But can you wait a bit? We all need to clean up."

"I have no choice," Pluto said grimly. He seemed about as eager for the nuptial as Eve had been to become a plaything without it. But the Demon bet bound him.

Eve climbed out of the cocoon and smiled at him. "Do you really mind?"

He gazed at her, wet despite her time in the cocoon, her hair plastered half across her face and her dress matted across her chest. "You're beautiful."

She kissed him, and Jumper thought he could almost see her soul enclosing Pluto, starting to impose decency on him. He was already a handsome man, externally; he would soon be handsome internally too. She would have an excellent marriage. That had, almost incidentally, solved the problem that had brought both Eve and Dawn to the mission: competition for the same man. They would not be competing anymore.

Actually, all the girls' problems had been resolved, not necessarily the way they had anticipated. Wenda had wanted to have a whole body so she could interact normally with men, but now had a man regardless. Maeve had wanted escape from the stork, but now she was satisfied with the baby it had brought. Olive seemed satisfied with her talent as it was, thanks to its usefulness for her crazy writer. Phanta was no longer afraid of Gheorge Ghost, thanks to Shepherd and Ram Bunctious. And Haughty was satisfied to change to Hottie anytime, because Charon liked both her aspects and was turned off by neither.

There was a pond not far distant. The girls and men stripped and went to it to wash, leaving their clothing to dry in the sunlight. Only Jumper was left, in more than one sense. He couldn't help noticing how the increased gravity affected the bodies of the girls as they ran. He wished he had a girl of his own. If only Sharon had not proved to be ultimately fickle.

He had achieved his mission. Now he could return to his natural state in the smaller realm. The Good Magician would surely provide him with another narrative hook or something to return him there. Yet somehow he was unsatisfied.

He focused on his feeling, and realized that it was because he no longer really wanted to go home. That life had been fine for him before, traveling from weed to weed and biting the heads off bugs. But there were no human girls there, no camaraderie of a shared mission, no human-style friendships. No bra-and-panty teasing, or spot seductions. No true love. Having experienced these things, he found he was reluctant to leave them behind. He would be lonely in a way no other spider would understand.

And of course he would be dead by the time the year was out, because the normal lifespan of a spider was under a year. He couldn't complain; it was, after all, the natural order. It had not bothered him before. Yet somehow he grieved for what was never his destiny. He almost wished that he had not been shown this fantastic alternate existence. It had implanted a dream in his imagination that was ultimately as false as Sharon's love.

He was a spider. An arachnid. A creature who related to this marvelous realm only peripherally. He would simply have to accept his role. Maybe the Good Magician would have a potion that would make him forget the rest.

Then he saw the ghost. "Button!" he exclaimed. "Truly, without you I couldn't have done it! How can I ever repay you?"

But the ghost could not answer verbally. Instead he held up a sign. THERE MAY BE A WAY.

"Anything!" For this was a kind of debt that should be repaid before Jumper departed. The completion of the mission had not freed Eris, yet she had sent her ghostly minion to help. Her generosity should be rewarded to the extent possible.

ASK DAWN.

As it happened, Dawn was returning, gloriously nude, along with the others. "Dawn, I have to ask you—" Jumper started.

"Yes, it was my bright idea," she said. "Now let me see if I can implement it."

"But you haven't heard my question."

"There's no need. Just be patient."

She knew what was on his mind. But what was on *her* mind?

The others returned from the pond. Now Dawn addressed them. "I think we owe Jumper a vote of thanks," she said. "He persevered when most of the rest of us were ready to quit, and he showed us how to work together, and he spliced the cable back together. He saved Xanth from the loss of its imported gravity. He's a hero."

"You are all heroes," Jumper said. "You should all be honored. It is true: we needed every member of our party, and then some. And that is my concern. Without Button Ghost's help—"

"In fact, why don't we vote him a sufficient title?" Dawn asked, ignoring his comment. "Such as the Honorary Prince of Spiders."

"Yes!" the others agreed.

"No, this isn't relevant," Jumper protested. "I don't care about honors. I just want to repay—"

"All in favor say Aye."

"Aye!" they chorused.

"Done," Dawn said. "Now you are a prince, Jumper. Do you know what that means?"

"No," he said, baffled by this silly business. They all seemed to be up to something, but it wasn't helping the one who deserved it.

"But Button does," Dawn said, looking at the ghost.

Jumper looked at Button. And was amazed.

Button was changing. In his place appeared the ghost of Eris, lovely in the gown she had danced in. She was just about the most beautiful creature Jumper had seen, and he had seen a lot of beauty recently. In fact much of it was standing before him, nude. But it was more than that: around Eris was the outline of her spider form, and that too was beautiful. The way she had danced with him—

Ghost Eris held up a sign. PRINCE JUMPER—WILL YOU MARRY ME?

Jumper almost fainted. Was it possible? Could an honorary nonhuman prince marry her and rescue her from her captivity? This seemed utterly crazy. Yet the Demons had their own rules for their wagers. Had there been a loophole in this one?

Then he thought of a problem. "Don't you need to marry a mortal with a soul? I'm a spider."

"While it is true that generally only humans or those with some human ancestry, such as crossbreeds, have souls," Eris said, "there do seem to be some exceptions. You have associated so long and intimately with several souled folk, in human form, that you have absorbed a portion of their souls. You do now have a soul of your own. You are fully worthy, Prince Jumper, in whatever sense you wish to take it."

Jumper realized that there might have been more of a point to his relationship with the girls than he had realized. Could the Good Magician have known?

"Don't keep her waiting in suspense," Dawn murmured.

Oh. What was there to lose? If it gave the Demoness what she needed, that would certainly be fitting. "Yes."

Eris stepped into him, embracing him somehow in both human and spider form. She seemed to be partly solid now. He realized that the anticipation of marriage was starting the soul transfer, and enabling her to break free of her prison. So her ghostly aspect was being replaced by her real body.

"Let's set up for the ceremony," Dawn said. "A double or maybe triple marriage."

"Hey, what about us?" Olive demanded. "We want to get married too."

"Then everyone," Dawn said. "Form your couples and stand before me." Her mouth quirked. "Clothing optional."

They lined up before her nude, men and women. Pluto with Eve, Charon with Haughty, Warren Warrior with Maeve, Prince Charming with Wenda Woodwife, Dick Philip with Olive Hue, Shepherd with Phanta, and Jumper now in human form with Eris. Seven couples of assorted natures.

"Do you, severally and individually, take your partners in marriage?" Dawn asked. "The correct answer is Yes."

"Yes," they chorused, some more eagerly than others.

"Then by the power vested in me as an unattached princess, I now pronounce you severally and individually, husband and wife. You may kiss your spouses."

They kissed, severally and individually, while Dawn stood alone, seeming sad. She had no man of her own to marry. But surely her time would come, for she was a lovely princess and Sorceress, and a wonderful person. She was surely also relieved that she had not had to change her gender to accomplish her agreement.

Then they broke into smaller groups, bidding farewell to each other before getting started on their assorted married lives. The mission was over.

Sharon appeared. "Damn! I chose the wrong side—again."

"You were always a fool," Pluto called. "I wasn't going to marry you anyway."

"But you promised!"

"Funny thing about Demon promises," he remarked. "They don't mean anything unless couched as Demon bets or disciplined by half a soul. Deception is merely a means to an end. So long, sucker."

Jumper kept his face as straight as he could. Pluto was repeating exactly what Sharon had said to Jumper. He must have been watching the action all along, and served her as she had served Jumper. It was hard to feel sorry for her, yet Jumper did, to a degree. He had never completely trusted her, but had liked her, and would have married her if she had been straight with him. But as she had said, she had chosen the wrong side. Again. In retrospect, he was glad that she had. He was surely far better off with Eris, for the time that remained to him.

"Oh!" Sharon exclaimed, outraged. Then she reoriented, assuming her most luscious nude form. "But you, Prince Jumper—you could probably use a mistress, for those dull intervals when your spouse is busy or asleep." She bounced in place, impressively. "How would you like—"

"He does not need anything of the kind," Eris said so firmly that small sparks flew from her words. "Nor will he in the future. I will assume any form he might like, for whatever purpose, including your form."

"Not that form," Jumper said quickly. "It would make me nervous."

"You're still impossible," Sharon said, and vanished in a cloud of acrid smoke. Jumper hoped he had seen the last of her, so that he would never again be tempted.

Now was the half-sad time for his leave-taking. "I will miss yew," Wenda told Jumper tearfully. "But I wood knot change a thing about this day." She kissed him and departed with Prince Charming.

Jumper gazed after them. Of all the girls, he cared for Wenda most, and was most glad for her happiness. As Charming put it, she might be half there physically, but she was all there in spirit, and that did count more.

"She will fill out when the stork delivers," Eris murmured. "It is love fulfilled that makes a woodwife a full woman."

That was gratifying to know. Wenda was certainly deserving.

The others said similar things as they left. Jumper knew he would miss them all, especially Phanta and Eve, who had loved him in more than the routine manner. But all of them had the considerable compensation of their spouses, and knowledge of their joint achievement. All except Dawn, ironically, who had found the key to Eris's salvation and his own.

"Too bad you didn't make it also with Dawn," Eris murmured. "Now, of course it is too late. You're married."

He stared at her, appalled. She could read his thoughts!

"Of course," Eris agreed. "I'm a Demoness. That's how I knew you were such a good person. Do not be concerned; I am not jealous of your prior experience. I will give you future experience to make it pale in comparison."

"Uh, thank you," he said, as another couple approached. He was glad he had married her, but realized that there would be considerable adjustments to make. She was no ordinary woman.

"Correct," she agreed, squeezing his hand. "But now I have half your soul, and that tempers my Demon nature. I married you for my freedom, but already I am discovering the joy of my burgeoning love for you. I will devote my considerable expertise to making you the happiest creature extant."

He was unable to reply, as the couple was with them now: Pluto and

Eve, he looking not as regretful about acquiring the moral discipline of half a soul as he might have been. But of course Eve was about as lovely and talented as a mortal girl could be; that was very likely some compensation. "Fare well, Jumper," Eve said. "I know you will find your marriage to a Demon well worthwhile."

"I surely will," he agreed. "Fare well." He felt his crush on Eris solidifying like her freed body, fleshing out as it were into complete and enduring love. He couldn't do much about it at the moment, because Phanta and Shep were approaching. The forms had to be followed to the end, and Phanta, too, was special.

Finally Jumper was left alone with his bride. Eris, becoming fully soft and solid, murmured in his ear. "There will be a complication, now that you are my prince consort."

Not another complication! But he needed to know it. "What is it?"

"Marriage to you, a mortal prince, freed me from captivity. I am duly grateful, and expect to see that you are never sorry for saving me. But there will also be an effect on you. A leakage of my power that can't be helped if we are to be close, as we shall be." She kissed his human ear, and squeezed him in an intimate place. "Very close."

"What is it?" he repeated grimly.

"You will be immortal. That is to say, no longer mortal. You won't die in a spider's life of months or a human being's life of decades. You will remain young and healthy indefinitely. It can't be helped, in this circumstance. I hope that does not annoy you unduly."

He stared at her. "This is a joke?"

"No. I'm sorry if it disturbs you."

Jumper knew it would be some time before he fully comprehended the significance of it. But at the moment all he had was his first impression. "I can live with it."

She laughed. "You will have to." She kissed him again. "Now come with me into my parlor. We have experiences to explore together."

"Yes, dear," he agreed, not at all reluctantly.

Author's Note

This is Xanth #33, six novels into the second magic trilogy of three cubed. Some readers want the series to continue forever; some critics fear it will. I have tried to slowly age the material, so that some four-letter words are used though generally bleeped out, and some adults signal the stork onstage instead of in the unmentioned background. But in general this remains a fun series, suitable for mature children if not for the freakable mothers of teens.

Some readers complain about all the puns. Well, other readers are busy sending them in, and I must either use them or throw them away, which seems wasteful. Even a pun has some right to exist. If I try to discourage readers from sending them, they get mad and send them anyway. Some send pages of puns, or complicated plots. One problem is that some characters or ideas deserve a much fuller treatment than I can give them, so they get passed off incidentally, and I feel guilty about that. Sometimes they get their fuller treatment in a later novel, as was the case with Olive Hue and her imaginary friends. So I use what I can, in the context of the ongoing story, thinking of it as being like nuts in a fruitcake or decorations on a fun house. One example is the five marvelous children in chapter 13, credited below: Seva Yugov sent about six full pages of descriptions of their talents, with all the nuances. He had really worked them out. But here only a fraction of that appears, because unless the characters are major, I can't spare the space to round them out completely. Sometimes it seems a shame. The truth is it would be easier for me to write these novels without any reader input; I use reader notions as a courtesy rather than from need. My fan mail still takes a significant portion of my working time, perhaps a third of it. No, I don't consider that time wasted; I learn things from my readers, and they are worthy people. But it doesn't make my writing easier.

Another feedback I get is about the naughtiness in Xanth. Xanth consists of magic, wordplay, puns, literalism, honor, wonder, parody, and other forms of humor, as well as adventure and romance in a land that resembles the state of Florida transformed, but it's the one percent naughtiness that conjures some folks' ire, as mentioned above. Ministers, older women, and the parents of teens tend to get nervous when panties are glimpsed. This novel, with half a slew of glimpses of bras and panties, abetted by the protagonist's discovery of love and sex, is apt to cost me some readers. But Xanth is and always was an adult series; it's not even listed for children. If I limit it to what some folk think is suitable for children, it will become an unrecognized children's series and lose its adult readers. Let's face it: a person who freaks out at the mere mention of panties is going to have a problem with all adult literature, movies, television, and games, not to mention real life. Children who insist on reading adult fantasy seem to be able to handle Xanth readily enough, even if their parents can't. Girls have even sent me panty notions; they like panty power. Boys seem to like sneak peeks. As far as I know, it does not send any of them into criminal careers. So Xanth is as it is, and readers who are alienated by this sort of humor are free to take their business elsewhere.

I am getting old, seventy-three at this writing, and perhaps getting crusty in my dotage. I try to keep fit with exercise and healthy diet, but the maladies of age are creeping up on me nevertheless. I live in Florida, on our small tree farm, but never quite discovered the address of the Fountain of Youth. As I started writing this novel I was undergoing physical therapy for an inflammation of my right shoulder joint that incapacitated my arm. I couldn't even do my hair, which I have grown out since my wife is no longer able to cut it monthly; now it's over a foot long and I wear it in a ponytail. So I notice ponytails on men and women. In general the women have neater ones, though not always. When I wear my hair loose around the house, it warms my ears and neck; maybe that's its natural purpose. But I was unable to reach it with my right hand, and so for a few days my wife did it for me. One day she even braided it. Fortunately the therapy was effective, and now my arm is functioning again. It never interfered with my typing, which required only very limited motion of my arm.

My wife had heart surgery. Technically, it was a replacement of an aortic aneurysm. That is, the largest artery in the body had swollen as it left the heart so that it looked almost as big as the heart itself. If it ruptured, she would have been dead in seconds. They set a new section inside, like filling an old stretched hose with a smaller tighter hose. The surgery was successful, and her slow recovery continued as I wrote the novel. I had already been doing the meals and dishes; for several months I did the laundry too. I also go with her when she leaves the house for shopping and doctors' appointments, just in case. We have been married fifty-one years, and we each do what it takes to make it work. But I no longer write novels at quite the rate I used to. It's a kind of payback; early on my wife went to work to earn our living so that I could stay home and try to be a writer. Otherwise I would not have made it. I have not forgotten.

Those who want to know more about me are welcome to visit my Web site, http://www.hipiers.com, where I have a bimonthly blog-type column and maintain an ongoing survey of electronic publishers and related services. The idea is to help make it easier for writers who are starting out and can't get the attention of traditional print publishers or literary agents. Writing is still likely to be a soul-crushing enterprise, but at least there is some faint hope.

Now here is the list of contributors, in the approximate order of the use of their ideas in this novel.

Flies in ointment, tangled web, running gag, fruit bat, soul food plant, draw bridge magic, rattler as baby ogre's toy, fish quartet, Ice

Cap, Cocoa Nut Tree—Robert. Wood Wife to become Mother Board—James Patterson. Anti-streaking agent—Michelle Johnson. No Gard (dragon)—Dale Dellatore. Biting Wind, Headphones—Sondra Lynn Holzmann. Oxalate, controlling oxygen—Jordan Kirby. Maenad trying to flee the stork, Infectious laughter, Cooking up a storm—Heather "Heatherlark" Ennis. Keeping an eye on someone—Sara Cornelius. Inanimate objects hide in the last place you look—Aftyn Skye. Shield that protects a person too much—Joseph Gruber. Harbinger-binging messenger—Christopher Ward.

Haughty Harpy/Hottie Harpie—Daniel Forbes. Phanta, who becomes a ghost—Erin Patterson. Olive Hue—who makes imaginary friends with real talents, from *Pet Peeve*—Tammy Yuen and Evan Mc-Coy, with the suggestion to use her here by Lisa Nicole from alchemy unplugged.com. Gene Blue, with talent of making blue jeans—Sondra Lynn Holzmann. Jamie, who makes things heavier—Paul Michael Patnode. Portable section of an enchanted path—Jestin Larson. Hail Mary, Ro-boat, Quarter Pounder, Mountain Bike, D Tergent, the sticks, The Cate family—Tim Bruening. Cottonwood—Rebecca Fanning. Fenfen—Rick Baker. Explosive Bamboo, Seal, Steel reaches out to take things—Ianus Stanton. Mercury Merman, who changes the temperature of water—Daniel Forbes.

Talent of turning wine to water—Caitlin and Shannon. Talent of pushing water away from the body—Ian Doig. Talent of transforming his arms into anything, Para site—Anthony V. Eye of the Bee-holder—Todd Snowder. Talent: turn gold to lead—Michael Eddy. Miss Gesundheit, who sneezes her head off—Nada. Auntie Depressant, who affects depression—John Urschel. The Burr Family—Davis Hunks. The Tard Family—Gordon V Pemrich. Ring Bear—Richard B Lively. Hedge Hog—Noah Hibbard. Porky Pine—Dallas Smith. Census Burro—Bev in Bellingham. Aukward bird—Ave Ornstein. Wall-rus—Carol Jacob.

Pluto demoted by Demon bet—Daniel Colpi, Sparrow. Pluto reduced to a regular character, dating Dawn & Eve, Samantha—Zachary Smitherman. Half Jumper's legs positive, half negative, to straddle Internet and Outernet; Demon Pluto knocks out the cable—Misty Zaebst. Angie Ina, heart throb, drop dead gorgeous—Dexter L Davis. Talent of touching a picture and being transported there—Michael Lindsay. Bicycle in Xanth—Don Hallenbeck. Luters, who steal from abandoned music shops—Tom Marrin. Stretcher stretches user—David Smith. Curse of falling in love only with committed folk—Chelsea J Young. Hugh Mann, who can change the description of things—Della Mae Stouder and Brother Rocky. Moosical—Michelle Webber.

Fiddler crabs—Moniqa Beatty. Jelly from jellyfish—Ariane West. Okra Ogre ogle riddle—Gary "Kaa" Henderson. Drakin—winged humanoid dragons—Dale Ashburn. C Duce the Cemoness—Tom Marrin. Sir puns—Mitchell Wooden. Sammy Cat and Claire Voyant have cat o'9 tails—Judi Trainor. Kitten Kaboodle—Michael VanderMay. Jenny Elf and Sammy Cat on the Lost Trail, Found Cabin, and contents. Dora and the spirit of Hope, Drums of Dole, Blue Funk—David Deschampheiaere. Talent of Empathy—Jose "Jj" Valest. Flion—winged lion who can speak—Leonis Lelan.

Conjured grape jam, Coven Tree—Jim Gandee. Anna Phylactic, with allergy—Deb Murray. Willie–Nillie twins—Jay Yates. Talent of Centaur Persuasion—Willie Pryor. Booby trap—Glenn E Moss. Machine and Pa-chine—Caraleigh Daugherty. Sun glasses—Jeremy Leask. Little Foot becomes Doll Fin—Todd Ross. Coy koi—A DeKrey. Fat Farm, Bare Lake, Anne Orexic—Dave Thomas. Sati Sfaction, who can sense ghosts, Belial Sfaction, who can make dust creatures—Stefan Sanchez. Porkypine—Phil Giles, Katy Gaston, Noah Hibbard. Hook Up—Moniqa Beatty.

Irrelevant—David D'Champ. Roger Roadrunner—Roger Vazquez. The Exception—Zachary Garrison Tieman. Show history of Button Ghost—Nada. Hemo-goblins—Dave Morgan. S R "Shep" Sheppard—Andrew Pilon. Conjuring a bit of the Void—Davis Hunks. Gin and Tonic—Malin Tirfing. Chocolate Kisses, Sage—Kerry Garrigan. Auspice—Jessica Gallant. Cook Book—Dakota Lorber. Aura Dawn—Chandra Phipps. Five remarkable children—Seva Yugov. Four-Letter Commands—Joseph Bauer. Oceana Rain Fields—Peggy Roberts. Diaper service in Xanth—Elizabeth Cember. Blending living and nonliving things—Leslie Patterson. Twins who conjure things into or out of bottles—Joyce Yang. Talent of making self ill at will—Philip Bauer.

I have dozens of puns left over, but tried to give first-time contributors their chance before using repeat contributors. A few that relate to characters who don't appear in this novel are also waiting their later turns. My cutoff point was the end of OctOgre 2007, so I could edit the novel in NoRemember.

I wish all readers well, until we both visit Xanth again. There should be at least a little magic in every life.